# I, CONKER ...

# I, CONKER...

Tom Davies

First Impression—April 1994
ISBN 1 85902 100 X
© Tom Davies

Printed by J. D. Lewis and Sons Ltd.,
Gomer Press, Llandysul, Dyfed

## Acknowledgements

This is to thank
Peter Jones, John Humphries and David Hughes—
three angels in heavy disguise.

Being the true
confessions
of a
postmodernist angel
with special
responsibilities for
wales

# First Book

It was dark for a moment and then an explosion of flame began throwing out fleeting gold rings. The first of the rings were bright and brilliant until they became slower and thinner, leaving just the hard kernel of a flame hanging there, yellow on black, with a hissing purple heart. The flame moved around hurriedly like the pencil of a quick sketch artist, actually drawing on the surface of the darkness, creating a huge lumpy landscape with high dark mountains which seeemed to be floating in the rising dawn.

I had come to the slopes of Snowdon on the very roof of Wales and it was winter as the flame sketched in more detail. All around me there were bleak, brown slopes with the winds quivering in the iced grass. I took one step forward over a pool of ice. The temperature had to be a good six degrees below and I was really sad that I wasn't home. It's not all that warm at home either at this time of the year but, after centuries of unremitting toil, most of us have got this look in our tired eyes and it would be terrible to miss out on anything.

But this was my patch and there was work to be done; a lot of work to be done and, the sooner it was done, the sooner I could get home again.

By now the dawn was flooding down the mountain and the surrounding fields were dusted with a thick film of frost. This glazing of frost even made the oval pellets of the sheep dung attractive. The hanks of sheep wool on the barbed wire fences were stiff, even brittle, to my inquisitive touch. Every molehill was frozen and cracked.

They said that I had better come here to Snowdon to begin my final report. They've always had this taste for the symbolic so here I am, walking through the mystic home of the Welsh tribe and so much of her history, but cold, fed up and homesick. Why I got Wales I'll never know. Some of us got whole Caribbean islands with nobody living on them and the sun shining all the year around. My closest friend Tractus got France—with problems enough for any angel—but at least he got Chartres Cathedral while Bimmimus never did like Spain but he did get Santiago de Compostela.

But I've always had this kingdom of rain—with not much by the way of perks—and it has to be said that the Welsh have always been nothing but hard work and trouble. My career here hasn't been without successes but, for the past hundred years or so, there has been a lot of exhaustion and failure and my flock has become a lost and wandering tribe more worried about drink and television than almost anything else. Aye, aye. I really did get the short straw if ever there was one.

I've had it right up to here with the Welsh and Wales if you really want to know and, what with all this rain, I would have been disabled by chronic athritis centuries ago if it had ever been possible for angels to fall sick. But the only place I ever get sick in is the heart; I've always cared about my work but it's given me almost permanent heartbreak for as long as I can remember. Ah, these Welsh. Give them a pint of beer and a television programme and they're beyond the reach of almost everyone. Bimmimus has found ways of breaking televisions but they only go out and buy new ones. Anyway I've never seen it as part of my job to go around breaking up anything at all. My name is Conquistadorious, by the way, but my friends call me Conker.

The sun had now been working on the ice and the stones had become wet and glistening. The frozen streams had also freed themselves in the thin sunlight and, deep within the tongues of ice on the rocks, you could see fat drops of water wriggling down inside them like huge dark tadpoles. Directly behind me and across the valley were the high jagged slopes of the defunct Llanberis slate mine. With its symmetrical tiers and romping cascades of stone it looked like the first scaffolding of some great cathedral that was going to be sculptured out of the slopes. But they don't build cathedrals anymore. I actually watched over the whole building of St David's cathedral down in Pembrokeshire and that was one of the toughest jobs any of us have ever had. I wasn't there all the time but I only had to turn my back for five minutes and roughnecks were slicing off labourers' noses or the bishop was stealing lead off the roof. But I'll explain that whole sorry saga when I get there.

Gerald of Wales, Geraldus Cambrensis—the first of the modern travel writers, some called him—once made a famous journey through Wales which went this way in the twelfth century. I never really bothered with him much but used to check on his progress now and then out of curiosity. It must be said that he took the most appalling liberties with the facts. I've been known to twist or colour a fact or two but I never reached his heights. The lakes of Snowdonia, he said, had an island which kept surging from side to side depending on the weather. Also, he added, all the fish had one eye. His book was full of stuff like that so we'd better take what Geraldus Cambrensis said with a big pinch of salt.

I was still the lone wanderer in my kingdom of ice when a walker burst out over a scree, bearing down on me in that urgent, ungainly way that walkers always have, but then striding straight through me without saying so much as a word. But they only ever see me when I allow it. Most of the time they might catch my breathing or laughter but that's about all; it doesn't do to get too involved with anyone in my business. But these walkers are always out on the darkest slopes and walking through me when I least expect it. It's the way that they are always hurrying that I never understand. They are forever stumbling to distant places like frightened mothers with their babies tied on their backs and fleeing another plague or new Herod.

Occasionally I stopped still, listening to the song of the mountain. There was a faint music in the air but mostly it was the sounds of the winds whispering in the grass or else making the brown bracken of the dead ferns rattle together softly. Now and then crows called out to one another as they went about their crow business.

And then, right in the middle of nowhere, I came across the rubble of a broken-jawed chapel, just sitting out on the slopes. The roof had long collapsed as had the floor and the whole end of the building. Inside there were the bare remnants of the vestry and marks where the pews had been. Sheep skulls, bleached by the weather, dotted the ground near the altar and gaping windows framed immense views of the mountain.

Well, I suppose any report on the past and present spirituality of the Welsh would have to begin with a ruined and pillaged chapel wouldn't it? The chapel had made the Welsh what they were and, just standing near the pulpit, I wondered how many thousands of times I had sat in a chapel just like this, smiling and marvelling as a glittering dynasty of great preachers pounded out the Welsh souls in pulpits like these. You will have observed already how I even sometimes talk like them. All Welsh preachers absorbed the language of the Bible and revived it in a stately oratorical way and I've been shepherding the Welsh for so long that I often find that I'm at it too. The use of language is one of the great threads in the tapestry I'm about to weave.

But everyone had tremendous times in these chapels and, just standing here in this particular one on Snowdon, I could hear the old hymns, feel all those lost years of prayer and see the faithful struggling to get here through storms for the Sunday morning services. It was a pleasure being an angel shepherding his flock then and, although I do tend to complain a lot, I have to admit that, particularly for most of the eighteenth and nineteenth centuries, I did have a lot of job satisfaction. Everything seemed worthwhile then.

The others often ask me who was the best preacher of them all and I would have to say Christmas Evans. I always liked to be around when he made his great graveyard sermon—and even dropped him a few of his better lines. I also spent a lot of time watching out for him since men like him were one-offs—Eight Inch Nails, the Welsh called them—so they always gave me specific orders to watch out for them and make sure that they didn't fall off their horses and break their necks before their time or anything stupid like that. Not that Christmas Evans ever gave me any difficulty—except he did have an extremely unfortunate habit of falling asleep on horseback—unlike some of the others like Bishop William Morgan who, with all those feuds and guns of his, gave me nothing but headaches almost for as long as he was working on his translation of the Bible into Welsh. They really wanted him kept alive for that but it was touch and go sometimes I can tell you. Very touch and go.

Ah yes, I spent a lot of time standing around with old Christmas Evans and he always gave me pleasure; everything he did made me happy. Just look, there he is now riding Lemon, that clapped-out horse of his, down near Llanberis. As soon as he left his house just over the Menai Straits in Anglesey the bush telegraph would get busy and word of his arrival go out through Snowdonia. They came from everywhere, from up the valleys and down the hills, on horses and in carts, some in tears and others shouting, welcoming their own one-eyed prince of the pulpit. Only people with great hearts ever managed to generate such feelings in the Welsh and his heart was one of the greatest.

He was also the scruffiest of all my preachers, largely because, much to his wife's despair, he kept giving away his clothes to poor people on his travels. He even once gave away his eye-patch and his hat was always battered because he used it to water his horse. 'I am never going to have any property in this world until I have my own grave,' he liked to say.

He would also stand on a rock at twilight, his one good eye looking about and saying nothing as more and more people gathered around. His eye was lost after he was attacked while young and the socket tended to pain him, particularly before a big sermon, so he might take a phial of laudanum out of his waistcoat and dab his blind socket with that. His face had thick Celtic features with beetling eyebrows, a square jaw and a nose you could break up rocks with. But, when he spoke, he always managed to catch the *hwyl*, making his congregation weep with strange emotions as he drew them into the ever-tightening net of his golden oratory. He gave his most memorable sermon right over there on these mountains when he presented the world as a graveyard in which the people were perishing. All the dogs of darkness were gathering as gales of fire swept down through a valley of dry bones. The dying people were only finally starting to be redeemed when Justice and Mercy entered into the fray until, in the finale, he would show all the battered hosts of evil in retreat from the cross.

His words were rooted in burning conviction, based on the most detailed knowledge of the Bible and a rock-solid faith. With all its bardic and poetic splendours this was massive preaching designed to arouse primeval instincts. But then all sermons needed broad and dramatic brushstrokes to keep everyone attentive and attentive they certainly were, as his strong voice wove his parables of punishment and hope in the air. Men like Christmas had the rare gift of being able to move the furniture around inside society and, as I said, he always kept me smiling as if he was my first-born.

Like all my best preachers he also understood the devastation of sin on the human personality and knew everything about the workings of the human heart. His every word sprang out of the purity and goodness of his own heart. 'Never raise the voice while the heart is dry,' he said. 'Let the heart and affections start first—let it commence within.' To reach the heart of others you must also touch your own heart, was another of his little sayings.

I carried on up the mountain, passing a derelict farmhouse, when a huge black cloud came sweeping in from my right. Far away there was a flash and an explosion so loud it even made me jump. The air all around had become dark and stormy with freezing rain coming down by the bucketload. I pressed on around frozen pools, moving ever higher up into the peaks. It's the winds that are the worst around here, sometimes so strong they can whip straight out of Devil's Kitchen and blow a Royal Air Force helicopter backwards.

But even in all this I kept going, following a long ridge and coming out onto the summit where the rain was still pouring down through the thick cloud. The winds were screaming with a real fury. Not that it lasted for long since, as ever in these mountains, no sooner had I sat there, than the sky began turning into the clearest and most ravishing blue and I could see for a hundred miles in every direction. Parts of the mountain were brown and gold but, deep in the dark shadows not yet touched by the sun, there were still huge tongues of ice with odd climbers trying to climb them. These climbers are mad. Occasionally I help them out if they get into difficulty but mostly I leave all that to the Royal Air Force. Anyway I've only got one pair of hands. It had better be understood straight away that, while I can move through space faster than anyone, I can never be in two places at once. Even angels have their limitations.

The whole of the mountain range began filling up with a golden, warm sunshine and I found that, as long as I kept moving pretty quickly, I could actually leap across all these rolling artefacts of light, using them like a giant staircase which would take me across the Menai Straits to Anglesey. Over the years I've found that I can do anything with light: it's when the darkness thickens up—particularly if there's no moon—that I get into trouble. I suppose I had better also explain that while I do have a set of wings—unlike most angels—I almost never use them. In exceptional circumstances like a storm or a fight with a dark angel I can unfold them if I am getting into difficulties. But the dark angels haven't shown their faces around here for some time now.

I've always had a soft spot for the island of Anglesey or Môn Mam Cymru, the mother of Wales. Everything seems to move at a gentler pace over here and, on mornings like this, I like to hang around on the Menai Suspension Bridge staring out at the swirling tidal eddies of the Straits, known to everyone as The Swillies. But there again I've always thought of Anglesey as an island of battling tides which come surging around those headlands at anything up to 10 miles an hour, changing their direction every 12 hours and 25 minutes until you can often see those moonstruck surges struggling in the opposite directions at the same time.

This flat island of sleepy villages and even sleepier farms is also surrounded by huge intertidal zones where you can paddle in rock pools, collect shells and driftwood, watch the passing herons and other important pastimes like that. Often the crows pick up the mussels and carry them high into the air before dropping them down onto the tarmac roads to break them open. The beaches can be walked on for miles without seeing a soul as gulls wheel overhead and cold waves come crashing in. Ah yes, I've always had the most tranquil moments around here.

Also the people up here are very different from the rowdier lot down in South Wales. They don't seem to feel the need to be forever poking their noses into everyone else's business for a start and their accents are different as are the kinds of Welsh they speak. A North Walian—or Gog—is said to be not exactly insular except that he believes that all traffic lights going north should be red and all those going south should be green. They still have a small but abiding fear of the English and any newcomers here might take years to be accepted into the community and maybe not even then. But rural communities have rural ways and always tend to act like large and private families. I can't say that almost anyone here has ever created any particular problems for me; a few are still faithful and I know a number of houses to call on if I ever need to listen to prayer.

Listening to believing prayer is my main source of enjoyment and relaxation. Prayer actually revives me and, if I do get into difficulties or become exhausted for any reason, I like to fly down to some monastery and spend a day sitting in the rafters listening to the monks. Llanthony Priory with the Cistercian monks was once a great favourite of mine but that's been a rubble for a few hundred years. Now my main bolthole is the monastery on Caldey Island just off the Pembrokeshire coast. These are serious devoted men who are still maintaining the contract of prayer and there are times when Caldey seems like my first home. Another way of reviving myself if I get too exhausted or fearful is to fly up to Holywell in North Wales and take a bath in the holy waters in the shrine there.

But I can enjoy myself in other ways too and sometimes, when I'm in Anglesey, I might go along to Pwllfanogl, a beautiful small foreshore tucked between Menai Bridge and Plas Newydd, the home of the present Marquis of Anglesey, where I might spend an hour or so in a garage watching that marvellous landscape painter, Kyffin Williams, getting on with his work.

For me he has always brought out the very Welshness of Wales; somehow managed to make his art take root in the land. I've often seen him out on the mountains sketching derelict cottages, old chapels or painting sheepdogs. But then he will come back to this little garage around the back of his house and, with thick lumps on his palette knife, put together landscapes which are always vivid, strong and full of sensuality. The Welsh have always been a very sensual race; they like to deny it in public but it's there all right and it's caused me more than a few problems over the years.

'If my painting is sensuous it is so because of the sensations aroused in me by the land of my birth,' Kyffin says. 'Some sort of style has been bestowed on me by the land, so well known to me and my forbears. There must be some explanation for an almost total lack of influence by others. People tell me that my paintings are very Welsh. If they are I am glad, but there has never been any intention to do anything else other than to paint my own land in my own way. What I do find in this country is a mood which touches the seam of melancholy which is in most Welshmen.'

So we're already getting something of the kind of people I've got in my flock—sensuous, often insecure and, on occasion, stricken by the blackest melancholy. Some of my best preachers have orchestrated this melancholy to wondrous effect. But the Welsh have always found a glamour in melancholy; they seem to absolutely relish any sort of spiritual pain. Indeed there have been times when all of them seemed to have graduated with honours in depression, particularly if they came from Aberystwyth.

But Kyffin's family were always solidly religious. Two grandfathers, four great grandfathers and sundry great great grandfathers were all parsons in North Wales giving their sermons in Welsh. Kyffin himself thought of becoming a minister but decided that he couldn't accept the rules. Then there was his cousin Dora who habitually hid her false teeth under her geraniums and his grandmother whose carriage was drawn by ostriches through Hyde Park. His great grandfather had an Indian mistress whom he kept locked up in the stables of his house in Bangor. On some nights you can still hear her ghost howling, it is said by some. But I've never come across her.

But, following the death of his brother Dic, Kyffin no longer has any family left and he now lives on his own in this small house which is an immaculate jumble inside with family photographs, paintings and sculpture dotted everywhere. On the hearth above the coal fire is written, in Welsh, on a huge slab of grey slate: 'As the cry of the stag for the watery streams such is the longing of my soul to be with thee oh Lord.'

Yes, Anglesey is a perfect island for the working artist; perfect in its light and tranquillity, perfect in the way that people rarely bother one another and, perhaps most importantly of all, perfect in its sudden glimpses of beauty which can ambush the spirit without warning and hold the heart in a warm and beautiful cocoon. You never quite know when it is going to happen either. I was walking along the foreshore just beyond Brynsiencyn later that afternoon when I noticed that the sun was going down in a huge red and gold storm.

I rose up and flew towards it with tears in my eyes since, directly across the full pink sea, the snow-capped mountains of Snowdonia were trooping across the horizon. There was the sparkling foreshore of Port Dinorwic and, further along again, the enchanted circular towers of Caernarfon Castle looking as if they were actually spinning up out of the sea. Just below me a few men, black on red, were messing about in boats.

I know I do tend to complain about the country a lot but it can still get right into my blood rather like the drugs that young people seem so fond of these days. This is my Wales and, carried away by the rapture of it all, I turned and turned again threading back and forth through this red and gold explosion. People often talk of Wales as being but an old woman gone in the teeth but her beauty is still alive and throbbing. The country still sits here waiting for the artist's brush and the admiring eye, forever managing to be both as melancholy as a funeral but also as sensuous as the Venus de Milo.

The moon was barely visible but the sky was spangled with a lot of stars that night. It's not easy to fly by starlight; it requires a lot of concentration and balance but it can be done. Also you need to adjust your weight slightly and that gives you a better edge and a lot more speed. Not that we ever need tackle anything with too much speed. As I explained, things are hotting up but no one expects us to go rushing around the place with wildly flapping wings or anything like that.

But, if the stars themselves get covered by cloud, I've still got a trick or two up my sleeve. I have never gone in for showing off by travelling around in chariots of fire or any of that flash stuff—not like some I could mention—but a few exploding rings can give me a good boost for up to an hour and, if the worst comes to the worst, I can always call up that yellow flame with the hissing purple heart. I can even use that flame to change the times of day, if you really want to know. That flame has got me out of more than a few sticky situations in the past. But I'm not going to explain too much about my little tricks. An angel has to keep some things to himself.

I say 'himself' but I had also better explain that none of us is either male or female. We do not marry or fall in love; neither do we ever fall ill or grow old or even die. There are the odd parties, particularly when a sinner repents, but, to be honest, I can't offhand remember the last time a sinner repented in Wales, certainly not in any numbers since the 1904 Revival in the South.

I can still remember the times when evangelical religion provided the fabric of this society; it was about the only subject for intelligent conversation from the elementary lessons of the catechism to the relationship between the universe and the mind of God. But that's all gone now. As I said earlier, it's been downhill all the way for almost the whole of this century. The decline of the Welsh language didn't help and the Church also lost control of education and political leadership. Those two world wars were also disastrous, of course. No one understood how a divine creator could have allowed all that carnage and the resulting scepticism all but wiped out my business. Aye, aye. The Welsh coal miners were always banging on about how hard their work was but, compared to an angel working a country riddled with scepticism and doubt, they've had it easy. The bonuses of patrolling this part of the world— apart from the scenery—have been few and far between for a long time now and that's a fact.

Yet Anglesey looked calm and beautiful enough that night, with the dark mingling with the cool and only the odd headlights from the passing cars revolving in the shadows. In fact the night was so clear I could even see the street lights of Caernarfon across the sea a good four or five miles distant. The flat countryside was dotted with the odd farmhouse or hamlet and, just passing the front windows of the houses, I could see that the people inside were, more often than not, sitting watching television. Television has also undermined my work in the most fundamental ways and I can barely mention the word television without feeling a severe shortage of breath. Suffice it to say that my one golden and unbreakable rule is that I never go into a house where there is a television switched on. Not that I have any particular objection to modern technology as such. Modern technology has done much to take the sheer drudge out of life while also making society more efficient, healthier and richer. Finius—who has got Africa—is always complaining that more technology there would make his work a lot more bearable.

Right at the top of that road, in the town of Llangefni, there's a small museum and, in one of the rooms, they've recreated the interior of a chapel. This is a marvellous example of how modern technology can work well. Visitors walking into a darkened room trigger sensors and my old favourite Christmas Evans comes alive in the pulpit again, preaching as a dying man to dying men. The sensors turn on the lights and there's a full-size model of him standing in the pulpit with arms held high and one hand holding a Bible aloft. His face is built out of a flickering hologram and his lips move as an actor's voice reads one of his sermons: 'The godless must turn out on a dark night full of fear, in winds and storms and raging tempests ...'

Old Christmas always loved conjuring with storms and tempests. Another of his favourite metaphors concerned the lighthouse just off the coast here: 'I was once told by a man who kept a lighthouse between Anglesey and Ireland that, on dark and tempestuous nights, multitudes of birds, having lost their way and seeking shelter, flew wildly against it and were found dead in the morning. So many souls, who have not "lodged in the branches of the great tree" the night before have also struck against the great lighthouse of Sinai's law, seeking shelter, but in vain.'

This great man of thunder and dew came to begin his work here in Llangefni in 1792. Then it was called The Dark Isle, famous for smuggling and wrecking. Christmas and his wife Catherine encountered such a spiritual chaos he immediately turned over one day a week to prayer and fasting. Always fervent in prayer he also ministered to nine other congregations.

His small house, which still sits next to the Cildwrn Chapel, was as mean and lowly as the manger. It was little more than a shed when he moved in, unsure if it wanted to stand up or fall down. The furniture could have come straight off the Ark and his broken bed was supported by a few large stones. The horse stable was also in the house and poor old Christmas—who was six feet tall—was forever cracking his head against the low beams of the roof. The one decent stick of furniture he owned, his chair, was pitted and pocked with knifemarks since he liked to nick bits off it with a knife while he was thinking of his sermon.

His wife, Catherine, even had to go out digging potatoes in the season to supplement their meagre income and occasionally he ran off a pamphlet of one of his sermons to sell and raise a few much-needed shillings. Almost all his life he struggled to pay off the chapel debts, sometimes going on long 'begging' tours around Wales. But getting the Welsh to part with money—then as now—was a most difficult business and one of his ploys was to storm at the congregation that he was aware that there was a lot of poaching in the area and, on no account, did he want to benefit from any poaching. He would prefer to receive nothing at all. The collection always went well after that warning because everyone was afraid that they'd be labelled as a poacher if they didn't flip some coins into his battered hat which he held out himself at the vestry door at the end of the service.

But although in such abject poverty he always clung to the truth and could not even tell a lie about the knackered state of his old horse when he wanted to sell it. But, there again, there is never any need to tell a lie for God. Christmas never went around the place acting the royal prawn either, spending much of his free time collecting recipes for medical treatments or various specimens of herbs. He was—what would you say?—a full man.

The morning and evening light of the eighteenth century met in my dear friend Christmas but he was as innocent as lamb. Throughout his career, some of the Cogs were forever sniping at him about money and, on reflection, I should have protected him more from what he himself called the guns of scandal and swords of bitter words. Not that he couldn't stick up for himself well enough. There was once a rumour running around here that he received a half a crown for every person that he baptised. A crowd had gathered when he was about to baptise a farmer's wife and he announced: 'They say that I receive a half a crown for each person that I baptise. This is not true. I receive a crown—not a half one. They shall be my crown of joy and rejoicing in the great day.'

Fortunate in having a wife who was beautiful, affectionate and good at digging potatoes he was mad with grief and pain when she fell ill and suffered for almost two years before she died. I visited him a lot in those bitter hours, sitting with him and doing what I could to sustain this huge, rumpled social engineer whose preaching had brought the honour and respect of thousands.

After Catherine died the chapel elders began sticking the knives into him again and it was a broken sixty-year-old with little money who, like David, was forced to leave the city, uncertain when he would return. He left Anglesey after a ministry of 34 years, leading his horse out of this town on a drizzling morning to make his way down South on roads which were littered with rocks and gaping holes. He only had some bread and cheese to eat, stopping to take water from local springs and streams. But I stayed with him on that dark and doomed morning when it seemed that the very trees were crying too. I can't cure bodily illness but I do have a rare gift among my fellow angels when it comes to fixing broken hearts. There was going to be a lot more massive preaching from Christmas Evans before his work was finally accomplished.

23

'As soon as I went into the pulpit during this period I forgot my troubles and found my mountain strong,' he said, almost understanding that I was there for him. 'I was blessed with such heavenly unction, and I felt the truth like a hammer in power, and the doctrine distilling like the honeycomb into the rarest wine.'

Yes, I was there with him in the pulpit all right. It was me who was wielding the hammer of truth which kept pounding away at old Christmas Evans's broken heart.

The sea mists were hanging low on the land that afternoon, tangling up with the houses and trees like ghostly hammocks as I moved out towards Llŷn peninsula on the north-west corner of Wales. The Land's End of Wales, some call it, just 16 miles long and up to 10 miles wide which, by reasons of its isolation, may be one of the last bastions of Welshness. A sprinkling of Welsh monoglots still live in Llŷn and bursts of that most musical of languages can be heard on every corner. The faithful still attend the many chapels on Sundays. But here also be dragons.

Down there I could pick out ancient burial grounds, old holy stones and stone axe factories. Ruined villages still slumber in small valleys and there are any number of derelict crofts standing guarding those farm fields and dandelion lanes.

But what few people know is that the hills all along the peninsula are magnetic. Some sea captains have to be careful since these magnetic eddies affect their navigation compasses and, for some reason, they always manage to give me a bumping around too so I can never really relax when I am flying around this way, forever turning to check and correct my flight path or, if distracted, finding myself going in the opposite direction to that I intended, or bumping into a chimney pot or something stupid like that. You can't be too much of a daydreamer in this game; not out in this part of the world anyway.

Those sea captains have also got to be extra careful with all these treacherous and powerful currents around this way, of course, and no matter where you are in Llŷn you are never more than minutes away from the timeless roaring of all those waves beating their brains out on all those rocks. All along here is also an old pilgrimage route to Bardsey Island or Ynys Enlli, the sacred island of the twenty thousand saints which lies in stormy waters just off the peninsula tip.

The quintessential Welshness of Llŷn has always attracted artists and the distinguished writer Jan Morris has settled in David Lloyd George's village of Llanystumdwy, immersing herself and her work in everything Welsh. There is also a residential writers' centre in Tŷ Newydd, Lloyd George's old home, on the bank of the river Dwyfor where, each week, some 16 students are taught the tangled literary arts.

I always loved to hear Lloyd George speak, particularly when he was at the height of his power as our Liberal Prime Minister. Along with that other Welsh politician Aneurin Bevan he was our most accomplished orator and, in his mouth, words became an inspired song. So we're back to that business of language already. Orators and preachers like him were the natural heroes of the Welsh whose one great pleasure was listening to recited or chanted poetry. They would use language to convey meaning and arouse emotion. In their mouths the marvels of the world marched to the music of their own speech. Lloyd George was incapable of uttering a dead or flat sentence; just like all his ancestral masters of the pulpit, every word resonated in his mouth. Listen to him talking about the River Dwyfor on whose banks he is buried:

'That's where I was brought up, that's where I played as a child, that's where I found everything that I treasure most and all the treasure that kept me going under the weight of the world—they tell me that the old Welsh worshipped rivers and I'm not surprised because a river like everything that flows is always pure, always full of joy ...'

But even a stranger to Llŷn can tell, just by looking around him, that serious and dangerous tensions are beginning to grow here. Just along the coastline there are huge caravan parks owned, mainly, by English holidaymakers. Some of the old Welsh die-hards are already complaining that the caravan has replaced the leek and the daffodil as the national emblem of Wales. English-owned cottages have also been burned around here over the last few years and, just near that telephone line, where a crow is greedily pecking out the insides of a crab apple, there's an English metal road sign with a hole blasted right through it with a shotgun.

A man who has put himself and his work right at the centre of these tensions is the poet priest R. S. Thomas who lives in a small, whitewashed stone cottage in the grounds of Plas Yn Rhiw manor overlooking the bay of Hell's Mouth. A fat white seagull was sitting on the chimney when I went past and, dressed in his usual green worsted suit with brown brogues and a skinny red woollen tie, old R.S. was sitting at a table reading a book next to a wood-burning stove at the rear of his cottage. He has a fine big forehead, rheumy eyes and large hands which might be more suited to a farm labourer than a poet. *Cartref R. S. Thomas* was written in spidery chalk on his front door and his main room had a huge inglenook firegrate with piles of logs. The skulls of sheep were dotted over the old oak *cîst* and bookcases. Just next to a rug on the bare tiled floor was a portable radio. This was the home of a man, you knew, who would never put his grand nose inside an English-owned caravan.

To be perfectly honest I would have preferred to have ignored old R.S. and all his anti-English bigotry but no inquiry into the spirituality of Wales could really call itself complete without at least recording his presence. Many regard him as the finest Welsh poet in English and one of the three leading religious poets of the century. But his life and work also tell us something of the way in which the Welsh have gone up the wall.

Here in this cottage old R.S. has essayed the long contest between Cynddylan in his tractor and our Bert in his caravan. First there were the pitiless poems laying bare the inner workings of rural societies like Llŷn where the peasant leans 'to gob into the fire', or 'the hill farmer pens a few sheep in a gap in the clouds' or stoops to pull 'the reluctant swedes'.

But soon, in the next wave of work, his posture became that of a disillusioned romantic, full of that old growling melancholy, of whom there are at least half a million other such practitioners in Wales. Thus he began writing of woods 'vibrant with sped arrows'; of 'wind-bitten towers and sham ghosts' and, even more ominously, 'an impotent people, sick with inbreeding, worrying the carcass of an old song'.

This is the language of hatred and despair which he also began directing against the English tourist—'the exploiters'— with their cheap goods, horrible language and thoughts of carnal sex. These visitors are buying us all up, he began crying. It is all over; everything is far too late. Our culture is being destroyed, particularly by the excremental English language. (All this, mind you, from a man who was born in Cardiff, spent the first six years of his life in Liverpool, had an English wife and a son who speaks no Welsh and who writes all his poetry in English for which he actually accepted the Queen's Gold Medal for Poetry.)

But even in private conversation he gets quite steamed up about the English, raising his large hands into the air and getting quite screechy as he likens the English tourists to Biblical swarms of all-destroying locusts. 'I am just not going to welcome them here and, if nothing else, my work has sought to describe how our old way of life has been destroyed by the English with their rotten culture, media exploitation and second homes.'

But, in his later work, the search for God had become more intense and, with his usual incisive economy and metaphorical power, he has been busy entering the myths of the 'snake-haunted' Garden of Eden and gazing up at the shame of Golgotha. So we often find him praying alone on his knees in a stone church before a silent congregation of shadows. We watch him looking out at grey waters 'as vast as an area of prayer' or the simple ravishment of the 'sun breaking through to illuminate a small field'. In his work The Cross is 'untenanted' and God remains resolutely silent.

He has clearly hoped that, with bleak if beautiful metaphor, he can touch God Himself but the main problem throughout his work is that love is missing and hatred flourishing. God is not distant, silent or difficult to apprehend. He can be understood by a simple belief in His Son and, if He stands for nothing else, it is love. You cannot come to know God with hatred and bigotry in your heart; God is always distant and silent to those who hate.

But the real menace of this disappointed romantic is that he has become amazingly influential. I don't even much like going to eisteddfodau any more since there are always any number of grizzled R.S. clones there, all busy snuffling in the trough of despair or else bursting with tribal hatred because they've just spotted a few hairy Englishmen towing their caravan up a Welsh country lane. I've never had anything against caravans anyway. Not everyone can afford an old stone cottage with an inglenook fireplace overlooking the sea. And I've heard some fine prayers in caravans in my time.

Also R.S.'s postures have become the very incubus of the wall-dauber and those who burn English homes. Perhaps significantly the road sign with a shotgun hole through it pointed to his home at Rhiw.

It makes me so mad. All this pin-headed tribalism is not the Welsh way and certainly has nothing to do with The Path of the Cross. The Welsh grew out of long traditions of hospitality and kindness to strangers no matter what their language. They've always been instructed to entertain strangers since they might be us angels in disguise. Fellowship with every nationality has also always been central to the Welsh way and, as I continued moving above the coastline and rumbling surf, I reflected—and not for the first time—how those who so often are claiming to speak for the Welsh are also so often precisely those who are busy leading them into the gathering storm.

The wind came booming down the peninsula, pushing around the curving sheets of rain as the man stumbled and fell down the slope, sending the bier crashing forward. One of the dead hands then tumbled out into the cold rain. It was a beautiful hand, as cold as alabaster, with long, thin fingers which had gone blue at the tips. The stumbling man's mouth had opened wide to let out a moan which was muffled by the rain, making it more of a splutter than a moan as lightning ripped repeatedly through the dark skies.

The three other cowled figures carrying the bier did the best they could to steady it—even though they too found it difficult to keep their footing—as the man got up again with blood running through a wound on the side of his head. They carried on walking down the sodden slope and soon the rain had washed his face clean of mud except that there was still a trickle of watery blood running from his forehead. In all their difficulties trying to keep their footing they hadn't even noticed the dead hand still dangling disjointedly from beneath its canvas shroud.

I hovered around behind the slipping and sliding group as they continued on their way. They looked as if they would manage all right but I hung around anyway just to make sure. Still no one had noticed the hand so I slipped it back in quietly. Funerals need all the decorum they can get, particularly on the last pilgrimage through a night of storms.

There were no fewer then ten different groups coming down the peninsula that night—some numbering as many as a dozen strong—so it was a bit like being a policeman on traffic duty for me, just watching out for them and seeing them down safely. Another group was carrying a woman on a stretcher, her face as white and stiff as that dead hand. She was not quite dead but nearly so as they stumbled the last few hundred yards to The Pilgrim Kitchen on Aberdaron harbour. As they arrived another group appeared at the top of the lane. These were carrying a large wooden cross and their voices were sending up a ragged hymn into the dripping night. They don't always keep walking in these storms since there are a number of makeshift mortuaries along the roads around here where they can take shelter and surround the body with the protection of Corpse Candles until the storm has abated.

This has always been a busy time on the peninsula, particularly after a long, cold winter. The old have lost their resistance to the appalling weather and so, when they are close to death or actually dead, they are taken on their last trip to Bardsey, to be buried along with the other thousands already there. Many of these pilgrims have dragged themselves across the length of Wales, leaping every river, scaling every mountain, braving every storm, all lured by the sweet promise of holiness and an everlasting resurrection for their loved ones.

The small stone-built Pilgrim Kitchen at Aberdaron was already packed with those waiting for a window in the storm. Out in the harbour small moored boats were bounding up and down furiously as yet more waves came smashing up against the cliffs. The angry waves were also throwing driftwood right up on to the cobbled streets and even the flinty pigs were sticking firmly to the shelter of their sties. The chief hazard now facing the pilgrims was the two-mile Bardsey Sound which was treacherous even on fine days with constant vicious changes of direction of the currents and the rip tides. In such conditions they are wise to wait for the weather to turn. But most are not wise and many of them couldn't row across a duck pond safely so they still throw caution to the winds, particularly if they are anxious to get their sick and dying to the island before they do actually die.

I've seen them begin rowing out into waves the size of houses and, while there is not much I can do to stop them sailing into a storm—if that's what they want to do—all I can do is watch out for them and steady their boat up a bit, particularly if it gets so bad they settle for prayer. I've always been obliged to respond to calls for help on the prayer line. Even if they've been behaving stupidly I've always been obliged to respond to faithful prayer.

The other problem that night was that The Pilgrim Kitchen was now jam-packed and they could barely squeeze anyone else inside. So why get soaked here when you can get soaked at sea, a few must have thought since, sure enough, two groups in separate boats did indeed take off straight into the teeth of the storm. They didn't even seem scared as they rowed out steadily with the rain still pouring down and the winds ripping the very tops off the waves. They were even shouting encouragement to one another, suggesting that they should have some kind of friendly race even if most of their shouted words were blown away by the winds.

The further they got out into the Sound the more they were tossed around like dead leaves in a high wind with the waves carrying their cockleshell craft high up into the air and then flinging them hard down on to their bows. One second they were there riding the crests of the waves, almost as if suspended by invisible strings in those roaring silences, when, on the next, they were plunged downwards again, the body of the boats yawing one way and another. The volatile currents had also separated the two boats and they had drifted some three hundred yards apart, making my job of watching over them even more difficult since, as one appeared, the other disappeared.

The unruly clouds were cutting out the moonlight and that wasn't helping my flight either. I also began struggling in a few magnetic storms so I had to use all my complicated powers of intelligence just to hold my position in the air and, even then, needed to use a burst or two of the yellow flame with the purple heart just to do that.

The clouds sent down a whole new downpour and one of the boats began shipping a lot of water. There was a loud, wild cry—half groan and half prayer—and I veered towards the water-logged boat, where two of the pilgrims on the aft seat were busy bailing with scoops. Just then the woman on the stretcher died on the other boat. At least she had died within sight of the Bardsey shoreline and I actually saw her soul rising up into the storm, flapping yellow on drizzling grey, like a huge bedraggled bird trying to fight its way home. At that moment the soul seemed to stop still in the rainy air and I

31

hovered around it with alarmed hands outstretched when it began to rise again, faster and surer now than before.

By now the dead woman's boat had got into deep trouble and was in danger of sinking fast. But fortunately for them they had given up trying to bail or row and were calling for God's help in loud and fervent prayer.

That was one of the rare occasions when I opened my wings and, even though I say so myself, what great wings they are, stretching up to thirty feet in length as I used them to try and stabilise the storming winds. I had to keep pounding them up and down hard, displacing hundreds of tons of air, until they created a sort of still vacuum which calmed the seas and enabled both the boats to get to Bardsey. The pilgrims were too amazed and even fearful to look up and see what was going on. All they knew was that something very special was going on and that they would all send up a fine prayer of thanks when they got there.

But the real problem with using my wings is that it is a very exhausting business. I might need anything up to a week to recover after unfolding them and a lot can go wrong in a week, particularly here in Wales.

But today, in the year of our Lord 1992, there was no sign of trouble anywhere and the island was sunny and silent with cormorants flying as straight as arrows over the still sea. Guillemots stood around in silent conclave on the cliff edges. One side of the island rose up like a stray mountain and, right at the other lower end, was the white tower of the Trinity lighthouse. Down on the seashore there were lolling seals and the hissing noise of many barnacles.

There are many places in Wales which have their own special atmosphere. St David's is one and Tintern is another. But Bardsey's atmosphere seems to come throbbing straight up out of the very earth and, on occasion, can seem as loud as a power generator. There's the spirit of healing here and the sweet scent of holiness too.

As I moved along a twisting track the munching rabbits and grazing sheep looked up. Between them they have made the grass as short and neat as a tennis court except when, a few years back, the rabbits were devastated by myxamatosis. When I came out on the prow of the hill I could see right across the glittering sea to Anglesey on one side with the mighty sweep of Cardigan Bay down here and, right across the water, the Wicklow mountains of Ireland. A Celtic cross stood in the old graveyard next to a rubbled monastery with the inscription: 'Is it nothing to you, all ye who pass by?'

The monastery was set up on this island in the fifth century by Cadfan, the patron saint of warriors. This was the beginning of the Age of the Saints when almost the whole of Europe was being torn apart by so many quarrelling Druids and tribal fighting that God decided to introduce a number of men who were going to be holy riddles; new ambassadors for his thoughts. Rainbows kept forming almost hourly along the Welsh coastline announcing the arrival of these prophets who were going to rekindle the fires of faith everywhere. It was at this time too that I was assigned here—all that bumbling Druid stuff around those big stones was way before my time.

Cadfan was one of the first of these holy men and the fame of his new community soon spread to the extent that pilgrims were coming here from all over Europe. Pope Calixtus II—'in view of the perilous nature of the trip to Rome'—declared that three pilgrimages to Bardsey would, in future, be counted as the equal to one to Rome. It was also around this time that it became fashionable to bury the dead here. Almost everyone down to Aberystwyth wanted to be buried on Bardsey. Even a casual spade into the Bardsey earth these days will dig up a pile of bones and it seems certain that at least twenty thousand people were buried here.

But the Bardsey pilgrimage ended in the Reformation when the monastery was pillaged. Later it was farmed and, at one point, was taken over by pirates. The island was even ruled over by kings and when the last one, King Love Pritchard, turned up at the National Eisteddfod David Lloyd George welcomed him as 'one of those Welsh from overseas'. It is now run by a Trust, with a few farms and guest houses. A hermit, Sister Helen Mary, lives in one of the stables and there is a Franciscan friar, Brother Nathanael, who looks after visitors during the summer.

A Franciscan friar is always a great delight for me since, in a sense, their life is one long, secret prayer. Someone like Nathanael makes perfect company for any angel since, apart from the small private flash prayers he likes to direct at every pilgrim to the island, he also goes through the more formal prayers of Compline, the midday office and evening prayer.

So on a bright sunny day like this I just wandered around behind him, perhaps breaking off to listen to Sister Helen Mary's prayers. A perfect day came to a perfect end when there was a blood-red twilight with the sun sinking in a bright rage behind some fat, black clouds. Lovely warm winds were sweeping in from the sea as Manx Shearwaters began skimming the bobbing waves.

That atmosphere I spoke of earlier was there again and I caught myself smiling as my spirit began twisting around with those other spirits of holiness and healing. But there was something else moving around in the salt spray of that crimson twilight; something else was actually breaking up out of the earth and preparing to make the journey skywards. I didn't understand any of it and had certainly never felt anything like it since it was almost as if the twenty thousand saints were busy marshalling themselves for some brilliant new resurrection dawn.

There's something going on. I just know it and I'm going to get back home to check it all out since it would be dreadful if I missed out. There's nothing in my makeup that can deal with missing out on anything important. Could it be that we're all being finally prepared for the time when every knee will bow and every mouth confess that Jesus is Lord? In those times the saints will again take charge of the earth and the graves will give up their dead.

More spirits began growing all around me, moving through the salty redness, chanting choruses of prayer and praise. Even the shadows were taking on new shapes and forms, mingling with the breezes as the sunset faded and stars speckled the sky, creating their own brittle starlight. These are all signs and rumours but could it really be that the Age has again become so dark that The Boss will soon return?

Angels know most everything there is to know but they do not know the time when he will step back onto the stage of the world.

# Second Book

It was a dull morning with the sun trying to break through massing, dark clouds, fat with rain, as I made my way out of Dolgellau following the old railway track along the banks of the Mawddach estuary towards Barmouth. Spring was beginning to stir in the damp land with catkin branches dangling overhead and the gorse bursting into bright yellow puffs. I spotted a shy stammering of snowdrops near the old railway station of Penmaenpool but the buds of the marching armies of rhododendron bushes had yet to open.

It was almost as if winter did not want to let go of the land without the most prolonged and violent fight since, even with the stirring Spring, frost was glazing the granite chippings of the old railway track and those distant mountains like Cadair Idris were still capped with snow.

After a few miles I stopped to sit on a studded iron bridge beneath which a stream was gurgling out into the estuary. It might even have been the most beautiful sight that ever soothed a fevered brow. The incoming tide had made the whole estuary as full as an egg and golden chariots of light were being driven slowly across the water, their movements contrasting brilliantly with the dark reds and browns of the outlying woodlands and mountains.

I am always delighted by such huge cartwheels of light since, within them, I can often travel great distances when the mood takes me. Aided by my trusty flame and exploding rings

I can move straight back home to Israel if I want, hanging out with the others on Megiddo perhaps or even sitting next to a goatherd in Qumran. It would be warming up in Israel now with whole floods of purple flowers all over the fields of Galilee and thousands of migrating storks powering their way across the Jordan Valley. Gangs of us like to hang out on the slopes of Sinai, making music or singing. Angel music has all heaven in it; it is as sweet as the morning dew and as delicate as mirages. And I know of no sight quite so thrilling as the archangel Gabriel, with his great wings fully outstretched, gliding down out of the sun over Jericho.

Not that I have been home for ages and, even within these cartwheels of light, travel over long distances is almost as exhausting as if I had been using my wings. Also, as I indicated before, the sooner I finish my report, the sooner it will be over and I might then be able to stay home for longer than usual.

But I wasn't feeling too homesick that day, sitting on that bridge enjoying the perfect silence of that Mawddach morning. Oh there was the occasional intrusive noise of a jet scraping away behind those clouds or the screech of a few disturbed ducks, yet the dominant sound was silence and you would have had to listen very carefully indeed to have heard even the loudest cry of anguish on that blessed morning in Wales early in Spring.

As I continued along the estuary bank I also noticed the way in which the vistas were forever changing. Everywhere the land seemed to be shuffling the cards and laying down a new hand on which you could safely bet a huge amount of candles. One minute I was deep in some woodland and the next I was hovering on the edge of a huge expanse of water. The tide was ebbing fast by now and huge sand banks began appearing in the water like the backs of giant gold hippopotami, all lit up by the passing shafts of sunlight in brilliant promises of glory.

There again the Mawddach has always worn as many different faces as there are seasons. Winds can pick up those sand banks and hurl them around with a Jezebel fury. And gales can whip up the dangerous passions of those flood tides which can swamp or drown everything and everyone. I've seen sunsets here so fatally beautiful they can cause heart attacks. There's nothing quite like the dancing interplay between the dying day and the oncoming night on the ballroom floor of the Mawddach.

Yet it took until that morning to really understand why John Ruskin had once said that there was only one more beautiful walk in Britain than the walk from Dolgellau to Barmouth and that was the walk from Barmouth to Dolgellau.

The town of Dolgellau is a solid, no-nonsense slice of pure Welshness, built out of huge chunks of local stone and scattered around its own river under the shadow of Cadair Idris which looms over it like a big, friendly bear. The mountain seems to keep changing shape too, on some days near and friendly but on others faraway and vaguely menacing. Mountaineers gather in the Dolgellau streets to tackle those vicious slopes as do clear-faced young girls and the odd prowling traffic warden. The stone buildings have the most severe non-conformist air about them since the place is solid chapel—with a dab of Catholicism—with most of the chapels polished, burnished and well-attended. People don't spit on the street in Dolgellau and, if they must swear, they do so behind the back of their hands. Barely any advertisement hoardings disfigure the buildings and, as befits the former site of the Parliament of Owain Glyndŵr, every corner of the twisting streets are alive with the Welsh language in which it is almost impossible to swear in anyway.

The tranquillity of the morning deepened when, in the next rhododendron wood, I noticed that a figure was watching me. He had a purple and gold cloak around his shoulders and a fancy mitre on his head. A couple of pistol butts were sticking out of his belt as he stood, hands on hips, his jaw sticking out pugnaciously in his usual posture of defiance. Well I knew who he was all right and, for a second, I thought that he was going to start performing with those guns of his and only prayed that I could settle him down quickly before someone got hurt. He may have been a bishop but he was the biggest delinquent that

I've ever come across and I was just shaping up to deal with him when a single cloud swept overhead, throwing a shadow over the rhododendron wood within which my pistol-packing bishop disappeared. Light has always been my method of travel but certain figures in the older church can travel in shadows and the bishop was one of them.

Some dark angels also like to travel around in shadows and I really do hope that I don't come across them before the year is out and my report is finished. Anyway let's not talk about them. Let's merely record that the bishop had gone.

Way out on the other side of the water I could just about make out the old Clogau gold mine where they used to dig gold for royal wedding rings. The mine is closed down these days but if any future member of the Royal Family fancies getting hitched and wanted to carry on the tradition they could still buy a mining pan in the ironmongers in Dolgellau and try his luck on these estuary banks. Not that those wedding rings have ever brought them much luck, I hear. Of the last five royal weddings all have ended in acrimony, divorce or tears.

Just near the gold mine is a house where Somerset Maugham used to go to write and, further along again, is the house where Charles Darwin wrote *The Ascent of Man*. We had more than a few heated debates back home on whether or not we should cook Darwin's goose before he wrote all that evolutionary nonsense. But, in the end, we decided to let him get on with it. Angels have never been expected to interfere with people's thoughts and destroying anything at all—even televisions—has always been a bit iffy. As the prime movers of a loving Creator we're not supposed to be capable of any destruction even if I've been sorely tempted often enough.

In many ways it's been a shame that we've been circumscribed like this since angels are terrifically strong. When we get together nothing at all can stand against us. In the old days—when the rules were very different—one of my fellow conscripts destroyed the Assyrian Army. A whole army of us were also finally sent in to destroy the wretched and lost cities of Sodom and Gomorrah. I also actually met the angel who rolled away the stone from The Boss's tomb with a flick of his wrist. It was a whopping big stone as well but it could have been a tennis ball the way he handled it. Others have closed the mouths of lions and even opened locked prison doors but, as I said, they don't allow us to do any of that strongarm stuff any more. The job is mostly paperwork now but, even so, I do hope that this is my final report. I've always enjoyed writing; it's always come easily to me but they now expect you to go on and on. I far preferred the old papyrus days when nothing was longer than forty or fifty words. But now reports can be five hundred pages minimum and you're expected to throw in everything but the kitchen sink.

I finally came to that long railway bridge leading into Barmouth which that wonderful travel writer H. V. Morton thought the finest artificial promenade in Britain. The tide had ebbed fully and the huge sandbanks were littered with bright golden patches of busted cockle shells left by the birds. The rain had held off but a hard wind, thick with salt, was sweeping in off the Bay.

But soon after leaving the bridge the happiness of the morning began to fragment as I came into Barmouth. The main smell was that of frying chips and it was amok with places with names like Las Vegas Amusements, Chuck's American Diner and Takeaway or The Barmouth Rock Shop. In fact the town looked as if it had just applied to be twinned with Sodom or Gomorrah and I seemed, in one morning, to have walked straight from heaven into hell.

There was Ye Olde Smugglers' Bar and pubs with the usual fishing nets hanging off the bar ceilings or port-holes through which you could marvel at third rate paintings of some South Sea Islands, not forgetting the stools made from lobster pots. Shops were piled high with twinkling tourist rubbish but there was little trade. Empty and shuttered hotels with improbable names like The Sandpiper, Crystal House and Wavecrest stood cheek-by-jowl along the seafront. A deserted fairground peered out over an empty beach where two dogs were chasing one another and a man was digging for lugworms. But that's the way of all seaside resorts which make their living from tourists isn't it? Too empty in the winter and too full in the summer. Almost all the accents were either from Liverpool and Birmingham and all you could be sure of was that it would have all driven old Owain Glyndŵr bananas.

But the main point of my visit there, of course, was to report on the spirituality of the place and, on that front, I must say that I all but expired with disappointment. The congregations were thin to the point of invisibility and, no matter down which back alley I went, I couldn't detect so much as a trace of solo prayer, even if I could always pick up television or inane gales of Radio One. Oh to find a home without television or Radio One. They can't even play a few pop tunes either without some fool butting in and announcing details of a multiple rape in Manchester or some double murder in London. And I don't ever bother much with readers of *The Sun* newspaper either, if the truth be known. I've discovered that I can talk to *Sun* readers or show them visions until my wings fell off and they still wouldn't have a clue what I was on about unless I threw in a big bosom.

All the old chapels in Barmouth were either empty or up for sale. The Ebenezer Chapel, founded in 1881, was for sale through Madeley Evans estate agents. Another chapel, along with a blue burglar alarm, had a large red sign announcing *The Price is Right. A Recession Sale. Hard Times. Stock Liquidation. Big Cost Savings,* the sign boomed on.

Then there was another of those damned video shops fouling up the very air. I mean to say I pride myself on being one of the first post-modernist angels, who understands the stress and difficulties of these end times, but I can't even stand in front of a video shop and look through the window for fear of being overcome by evil gases that are swirling around inside them. The trade with all its 'terror, revenge and violence' has got so bad I can even see nests gathered above the counters with small black wings poking up out of them. A few times

42

now I've even fainted spark out on the pavement when I've been near them so I've got to give them a very wide berth.

Should you ever find an angel lying unconscious in the street you can be sure it'll be a video shop or a particularly heavy concentration of satellite dishes on the eaves of the houses. Just grab him by the ankles and pull him around the corner to another street or preferably an open field. He'll revive soon enough.

A few days later it was one of those usual Welsh mornings, full of rain and gloomy prophecy, as I continued my journey up the valley out of Tywyn. The first of the Spring lambs were romping about in the fields and, in Dolgoch, I wandered up a small valley and marvelled at a high waterfall, throbbing with bass thunder and ancient defiance. The sound of a waterfall must be one of the authentic sounds of rural Wales and they were all making a burly, angry music just now after a few days of heavy rain.

But there again, now I come to think of it, most all the authentic sounds of rural Wales have something to do with water, from hurrying streams to rain spilling off roofs into butts and fat raindrops hissing the bare branches of the trees. Also it's all the light that's forever playing on all this moving water that so often makes the Welsh countryside seem so magical.

There was that rich and yeasty taste to the land, stretching her loins after lying for so long in her winter bed. The aggrieved clinking of magpies hung in the air and just here was a pocket of new honeysuckle.

I returned from the waterfall to an empty railway station then followed the path of the Talyllyn railway up along the side of the lake where the rain was making numerous dartboarding ripples on the surface. The sides of the valley were mottled with browns and greens and all the surrounding peaks were steaming with mists as if being boiled on a giant stove. Then, as I came down to the edge of the lake, Cadair Idris—or The Chair of Idris—loomed over me before disappearing into rain clouds again. It was up to its old tricks again too. The closer I got the more the mountain seemed to change shape. One minute it was an impregnable medieval fortress and the next it was some great battleship sailing through a sea of storms. It also managed the almost impossible feat of seeming both vague and distinct at the same time.

It was no weather for flying anywhere and the rain mists kept swirling around me so thickly I decided to walk up those high slopes. Sometimes the mist opened and I could see the river falling out of the top of the mountain and chasing down that valley of stones in a continual angry rush. But within minutes the opening closed again and I saw little except the mossy rocks around my feet.

On occasion my path went almost vertical and I had to haul myself up with my hands, coming out onto another level where not only did I come across the foulest stink but also found an exploded sheep with hanks of wool dotted all around. Its pink ribs had been picked clean by the crows. But its head was still strangely intact and its eyes stared up at me miserably. Oh brother, look what's happened to me out here, those eyes said. Just look at the state of me.

The stench drove me on and, on the next plateau, there was yet another dead sheep and yet another which had no head at all. R. S. Thomas might have enjoyed the symbolism of moving through this old sheep's graveyard but I absolutely hated it and it was a relief to move out onto another wide path which would take me to the final slope to the summit.

Some ten minutes later it began snowing and I began counting the snowflakes dissolving on my hand. A bank of mist actually seemed to be following my feet and I could have been walking on some kind of mechanical elevator. The snow stopped after a while and now huge gaps were opening up in the mists again, giving enthralling glimpses of the valleys and waterfalls all around. Yet apart from the continual roar of the river—which was really a sound of the mountain—the silence went right through me and yet again I understood why so many people over so many years have come up here to pray. I guess—but it's only a guess—that I've picked up some of the best prayers of my career out here on the summit of Cadair Idris.

I just happened to be going by one day when I caught Christmas Evans deep in a three-hour session here, mainly asking God to bless his ministry in Anglesey. I spoke to Christmas on that occasion, telling him that he should enter into a fresh covenant with God and everything would work out fine. But it's not a big burning bush job when I speak to anyone. The way I work is to drop silent words into the brain as it prays. As long as it's fervent, believing prayer I can get through to them without any problems at all. The difficulty comes when they are determined not to listen. Not everyone who prays takes time to listen—as everyone always should.

The mists lifted slightly again as cold winds came booming up from the valley below. You really can see the shape of the chair on which old Idris was supposed to have sat but that story is a load of low nonsense if you really want to know. The Welsh have also long believed that, if you spend a night up here, you will go mad or blind or become endowed with wondrous poetical powers. Another case of low nonsense, I'm afraid, since you're more likely to get a bad case of pneumonia or hypothermia if you tried that. The Welsh have always had this weakness for believing just about anything you care to tell them. They've always suffered from a certain lack of scepticism.

Charles Darwin once walked up here to the summit and thought that the mountain was 'a grand fellow'. Not that I bothered to speak to him of course. Also Thomas Love Peacock was right on this spot when he reflected 'with astonishment and pity on the madness of the multitude'. I also spoke to the evangelist George Fox just over there in a vision and that was something else again.

But I never initiate visions as such. All visions come directly from God and I am merely their channel. So, while I might have a certain freedom in the form of the vision, the basic message or symbol is always God's alone. I can tart it up a bit, if I feel in the mood, but I'm not usually in favour of too much tricky business because people find visions difficult enough to understand as it is. I always prefer to give it to them straight so, with George Fox, it was just a case of a huge pair of hands reaching out of a fiery pit.

The purpose of these visions is two-fold. They are to deliver the simple message; in this case the saving grace of God's hands as a protection from any punishment. But also a vision can simply be God's way of letting someone know that their work has been anointed. This private knowledge, in its turn, gives them a secret edge. Every preacher needs great tenacity and perseverance since he is always railing against walls of doubt and evil so, we've long found, a private vision can work wonders in that department.

We had all known for a long time that Fox was special so, particularly as he wasn't strictly speaking from my patch, it was a huge pleasure to catch him up here and reward him like that. Once they've seen one of my visions they tend not to wander too far from the true faith. My visions may not be the prettiest of them all—you don't get too many shimmering pillars of fire in my work—but they've always have great elan and punch. Get a vision through me and you don't forget it in a hurry.

But, oddly enough, by far my biggest success in connection with this mountain was not with a man or indeed anyone famous at all. The greatest triumph I ever had out this way was back in 1800, with a sixteen-year-old girl and I can remember almost every detail of that day as if it was yesterday.

It was late in a summer afternoon with an unusual number of cattle being driven along the drovers' roads towards the English borders. I had counted five separate herds going across the Snowdon area alone, their flanks sweating hard and nostrils snorting with steam as they were pushed on by yapping corgi dogs and the drovers themselves on their Welsh ponies.

But everything was serene enough with the sun preparing to sink behind the bulky black outlines of the mountain range. I had been flopping about the slopes of Cadair Idris all afternoon keeping half an eye on an old clergyman who spent most of the afternoon puffing up the mountain and was even now puffing his way back down again. Old people should accept the limitations of their bodies, in my view, but he couldn't—or wouldn't—so, after he sent up a fine prayer for God to give him sufficient strength, I was tailing him quietly just in case. But then my spiritual antennae picked up a run of bright golden chimes in the cooling mountain air.

I had been getting the vaguest readings on the chimes all day—nothing of any great spiritual moment has ever happened anywhere in Wales without me hearing about it through the chimes—but I couldn't quite work out what they were about or indeed where they were coming from. Perhaps I hadn't been concentrating properly because that old clergyman really did look as if he was going to fall off a rock and break his neck at any second but, in the event, this last run of chimes indicated that something rather special was unfolding and, what is more, it might even be going on right here on the mountain. Then, floating upwards into a dusty twilight, I was checking around and all became clear.

A young girl was coming up the mountain path and walking with something of a limp because she had cut one of her bare feet. There was, of course, nothing unusual about a young girl walking on her own—whereas today no mother would allow such a young girl to walk down a garden path on her own, particularly in her bare feet—but it was getting late and, even though it was a still, warm evening, it would get cold almost as soon as the sun disappeared.

I immediately forgot about the clergyman and went to hover behind the girl. Apart from her injured foot she was also very tired and her lungs were pulling in breath in short, squealing gasps. Indeed she was so tired she wasn't even walking in a straight line, once swaying so dangerously that I had to reach out and hold her by the elbow to steady her up. But she was clearly a good girl and anyone at all would have been pleased to help her. She had short, badly cropped black hair and the largest hazel eyes. But her cheeks were streaked with dirt and now, with the sun going down fast, she was shivering and squeezing herself with her arms a lot. What was she doing out here and where was she going?

Well I soon worked out that she had come from Llanfihangel-y-Pennant and was walking the 25 miles to Bala. Even more interestingly she had three shillings and sixpence in her pocket—which she had taken six years to save—and was going to Bala to buy a Welsh Bible from Thomas Charles, a bright young Methodist minister who was even now compiling an important Scriptural Dictionary with lots of new learning about Wales. Mary Jones was her name, a weaver's daughter.

By now she had become so tired she could barely walk at all so, with the darkness thickening up, I moved out in front of her and sucked a lot of the oxygen out of the air just around her mouth. This is an angel trick which Bimmimus once taught me for putting people asleep safely and quickly. They faint as soon as they lose their oxygen and, as they slump downwards, you then pick them up and carry them to somewhere comfortable where they can revive their spirits and strength with sound sleep.

I put Mary under a juniper tree where the grass was dry and soft and, after arranging her head comfortably on one of her arms, covered the whole of her body with mine, warming it right through and taking her spirit deep into its sleep. Then I kissed the wound on her left foot better and sat with her through the night, warming her again when she got shivery and shooing away some inquisitive crows, until the sun began rising on the mountains and she woke up, sitting up with a mumble and rubbing her eyes with the backs of her hands.

She was very calm and relaxed by now, not even wondering unduly how her wounded foot had got better. Neither did she seem surprised when she found some fresh bread and a jug of water next to her. She wolfed down the whole loaf hungrily before washing it down with the water when, stiffening her back and letting out a most unlady-like belch, she got up and carried on her way.

The chimes around her again became quite strong so I stuck with her as much out of curiosity as anything else. As I've already explained we angels already know almost all there is to know but can never see into the future. So I followed her the dozen or so miles into Bala where she called on a bakery and asked the whereabouts of the Reverend Thomas Charles.

His wife, Sally, opened the door of their fine manse near the lake, looking Mary up and down with a mixture of wariness and contempt. I may have fixed the wound on her feet but I really should also have done something about her dress which was by now almost in tatters. In any event Mrs Charles merely closed the door again. I couldn't believe it. Here was a most promising Christian household—which might even one day become famous—and they were slamming the door in the face of a little girl who had walked 25 miles to be there. Mary just walked back along the path and sat on the edge of the roadway crying. Outraged, I went to the door and gave the knocker one hell of a belt. Mrs Charles opened the door almost immediately and, on looking around and seeing nothing, closed it again. I gave the knocker another banging and almost shook the house down. By this time Thomas Charles himself had come to the door, in his shirt and braces, to see what all this banging was about. He couldn't see anyone, of course, but, on walking down the path, he saw that Mary was still crying in the roadway so he invited her inside. At first she refused to budge but he took her by the hand and insisted.

In their living room Mary, still snuffling, explained how she had saved all her money for six years to buy a Welsh Bible. She had heard that Mr Charles sold these Bibles so she had decided to walk there and buy one. I must say as a performance it could hardly have been bettered and I doubt even if that great old sentimentalist Charles Dickens could have improved on her tale of scrimping and saving and all that barefoot hardship on the mountains. But Mary was Welsh, of course; let's not forget that. There's no one quite like the Welsh for turning on the taps when they get going.

Anyway no sooner had she got to the end of her story than Thomas Charles was in a worse state than Mary. Even Mrs Charles was crying, mortified by her earlier rudeness to the girl since she had assumed that she was a begging gipsy. They were all at it and the way they were sobbing it was as if they had been lifelong sinners who now understood that the time for the reckoning had finally come. 'Oh Mary fach,' Mrs Charles kept saying. 'Oh Mary fach.'

Even more sadly—given Mary's heroic efforts—Thomas Charles did not, in fact, sell Bibles either in Welsh or English. But, holding up his palm in re-assurance, he did say immediately that he would give her his own copy.

Now I have already explained that I could not see into the future but, even so, I couldn't have even started to have guessed what this tearful encounter would finally lead to. Five years later, with the example of Mary's zeal and thirst for Biblical learning still fresh in his mind, Thomas Charles paved the way to the creation of the British and Foreign Bible Society. So young Mary Jones became instrumental in the distribution of Bibles in the most remote corners of the world and I still count banging on that Bala door as one of the highpoints of my career. One of The Boss's strictest injunctions was that his secrets should be spread abroad.

For a while Thomas Charles made Bala the spiritual capital of Wales and he worked with the other Methodist leader Daniel Rowland for more than a quarter of a century. When Charles died in 1773 some 20,000 came to his funeral at Talgarth and six ministers preached nine sermons. Yes, there have been a few successes in my career all right although, next, I'm going to tell the story of another success which could so easily have been a disastrous failure.

A huge grey sky was moving slowly and determinedly over huge grey mountains of jagged grey slate as I stood on the corner of the town of Blaenau Ffestiniog. This grey seemed to get everywhere. Almost every colour appeared to have been drained out of every corner of the landscape with everything painted a different shade of the same grey—from those slow-moving skies to the jagged mountains and the curving terraces.

The insides of the slate mines were cavernous. Most have long been closed but the Gloddfa Ganol slate mine is still very much in business with a huge circular saw ripping through a block of slate in one of the cutting sheds. Small coloured locomotives stood around in the outlying yards like the discarded trains of some giant who has finally grown out of playing with them.

But this was no time to be hanging around so I cut inland, past a few old churches and a river, until I came to the small village of Penmachno. Once out on the other side I passed through a blasted woodland and careered down a long hill before coming across an old farmhouse called Tŷ Mawr which had a decidedly wonky chimney and sat at the bottom of the valley next to a hurrying stream. For me it was a bit like stumbling into some ancient, favourite dream as I went over to examine the small damp hay stack at the end of the yard before crossing the stream on an old stone bridge. All around the valley was a misty patchwork of woodland and sloping green fields.

Tŷ Mawr has been beautifully restored and was almost exactly as I remembered it when I first came here way back in 1545. There was no glass in the window frames and it had a cold flag-stone floor. An inglenook grate opened straight up into the sky and a steep, wooden staircase led upstairs. I paused in the inglenook and held my breath but could hear nothing except the tinkling stream and the distant chattering of a skylark.

The chimes first brought me here early in 1545 and right up that particular wooden hill I had stood in the corner of the bedroom watching the birth of William Morgan, the second of five children and a direct descendant of one of the 'royal' tribes of North Wales.

It wasn't a difficult birth—as they so often were then, particularly if they decided to come out sideways—since there was a beefy midwife in attendance who all but yanked William out before he had got going, then cut the cord before giving him such a hefty smack on the bum as she held him up in the air that I had to look away. But midwifery was all pretty basic then. Lots of hot water, a pair of iron shears and a good smack. And that was it.

The chimes became stronger as I watched his angry red face burst into a scream so I knew that I had to be careful with this one. I didn't know what he was destined to do, of course; all that had happened was that the chimes had alerted me to his importance and that they especially wanted him looked after while he got on with his work. I didn't even know what the work was going to be but, as it turned out, Wales owed that screaming baby a debt of gratitude almost greater than to any other, since William Morgan was the first man to translate the Bible into Welsh and, in so doing, virtually saved the Welsh language single-handed.

This farmhouse had long fallen into dereliction but the National Trust restored it to its former glories a few years back. Iola Jones and her husband now look after the farm, receiving some 4,000 pilgrims here each year while also lecturing on William Morgan's life and work to various schools and interested groups. But she doesn't tell them the real story of William Morgan. Only I know the real story behind that important translation and what a story it was.

After young William left Tŷ Mawr he went to Cambridge University so, for a while, he was out of my bailiwick and the responsibility of Sorroptus. Now the others have always accused me of calling a spade a shovel but let's not mince our words here. Sorroptus is useless. I couldn't even start telling you how many people have died years before their time because he was daydreaming somewhere else. Do you remember William Huskisson, the leader of the House of Commons, who was the first man to be run over by a steam engine while a large crowd, including his greatest enemy the Duke of Wellington, watched? You've got it. Sorroptus. And that English king who got an arrow in his eye? That's right. Sorroptus again. The same angel couldn't give a Sherman tank protection but, even so, William Morgan managed to stay more or less in one piece while he was studying in England where he also became one of the first golden children of the Reformation. He became a key figure in a new age of enlightenment when people everywhere were first learning the delights of the printed word. One of the key doctrines of the time was that the Bible was the unique revelation of God so, when William came back to Wales and was appointed curate at Llanrhaeadr ym Mochnant, he settled down to translate the Bible into Welsh working from original Hebrew and Greek texts. The publication of this translation was to become as significant to Wales as the defeat of the Armada was to be for England in the same year.

I left Tŷ Mawr to cross the countryside to Llanrhaeadr ym Mochnant, burbling along with my little jets, and, as I did so, I was already beginning to sense the shape of my final report since I was also coming to understand that there really was a coherent mythological map of the secret life of Wales. Everything from St David through to William Morgan, Christmas Evans and even R. S. Thomas had an organic spiritual unity, I saw. Each of them inhabited their own cave of praise in which the Welsh nation had finally been born. But these caves of praise were all inter-linked by the same underground river and they contained whole treasure chests of precious ideas and sacred prayers. These caves are forgotten places of scholarship and fine music; places of powerful preaching and personal holiness.

Llanrhaeadr ym Mochnant straddles the borders of Powys and Clwyd and there were eight ducks risking life and limb by walking down the middle of the high street when I got there. With its bed and breakfast signs, shops and pubs the village has all the utter perfection of the ordinary even if there is nothing at all ordinary about its waterfall Pistyll Rhaeadr—one of the Seven Wonders of Wales.

I clambered around the rocks next to it, enjoying its spray and thundering music, thinking again about our William Morgan who also used to enjoy sitting here, watching the changing seasons as this huge jet trumpeted the news of the spectacular marriage between water and gravity. But the foam was a disappointing bracken colour that day. The whiter the foam the cleaner the water, they say. I checked down behind one rock but, as I had expected, the pistols had gone.

And then I felt it again; the sense that he was watching me. He was out there all right, hiding himself in some passing shadow, but with his eyes locked on me like radar.

The house where he worked on his translation has long fallen into a rubble but there is a newer house on the same site which is another Bed and Breakfast: Llys Morgan Guest House. Inside there is a full-size snooker table, a television and video recorder, a computer and all the other electronic paraphernalia of a society on the rack. All you can be certain of is that William Morgan would not have been able to understand any of it.

Llanrhaeadr is now a small, relatively stable community but we have to remember that, back in the sixteenth century it was a harsh, gossipy place where jealousy and enmity were forever springing up. Assaults on parsons and affrays in cemeteries were common in these vigorous Elizabethan times although vexatious law suits were the most popular weapons of the gentry. Anyone who was anyone was there to be attacked— either with a fist or a law suit—and it was in this atmosphere that William Morgan took up his living here in 1578.

But it has to be said that he was as vexatious and pugilistic as any of them and the arguments and fights came thick and fast throughout his 16 years here. While he worked on his translation he was under my intensive care and he was the biggest headache ever. If I took my eyes off him for five minutes you could be sure that he was embroiled in yet another dispute or threatening to shoot someone. How he didn't get shot himself I'll never know because there's one thing I can't do and that's stop a bullet. With an arrow you've got a chance—if I'm around—but not a bullet.

Anyway the serious rows began when William persuaded Catherine Lloyd, a local heiress with legs that went all the way

54

up to heaven, to marry Robert Wyn instead of Edward Morris, her first choice. Why William ever got mixed up in these affairs of the heart I don't know—love should find its own way—but he did and so began his long-running feud with Ifan Maredudd, Edward Morris's uncle.

Then, as if to rub salt in Maredudd's wounds, William himself then married a woman from Oswestry, who herself had been widowed twice, once to one of Maredudd's relatives. William then made matters worse by testifying in public that Maredudd was living in sin with a woman.

Maredudd struck back with every weapon in his formidable armoury. He rained a flurry of law suits on William's head; he publicly called William's wife 'a wafer woman' of the 'lewdest order of life and loosest behaviour of any woman that in the memory of man dwelt in the century where she now dwellest.'

Then the plot sickened when Maredudd gave Raymond Powell, a local pig breeder, half a sovereign to go to the manse and thrash William to within an inch of his life. Now if I say that Raymond Powell was built like a brick outhouse and that, when he walked, he dragged his knuckles along the ground, you are doubtless getting the picture. Poor Raymond didn't have any brains at all and, such as he had, he kept firmly lodged in his knuckles.

But this was the worst time for me since you were never quite sure when Raymond Powell was going to arrive—either in the middle of the night when he would be drunkenly trying to climb in through the Morgans' bedroom window or in the middle of the afternoon when William might be working on the Book of the Apochrypha. My sense of smell has always been excellent so I could often pick up his piggy smell long before he arrived at the manse and so, as he was often drunk as well, I could merely trip him up into a stream and bring his head gently into contact with a big stone. That usually put him off for a few days because, no sooner had he regained consciousness and sat up in the stream, than he had forgotten whatever it was that he had set out to do and returned to the pub.

But one night late in the summer Raymond must have had his annual bath or something since I hadn't picked up his smell and he had got into William's bedroom and was about to make mincemeat of the poor man's head with a knobkerry until I just managed to grab Raymond by the wrist, twirling him around and sending him flying down the stairs but being careful that he didn't break any bones. Looking out for people's welfare at the same time as you are busy assaulting them has always been a big problem for us. Angels are not allowed to inflict damage on anyone and it was at least another hundred years before Bimmimus taught me that trick of sucking the oxygen out of the air around someone's mouth to lay them out.

But, fortunately for all concerned, particularly my good name, Raymond Powell decided in the end that he couldn't in fact thrash William Morgan to within ten feet of his life and ended up giving Maredudd his half a sovereign back. Maredudd even offered a whole sovereign and then five sovereigns but Raymond, in perhaps the only real insight he'd ever had in his life, said that he believed that there was a shield around Morgan and it didn't seem possible to be able to damage him in any way.

We all had some peace after that for a while and William finished the Book of Apochrypha when, for no reason at all, he called in the troops to make a show of force in the village on the day of the fair and then he threatened to burn down the cottages belonging to sixty poor people. This time it was my turn to almost faint from anxiety and I was very tempted to bring another big stone into gentle contact with William's fat head—or at least shove one into his mouth—because, for a moment, it even looked as if I was going to have to call in reinforcements since the villagers had become really unruly, gathering in some force outside the manse while also threatening to burn it down and all that was in it. I mean to say the Welsh language would never have recovered if that had happened.

As it turned out William's wife went out to reason with the mob, calming them down by claiming that her old man suffered from periods of insanity when he just didn't know what he was talking about. He was as mad as half a dozen hatters, she told them and certainly had no intention of burning down those cottages. She added that the family had already booked him a place in Bedlam where he was going to spend the rest of his days firmly manacled to a strong wall. That got them all laughing and I've always marvelled at how laughter is the perfect antidote for aggression and violence since, within ten minutes or so, they were all drifting back to the pub.

But perhaps William really had lost all his marbles since, the next thing, it's Billy the Kid meets the Archbishop of Canterbury because he was strutting around the village packing pistols under his clerical vestments. I was worried stiff that he was going to shoot someone in church if they looked at him the wrong way while he was handing around the communion cup. I mean to say how was he going to get his translation finished if he ended up in prison or got himself hung, drawn and quartered. He did shoot a mad dog outside the pub one day. The thing was foaming at the mouth and running around biting the children so William took out his pistols and drilled the poor beast full of holes. There was a big increase in the congregation the next Sunday after that. I had to steal his pistols in the end and hid them down by the waterfall. Now I suspect that he's found them again.

While all this was going on the court cases with Maredudd—who then publicly accused William of beating up his mother-in-law—stretched out for years but, nevertheless, William did manage to finish his translation by 1587 and it was published in the October of the following year. His small reward was that he was then made the rector of Pennant Melangell but he had to wait until 1595 before they made him a bishop. My period of intensive care was over after the main translation but he did also manage The Psalter and, the next year again, the Prayer Book. He was a fine translator too, mysteriously connected with the Welsh Bardic tradition, with an instinctive feeling for rhythm and sensitive to all the nuances of language.

When he died in 1604 a black hour spread over Wales. I wasn't in a black mood though. No longer having to worry about Bishop Morgan was a terrific relief even if the new Welsh Bible was a monumental work containing 1,182 pages of the Old and New Testament, with the book of Apochrypha, bound in leather and printed with black letters on paper imported from Normandy.

Later that night I was moving across the country again when I picked up a rare call for help on the prayer line. There was a time when I might have picked up four or five S.O.S. calls a day on this line to sort out some little drama or other but that's not the case any longer. Now I might get one a month, if I'm lucky. But, in any event, I am always on red alert if one of the faithful does send up a call for help and this one was from Llanidloes, a small market town in mid-Wales.

I scooted down there in a second finding a vicar in the manse in one hell of a mess because somehow—and I'm not at all sure how—he had managed to end up standing in his kitchen sink with his big toe stuck up the hot water tap. And he was still wearing his dog collar. What's going on with ministers these days? You just wouldn't believe what some of them get up to.

Anyway his frantic prayer obliged me to help him in any way I could—even if he was now using some terribly bad language which was quite upsetting me. I gave his ankle a couple of tentative tugs but couldn't see any way of getting his toe out without breaking it so I finally floated the butter dish over to him, pushing it nearer and nearer to him on the draining board until he saw it. If he wondered how a butter dish had come floating over to him he didn't show it—or see it, come to that—but, sure enough, he began rubbing the butter all around his big toe until he finally managed to work it loose and get back on the floor again.

58

At least he did manage to stop cussing and say a quiet prayer of thanks and so, suitably mollified, I got on my way.

A few days later the weather had brightened after endless showers of rain and I was lying in the ruins of Montgomery castle with my wings spread out soaking up the sun. It's not exactly elegant with me lying there with my belly poking up and wings flopped out all over the place but this constant Welsh rain really does seep straight into your system and a few hours of sunshine can do wonders for your undercarriage.

I've always been very fond of Montgomery; a small forgotten town that no one visits unless they have to or want to. For no apparent reason its railway station was built a couple of miles away and, when a cartographer drew up a map of the county, he left the town off it altogether. The houses are a bit of a jumble—either Georgian or Elizabethan—and, to be honest, it hasn't changed much since the seventeenth century. There is a town hall, a small museum, a profusion of small shops— including an ironmongers which has been mongering iron for more than a hundred years—and so many defunct prisons you would swear it had once been vying with New York to become the crime capital of the world. The old county goal which once, according to a sign, housed 'Debtors 3, Felons 10 and Lunaticks 3' has now been converted into flats, albeit with the old prison doors.

There is a robber's grave in that cemetery where lies one John Davies who was hanged in 1821 for allegedly stealing a watch off a local labourer. Davies died protesting his innocence and brought down the malediction of God on the community saying that nothing would grow on his grave for a hundred years. It didn't either but that was nothing to do with me although a rose bush and holly tree are now growing on that spot so vigorously you might have thought they were feeding off half a dozen grow bags.

Yet it was while lying on the castle ruins that I spotted some dark shapes spinning through the skies over the border in Shropshire. But no sooner had they come than they were gone again. I took no further notice and was lying back abandoning myself to the sunshine of the moment when another dark shape flew across the face of the sun and I sat up trembling.

The sky was still clear when, in the far distance, I spotted four huge wings come crashing out of the avalanching sunshine. The very air was shaking with all the authority of tropical thunder and, as one pair of wings was black and the other white, I knew that Sorroptus and Klang were fighting again. It looked a tremendous scrap as well, screaming a few miles one way and then back again, tearing a few drifting clouds apart with their crashing wings.

Other dark shapes were also wheeling about and I stood up, swallowing a lot and wondering if I should join in the fray. I've never been afraid of a fight with the dark angels but they have told us again and again that we should stick to our own territory and not get involved. Sorroptus may be a bit of a daydreamer but he was one fine hitter when he got going so he was more than able to look after himself. But if Klang had called in his mates for a show of strength I might have no option. That's the way it's always been with the dark angels. They never fight by the rules. Our side, on the other hand, have always been told to play it straight.

At least the sunshine had made my wings good and dry by now so I stood on the castle ramparts, warming my body up by beating my wings up and down slowly, still uncertain what to do, when the skies cleared again and the thunder subsided. It was just as well, I suppose. Had I used my wings and got into a long bruising fight there's no telling how long I would have been out of action.

These are perilous times for us all and, with a great sadness and even a little fear in my heart, I saw that I had better get on with my work. Anyway all the dark angels may be getting their dues sooner than they expected. But even we don't know when that great day will be. As I've already said, the time and date for the return of The Boss are secrets, locked deep in the heart of God alone.

# Third Book

The hummocky shapes of the Berwyn mountains began to take shape within the exploding rings when I resumed my journey about two weeks later. These mountains do not have the rocky drama of Snowdonia but they do have undeniable charisma, wreathed, as they were today, in crowns of mists as the flame moved quickly through those lovely high valleys, sketching in twisting streams, lonely farmhouses and foxglove lanes alive with scurrying pheasants and bleating sheep.

I love it when great hoops of sunshine go rolling slowly down these slopes and, like a shouting child on a toboggan, I can go rolling down inside them. Local people have often remarked on the sound of loud unexplained laughter hanging in the Berwyn air but, as likely as not, that will just be me fooling around. We angels are complicated spirits but we are just children at heart.

These mountains were the stamping grounds of Owain Glyndŵr when he was launching his guerrila warfare against the English at the turn of the fourteenth century. Ghosts have lived unmolested in those graveyards long before that and, on dark nights, there are always strange, suspicious movements in the hedgerows. Ah look, there's a hawk's wings trembling on the wind before it twists and dives, snatching a sparrow off a branch in a burst of tiny, terrified squeals. I suppose I could have saved the sparrow but hawks have to eat.

The spiritual history of Wales, I will be anxiously emphasising in my report, is not something which has entirely lived in the past since it is still very much alive in the present. It is true that the Welsh have deserted God in droves but there are still keepers of the faith and one such keeper is Alice Thomas Ellis, the novelist, who has a traditional Welsh longhouse here in the valley of Pennant Melangell on the edge of the Berwyns deep in Powys. The house nestles, with a few outlying barns, at the foot of a high hill afforested with lines of pines. Huge chutes of rain come driving off that mountain and already you can see the Spring moving with extraordinary power in the land with everything coming up with some urgency as bandy-legged sheep totter about the fields.

Alice found the house in a derelict condition about 20 years ago. It had been built on the foundations of an old convent and, when she first saw it, the roof and floorboards had gone and a river ran through. It took six years to make it habitable and she and her family often slept in it without roof or windows. 'But we're still working on it. Thomas Mann said that when a house is finished then life is over.'

It has a soothing atmosphere with flagstoned floors and walls which have been created out of the timbers of the old convent. The silence of the rooms and surrounding fields is almost deafening and, apart from the occasional crucifix, there is also a noticeable absence of ornament.

This is the house of a woman who is struggling to come close to God, you might guess, and you would be right. In the autumn of her years Alice Thomas Ellis—her real name is Anna Haycraft—wants to build a relationship with God in this house. She wants to sort it all out with Him before she goes.

'I love living here because there is a unique and magical quality about the Welsh countryside which is not easily distinguished from heaven. There's something immeasurably ancient yet vital in the landscape—something which always makes you think of God. I love the greenness of the green, the greyness of the walls, the sheer ancientness of it all.'

She has a wonderfully warm face etched with a few tell-tale lines but beautiful still, with the large brown eyes of a Boxer dog, full of mischief and sparkly with intelligence. There is also a marked stillness about her, except for her hands, which always seem to be fiddling about, dealing either with a cigarette or another drink. But it's those eyes that people always watch as she talks, which she does almost incessantly, full of wicked mimicry, enthralling stories and little jokes, almost always against herself. But it's rarely for long before she has returned to her favourite subject.

'I believe that the Church has abandoned me. I don't believe in all this ecumenical rubbish and I don't like the charismatics or guitars on the altar at all. The only way to find true holiness is to gear your personal search towards God. I get bad periods with God sometimes and recently began thinking of Him as remote and having packed it all in. But then I decided that it was all our fault and not His. If He's not there we're all finished. There's no point to anything.'

Her faith is long-standing and deep-rooted, growing from an experience which made her change course when she was young and decided that she would be a nun. 'The experience was of hell. It was of unremitting light with no shadows; the absence of God. It could, of course, be described as a nervous breakdown but it's almost impossible to talk about it to someone who wasn't there.'

Perhaps I had better interject here that I wasn't there either. I'm not very big on shadowless experiences of hell and it's not really in the style of my work at all. The dark angels don't go in for visions either; they just take pleasure in promoting violence and criminality. If anything her bleak vision sounds more of the school of Sorroptus whose work has always been rather more of an abstract nature. All my work is more concrete and direct. Subtle as a sack of nails that's me.

She did become a nun after seeing that vision but her time as a postulant was short-lived since she suffered from a slipped disc. The doctors wanted to operate but the nuns said no. They felt that it was the will of God and decided that it was time for her to leave. Instead she met and married the publisher Colin Haycraft, becoming his fiction editor and mother of seven children. Now she has based herself here in Pennant Melangell where she writes a stream of books in which she is something of a prophet of old, standing up and denouncing evil wherever she sees it.

She's also continued practising her earlier Carmelite calling, reading The Divine Office daily with the regular discipline of prayer. Indeed she even has plans to restore her home into a working convent, complete with plenty of austerity and hard work. She has been working out the details with one of her closest friends, the novelist Beryl Bainbridge.

'Beryl is going to do the gardening and I'm going to do the cooking. We're going to have plenty of fires so it's not going to be too cold. And we're just going to have the odd sherry in the evenings. We have lots of other lady friends who are also quite keen but first they want to know our rules on gentlemen callers. We haven't worked them out yet.'

Ah, a faithful and feisty heart has always been a great joy to me and, on warm summer evenings, when I've been passing this way, I've often stretched out on the mountain behind her house, merely to be close to her. Sometimes she has actually heard me breathing in the warm night air and lots of her friends have heard me too. I've even flung a few things around in the barn to entertain her guests but had to put a stop to all that when some woman came out of the house one night and proceeded to try and exorcise me with prayer. *Exorcise me!* Well some of them had clearly misunderstood my presence there so I decided to start behaving myself and stop all that heavy breathing lark. Now, when I'm out this way, I'm simply content to sit on her roof with my hands folded on top of one another, quietly listening to her prayers.

But with spring still busily colonising the mountains I got on my way, cruising through the heart of rural Wales and marvelling at her song. For this is the world of chesty crows and the bell-heather; of high winding roads and broken dry-stone walls where, even this late in the year on the steep slopes, you still came across large lumps of snow. The winter was still clinging to the land and only the odd hill farmer moved, black on grey, through the cold mountain mists.

In the brilliant early morning light I came down to the edge of Lake Vyrnwy with its mirror-calm waters, pine forests and Victorian water treatment centre which looks like a half-finished Walt Disney castle. The odd smoking chimney rose up out of the pine forests and, in a nearby field, the nostrils of long-haired Highland cattle snorted with plumes of warm air.

I always feel a little tense here on Lake Vyrnwy since I remember all too well the days when the R.A.F. were testing the bouncing bomb here during the last world war. Those bombs went on to burst dams and kill thousands of people in German valleys such as the Ruhr and all I could do about it was stand here and watch the bombers come in low and drop their little bouncing messengers of hell on the lake.

That war was a most depressing time for all angels. We did what we could but they told us to stay out of it since matters had got so sticky in Germany they could, alas, only be fully and finally sorted out by the use of force and a huge loss of life. I count that war as the lowest point of my long career, as I hung about here in Wales watching my work—and much of the country's faith—being destroyed right before my very eyes. We angels should have been allowed to become much more involved in the war, in my view, but I am merely another foot soldier and foot soldiers are always expected to do as they're told and not have any views. That's the way Michael sees it anyway.

But on that fine morning on the edge of Vyrnwy I was, for some reason, feeling a little tense and headachy. That's not normal for us and certainly not normal for me especially with all this spring sunshine pouring through the air. There were lots of faint warning vibrations around. Then I caught a glimpse of some fleeting dark shapes in those big skies but couldn't quite make them out. Could it be them? Surely not. Dark angels don't usually come this way and certainly not in any numbers but, there again, you can never be too sure what they are going to do next.

Anyway I tried some somersaults and rolls in the sunshine but that didn't do anything to change my depressed frame of mind either. A prayer from someone—anyone at all—would have helped but I couldn't latch onto anything at all in that line. It had also been a long, long time since I had even picked up the faintest run on the chimes so I was becoming increasingly desperate when, in a forest clearing, I came across a sight so appalling that my blood ran cold and I knew that I hadn't been depressed for nothing.

Right there, near an abandoned old Fordson tractor, was a large black ring, about twenty feet across, as if a giant bonfire had been lit there. The ground was still warm with charred wisps of smoke drifting up out of it. Even more ominously there was a ring of bright white slime around the edge of the smoking black ring so I knew immediately that a gang of dark angels—perhaps as many as six of them—had settled down to spend the night here. Six of them. Oh blimey.

I all but shot up into the sky and was just hovering there, searching the skies to check that they had really gone, when I spotted another smoking, blackened ring about a hundred yards away. I turned and turned again. Just what were they doing out this way? And, more to the point, how was I going to fight all of them? By now my headache had tightened into a sort of vice-like migraine but, even in the depths of that, I had an idea and—steady now, mind that electricity pylon—hit the flames at full throttle, disappearing into explosion after explosion of gold rings.

The people of North Wales may well have thought that I was just another R.A.F. jet screaming low over the mountains as I headed straight up to Holywell on the coast. Indeed I might even have left a bit of a vapour trail behind me as I scorched through those blue skies, as if I had a Springer missile right on my tail, before banking up high and swooping directly down into the waters of the well, feeling the refreshing coldness of the water reach up to engulf the whole of my being as I let everything go and became as one with the water, feeling myself break down completely as I moved around and around in the hurrying currents, losing those awful images of circles of slime and smoking black rings from my consciousness as I surrendered myself completely to the well's holiness and purity.

Within a second my headache had lifted and within two I was my old ebullient self, skylarking about in the water and looking up at the ageing pillars as the gorgeous sunlight mingled with the water which was spilling up out of the ground and over some smooth brown and green rocks.

This is the Bethesda of North Wales, a spot hallowed by centuries of prayer and healing where I have often come before to take a dip which will re-inforce my vocation and re-arm my holiness. Dark angels can't do any harm to anyone when their holiness is strong. Take on the whole breastplate of God, it says in the Good Book, by which it means that you should acquire all the characteristics of holiness and then you will be invulnerable. And not only will you be invulnerable but you will also be able to fight a whole Himalayan range of evil.

Holiness comes from the Anglo-Saxon word *halig*, meaning something which is complete or inviolable; something which is of high moral excellence, spiritually perfect, of God. Islands can mediate the concept of holiness to us since they are one, whole, apart. They are places of solitude where the wondering mind can grapple alone with the mysteries. There is no grandiosity about holiness either; you can only ever locate real holiness amidst the poor, the broken and the lowly. When The Boss went into Jerusalem, we should remember, he did so on the back of an ass.

But to understand the real nature of holiness you also have to understand the nature of water. The water bursting up out of this well, for example, is complete, perfect and of the highest moral excellence. Water, as the bringer and giver of all life, is God's most basic tool. Water also washes away sin and regenerates faith so it is most natural for a hot and bothered angel to seek out holy water like this to get him back into

67

shape. By mixing every part of himself with holy water he can be cleansed and re-born. He can also be re-armed to fight again.

A man in a bathing costume sank down into me and the waters, immersing himself three times before coming up to pray. Some can stay in these freezing waters for a long time. One pilgrim, John Gerard, wrote in 1593: 'I came here on the day of St Winefride's feast. There was a hard frost at the time and though the ice in the stream had been broken, by people crossing it the previous night, I still found it difficult to cross the next morning. But frost or no frost I went down into the well like a good pilgrim. For a quarter of an hour I lay down in the water and prayed. When I came out my shirt was dripping but I kept it on and pulled my clothes over it but I was none the worse for the bathe.'

Now the man in the bathing costume was out in the adjoining pool and kneeling on a large stone saying a prayer to St Beuno. Built directly over the spring was a stone gazebo which, in its turn, was surrounded by an old stone chapel with fan vaulting and small, witty sculptures of little animals and flaking faces. One carving was of a pilgrim carrying another on his back through the stream.

This shrine has been a place of unbroken pilgrimage since the seventh century. Here the deaf have heard for the first time, the crippled have walked, the blind have seen and the dumb have discovered songs of love in their mouths. Even in the violence-fouled days of the Reformation—when the shrine was broken down or locked up—pilgrims continued to come here, often at night and at great risk, for services conducted by priests in disguise.

Directly in the corner was the stone statue of St Winefride herself, the 'fair flower of Wales, hope of distressed pilgrims and patron saint of Holywell.' She had a crook in one hand and a palm of martyrdom in the other. A stone gown flowed down around her shoulders and there was a thin white line around her neck. There is quite a story attached to that thin white line since it was about the only time that I actually managed to restore life after it had been terminated. Only The Boss can normally do any of that Lazarus stuff but there was one unusual factor at work in Winefride's case.

It was November 3, 660, when Caradoc, a Welsh prince from Hawarden, returned here, feckless and frustrated after a day of hunting. I'm told that a day of bouncing around on a horse can shake up a man's hormones in a most unfortunate way and it hadn't helped that he hadn't caught anything while out hunting either. Anyway he kept pacing around in a positive white heat, shouting at his vassals to find him a woman on whom he could vent his frustrations. But when none were forthcoming he finally made advances to Winefride. Well she was beautiful enough but not at all interested in any of the old malarkey, telling him in no uncertain manner to get on his horse and be gone to some whorehouse in Bangor.

At this Caradoc, who had clearly had a very bad day indeed and was still as randy as a labrador, took out his sword and threatened her. That didn't do anything to improve his chances either but, when she saw that he really did mean business, she ran for the sanctuary of a church. Caradoc ran after her unsheathing his sword and, swinging it around with both hands, hacked her head clean off her body.

At that moment Winefride's uncle, St Beuno, arrived on the scene and, in a screaming fury, laid the curse of God on the murderer who promptly disappeared into the air. Then the old saint went down on his knees and prayed that the young girl's life should be restored. That's where I came in.

It was a brilliant, fine prayer which I picked up on the prayer lines from about a hundred miles away. I got there almost immediately only to find this most distressing scene with the severed head lying some eight feet from the body and blood splashed all over the place. But here was the unusual factor: her orphaned soul was still there, sitting by the side of the small stream rather like a fawn that was so frightened it didn't know where to go. A situation like this is most irregular if not unique. Souls normally can't wait to get home and, as a rule, don't even give the old body a second thought. Some do get into difficulty on their last flight, usually because of their anxiety to get home, but none that I've ever come across have ever actually hung around like that. Perhaps its unusual reluctance said something about Winefride's nature.

Anyway Beuno was still praying so I spoke to him firmly, telling him to pick up the head and join it to the body. Fortunately he was listening as he was praying but I have to say it was a pretty gruesome sight when he did pick up the head and just stood there, blood running all over his habit, still weeping and unsure what to do next. Go on man. Put it on her body. On her shoulders. Then, just as the head did touch the body, I waved the soul over to me and bundled her into the whole lot. Now I know all this sounds easy—when, in fact, it was highly complicated—but if the timing of the operation is right and there is real quality in the prayer, these effects can occasionally be achieved. But even in the unusual circumstances of the soul still being around there is still, mind you, a lot of luck involved as well.

A line remained around Winefride's neck for the rest of her life but she did go on to become a nun in a community at Gwytherin where she later became the Abbess. Beuno moved on to a monastery at Clynnog Fawr.

Soon after her death this well became a holy shrine famed for its healing and Winefride entered into Welsh mythology as a symbol of the inviolable status of womanhood. When Caradoc attacked her he was striking right at the heart of the family. His actions were also motivated by lust, the hallmark of the barbarian. No one could henceforth strike a woman in Wales though her husband could touch her lightly with a thin twig just below her shoulders if she gave away his harp, cloak or cauldron.

I continued lying around in the water for almost an hour as yet more pilgrims turned up, some filling up bottles and petrol cans with water before going away again. Children began splashing about the larger pool too except that the curator

70

shooed them out. Some twenty to thirty thousand pilgrims still come here every year, mainly from Liverpool and Birmingham.

During the regular morning services the pilgrims are shown Winefride's fingerbone and told that they too can become holy by thinking about holiness. They are reminded of the strength of prayer in the shrine and its unique place in the history of pilgrimage. I always smile when I hear that line. This shrine is certainly unique in my career and that's a fact. When the word got out about it back home all the others were asking me about it but I just got all evasive, claiming that it was all a bit of luck; a pure fluke which, in a sense, it was.

I guess that the one angel who has had more problems than most with the premature death of his charge is Hangopholus in America who, perhaps predictably given his patch, has become known to us all as Hank. Fortunately we need hardly any sleep but, even so, Hank has been hard at it for more years than you can shake a stick at. I mean to say he's got the whole of America—the home of Hollywood to boot—and that's too much for even a dozen angels.

At one stage Hank was struggling to keep Marilyn Monroe and Elvis Presley alive and look after the rest of America at the same time. Why they were so keen to keep these two entertainers going I was never sure. They were even upset when Hank lost James Dean in a car accident and were most insistent that it didn't happen again to Marilyn or Elvis perhaps because they were thinking of some sort of Cliff Richard public evangelist role for them in the future. But Hank just couldn't keep up with it all in the end. Lucifer's agents were busy pumping pharmaceuticals into Marilyn and Elvis as fast as they could go and Hank didn't have the technology to keep them clean twenty four hours a day.

If I tell you that they had also started worrying about the safety of the Kennedys about that time that'll give you some idea of how busy Hank was. And we all know what happened to the Kennedys. I even lost Dylan Thomas over in America and Hank didn't have a spare five minutes to keep an eye on him. Dylan was my best ever poet too and I might just have kept him alive had he stayed in Wales or even, at a push, England but as soon as he got into all those whisky-sodden parties in New York his time was up. I'll explain all the problems Dylan Thomas gave me when I get down to Swansea.

When I last saw Hank back home he was telling me that the dark angels have now more or less taken over the whole of Los Angeles and New York. In fact he said that he never goes to either city any longer and couldn't even remember when they had last asked him to look after anyone in the entertainment business which had also been more or less taken over by the dark angels. It's all violence, cruelty and perversion over there now, he says, which, as we all know, is red meat to a dark angel.

There was some talk that Hank might have to keep an eye on that pop singer Madonna but then it turned out that even Lucy wasn't interested in her so Madonna was left to look after herself. I know it might sound heretical but I've always been rather found of Madge's music but I would have to say that my favourite pop record of all time is, perhaps predictably, *Stairway to Heaven*. But I also like to relax to traditional jazz and have had some really happy times on holiday with Hank down in the Old French Quarter in New Orleans. If I'd never had a harp I would have learned the clarinet.

But I haven't seen Hank for some time and did hear from Sorroptus that he had got himself into some real difficulties and it had got so bad that he was downing a bottle of Jack Daniel's a day before breakfast. But they had a word with him finally and he managed to get his act together again. I'm not sure what they said exactly but it seems that the basic thrust was that it wouldn't be long now.

Later I called at St Asaph's Cathedral, as I was in the area, and stood in the corner of the nave, enjoying the Sunday morning service with a congregation of about sixty. The sun was blazing down through the stained glass windows and onto the floor of the squat low Cathedral in luminous rosettes of splashy light. I particularly enjoyed the minister's prayer and even giggled a bit during the sermon, which got a few people looking around. But the singing was also quite good which was something in these tuneless, off-key times.

This cathedral was founded back in 560 by St Mungo, the patron saint of Glasgow, exiled here by jealous Scottish chieftains. Mungo's big pleasure was to stand in an ice cold stream when he went through his daily offices until he finally died in 603 from the shock of sitting in a hot bath.

But what architectural form, I wonder, is lovelier than stained glass? These windows are transparent music and I don't think I've seen anything in the world quite so inspiring as Chartres Cathedral when Tractus showed me the astonishing stained glass works there. St Asaph's isn't Chartres, of course, but it is lovely still with one big window depicting old Mungo himself in the north aisle with his logos of the salmon and the ring.

These windows were the medieval counterparts to our cinema and videos; they were the first and earliest of all our media designed to tell ordinary people about the parables, miracles and the kind of work we angels get up to. These windows represented the media before it was corrupted by all the dark demons of hell. There was an old catechism which said that, as soon as you entered a church, you should take the holy water, adore the sacrament then walk around the church and consider the windows.

There is also a Translator's Chapel here which commemorated William Morgan's translation so imagine my surprise, then, when I looked into it and spotted my old pistol-packing bishop kneeling there before the altar with his eyes closed and head bowed. I wasn't at all clear what game he was playing with me these days and it was almost as if he had decided to follow me down through the centuries. But why? His real problem was that he was so unpredictable and temperamental you were never quite sure what was on his mind. But surely after all I'd done for him—particularly while he had been working on his translation—he couldn't mean me any harm? Could he?

73

I moved a little closer to his bulky kneeling frame but, if he was aware of me directly behind him, he wasn't showing it. His breathing seemed to be a bit asthmatic—as it always tended to be in the winter—but I had never really known what he had been suffering from. I couldn't make out what—if anything—he was praying about either. Yes, a strange, strange game this was but I wasn't going to take any chances of upsetting him or those pistols of his so, taking a few steps to my left, I slid up a long shaft of stained glass sunlight which was conveniently lancing down through one of the chapel windows.

The next stop in my inquiry took me to the farm of Dolwar Fach in the Montgomeryshire hills. We could have been on almost any Welsh hill farm here with five white ducks jerking around in tight formation in the yard and a ginger tom cat lying on its back in the porch licking its belly. A burbling stream ran down the side of the raised farmhouse and cows shuffled about in the stable where a fox bush hung off one of the rafters. Sheep dotted the fields all around.

An ordinary-looking farm, sure enough, but also one of the great spiritual and cultural power points of Wales since I was present right here one day when the Holy Spirit actually moved through a young woman called Ann Griffiths. The faith of Wales was renewed in these fields, as it always has been in times of doubt and exhaustion, usually through a lowly person in poor and unpromising circumstances.

Ann was born here in 1776 and was converted to Methodism after falling under the oratorical spell of the Rev Benjamin Jones of Pwllheli. In fact all her family converted to the chapel—except the dog who continued going to church—and Ann became a seminal figure in the flame and flood of the Methodist revival when so many chapels were built throughout Wales.

I had known about Ann's importance through the chimes for a long time so I was keeping a very careful eye on her but it wasn't until she actually came back to this farm that the Holy

Spirit caught her out in that field and poured his mighty, creative energy through her. I can't say I saw much of the Holy Spirit—only Michael, the C. in C., ever meets the spirit with any regularity—but the first I knew that something was up was when I spotted lots of flashing, coloured lights dashing through the air rather like a swarm of incandescent minnows. There was a faint trembling of harps too as this swarm circled Ann twice then gathered into a tight bunch and just seemed to funnel down through the back of her neck. If I were to describe the moment at all I would say it was as if a tumultuous zest had whipped through the air and then disappeared straight into Ann. She was a very tall girl who just raised her hands a little and smiled with pleasure but only I knew that, at that moment, this humble and uneducated girl had been given the rare and precious gift of bardic praise.

Perhaps I had better explain here that this gift of bardic praise is only ever bestowed on a few but the tradition goes back to the sixth century. The deep secrets of the praise tradition are these: when there is an object to worship only then has life an abiding meaning. The act of praise affirms one's human identity and enables man to take root in the sacred mysteries. In praise the praiser can then find his place and meaning in the whole human story.

One of the first men to be given these secrets by the Holy Spirit was the Welsh praise poet Taliesin of Rheged, the lost kingdom of south-west Scotland. He was known as The Chief of the Poets whose job it was to defend and sustain the social order. As the king was then the lynchpin of the social order Taliesin's dutiful doggerel to the king would begin like this: 'Defender of Rheged, Land of my Praises, your country's anchor ... You are the bridge from the past to the future, the best of your breed, the head of your race.'

But Taliesin also extended the range of praise poetry to include God and love. The bardic dynasty which began with Taliesin used poetry as an act of worship. Dafydd ap Gwilym, the Welsh Chaucer, wrote prolific love poems while Morgan Llwyd transposed the Taliesin tradition into prose. 'The first act of the skylark at daybreak is to praise his master: and that should be the first act that man should be obliged to do, praise God from the depth of his heart.'

So it wasn't too many more years before I was watching Ann Griffiths being given the bardic gift; a tradition which was almost as old as the Welsh nation. 'You cannot pluck a flower of song off a headland in Dyfed in the late eighteenth century without stirring a great northern star in the sixth century,' the writer Saunders Lewis said of this glittering tradition.

Ann used her gift to compose letters and hymns which both evoked the heady atmosphere of the Methodist revival and are widely thought be the sublimest prose in any language. Saunders Lewis described her longest hymn as one of the greatest ever religious poems. Her hymns of praise spoke to the hearts of many people of diverse faiths throughout the world and down through the centuries.

Here we see a mature mind trying to unravel the mysteries of faith and expressing its wonder with a classical balance and in a melodious language. In this work the small begins to find a relationship with the infinite. We also come to understand a vision in which man can reach out for the hand of God and is therefore rescued from a sea of meaninglessness. Ann also understood the necessity of purity of heart and the hidden potentialities of that heart. She also knew how the true qualities of holiness can be learned from God alone.

Modern academics have often pondered the texts of the hymns and found them astonishing both in their complexity and understanding of the mysteries. Her detailed knowledge of the Bible, of course, would have come from the pulpits of Thomas Charles and her friend John Hughes of Pontrobert. She would also have known the Book of Common Prayer and the plygain carols. But the deepest wonders of her knowledge came from the Holy Spirit alone since, in this small marvellous body of work, we can detect other larger sweeps of scholarship from the devotion of the Middle Ages to the Biblical learning of the Reformation and even the warmth and love of the common people. These are the deep things of God alone which made the Welsh a strong, stable and secure people; the clean rain of heaven which nourished the people and made them great.

Ann died a year after marrying her husband Thomas Griffiths of Meifod. Within ten months of the marriage she gave birth to a daughter Elizabeth. The baby was christened but died within a fortnight and Ann died a fortnight after that. There was little I could do for her since more than anything—more even than her own life—she wanted to be with her baby again. I even made it my business to personally carry her soul in my arms across the Jordan and up to heaven. The other angels wept too when she was reunited with her child. Ann cried and kissed her little babe and I left them to themselves for a few minutes before ushering them both into the presence of God. There are no moments of happiness quite like the moments of happiness in heaven. Here there is an eternal rapture and love reigns. The last enemy of death should hold no fear at all for the true believer; it is the door to the resurrection where all those you loved and lost will be found again.

Ann's body was buried in her small chapel in nearby Pontrobert and there is a granite obelisk to her memory in the parish church of Llanfihangel Yng Ngwynfa overlooking the Berwyn mountains.

Ann never made a fair copy of her hymns which were all handed down through oral tradition. Nevertheless they became the very fires of the Methodist revival, ensuring that they would burn for years to come. So this farm at Dolwar Fach is a sacred place where man and God still meet. The poet Cynan spoke of the inseparable union that now exists between Dolwar Fach and the resurrection. Pilgrims still come here from all over the world to be welcomed by the burly shape of the farmer David Jones and his wife.

And oh it's a lovely farmhouse still, full of old bees-waxed furniture and oak dressers stacked with fine plates. One dresser has small patches of wood in it; bits which have been taken from the coffins of various members of the family. 'That's Uncle Will's there and great grandad's—the whole of the family is in there somewhere.' Sepia prints of aunts and uncles troop across the piano but there is no photograph of Ann, only a drawing showing her with long hair and big eyes. She actually had smaller eyes than that and the drawing gives no idea of her tallness either.

David Jones—when he is not complaining about how hard it is being a hill farmer—will also show the pilgrim a sheep horn and a scythe sharpener which belonged to Ann's father. Lots of pilgrims pitch up at Dolwar Fach and he will also proudly haul out his visitors' book to show them the autograph of Enoch Powell who gave his address as The House of Commons.

'You get these different stars from one generation to the next,' he says of Ann. 'Most people can't do it no matter how much education they get. But some just do it. They are picked and that's it. One famous bard said that he would have given away everything that he'd ever done if he'd written just two lines of any of Ann's hymns.'

Another secret of praise is that other bards recognise the gift immediately.

Just then Spring finally burst all over the land in a profusion of growth and new colour, adding a fresh lustre to the mountains and valleys of central Wales as I cruised the speckled peaks of the Cambrian mountains, simply revelling in this great thrilling romp.

I had been over in the market town of Rhayader again and was turning up into the Elan Valley when I noticed that everything had finally got underway. It was just wonderful swooping around and around in all that sunshine and reaching out to touch everything: the primroses and nodding daffodils in the hedgerows, the white strips of hawthorn hanging in the lanes and the lush green fields with all their frisky lambs.

There are six million sheep in Wales—about twice as many as people—and it is one of my pleasures, at this time of the year, to fly around the fields and help out a labouring ewe if she has got into distress. Sheep are the dimmest of animals so, if the lamb is stuck, I might give the wet fetlocks a good tug to ease it out. Even as an angel, who has seen just about everything there is to see, I still love that moment when the mother begins licking the mucus off the slippery bundle which will suddenly open its mouth and let out a quivering cry of new life. The miracle of birth is always miraculous—no matter how many times you've seen it.

I also like to flit among the newly returned swallows or with the madly chattering skylarks. If you stand and watch carefully you can pick out the baby brown trout feeding in the Elan river. Also there are the curling tongues of the tiny fern growing in the brown bracken.

It is entirely appropriate, I suppose, that all this new growth comes to the Valley at Easter since this is also the time when the sun traditionally comes out and dances with joy to celebrate the resurrection. Some also believe that sun playing on water at this time is an angel dancing. Others believe that the Boss's blood still surges through the world and that, each Spring, it is his own life which brings all this new energy into the land. There's a lot in that too.

But Easter always arouses a great mixture of emotions in me because I was one of the foot soldiers in the twelve legions of angels who gathered around Calvary as he died on the cross. I had never known a moment like it. There was this man who had only ever done loving things and he had a crown of thorns on his forehead with nails in his wrists and his legs tied to the upright. His every single joint was aching and the normal way for a person to die in crucifixion would be for his lungs to rupture and for him to drown in his own blood. If he had not died within a few days he would be pounded to death by a mallet.

The Boss's every movement was an agony—particularly as he had been reviled and deserted by all, including his disciples—and we were all there, with tears in our eyes and swords drawn, ready to cut him down in a second. But he refused, of course. His final exhibition of love had to be supreme and without any possibility of reward. 'It is finished', he said finally and died with a child's goodnight prayer on his lips.

We all remained there with him as three hours of darkness descended on Jerusalem. We angels had suffered as he had suffered and even Michael was so overcome by grief he couldn't tell us what to do. In the end I slunk away with Tractus back to Megiddo and there we all stayed more or less in a state of despair until we were told about the resurrection three days later. Ah, so that's what it was all about. The work of God is always a mystery but it all does come clear in the end.

I stayed on the Megiddo plains for almost five hundred years before they finally came and told me that I'd got Wales. 'I've got what?' I shouted, throwing my harp down onto the ground, thinking they'd given me the whales that swim in the sea. 'I'm an angel with wings. How the hell can I spend all my days swimming around under water?'

'Where's your brains, Conker? Not the whales that swim dopey. Wales, the country that's stuck on the side of England.'

'England? Where's England?'

Well Sorroptus got England, Tractus got France and I got Wales, with all her bleating sheep, pouring rain and melancholic people. How I hate Wales sometimes. But not today since I was spinning down past the gold and brown slopes of the Elan Valley, playing and whooping in the warm sunshine which was glazing the lakes with acres of golden fire. Shelley, one of the greatest lyric poets in the English language, lived here with his wife Harriet in Nantgwyllt briefly after they married. The poet was hoping to make it a community of ideal friends until, as usual, he was chased out by a swarm of debt-collectors. Poor old Shelley always had this thing about debts: he just didn't like paying them.

An old farmer stood in his yard and, although he looked a bit daft, he turned out to have the mind of a marvelling poet. 'I love everything about the land at this time of year. The swallows came back on the river bank yesterday. The buds are coming up and the flowers are out. Everywhere there's frogspawn and I do love to hear all those old frogs groaning away together.'

This is reservoir country, with huge curtains of white water cascading over the high dams. The water flows don't have the jagged patterns of most normal rural waterfalls and come down in high symmetrical walls of foam all busy playing with the astonishing light of this mountain fastness.

This valley was drowned in 1893 when a hundred people and 24,000 sheep were moved to provide a reservoir of fresh water for Birmingham whose children were suffering from high rates of typhoid and smallpox. It took eleven years to build the four dams and they are something of an engineering triumph sending 70 million gallons of water a day to Birmingham using only gravity and without the aid of a single pump. The water takes three days to get there.

There is certainly a pleasant timeless quality about the whole valley and life has barely changed for the farmers here for almost a century. Mrs May Lewis didn't get an electricity generator until 1969, using oil lamps and Calor gas before that. She also only had her first washing machine twelve years ago and still hasn't got a telephone or television.

The one problem the farmers here were having this Spring was that the crows were attacking the young lambs, taking out their eyes and tongues. But it's difficult to shoot a crow since they know the difference between a gun and a stick, merely flapping out of range when they see a gun, then sitting on a branch and looking down at the farmer. 'When we were kids we used to go out and push the crows' nests off the trees but the kids don't do that anymore,' said May.

Further up the valley there was a dead badger on the road but there would be no decent funeral for old Brock since he would just be left there for the birds to scavenge. There were plenty of birds everywhere too, all getting into furious fights since this was nesting time. Buzzards, magpies and ravens were all at it and, as I went by, it sometimes looked as if the whole sky was full of fighting.

Just by here also was 'The Flickering Lamp', a small bed and breakfast run by Laurence Dowden and his wife Maggie. Laurence first began coming here as a holidaymaker but then gave up a successful career in computers to stay here permanently. 'I got fed up earning a lot of money and living in a house I never saw. I wanted a living where I could stay at home and here it is.'

Water comes from their own spring and the electricity from their own generator. There is no television and they don't even bother to try and keep out the sheep who are forever foraging in their garden. There are also bats in the eaves and, early each morning, a pair of rare and beautiful red kites come and hover over their house since, Laurence suspects, they'd got their eyes on their little boy's guinea pigs. But he also leaves bits of chicken on the garden post for the kites which they take if the bits are sufficiently rotten.

Being an RSPB warden he is most protective of his kites and, at this time of year, when the kites are about to lay their eggs, virtually the whole of the valley is on a red alert and on the look-out for any of those dreaded egg-collectors. They even have the car numbers of most of the main egg collectors and work in close contact with the police. Last year some Gurkhas spent six weeks guarding one nest in Elan and an egg collector who had tried any of his nonsense would have been very sorry indeed.

Yet what with taxidermists and myxomatosis the kites have had a very hard time indeed over the years and there are only two pairs now breeding in the upper parts of this valley. They are very sensitive to disturbance and an added hazard is posed by the other birds like cravens and crows who would actually take the eggs or fledgelings from the nest.

Also the kites have been forced out of their natural oakland habitat since the sheep have been busy eating the seedlings there and, as the rangers have found, it's awfully hard keeping sheep away from any kind of food. The mass intrusion of motor cars into the valley hasn't helped anyone, of course, least of all the sensitive kites. Why don't they just ban cars from everywhere and be done with it?

The urge to fly with these marvellous kites proved irresistible and soon I was up there with them too, soaring over this great Welsh fastness or else gliding around in widening circles as we rode the thermals together. I thought I knew all there was to know about flying but these birds were complete masters of the air, either making long sideways glides without moving their wings an inch or banking up high again, orchestrating their every move with the distinctive forks of their tails.

All right if that's the way you want to play it . . . I shook out my own great white wings and glided with them too, holding everything perfectly still as ghostly puffs of wind took us up and down. Then I swooped and stalled in mid-flight, showing them one of my better aerial tricks. But, if they were impressed, they didn't look it and, in fact, one of them abruptly broke off flying with me and dived almost vertical since he had spotted a water snake sunning itself on a stone on the edge of the lake.

But the other one stayed with me for an hour or so, making his distinctive mewling calls as we swept back down into this cocoon of rural rhapsody, past the water tumbling over the dams, above those old groaning frogs, along the hawthorn lanes and up into the red and gold flames of a perfect Spring day.

# Fourth Book

As the whole of Wales waited, with bated breath, for a gaudy summer to begin rolling a carpet of sunshine and warmth all over the land, the skies, as usual, poured with cold rain. Floods blocked up vast areas of mid-Wales and bilious black clouds kept sweeping in from England dumping yet more squalls of rain on all and sundry.

I had got to Welshpool, the main market town of mid-Wales, coming to life within my exploding gold rings but then, just as quickly, disappearing again. All this rain was taking the zip out of my rings and no messing about. I was feeling pretty damp in myself too, taking one look at all this gusting rain and fading back into the air. It isn't that I can't actually operate in the rain; it's just that all this rain makes me so fed up I don't want to operate. Sunshine is my medium and where I'm happiest so there I was skulking along that fine rainy border between being and nothingness, neither in nor out. That Monday morning feeling some call it. But others call it the blues.

Anyway, miracle of miracles, the sun did break through for a few seconds and I did finally get down there on those streets, standing in a puddle and right next to a milkman who was going about his business accompanied by the staccato music of his chinking bottles. A sodden dog began harrying the milkman and, for a moment, I thought he was going to bite him so I reached out my hand to calm the dog down. The dog, unsure of what was going on, stopped growling and began whimpering, his tail dropping well down between his legs as his aggression deserted him.

Right up that hill was the Welshpool and Llanfair Railway Station—The Farmers' Line—built at the turn of the century to bring the people and their produce to the market here. It might be one of the most picturesque lines anywhere, puffing through valleys and along the sides of lakes with crazed-looking locomotives from Germany or the West Indies and carriages from Austria or Sierra Leone. But the station itself was locked that morning so I ambled back down through the town to watch everyone setting up the livestock market which, with an annual turnover of some £28million, is one of the largest of its kind in Europe.

Some great characters used to hang around this market and, whenever I was in the area, I might pop in to listen to the patter of Rattle-snake Joe who came here with a few snakes in his suitcase which he used to drum up custom. Joe sold oil to cure rheumatism, even soaking strips of leather in it and shouting that everyone should think of these leather strips as being like the human body. Those snakes of his could have done with a good rub down with some of that oil if you asked me, both of them looking extremely flaky and as if they had terminal arthritis.

Then there was Dixie King, an old con man who came here selling powdered brick in envelopes claiming the powder cured indigestion. Some swore that it worked too. Anyway Dixie King used to sell his 'cures' stripped to the waist in the middle of winter but this strange sales pitch, alas, ended up giving him a fatal bout of pneumonia for which there was no known cure—not even his powdered brick.

Even as I stood near the main gate more and more trucks were rolling up in the rain. The sheep and cattle were then taken off the trucks and driven into separate sheds with their pens of thick metal bars. The farmers took no notice of the rain, of course. These Welsh hill farmers knew all there was to know about theirs, the wettest work under heaven.

The cattle bellowed with the effrontery of it all and their eyes were big with fright as the drovers whacked their backsides with sticks. The sheep, all as daft as daffodils, bleated pitifully as they were squeezed into their smaller pens, some trying to climb onto one another's backs as they tried to escape from all that crowded madness. Everywhere you turned the air tasted of animal dung.

First the sheep were graded by a tall man with big hands who prodded and poked them before another man put a daub of green paint on their heads, showing that they were fit to sell. 'This one's about to lamb,' he told one farmer as he turned the sheep over on her back.

'No, she's not,' protested the farmer.

'Well, if you say she's not, she's not. You should know. But farmers tell you anything in this place.'

When the sheep auction finally began with the tolling of a handbell the auctioneer stood on a plank above the pens and all the purchasers crowded around the pens with many standing inside them. Then, as each sheep came up for auction, everyone prodded the luckless sheep with their fingers trying to decide if it was too fat or too lean. Each sheep might be poked at least a dozen times as bids were made in a mysterious series of grunts, nods or little waves in the air. As far as I could make out each sheep was going for around £30 which, according to the farmers, was about a middling price. When each sheep was sold it was daubed with another colour and, by the time the day was over, your average Welshpool sheep's coat had about as many colours as Joseph's.

The cattle auction took place inside a sort of enclosed cockpit in which the flat-capped punters all stood together on concrete tiers as heifers and bulls stumbled and slipped on the dung and urine in the pen in front of them and the auctioneer, Jim Evans, went through his babbling, high-pitched spiel. Jim was picked for this job after someone heard him reading the lesson in church. He explains that, in this job, all you've got to do is know the signs and remember the names. 'I don't mess about. It's got to be sharp when I do it. But some farmers will stand on my foot if they think I'm going too fast. One nearly took my foot off the other week.'

But it was difficult not to feel sorry for the animals, constantly beaten and poked as they moaned furiously about the indignity of it all. Some say the animals can smell their impending death but that's not true and they don't anyway have souls like humans. But a few bulls have escaped over the years and all hell has broken loose as they charged around the market looking for someone to gore.

I was standing there watching yet another unwilling bull being beaten into the auction pen when my eyes fastened onto a trio of strangely dressed people standing together on the top concrete tier. My eyes looked away and then turned back again since one of the men had a missing eye, another was a tall lady with long dark hair and, although I didn't recognise him at first, the other was no other than Bishop William Morgan. They were all staring down at me but showing no emotion and as motionless as an old Rembrandt master. It didn't take me any time to work out that the other two were Christmas Evans and Ann Griffiths, all three of them clearly tailing me down through time and history. Now then. What was this all about?

Their manner wasn't threatening or hostile but they were making me desperately uneasy nonetheless. Angels like to understand what's going on—they *need* to understand what's going on—but even my angelic intelligence couldn't start to work out the structure or reason for these illusions which were clearly playing hide and seek with me. There was no meta-narrative to hand at all. All they seemed to be doing was breaking all the known rules and I didn't know why. Ah well doubtless there was some explanation for all this strange behaviour but, if there was, I couldn't get hold of it. Perhaps even angels can't find any ready answers in a postmodernist age. Even we are being baffled by the complexity of a world struggling to find meanings in an age of crisis. And certainly this trio of holy ghosts wasn't about to explain anything since there was a change in the light in the window, following another ferocious downpour of rain outside, and they vanished.

I made my way out of the auction shed, cautiously looking around at the crowds, scanning each corner for signs of any more irregular characters when, absurdly, the market was invaded by a huge media circus all whirling around the Liberal Democrat leader Paddy Ashdown. The country was in the middle of a general election campaign and he was surrounded by police and security people but, as one farmer told another, they wouldn't be throwing any eggs at him because eggs were too expensive.

Ashdown tore through the market as if his back was on fire, shaking hands here and there before making a short speech from the bed of a lorry in which he assured the farmers that he had their interests at heart, he worried about them day and night and, when elected, he would sort out all their problems immediately. Ah, how I love to listen to the glib promises of politicians. If all those glib promises turned into real actions this world would have become a heaven years ago.

'It's a pity that only those in opposition seem to know what to do with us farmers,' one of them said in the bar afterwards. 'As soon as they get into power they're clueless.'

Others there talked about the 'soft' prices and how the sheep prices were still disappointing. One of them said that one of his neighbours had become so plagued by debt that he had taken a shotgun to himself. Even more tragically he had messed it up and was now in hospital after taking away half his mouth.

There are things I can do for people on the verge of suicide and why they don't try prayer any longer I just don't know. The Welsh in these parts always understood the power of prayer and around the turn of the century, I was busy around these parts night and day. But, apart from the usual, predictable houses—where the prayers have become rather more ritual than heartfelt—I can't remember when I last heard a decent and prayerful plea for help from the helpless.

I wandered back up to the northern coast, still feeling depressed and unfocused. It was also difficult to get any real sort of handle on the substance of my final report too since, no sooner was I picking up a bit of stride, than I was being thrown completely by these mysterious pursuers who, of course, had once been among my most special charges. That was the real problem. They couldn't be menacing me after all I'd done for them. Could they?

But there was still no sign of them by the time I got to Porthmadog where, I noticed, there was a poster announcing that the National Eisteddfod was getting underway in the next week or so down the coast in Aberystwyth. Perhaps that would take my mind off things for a few days and I certainly needed some sort of break from all this mental stress.

As I was walking to the railway station I noticed that it was a brilliant day with the sun blazing down through a clear blue sky. It almost looked as if summer had really come at last with white butterflies dancing in the heat hazes in the fields and, on the station platform, everyone was in their summer clothes as they waited for the train.

The small trains of Wales begin their seasons after Easter and I always like to travel on one where possible, enjoying both the scenery and company. The pilgrimages of old were always about the journey, of course, with the arrival being of almost secondary importance. On a journey you could always enjoy the fellowship of the other pilgrims; all settling down at the end of an exhausting day for a few hours of food and story-telling.

Everyone liked to get on the road in the fifteenth century, particularly after Easter. Some went for reasons of piety or devotion but mostly they were attracted to a change of air which would do themselves and their bodies some good. There would be farm workers taking time off from the land, the rich on horseback followed by wagons and uncouth archers, quacks selling cures for the bites of vipers and minstrels who would entertain with their songs. There might also be falconers and mummers or slaves early out of bond, not forgetting all the bear-baiters, clippers of coin and other crooks like those pardoners selling indulgences which promised full remission in hell for sins down here.

My friend Sorroptus actually watched over the same pilgrimage as the English poet Geoffrey Chaucer back in the fourteenth century which, in its turn, led to the famous Canterbury Tales. Sorroptus said that he had long known about Chaucer through the chimes and just followed the group from inn to inn all the way to Canterbury and the shrine of Thomas a Beckett. The pilgrims did indeed tell some wonderful stories, it seems, until all that mead took a firm hold on their brains and they all began talking the most unutterable rubbish. But, by that time, Chaucer himself was also so drunk that he couldn't tell the difference.

The rail route down from Porthmadog is particularly pleasant, following the coast down past the lowering range of Snowdonia and right next to the mighty castle of Harlech. At each station people got on and off and I was trying my best to relax as I stretched out in the luggage rack looking out at the green marshes dotted with sheep and the tides washing right up against the brown sea walls. The train arrived at each station with a noisy burst of its horn and every head jerked back when it took off again.

The real trouble with me is that once I start worrying about one thing I start worrying about everything. If angels could get ulcers I would have died years ago. Unable to reach any conclusions about William Morgan and company I then began worrying about the build-up of the dark angels, even though I hadn't seen any signs of them since that morning on the edge of Lake Vyrnwy. But the time you don't see them is precisely the time you need to be really worrying about them since you can be sure that they're up to something. You can safely bet your very last harp on that.

Klang was never much of a one to go skulking around in the shadows; he would always do his evil business right out in the open. But, with so many strange things going on, I suppose my biggest worry was that my ancient adversary Splachnik had finally crawled back into the fray. I always thought I'd cooked Splachnik's goose after that nasty business with that boy, Tommy Jones, back in the Brecon Beacons in 1900. But, as you can never really kill an angel, no matter whose side he is on,—even if you can incapacitate him for a few centuries—it could well be that Splachnik had found some way out of that lake and had set up a new base on some poor council estate in the mining valleys down in the South.

That's precisely where dark angels like Splachnik always worked the best, of course—among the poor, the uneducated and the unemployed—and I have to admit that I thought of him the other day when I was reading in a newspaper that a Neighbourhood Watch caravan had been set up on one such estate and the kids had locked the watchman inside and then proceeded to burn it down. That act of vandalism sounded straight out of the school of Splachnik. It had his fingerprints all over it and, if he had gone and found himself a gang of impressionable dark angels and they were travelling around Wales together, there was no telling what havoc they were already wreaking.

A large shadow fell over the window of the railway carriage as we were reaching Aberystwyth and I had to admit that I jumped a bit until I realised that it was merely the shadow of a tree which had been caught by the sun.

Oh these are tough times all right. Who'd be an angel eh? Our hours are as endless as our work and we're not even paid anything for our labours. The triumph of the good, they are always telling us, is a reward unto itself. Well, as the good doesn't seem to be doing much triumphing around these parts any longer, perhaps they can think of some sort of better reward?

I'd be partial to a new territory; that's what I'd like the most. Some quiet island in Polynesia, where the sun shone all day and there were no sheep, and I could sit on the branch of a banyan tree, coming up with new tunes on my harp as dusky maidens played ball on the beach with clear blue waves breaking on the golden sand. Now that's what I call a decent reward for the amount of work they expect us to put in. And if I couldn't have it on a permanent basis then just a month a year would be enough. I could take any amount of sheep, rain and melancholy if I had a month of that to look forward to every year.

But the sheer vibrance of Aberystwyth soon perked me up as I hung around the busy corners with people and cars milling around as the fat smell of chips came drifting from all directions. Aberystwyth is a very fish and chip sort of place, cheap but ebullient, vulgar yet substantial, all of it as amiable and unpretentious as a boomtown bookie on a winning streak.

With the tourist season well underway—and the Eisteddfod about to begin—there were buskers out in the doorways entertaining the people in the usually vain hope of a bob or three. Traffic wardens lurked behind lamposts planning punitive sanctions against unwary motorists and, just next to the railway station there was an exhibition of local memorabilia—'Aberystwyth Yesterday'—which included all kind of items from Edwardian baby clothes to railway signs, door knobs to postcards and old shoes to Welsh Not signs.

But one of the undoubted stars of this centre of tourism and learning is the long curving Edwardian sea-front packed with hotels and guest houses. Almost every five minutes you can hear something else falling off this tatty, sea-bitten facade as the elderly sit in armchairs in the hotel windows, either asleep or staring out into the rain.

Yes, it had begun raining again which was just as well since most people found the pebbled beach almost impossible to sit on and the cold sea-weed clogged sea almost impossible to swim in. A Polynesian island it ain't and that's a fact. There was an amusement arcade of spectacular and noisy vulgarity on the front and a camera obscura on the top of a funiculared hill in which anyone can examine that crumbling sea-front in glorious detail.

In the winter the town is taken over by students from the university who largely seem to be studying alcoholism, and make more noise than a football crowd. But there's none around here at the moment with just the holidaymakers soaking up the rain and wishing they could afford to go to Spain.

The other star of the town is the National Library—with its three million books—which sits on top of a high hill and overlooks the town. I go to the National Library often, usually in the dead of night, if I want to spend a few quiet hours reading and relaxing with a good book. But, at other times, I might go there to remind myself of my life and achievements. Let me explain, with all due modesty, that there's a lot of old Conker in those books.

When I just want to relax I might pore over the first edition of Euclid's geometry or even read a few of the original tracts of the American Civil War. But, if I'm in a rather more aesthetic mood, I'll take out something like the Llanbelig Book of Hours and enjoy the colours, the care, the craftsmanship.

But, on the other hand, if all that Welsh rain is getting to my nerves and I'm in need of reassurance, I might take down the first edition of William Morgan's Bible and smooth its pages or hold it to me, reminding myself that all that time and trouble looking after that cantankerous bishop wasn't in vain. Then there is one of Ann Griffiths's letters in her own hand and the pure memory of her work makes me proud as does re-reading one of the letters of Dylan Thomas or the original version of the Welsh National Anthem as written by Evan James and his son in Pontypridd in 1856.

Ah we had a lot of fun composing that anthem together. We knew it was a strong tune right from the beginning but I had no idea that it would go on to embroider the nation's soul and get sung at almost every rugby international for ever. I always feel a swelling of pride at rugby internationals when I hear the anthem and I've even been known, on occasion, to gently interfere with a game, particularly ones against the English, if the ball's not been running the Welsh way. A rugby ball is such an odd shape any angel worth his salt can get it bouncing in more or less any direction he wants.

There are also lots of other books here in which I had a part: copies of the poems of Taliesin or the White Book of Rhydderch or The Black Book of Carmarthen, the earliest collection of Welsh poetry. They are all here, catalogued and stored in the right atmospheric pressures which are constantly monitored, for all eternity. So, much as a novelist might enjoy standing in front of all his published works and telling himself that's what it was all about, I can also come here to the National Library and stand in the polished shadows, looking up at all the shelves and stretching my wings out wide, feeling a proud surge of the tribe as my chest swells and I tell myself: 'Conker boy, you were there. Conker, this is what your life and career has all been about. It was through all these books that the Welsh became what they were.'

It's been some achievement, when you come to think of it, and—whatever I might say about a Polynesian island in my more depressed moments—I am very proud of what I've managed to achieve over the centuries in this small land stuck on the side of England.

Then the Eisteddfodwyr came to town.

It is almost as if the whole country has been put on a war footing when the National Eisteddfod begins because about a quarter of a million people throughout Wales suddenly take to bus, car or bicycle. They also catch a train, horse and cart or use their own two feet. There are silver-haired professors and shaggy language activists; wild-eyed poets and beefy, well-fed vicars; young girls flaunting the disposal of their bras and Rhiwbina romantics worrying about their latest short story; teachers busy moaning about their rates of pay and children togged up in their chapel best; whole choirs with a thirst as big as their voices and harpists risking a double hernia by lugging around the largest of harps on their shoulders.

The whole lot of them travel up hill and down dale to come here and celebrate the poetic heart of Wales with its love of rolling rhymes and singing visions. The Welsh must be the only race in the world who gather every year in a muddy field to crown a poet. And here they all were again ... all come to Aberystwyth to revive themselves with a bathe in their own cultural Lourdes; all gathering together for a bit of crafty harmonising and the spinning out of impromptu verses; catching up on all the latest gossip in the Principality or else hatching new plots or picking the Welsh rugby team all over again or assassinating characters or starting whole new rows with public calls that it was about time that Offa's Dyke should be electrified, the better to keep out the English and protect the Welsh language. The tribal drums get walloped loud and hard at the Eisteddfod.

As for myself I like to hover around the main field as they all slosh around and around in the mud in their wellies, opening their arms wide and falling on some distant relative or friend whom they haven't seen since the last Eisteddfod. You don't send Christmas cards to relatives in Wales since you always meet them every year on the field. Then they will gossip like mad about who's doing what to whom, where, when and why.

Eavesdropping on these conversations, as I do constantly, I can then get to know what's going on in almost every corner of my patch since these people are almost all keepers of the culture and there are not many pies being cooked in any part of the country without one of them having a dirty finger in them somewhere.

Meibion Glyndŵr, for example, is a tiny group of Welsh terrorist extremists who periodically burn down English-owned homes in Wales. Now I have often felt the urge to hand these daft twits over to the police but, to a certain extent, I am bound by the rules of the Confessional. But I can tell you this: there are only three of them—one of whom can't even speak Welsh—and they couldn't organise an explosion in a firework factory. Furthermore they are mostly content to conduct their campaign by sending anonymous letters to a gullible media.

In the various tents, caravans and stalls around the field you can buy hamburgers, lollipops, wood crafts, paintings, glass sculptures, Welsh language kits, pugnacious car stickers—KEEP WALES TIDY, DUMP YOUR RUBBISH IN ENGLAND—and even electronic harps. But the harps for sale here are a good deal bigger and—dare I say it?—a lot clumsier than the type I like to play.

I was practically born with a harp in my hands with my fingers forever playing those lovely little runs which so beautifully evoke the atmosphere of heaven. Indeed the harp is the original instrument of heaven and, as such, the oldest musical instrument in the world. I first introduced the harp into Welsh culture more than a thousand years ago when I happened to come across a master carpenter in Denbigh. His chisels could make wood sit up and sing so I held the shape of a harp in his mind for a couple of days. He couldn't understand it at all and kept complaining to his wife of a strange-shaped headache until he just had to give form to that shape if only to get it out of his mind. It was the most lovely instrument too and, since then, I have been fortunate to have heard harpists play some of the most sublime bursts of music.

I must say that the Welsh had no difficulty at all in taking to the harp. They always regarded them as sacred to the extent that, back in the twelfth century, it was decreed that any man's possessions could be seized for debt—except his harp.

At the Eisteddfod the gorsedd—or circle of bards—who are all dressed in green, white and blue nightshirts and all look as if they've been freshly dug up, gather for a neo-Druidic ceremony early in the week when the Horn of Plenty is held aloft and all that. As a strictly Christian agent of God I have never had much truck with Druidism or any of that fertility oaken wand stuff.

But the main purpose of all the proceedings, of course, is for the competitions. Prizes are handed out here, there and everywhere for choral singing, poems in a strict metre, poems in a free metre, translations, plays and short stories. Harps twinkle and parents of lost children are appealed for. Amidst all this intense cultural efflorescence swords are unsheathed and red-faced trumpeters blam away as if advancing on the crumbling walls of Jericho.

Even as I ghost around the backs of the tents I pick up a lot of quiet prayers from the competitors for crowns and chairs but there's not much I can—or want to—do about them. I do not classify such self-seeking 'prayers' as proper prayers and would rarely do anything about them even if I understood all too well what a great joy it must be to be crowned bard for the best poem in a strict metre.

This crowning is the theatrical highlight of the week. *'A oes Heddwch?'* shouts the Archdruid as the Great Sword of the Gorsedd is unsheathed—'Is there peace?' *'Heddwch'* The crowd shouts back and the sword is put back in its sheath. The lights are then dimmed and a searchlight rolls around and around the gathered spectators. The Archdruid announces the name of the winner who must then shout *'Yma'*. (Here.) Even I can get quite tearful when the winner, after a suitable and traditional show of reluctance, is then escorted to the stage to rapturous and prolonged applause. There he is seated on the bardic throne and made a fuss of by children dressed as elves, nightgowned druids and trumpeters. Oddly the winner has always just had a haircut and is wearing a new suit.

This is the best side of the week's events but I've been noticing for some years now how even the Eisteddfod has been catching the great terminal disease of our time by which I mean the modern artists' attachment to perversion, cruelty, violence and despair. This is yet another manifestation of the work of the dark angels of which I have been complaining about so much. You know what I mean: the way in which everyone has become an alcoholic child abuser with brothers who have turned gay and a father who was once chief hit man with the Mafia before he settled for getting drunk on Saturday night when he came home to beat up mother and wreck the house.

The modern artist has totally lost the ability to celebrate the ordinary and that loss has affected everything.

The other year in the Eisteddfod at Newport all these graduates in gloom were so noisy that I had to leave earlier than usual. The crowned bard's winning poem was about a Carmarthenshire farmer who, suffocated by the English and their barbaric ways, killed himself. Another portrayed the new road from Liverpool as a snake giving Merseyside criminals easy access to North Wales. No one won the prose medal because the judges looked in vain for something other than disease and alcoholism in the entries but the actress Siân Phillips then cheered everyone up with a story about the terminal illness of a Glamorgan cricket fan. A poem about cancer won the strict rhyming section and the winner of the painting gold medal was of a tombstone.

So you can see what gets me down so much. As I've said often enough before: to suffer and despair has become almost a sacred necessity for the Welsh; they absolutely glory in lament and weeping. They even have a word for it—*dwysder*—which, although it has no exact counterpoint in English, means a consciousness of a mighty burden; the wailing in the dark night of the bardic soul.

There wasn't so much of that in Aberystwyth that year—even if there was some—but the harps tinkled, the choirs sang and the rows were as wonderfully bitter as ever. The best row in recent years came after Clive Betts, a reporter for the *Western Mail*, named the crowned bard in advance of the occasion. The premature unveiling of this holy secret led to a peculiarly Welsh row, conducted with red blustering faces and in major spluttering decibels, which managed to keep going all week. The Archdruid even gave Betts a rollicking from the stage for spilling the bardic beans.

The Eisteddfod proper began in Cardigan in 1176 and its main function was to systematise the affairs of a growing rabble of 'rhymers, bards and minstrels' who were busy springing up everywhere like nettles after the rain. This new Bardic Order was supposed to lay down strict metric rules and give proper licences to such poets who had been deemed to have served a suitable apprenticeship. The intention was to try and regulate the increasing numbers of these poets who were forever wandering all over the Land of My Fathers polluting the air with their rubbish rhymes.

But this licensing system soon broke down only to be revived in the eighteenth century by one Edward Williams or Iolo Morganwg as he came to be known. I always had a soft spot for old Iolo but, if you detect a certain scepticism in my voice with regard to the Eisteddfod, it is almost certainly to do with the fact that I knew that old forger better than most and understood all too well how his bad habits had, in fact, done much to create the spirit and ritual of the modern Eisteddfod. Oh I knew everything about old Iolo all right.

I picked up the oddest sounds when Iolo was born in Llancarfan back in 1747 which were not so much ripples on the chimes as a series of cracked notes. Indeed I kept an eye on him for most of his childhood and couldn't quite work out if he was going to become a saint or a mass murderer since, while he clearly had a lot of talent, he used to like spending hours dropping live ants on spiders' webs and enjoying seeing them eaten or else he would go out into the Vale of Glamorgan and tip eggs out of birds' nests just for a lark.

He also had the peculiar pugnacity that often comes in small men; an image which wasn't helped by the huge black hat he liked to wear everywhere together with a black cloak and a black canvas bag full of books slung over his shoulder. All he needed was a broomstick and he could have flown around everywhere like some demented old witch. His ideas didn't come any odder either. He would never travel by stagecoach, he said, because he was too fond of horses. Despite this concern for the souls of horses he still enjoyed killing ants on spider webs until he was quite an old man and even took to carrying around vipers in his book bag. It was also his habit to wash his hands and then urinate. Come to think of it I've never known anyone with such mental energy for creating ideas—crackpot or otherwise—but usually crackpot.

Yet he used to write quite a lot of interesting prose—both in Welsh and English—until he picked up a rather nasty opium habit to help with his arthritic pains. He couldn't get off the opium again and it wasn't too long before he was writing all kinds of forgeries and fantasies—in Welsh, English and Hindustani—while his dress kept getting odder and odder and he was seeing all kinds of strange shapes and colours in the air. I never felt the need to watch over him much—particularly as he was stoned out of his brain for most of the day—but I did take his hand and fish him out of a river a few times when he was in such a state he didn't know where he was.

But I must say that he was never boring and never happier than when trying to charm the ladies or forging manuscripts and claiming that they were the original works of the poet Dafydd ap Gwilym, say, which he then tried to sell for huge amounts of money.

I used to drop in on him from time to time and just stand behind his desk shaking my head in disbelief since he had invariably hit the laudanum bottle again and was cooking up 'medieval' poems which turned out to be so convincing that they were going to send scholars dancing up the wrong garden paths for years to come. I just didn't know where he got it all from but it flowed out of him in half a dozen directions and a dozen styles all as effortlessly and enthusiastically as a mountain stream after a week of heavy rain.

Then, for many years, I lost track of him in Wales since he went to London where he was busy conning everyone. Sorroptus reported to me that he was pals with such as the poet Robert Southey and wandering the streets telling the sceptical Londoners that he was 'The Bard of Liberty'. Sorroptus couldn't stand the sight of 'that little git in the black hat' and was always asking me when I was going to have him back. Iolo was leaving a bad odour everywhere, it seemed, usually through a string of businesses which within weeks, if not days, of starting up were floundering in a sea of acrimony and debt. One day he was a mason and the next a journalist. Then he ran a grocery business followed by a lending library.

He even had a trading schooner which did all right until it sank so it was clear that he wasn't going to be staying in London for long.

I picked up on him again when The Bard of Liberty was flung into Cardiff prison—for debt, predictably enough—where he was feeling exceedingly sorry for himself for five minutes until he got the materials to start working on his forgeries again. No sooner was he released than he was again the champion of Druidism and, in a Carmarthen pub, introduced the Gorsedd into the Eisteddfod.

He'd got the idea of awarding bardic degrees in an opium dream but I have to say that it was his fluent and extravagant pen that set the seal on old Iolo's opium dreams. So he announced his grand resurrection of the ancient order of bards with this elegant claptrap:

'When the year of our Lord is ——, and the period of the Gorsedd of the Bards of the Isle of Britain within the summer solstice, after summons and invitation to all Wales through the Gorsedd Trumpet, under warning of a year and a day, in sight and hearing of lords and commons and in the face of the sun, the eye of light, be it known that a Gorsedd and Eisteddfod will be held at the town of ——, where protection will be afforded to all who seek privilege, dignity and licence in Poetry and Minstrelsy ... And thither shall come the Archdruid and Officers of the Gorsedd and others, Bards and Licentiates of the Privilege and Robe of the Bards of the Isle of Britain, there to hold judgement of Chair and Gorsedd on Music and Poetry concerning the muse, conduct and learning of all who may come to seek the dignity of National Eisteddfod honours, according to the privilege and customs of the Gorsedd of the Bards of the Isle of Britain.'

Ah yes old Iolo was a half-mad, hypochondriac, big-headed junky all right. Rather in the style of the modern tabloid journalist he just could not separate fact from fantasy and he'd knock you down sooner than look at you. But despite all this—

or perhaps because of it—the Welsh took him right to their bosom and what you see on the Eisteddfod field today is nothing less than an astonishing tribute to old Iolo's opium visions.

It was absolutely terrible that night. You know how it goes. You do nothing for months and even years then you're scooting all over the country with barely time to change your mind.

I had been enjoying listening to a child's bedtime prayer in a farmhouse just outside Aberystwyth before taking off into the dark countryside in the strangest of moods, feeling both bored and happy, dreaming and awake, riding along iridescent lines in the darkness, touring the nether regions of time and space when I picked up a call for help on the prayer line way out in the Irish Sea.

The Irish Sea is not technically my patch since it falls under Ireland which belongs to Victor. But there's something of a mystery about him since he's disappeared into some Bermuda triangle and been missing for more than two decades now. None of us can understand it. Victor was always a feckless sort who didn't exactly overtax himself with anything—but he was usually there for any sudden cries for help. But then he just vanished like a ghost at dawn.

There was even talk back home that he had been suffering from sort of strange identity crisis, following the collapse of the Church on that strange island, and that he had decided that he was a leprechaun and gone to play with the little people. But this didn't make any sense at all and, one quiet weekend a few years back, me and Sorroptus went over to Ireland to look for him. But we didn't get a whiff of him—not a whiff—even if we did pick up the strongest smell of a few patrolling dark angels over near Croagh Patrick. We hoped that Victor's disappearance had nothing to do with them but, if that was the case, we never got to the bottom of it.

You may have noticed by now that there has been a certain deterioration in the quality of angelic service in recent years so I had better clarify one point right here. As I indicated before angels do not fall in love, marry or die. We are also as old and durable as the Himalayan range but we can get tired, injured and, in certain exceptional circumstances, incapacitated for a while.

But our real problem is that we suffer—if that is the right word—from human emotions. We get happy and sad; tearful and courageous; exuberant and pensive ... And it is this range of emotion, I think, which has slowly but inexorably been leading to our undoing by bringing us too closely into the fallen reflections of the postmodern condition. Hank hit the bottle to deal with depression and overwork; Victor probably developed some strange schizophrenic disorder and just vanished. I also know for a fact that Bimmimus would have given anything at all not to have had Spain, particularly after they were knocked out of soccer's World Cup when the whole nation took to its bed and didn't seem to want to get up again. 'And you think the Welsh suffer from the glooms,' he told me.

The only angel I ever knew who was always cheerful and happy, despite lots of difficult famines and droughts, was Finius in Africa but even he's been getting the hump these days, mostly about what television is doing down in South Africa. Get him on that subject and he never shuts up; how just one television camera can keep violence swirling around the townships for days on end. Well, we've all got that problem haven't we? Sorroptus nearly lost almost all his prisons the other year just because of that one camera that covered the Strangeways riot. You mark my words: this television thing is going to do us all in before we get much older.

As for my own work and patch you will have noticed by now that it's more or less a love/hate relationship all the way with these Welsh. Well I can live with that; let's face it, I have to live with that. You won't catch Conker running away or hitting the bottle. I'll do whatever is necessary—and fight whatever fights need fighting—right up to the final hours which, I'm beginning to believe, will not be too far away now.

Anyway I picked up this call and sped straight out into the Irish Sea on the wildest of nights with thick curtains of sea mists hanging over every wave. I couldn't even locate the source of the call for a second or two because the winds were becoming really strong so I had to keep frantically quartering the waves until I finally found this small fishing smack with two oil-skinned Irish fishermen down on their knees, with fish and crabs slithering all around them, as they prayed to the Lord in the most pleasing and fervent manner.

Their engine had packed up because they had run out of petrol and they weren't even trying to steady the boat by using the wheel, clearly having decided to stake their all on prayer so I thought that I'd just quietly tow it back to land when, blow me, there was a traffic accident right outside Conwy Castle so I had to leave the stricken fishing boat and get back there, catching the spiralling car and giving it a few more spins so that it landed the right way up, making a quick check on the vicar, still sitting there with his eyes wide with a mixture of terror and disbelief, before returning to the Irish Sea through the thickening storm only to find that the winds had really got up by now with the fishing boat bouncing around in the most dangerous fashion and in danger of capsizing at any moment.

I never like doing it but I had no other choice except to open my wings, stretching them out wide and fighting hard against the winds until I had created a small pool of tranquillity right in the middle of the storm. This, by any stretch of the imagination, takes tremendous strength and, just when I was pondering my next move, one of the praying fishermen jumped up from his knees and shouted to his pal that he had just remembered that he had a spare gallon of petrol under his bunk. I continued keeping the boat steady as he got it out and, within a minute or so, the engine was back in action and they were spluttering safely back to port.

No wonder Victor had gone missing if these two doughnuts were in any way representative of his flock.

But then I had to turn back again and go screeching right across Wales since a man was about to jump off a church spire near Presteigne on the border and, to make matters far worse, he was also very drunk, just clinging to the church spire as he wept and prayed alternately. You know the kind of thing: 'Oh dear God please help me. I've had enough and I want out. Please God don't turn your back on me now. I'm ruined—my life is over.' I hovered around him for a full five minutes waiting for him to make up his mind what he wanted to do. If they really want to kill themselves that's their business—free will and all that—but, if they are actively seeking God's help, then it becomes my business.

But the trouble with this twerp, who clearly had all the intelligence of a breeze block, was that he was so drunk he didn't seem to know if he wanted to live or die, now shinning even higher up the spire and clinging to the weather vane. Well I couldn't hang around here all night waiting for him to make up his mind—assuming, of course, that he had a mind to make up—and I was dead tired after using my wings in that storm so I decided that I'd had enough of all this nonsense and, perhaps cruelly, flipped him around a few times on the weather vane, where he looked like a toy aeroplane whizzing around in circles on the end of a piece of string, before he let go and went whirling out into the air and I caught him as he fell, sticking my hand over his mouth to stop all his hysterical screaming, then letting him down onto a tombstone in the graveyard with the gentlest of bumps.

The fright of the fall had sobered him up completely and I had to laugh as I looked down at him lying there and gazing up into the darkness wondering what had happened to him. His hands even began feeling parts of his body to make sure that they were all present and correct as his huge wide eyes kept sweeping around in the darkness trying to work out where all that strange laughter was coming from.

I left him where he was and slunk off into that summer night, looking for somewhere quiet to have a rest. We never need to sleep but I do have to rest for quite a long time after such a busy night and using my wings like that. We angels are not gods after all; we're just the lowly conscripts in a mighty army doing what we can where we can.

# Fifth Book

It was an awful self-indulgence, I know, but, after my busiest night for years, I just lay in a warm field outside Presteigne for almost all the day soaking up the psalms of summer.

It's also probably as well that I can only be seen when I choose since it can't be a pretty sight with my wings stretched wide and legs splayed apart as I enjoyed the way all that sunshine went right through to my tired marrow. If you face the sun and close your eyes you can also get a nice celestial blaze in your brain which is a good glowing state in which to say your prayers.

But it's also nice to feel close to God's creation; to lie here with the bees and wasps whizzing through you as they go about their business; to watch a damsel fly hovering in the air before moving forward at speed again; to count the thick green leaves on the trees and savour the hundreds of scents that can come together in a summer field. If the conditions are right you can even hear the flowers growing or the drunken flutterings of the butterflies. All growth is the gift of God and it is good to do nothing sometimes, feeling primal and unconcerned, rolling back and forth in the very heart of life while having a good stretch or mindlessly fingering your belly button.

This went on for hour after lovely hour when, late in the afternoon, something black and shadowy fluttered over my closed eyes and I jerked upright with a start, looking around anxiously. This black shape could have been a crow but it was surely too large for a crow and there were no eagles in these parts. Then my radar picked up some curious warning vibrations hanging in the midge-swarming air and I knew something was up. It couldn't have been, could it? Every part of me was on full alert. But those vibrations were still vibrating, telling me that the black shape might even have been a baby dark angel. Dark angels can have babies, when they are feeling strong and daring enough to protect them. Yet, having said that, I haven't seen a baby dark angel for at least a hundred years and certainly never in Wales.

There was a time—particularly in Victorian London—when Sorroptus was fighting and fixing baby dark angels on an almost daily basis and most of them were soon cleared out. Yet if that really was a baby dark angel flying around here then we were all in far bigger trouble than even I had dared imagine. Those babies have always meant that dark angels are prospering and gathering in great numbers. Even the small ones can fight like hell too—if you can manage to track them down in the first place which is easier said than done. Real evil is always difficult to spot: it has a way of being missed even by us white angels. I've always been quite good at spotting them but I don't suppose that even I see all of them by any means.

Anyway one thing I did know for certain: that fleeting dark shadow had completely ruined my summer reverie so I decided to return to Presteigne and see what was going on there. Who knows, they might even be gathering somewhere around the outskirts of the town and, if they'd got babies as well, I'd definitely have to do something about that.

Presteigne is the smallest county and assize town in Wales. It is also a curious place since it is on the border where the people do tend to stand around watching out for any strangers. They also like to ask lots of questions but are less keen on giving any answers. It is also difficult for them to know if they're actually Welsh or English, having been over-run so many times, by both sides, in endless bloody battles down the centuries. It's not a place I'd ever dash to first but pretty enough. Oh yes, pretty enough.

The town also features in George Borrow's travel book, *Wild Wales*, in which he immortalised a 'land of renown and wonder, the home of Arthur and Merlin.' Borrow thought that the Welsh were racy and robust, yet loving the magical. 'Wales is a bit crazed on the subject of religion,' he wrote, 'but still retains old Celtic peculiarities and still speaks the language of the bards.'

For myself I always thought that old George was a bit crazed, particularly on the subject of religion. He seemed to believe that he would discover the secrets of life in the bottom of a pint glass and was forever whacking down the stuff but, when he wasn't actually drunk, he was going around the place upsetting people with his endless nosy questions in his dictionary Welsh.

Thus his idea of a good chat with a maid in the Radnorshire Arms in Presteigne was to ask her dozens of questions. Was she a native of the place? Were her parents alive? How did her mother support herself? Were her mother's lodgers quiet? What did her mother do when the lodgers were not quiet? Of what religion were the lodgers? Of what religion was the maid? Had she always belonged to that religion? And so on and on and on. In fact the one thing the maid did tell him was that Presteigne was not in England or Wales but in Radnorshire.

Yet I was still feeling quite tense as I entered that Presteigne dusk; still had that fleeting black shadow flickering about bat-like in the back of my mind. History has always told us that whenever there are baby dark angels there is always lots of trouble; they actually thrive on crime and violence of all sorts; baby dark angels really are the spirits that work in the children of disobedience.

I came to the Radnorshire Arms, which was built in 1616 and looks every hour of its great age with log fires and oak panelling. There are also hidden passageways and priest-holes inside; a veritable gorgonzola of ancient escape routes. And what were they talking about in the bar? They were complaining about how difficult it was to get a taxi to come out because the drivers were afraid of getting beaten up.

The daylight was now breaking up fast as I moved further along the high street down past the Spar supermarket, brilliantly lit up like an aquarium with a few people walking around the shelves inside. The Top Hat restaurant had yet to open but then I wobbled and gagged a bit and had to move right across the road to skirt around the next shop, Video Visions, with its appalling stench and usual cloud of evil leaking out over the pavement.

With its deep-rooted and romantic attachment to everything that is violent, cruel, horrific, morbid and perverted the video industry has driven a stake of the purest evil right into the very heart of this society. The violent imagery of many of these films is breeding violence on a massive scale—particularly among the young, the poor, the unemployed and the uneducated—but, even deeper than this, it's also a matter of the criminal ideas and concepts in these films which are always dealing with such as terror, alienation, violence, revenge and horror. These films are always busily promoting ideas such as the cathartic purging of violence, the necessity for bloody revenge, the ways in which justice can be achieved by crime.

All this is a far cry from the teachings of my old warrior ministers of the pulpit like Christmas Evans who nourished the Welsh with such ideas as the inspiration of purity of heart, the white flame of absolute goodness and the destruction of the self. They taught the simple joy of honesty, the certainty of the resurrection and the way every relationship comes alive in love. These video shops are pouring out the black rain of hell which is turning the young into vandals and criminals; exposing them to violent sex in films such as *Cape Fear* and *Basic Instinct* and positively inciting them into war with our police with such anarchic individuals as Rambo. A society always goes rotten in its education. Corrupt teachers with corrupt ideas create corrupt societies. The Welsh grew under the shadow of the

110

pulpit and are now dying in front of the window of a video shop.

Ideas govern everything people do. The world is merely the sum of a person's ideas about that world and that person is but the sum of his ideas about himself. It's criminal ideas that are responsible for most crime—not poverty or unemployment or even drugs as is so fondly imagined. Poverty, drugs or unemployment may be motives for crime but criminality lives in a deeper and more subtle cave along with the dark angels. Crime begins and ends in the way a person thinks; in the way he thinks of himself and his relationship with the world.

Only the Chinese have ever properly understood crime which, they say, is merely a matter of disorganised ideas. If you steal an apple from the commune they just keep talking to you until you understand the folly of your ways. China hasn't got an angel of its own, oddly enough, but there again we can't ever do much if there's no prayer. Such work as needs doing there is done on an ad hoc basis by whoever happens to be free.

So here it is in this Presteigne twilight—another tiny video outpost in Lucifer's growing empire of lawlessness with the face of Hannibal Lecter staring out of the window at me. 'Brilliant, cunning, psychotic', the poster says in reference to Hannibal's performance as a human cannibal in the film *The Silence of the Lambs*. This film—with its relentless emphasis on violence, cruelty and perversion—is perhaps a classic definition of the evil which is now busily destroying the world and, to make matters far worse, this same world has become so blind and mad that it has actually heaped international honours on it with a handful of Oscars. Even worse than that, Hannibal Lecter was played by Anthony Hopkins. From Port Talbot in South Wales! One of my flock! *One of mine!*

Now I've always had an uneasy relationship with the stage and have never really taken much notice of actors, no matter where they were from. Their births have never been accompanied by any runs on the chimes even if Wales has produced some quite talented actors in recent years particularly in the shape of Richard Burton and Anthony Hopkins.

Yet I have never been much of a fan of a lot they both did and there was also the added problem that, for many of their waking hours—particularly Burton's—they were usually so drunk there was no point trying to talk to them about anything at all. There's not much even I can do in the face of chronic alcoholism and, especially after he began to repose in the beefy arms of Elizabeth Taylor and all that destructive madness that is Hollywood, I lost my passing interest in Burton and his career.

Anthony Hopkins, on the other hand, was a very different character since he was much softer and without the relentless selfishness and even silliness that characterised Burton. Yet, having said that, I never really bothered much with Hopkins's career either—he did some good Shakespeare and Sorroptus raved about him in Pravda but, as his career blossomed, I saw less and less of him anyway since he was spending a lot of his time in Hollywood and hence out of my area.

Imagine my surprise then when I learned that Hank had caught up with Hopkins in Los Angeles in the winter of 1975 and did quite an effective number on him. Hank and I have always got on well but he's often admitted that he's still feeling bad about losing me Dylan Thomas. Maybe this was his way of making amends and maybe it was for other reasons. I don't know but, in the event, he caught up with Hopkins when he was in the right mood in Los Angeles and told him straight that, if he could get out of his alcoholic maze, he would be spared all the ravages of hell. There was no need to feel so empty, so careless, so drunken ... 'So stop drinking and get on with your life and live it and have some fun with it,' Hank told him.

It was a grittily economical vision with simple words that Hank does so well—he's also got too much on his plate to go in for any of the more elaborate pillars of fires stuff—and he threw in some good practical advice—'And remember to sling your arse down to Alcoholics Anonymous'—and Hopkins has not had a drink from that day to this. He has also become a nicer, warmer person who shows a lot of gratitude by working with other alcoholics.

So why has he gone and got himself mixed up in nasty, brutish films like *The Silence of the Lambs*? I don't know and neither does Hank. The film happened to be mentioned when Hank and I were chatting together back home and he said that if he'd known Hopkins was going to go on and make appalling rubbish like that he would have left him the miserable piss-artist that he was.

Yes, Hank has a very vulgar turn of phrase, unusual for an angel. But, as I mentioned before, we do tend to take on aspects of our flocks and Hank reckons he's had America for far too long. Oh let's face it—we've all had our flocks for far too long. And there's not a single one of us who now believes he's winning.

By now the night had really thickened up and the curfew bell was being rung in the church. The soft, doleful clanging went sliding over the Presteigne rooftops telling the townsfolk of the end of another day. The bell-ringer, Harry Hatfield, has been ringing the curfew here in St Andrew's for most of his long life and this unique tradition goes back hundreds of years, recently saved by a donation by Mike Oldfield of *Tubular Bells* fame. Women sometimes ring it in summer months but don't like doing it in the dark on their own. 'There *is* something in the church,' says Harry. 'I don't know what it is but you always feel that there's something in there when you walk inside. Put it like this: I'm always happy *after* I've put the light on.'

Swallows flitted around the old tombstones of the surrounding cemetery where only the coldness slipped quietly through the shadows. One of the tombstones marked the grave of Mary Morgan, a 16-year-old servant girl who killed her bastard child. She was taken to Presteigne jail in 1804 and was later hanged in nearby Gallows Lane, the last woman in Britain to be hanged off a tree.

'In memory of Mary Morgan, who young and beautiful, endowed with a good understanding but unenlightened in the sacred truths of Christianity,' it says on her lichen-speckled tombstone, 'became the victim of sin and shame and was condemned to ignominious death in April 1804 for the murder of her bastard child. She underwent the sentence of the Law the following Thursday with unfeigned repentance and a fervent hope of forgiveness.'

There was, I was pleased to note in this graveyard twilight, a bunch of flowers on her tombstone, the only one to have flowers on it.

It was the climate of superstition and ignorance which really killed Mary Morgan. I have long noticed that, when a Christian church or chapel becomes strong, they drive most superstitions out of the area since rationality is the very basis of Christian faith but, where the churches and chapels are weak, you just never know what's going to happen. All sorts of barbarism triumphs when a country loses its faith.

The quality of faith has always been patchy around here which, in its turn, particularly around Mary's time, encouraged strange businesses like the burning of the Wicker Man or sin-eating. All that sort of stuff really used to give me the willies so I usually just gave a sigh and a shudder before scooting out of the way with a quick burst on my exploding rings.

The main difficulty with all that sin-eating stuff was that the local Church leaders were so faithless they got into it too. Once thirteen parsons got together and decided that they were going to exorcise a ghost, Black Vaughan, from this very graveyard since, they believed, he had been causing a lot of trouble in the neighbourhood.

Now I knew this ghost, a sad little poltergeist whose idea of a lot of trouble was to throw a soup ladle across a kitchen, so, perhaps childishly—but what the hell?—I decided to have a little fun at the expense of these thirteen holy exorcists. We angels always had the time for a bit of fun then, come to think of it. Whenever we were together back home a few centuries back we were always boasting about our pranks, but not any longer.

Anyway these thirteen parsons came to this graveyard carrying their bells, books and candles, summoning up the spirit of Black Vaughan so I did my Hamlet's-father-on-the-battlement-bit, walking a few feet above the tombstones towards them while clanking a lot of rusty chains and carrying my head under my arm.

The whole lot of them fainted spark out, as if they had been freshly chloroformed, except for one who was so stupid he must have been a bishop. He then claimed that he had somehow managed to trap me inside a snuff-box which he showed the others when they regained consciousness. He took the snuff-box to that well on the other side of the cemetery and dropped me down it. All their heads peered down into the well as the box fell into the dripping darkness but they then turned and looked at one another when they heard several ripples of my best sardonic laughter hanging in the air. 'I don't think he was inside the snuff-box at all,' one of the brighter ones pointed out. 'You can't laugh like that inside a snuff-box can you?' he went on. Well perhaps not all that bright.

So, to be honest, I've long avoided this area until young Mary Morgan got into all that trouble with the mobs gathering daily outside the prison waiting to see the public hanging. She was a strikingly pleasant girl with dark curly hair and a slight twist in one of her large brown eyes which kept glistening with tears. There wasn't a trace of flirtatiousness in her either with lovely prayerful hands and a long thin neck. She had been abused by a squire in a local castle who was going to get his comeuppance later. It was him, in fact, who had forced her to kill her baby.

Certainly Mary shouldn't have been in that cell, still less facing a hanging and I followed her prayer lines straight to her on the first night she was locked up. There was no point in trying to be too clever at that stage so I just appeared before her, told her my name and business then offered to help her escape and even fix her broken heart. She continued blubbering for a further five minutes when she stopped and looked up at me. 'Are you really an Angel?' she asked me with a child-like innocence which I found most touching.

'Yes, I really am.'

'Can you really fix broken hearts?'

'I can fix almost anything at all, Mary. You break it and I'll fix it. So what about it?'

'You couldn't fix my heart. It's in too many pieces. Oh Conker, I just want to die; that's all I want.'

'Well, if that's what you want Mary, that's what you will have. But we angels do like people to die of old age. That's what we like the most.'

'I just want to be with my baby. Can you fix that perhaps?'

'Oh yes. That's my job and, as long as you die with faith in your heart, I will take you straight to your baby.'

'Let's settle for that then shall we, Conker? Let's just settle for that.'

'You're in charge, Mary. I'm only here to do what you want.'

'Well I'd quite like it if you gave me a little kiss. Could you do that?'

'Oh sure. I can give you as many kisses as you want.'

'Just one would be nice.'

She could have changed her mind right to the end, of course, and I would have taken her off that rope in a second if she'd called out for help. But she even smiled at the gathered crowd and her heart was alive with prayer when they slipped the noose around her neck. She hardly suffered for a second either as she dangled from that cursed tree before I took her soul in my hand to take her across the Jordan. One of the Seraphim, who had six wings and whose normal business was to praise God, actually came down to meet Mary holding her baby. It was a most moving moment and the rest of us all averted our eyes as mother and child spent some joyful moments together. Then I told Mary we had better be moving on and, with an arm around her shoulder, escorted them both in to be eternally emparadised with God.

(I was having quite a lot of practice in these tearful heavenly reunions about this time since Anne Griffiths and her baby died the following year.)

Later, I left the graveyard at St Andrew's and walked down to the River Lugg which rises some ten miles from here and marks the border with England. Dragon flies and the odd kingfisher knock about on this river, but not tonight, since all I could hear were its cold waters chuckling in the darkness. Trees hung over me like leafy whips and far away was the faint roar of traffic. The mackerel sky had black wisps of cloud hanging in it. I crossed back through the town and came to Warden View where lots of executive bungalows were sitting cheek by jowl on a hill. Televisions were flickering brightly in the living rooms with people watching the *Nine O'Clock Violence* on the BBC. Their every head was transfixed by savage images of murder, fire and looting in Los Angeles.

I wandered back past a deserted school with a 'Vote Tory' sticker on the main door. Almost every living room had a television set in the corner with its thin blue light neutralising the colours of the wallpaper. A man was firing a machine-gun. Another warehouse was going up in flames. The heads were still transfixed by the murder, fire and looting.

I thought of Hank and how he must have been suffering so much with all this going on inside his area. He says it's pointless for him to go into L.A. any longer since there were whole areas where the dark angels were openly sitting on the rooftops. He always said he had seen it coming, of course; he had always said that no society could be subjected to such a high level of violence, through its media, without turning on itself in the end. Nevertheless I said a quiet prayer for him, hoping that The Boss would be there for him and give him all the strength he needed for his struggle.

The real trouble with all this evil that we seem to have been fighting almost for ever is that it keeps changing its face. I mean to say *The Silence of the Lambs* is clearly an evil film and films like that will have played their own role in the L.A.

disorders. Those people shooting one another and looting the shops are also in thrall to that evil but, even worse, is the evil that is carrying all this violence into every home in the world. Modern journalism is so pious in its sacred insistence on pouring the world's violence into every home and can't actually see that it is modern journalism, especially on television, which is also creating a violent world in the first place.

Perhaps I'll ask Bimmimus precisely how he manages to put a television out of action when I see him next. If the operation took a minute, say, how long would it take before I got around the million-odd televisions in Wales and, more to the point, how long would it take before they got them fixed again? Ah, dreams, dreams. Where would we be without our idle dreams, eh?

I turned back out of town, passing a street lamp shining on the blossoms of an espaliered apple tree. Many of the blossoms had fallen, like fresh drifts of dusty snow, onto the pavement. Next I crossed a playing field before coming out on Gallows Lane where the self-same oak on which they hanged Mary Morgan still stands.

Cars roared back and forth along the road with their revolving headlamps making the hedgerows shimmer and dance in the darkness. But, the closer I got to the tree, the more I began to feel danger. Warning sounds in the air became louder and louder until I stopped still and searched the whole of the night with my senses. Everything kept bringing me back to that tree so I edged closer and yet closer to it until I saw something which sent my every emotion surfing hot and cold inside me. There were patches of slime all around the base of the tree which had burned into the ground and killed all growth.

I moved closer still and felt quite jangly when I made out the silhouettes of two dark angels sitting on one of the main branches with a baby sitting in between them. In fact none of them looked all that big since their general lines had a way of

118

melting straight into the night. So I hadn't been wrong about that baby either who was snoozing quietly along with the other two. It was difficult to be sure from this distance but one was almost certainly Klang and the other probably some popsie he had picked up in some low dive in another corner of the world. There was no telling how old the baby was but it was one of the ugliest little monsters I've ever clapped eyes on just perched there, alternately chomping and snoring with slime dripping off its wings and bits of old food dribbling down the front of its chest.

I walked away from them wondering what to do. They would be extremely difficult to overcome in a fight and Sorroptus, who could really handle himself, had been fighting Klang almost for ever. I doubted if I could even manage his popsie, come to that. But we have always been under instructions to attack and destroy baby dark angels wherever possible. Just use your sword and chop their heads off, Michael once briefed us. You will always be attacked by the parents in return but that's what you must always do. Get the baby first and then fight your way out as best you can.

'And remember what I have always asked of any soldier in this army. You already think like angels but you must also always speak with tongues of fire and fight like ancient warriors. The very honour of God is always at stake in everthing you do.'

Well I can fight as well as any other angel but I've got to confess that I've never liked it much. Violence against anything at all has never been my style or to my taste except, of course, we are talking real evil here. It was MacMac who always loved long bar-room brawls with dark angels—the longer and bloodier they were the happier he was—which was why, I guess, they gave him Scotland, particularly Glasgow which at times is one long bar-room brawl.

But scrapping has never been my cup of tea. In fact I have to admit that the first thing I did was check out the position of that tree, wondering if I could argue that it was in England and hence the responsibility of Sorroptus. But it wasn't. Not by a few hundred yards it wasn't. A shame really because Sorroptus also enjoyed fighting with dark angels. He once told me his idea of a perfect day was a long fight with one of them. Well, we're all different aren't we? There's none of us the same.

Oh come on, Conker. Try living up to your name eh? They're here in Wales, which is your territory, so you've got to fight them with everything you've got and get that baby or else there's no telling what will happen if that baby has babies and they start breeding in large numbers. How are you going to manage then?

So I drew up a battle-plan in my mind and went through it slowly and carefully. I would have to do what I did when I last fought and overcame Splachnik; call up the spirit of the old Welsh dragon. On that occasion I rounded on Splachnik belching smoke and fire and half-frightened him to death before I lopped off limb after limb, bound him up in chains and threw him into that lake in the Brecon Beacons.

There were, of course, three of them to sort out this time and, while I might get the baby, there was no possibility at all of overcoming Klang and his popsie so I would just have to fight like mad until they gave up and slunk away.

Our rules of engagement are most strict that we must always attack face on and issue an appropriate warning, so I finally took up my position about two hundred yards away from the tree directly in front of them. Then I had to adjust my weight to suit the thin moonlight and use my hissing yellow flame with a purple heart to draw myself a full length sword. A few quick bursts on my exploding rings followed and I began a full metamorphosis into a flying Welsh dragon with flaming red wings, huge bursts of fire erupting out of my mouth, smoke coming out of my nostrils and my long scaly back arching with terrifying power. Then I reared up on my back legs and attacked.

You would think that with all these bursts of fire and general racket I was making out in that field they would have at least woken up by the time I got there but their heads were still dropped with their eyes closed when I slashed away a lot of the foliage with the first stroke of my sword the better to get at them. 'This is Wales which is under the full protection of Conker,' I was then obliged to roar, raising my sword and giving Klang a burst of fire straight in his face. But as long as I live I will never forget the face of his popsie whose eyes opened wide in terror as she took in my fiery details whereupon she fell into a straight swoon and fell off her branch backwards. With Klang still confused and blinking from all my fire and smoke I knew I was doing well as my sword came downwards and sliced his baby right down the middle into two more or less equal bits. My blow even cut through the branch on which they had all been sitting and it wasn't until Klang was actually falling to the ground and almost landing straight on top of his popsie that he woke up and hit back. And what a hit it was!

He came screaming up at me and head-butted me with such force that we both might have gone at least a mile up into the air before we grabbed hold of one another as our huge wings fought to get some lift in the air and we both fluttered downwards like a pair of aeroplanes in a dog-fight.

Wings are everything in a fight like this and I kept trying to steady myself for long enough so that I could get a good slash at him with my sword and so destroy his ability to fly properly. But this wasn't Klang's first fight with a sword-carrying red dragon by a long shot so he kept working away at me at close quarters, raining in blow after blow on my chest and all but knocking the fire and puff out of me as we spiralled down to earth where we landed in a field with such a thump that it caused a crater a good twenty feet wide.

I had caught his wings a couple of times but hadn't inflicted any real damage on him and was further distressed by all the corrosive slime he kept leaking over me. This slime is murder if it gets into your eyes and all I was thinking about was how to get far enough away from him so that I could wield my sword properly when the very heavens farted. Hovering over me was Klang's popsie and, judging by the blazing anger in her eyes and the obscene screams coming out of her mouth, she was madder than all hell about the way I'd just halved her baby. Oh blimey, this was going to be a night and a half this was.

I made as if to roll one way then rolled another, managing to wriggle out from beneath Klang when the popsie landed right on my back. There was no way I was going to get my sword into her while she was on my back and, to make matters far worse, Klang was up and standing right in front of me and I could see that any second now I was going to be the raw filling in the middle of a dark angel sandwich.

She even prevented me from getting a good lunge at Klang as he grabbed me by the throat so hard there was no chance at all of bringing up any more fire. In fact I was wondering if I was going to be the first angel in the history of the world to actually get killed in action when there was scream of white light whirling around and around us, accompanied by the sound of a rescuing calvary charge. Ah I knew whose idea of fun this was. This was Sorroptus arriving in the nick of time to save us from the Red Injuns, shaking out his wings with an exuberant yell and shouting, 'This is England under the full protection of Sorroptus' before grabbing Klang by the ears with both hands and pulling him straight up into the air where they both heaved around like a couple of bull elephants fighting deep in the jungle.

The snag with all this was that Klang hadn't let go of my throat and I was just being shaken around like some useless bauble dangling on a storm-tossed Christmas tree as they both got down to it. Well at least we clearly weren't in Wales any more and had got into smelly old England. That much was clear.

But then Klang's popsie also got up there fighting with us, using her feet, legs and whatever—where these women learn all these tricks I don't know but clearly even dark angels also watch too many movies—and I was dropped to the ground, still too dazed to stand up properly and feeling a huge fall of soot in my chest. It was an extremely fagged-out dragon which finally managed to get to his feet when the dreaded popsie landed on my back again and was trying to work her fingers into my eyes. I didn't mind the fingers: it was all her slime and constant obscenities that were getting on my nerves so I decided to fix her once and for all and was busily trying to tumble her over my head with Sorroptus and Klang now fighting a good three miles away—you could just about make out the flashing tips of their wings like distant, waltzing meteors—when something so bizarre happened that I still haven't been able to work out its meaning or significance properly.

A shot rang out and the screaming harridan on my shoulders suddenly went limp and began sliding to the ground. So what was this all about when it was at home? She had actually been killed by the bullet of a gun and was even now shrivelling up like one of those pantomime witches on the stage after being cursed by the good fairy. I just couldn't believe it. Dark angels don't die but that dark angel was as dead as a dog and no messing about.

I looked around me and there, about twenty yards away, was the unmistakable figure of Bishop William Morgan in his unmistakable red and gold clerical vestments and his unmistakably pugnacious jaw. Now he was blowing the smoke off the barrel of his pistol, nodding to me as if reassuring me that everything would be all right. I mean to say, everyone is watching too many bad movies now.

Well, well, well. This was a complete turn up for the books wasn't it? The protected had finally become the protector. The man I once looked after was now looking after me which also might explain why Christmas Evans and Anne Griffiths had started being around again. Perhaps all my mysterious pursuers were in fact all here to take me safely through my final journey.

These were strange, strange times and no mistake. I thought I was going to be making a quiet, routine report this year but it was turning out to be anything but. Still it all added up to one mighty conclusion—that we really were moving into the mystery of the final days and The Boss might be about to make a move sooner than anyone expected.

I lifted my arm to salute old Dead-Eye Dick. He accepted the salute with one of his own and disappeared into the darkness. But I knew then that I couldn't carry on with my work straight away. Now I needed a real rest after all these excitements and, when I need a real rest, I either hang around a working monastery for a few days reviving myself with their cycles of prayers or I like to listen to traditional jazz.

I was still quite shaken up when I got over to the other side of Wales again for the holiday weekend in Aberaeron. I've often picked up on this little jazz festival over the past few years, spending many happy hours lolling about the pubs with a glass in my hand or on the camping field as jazz musicians from places as far apart as Canada and Holland come together for hour after blissful hour of traditional jazz.

Traditional jazz is ramshackle music with huge zest which arrived in Wales via Cardiff's dockland from New Orleans. It also has the most unusual characteristic of being both mindlessly happy and heartbreakingly sad while, at its most typical, it has a strutting bravura which makes it good for dancing and jumping about to. Basically it's music for born-again delinquents although Hank and I—as far as I know—are the only angels who actually enjoy it. I've been telling him for ages to get over to Wales for this weekend but he keeps saying that he hasn't got the time. What's a lost weekend in the history of the world, I say to him but, despite his multiplying problems, he remains unusually conscientious.

For this weekend I might take a few days out and become a scruffy, half-drunk student from Aberystwyth with wild hair and a long beard, sitting near some stage enjoying the great romp of it all. The weekend certainly has ways of putting me back together after the rigours of the year and bloody fights with dark angels. Oh Aberaeron has done that more than a few times now.

The only trouble was that it was typical Welsh weather that weekend with rain coming down in stair rods and howling gales busy trying to rip off every slate in the town. The Saturday night also happened to have the highest tide of the year with huge brown waves whump-whumping against the breakwater or chasing one another down the length of the harbour. Piles of driftwood were washed up the slipways and dumped on the pavements of the streets. Lots of small ducks huddled for shelter behind the Hive on the Quay restaurant while the sleek launches on the harbour were all bouncing up and down like steroid-packed athletes on an eternal trampoline.

When the winds dropped the rain came sheeting down again. Democratic as ever, it rained on the chapels and the small spiritualist church; it rained on the aquarium and the fine Georgian square; it rained on the bakery and the restaurants; it rained on the small backyards and the crowded pubs.

Aberaeron is one of a few villages along this coastline which grew up on the herring shoals. Now the shoals have diasppeared the place lives on the rather stranger diet of tourism and jazz and it was to listen to that music that we had all gathered here again this stormy Saturday as almost every pub was amok with wailing trumpets, pounding drums, strumming banjos and those lovely flirtatious riffs of the clarinet. All a far cry from the Welsh and their harps, I know.

Not that this bad weather meant much to the thousand-odd delinquents who had gathered here, since this place is famous for its bad weather—there are those who believe that bad weather was actually invented here—and, back in 1986, Hurricane Charlie ripped straight through their little tented city in the field. Wally from Llanelli, a silver-bearded veteran of the Welsh traditional jazz scene, was staggering back to the camp site in 1986 after the pubs had closed and stood on a small hill above the field where he was rather amazed to see all those tents flying around in the air like a squadron of canvas flying saucers out on target practice. One tent was actually heading straight out to sea and two othere were flying around and around his head. 'Ooooooh man,' Wally thought with his eyes rolling around with fear. 'Ooooooh man oh man.'

He then decided that he had better get into his own tent and roll a special fag to calm his nerves. Next thing he was floating up in the air too, not sure if he was camping or hot-air ballooning. He began yelling out to the others to grab his guy ropes before he got blown away to Ireland and, the next thing, there were five jazzers hanging onto his guy ropes with Wally bouncing around like a demented kite somewhere ten feet above their heads.

No tents were actually blown away that night but, by way of a change, the sea came in over the breakwater and the jazzers had to paddle for their very lives. They even had to call the fire brigade in the middle of the night to drain the camp site but that's Aberaeron in the rain for you. The real truth is that most of them hardly care if they are about to drown or be blown away mainly because they are always far too drunk. Whole Olympic swimming pools of the stuff disappear down their throats during the festival and, at the end of each night, it's always the same sorry story of grown people trying to play golf on the top of snooker tables, losing their false teeth while throwing up in dark corners or later being interviewed by the police about some offence which they have always, without fail, forgotten committing. 'Who me? Don't remember a thing.'

One burly jazzer, Chris the Greek, wearing a T-shirt announcing that he was 'Half Man—Half Biscuit' was decidedly the worse for wear and on all fours trying to get into a sleeping bag in the darkness when a girl's frightened voice piped up: 'You don't live in here mister.'

But, as a scruffy student from Aberystwyth, no one bothered me and I enjoyed all the bands who played lots of those lovely old favourites like 'My Bucket's Got A Hole In It', 'Digging My Potatoes' or 'Ice Cream'. The banjo has such bounce and the trumpet such a powerful drive. But it's that clarinet that's always been my favourite, of course, with those wailing riffs, full of laughter and gaiety. I always have the same fantasy when I hear the clarinet: of strutting through heaven as if on a New Orleans funeral march blowing the clarinet and playing 'When The Saints Go Marching In. Oh Lord I just want to be in that number ...'

Then, lo and behold, the sun actually came out for the big parade through the streets on the Monday afternoon. Indeed I followed the Adam Adamant jazz band through the streets myself as the girls dressed up in their glad rags and danced around and around us, feeling quite relaxed and normal for a while until I spotted yet another mysterious figure standing on the harbour corner leaning against a lamp-post.

It was a strange aroma that my keen sense of smell picked out of the other street smells at first: the decidedly sick/sweet aroma of opium. Now all kinds of substances have been smoked in Aberaeron over the years but I have never quite picked up on this one which drew me straight to the man on the lamp-post.

He was wearing a huge black hat with a black cloak and had a canvas bag full of books slung around his shoulder. Oh aye, that was old Iolo Morganwg standing there smiling at me so it was time for fun and games again. I am not an especially paranoid type but all this illusory malarkey was beginning to get me down and no mistake. I'm in control of time not them. Just what were they all up to?

'You don't think you can win this game without us, do you?' he asked me when I approached him.

'?'

'This game you're on. There's no possibility that you can get through it—any of it—without us. There's no future in solo effort. These are the darkest days ever and everyone has to work as a team. You need all history.'

Perhaps unforgivably, in the face of all this gobbledegook, I laughed. Old Iolo hadn't changed a bit. That much I did understand. 'I need all history?'

'All history. When the time comes you'll need it all—even the bad bits. Keep an eye on the bad bits, Conker, and you might just have a chance. Use the thrust of all history.'

I knew I could ask him questions for ever but he'd never make any sense, particularly if he was back on that opium. But, in the event, he disappeared in a puff of jazz and all that was moving around the corner was the rest of the parade and all those cold winds still howling in over Cardigan Bay.

# Sixth Book

The flame moved around on the huge bright canvas of bare light, sketching a long and winding brambled lane which swooped down a hill and right into a square with a stone soldier from World War I standing with his rucksack and rifle on a plinth. There was one gold ring and then a second, dissolving right into the sunshine as I came parachuting out of all this brightness, landing as slowly and noiselessly as a falling leaf right next to the stone soldier.

Now the flame was moving quicker and with more confidence, creating a pub, a general stores and a garage. A smell of frying bacon hung everywhere and two old men were talking to one another in Welsh. A woman in an opened window shouted at the old men, but they just laughed and took no notice. All around were the rolling Cardiganshire hills, each of them still wearing their gaudy summer crowns.

I walked away from the village square, past a row of houses and down to a school where children were playing in the yard. Playing children are always the purest delight to me and I might join in their games except they sometimes get a bit puzzled—even frightened—when I cannot contain my laughter. It just seems to slip out and, while many children will take no notice or assume that the laughter is coming from somwhere distant, a few of the brighter ones will stop still as their eyes look around slowly and carefully.

I joined in a skipping game and, sure enough, began laughing like an emptying bath tub, making one of the little girls drop her rope and run away. That was my cue to withdraw discreetly, disappearing into a gold ring and coming out on the other side of it, getting a few hundred yards down the road before dancing back into the ring and coming out on the other side of it again. Now I was standing next to the railings of a chapel and looking out over a field at a small church with a tangled yew in the graveyard. This church is one of the most beautiful in Wales; it was actually built on a secret bed of Praise and much of the Welsh character lies coiled within it. But if I had to say just one thing about this church I would say that it has the eye of the sun.

We are in Llangeitho where, with a population of around 250, nothing much happens. They used to have a smithy, two tailors and three shops but they've all long gone. Last month someone broke into the school, which amounts to a crime wave, and the only headache the community council is now dealing with is where to locate a new playground for the children.

That flowing river Aeron is not what it used to be either. The water used to bend and twist over smooth pebbles with lots of brown trout darting for cover. But, in the manner of the modern world, they decided to straighten the banks with tractors which destroyed the trout pools and killed off the fish. Those tractors have an awful lot to answer for.

But you can still pick up all kinds of sounds as you stand on the river bank. There's birdsong, passing traffic, barking dogs, a tractor cutting a hedge and the occasional R.A.F. jet rifling through the skies. But mostly there's long stretches of silence and, looking down into this river and savouring the silence, it would be easy to forget that this village was once the spiritual powerhouse of Wales. The Welsh made a lot of progress in this silent handful of buildings, particularly under the leadership of one man who, even when he was sixty, liked to throw a leaf into this river and out-run it down through the meadows.

Daniel Rowland was his name; another of our Eight Inch Nails who was also one of the first masters of the pulpit.

I have already explained something of the role that Christmas Evans played in forming the character of Wales but it has to be said that he had at least a dozen powerful contemporaries who included John Elias, Howell Harris, William Williams and Daniel Rowland. These men, in their pulpits of fire, became the conscience of the people and their ideas became the ideas of society. Preaching festivals became people's holidays and through them the Welsh were literally fed the food of the Bible.

The preacher took the sermon and made it an instrument of social revolution. The sermon awoke consciences and attacked evil employers or drink; it destroyed bad customs and influenced manners; it encouraged the building of new chapels and nagged people to remember what they had forgotten. Revivals were always maintained by the preached rather than sung word and these charismatic revivalists were like the modern pop stars using the *hwyl* to work on the feelings and move the heart. Their appeal was always to the human heart as their lovely words flung sunshine and shadow over the faces of their congregations.

One of the great stars of the northern pulpits was John Elias, whose sermons were steam engines of reason fuelled by unrelenting feeling and detailed knowledge of the Bible. Crowds always turned up in such huge numbers to hear his daring and even dreadful attacks on sin that they often had to take the windows out of the chapels to make room for them all. People even fell to the ground under the impact of his words and a grief-stricken ten thousand attended his funeral. One of Elias's most endearing features was that he had always refused to believe in material progress and I liked that a lot. Everything that mattered had taken place already: material changes were no progress at all.

But pleasing as these great preachers were to some there were others who were forever attacking them physically and I had to be on constant alert almost throughout the eighteenth and nineteenth centuries shielding my boys from attacks with sticks or well-aimed rocks. These preachers had such tempestuous personalities that some people had a go at them for even walking down the streets, particularly Howell Harris who was forever getting himself arrested, stoned, beaten and thrown out of town but still coming back to haunt them like a bad hiccup, railing against all the 'ale-house people, the fiddlers and harpers' until he was flung out of town again. These were wild and dangerous times for all preachers. One of Harris's friends was actually killed while preaching at Hay-on-Wye—I only have one pair of hands and anyway picked up nothing on the prayer lines—and twice I had to pull Harris, half-dead, out of a ditch and bring him around.

Yet the big man of this period was Daniel Rowland who, here in Llangeitho, started the first Methodist revival in this very pulpit with powerful sermons talking of such as the 'stormy law', 'purity of heart' and the 'testimony of a good conscience'. It still only seems like yesterday as I stood on that window ledge watching him with a proud smile as the voices sang with praise and some jumped up and down continuously. His sermons were like nothing that had ever been heard up until that time and sometimes his words were so melodious and the music of his voice so strong and his arguments so clearly pleasing to God that I too would just weep and people near me would look up at the rafters and hold out their hands wondering where the leak was coming from.

Rowland knew the Bible off by heart and built all his meditations on the scriptures. Sometimes he made some notes on a few slips of paper but never referred to them. Even when he cried himself it never affected his speech which, in fact, became clearer. As Christmas Evans put it, his sentences were always terse, accurate and pregnant with good sense. Any power that seized him also seized his congregation and, in the common struggle, they became one and entered into the same binding covenant.

He had a high forehead with beady eyes and a sharp, aquiline nose. In the pulpit he always wore a black gown and, when he described The Agony, his voice was so charged with raw passion that he could electrify the whole congregation, making many faint, weep or jump with joy. They became known as The Jumpers and, when anyone criticised their antics, Rowland would retort 'Sleepers, sleepers.' He would also liken the Christian to the flea. 'The lower he crouches the higher he flies.'

Up to 5,000 would travel from all parts of Wales to hear him here on sacrament Sundays. Hundreds would stop at a well a few miles outside Llangeitho, drinking the water there and taking food. Rowland heard their singing as they made their way to his chapel. 'Well, here they come bringing all heaven with them,' he used to say. Many carts and horses were tethered out in the fields and six clergymen helped with the communion.

Whole movements were nurtured in the shadow of this sacred pulpit. Rowland converted Howell Harris who in turn converted Thomas Charles. William Williams of Pantycelyn, whose deep feelings and burly poetry still lives in the hymns of crowds in rugby internationals, added his music to Rowland's oratory and introduced his first hymn book, *The Sea of Glory*, to the people here. Now Wales had words to sing and a heart to sing them.

Rowland's sermons usually went on for an hour but on some days 'the fire came down from heaven' and he preached until the sun went down in the western windows. His ministry lasted for 50 years and inspired no fewer than five separate revivals. But Rowland also understood that words, however inspired, were not enough so he created tiny Methodist cells (*seiat*) which became the lifeblood of the movement. In these cells, with appropriate leaders, members could share their experiences, strengths and hopes. These cells also led to prayer meetings, Bible classes and Sunday Schools. The chapel was finally in business.

But not any longer, dearly beloved; not any longer. Barely a dozen came to these pews to worship last Sunday and not many more than that went to the church over the road. Television now claims Rowland's great congregation. The news readers are our modern preachers and the BBC's *Nine O'Clock Violence* is the new pulpit fashioning the sick souls of my wandering tribe. Reporters from *The Sun* are taking around the collection plates and Hannibal Lecter is in charge of the deacons on the Big Seat. It is precisely these wretches in their electronic pulpits who are now fashioning the souls of the people just as Rowland and Williams fashioned the souls of the people in their wooden ones. It is all too easy, from where I fly, to see why the country is up to its knees in a bog of violence and crime—and sinking fast. It is even easier to see why they are now stabbing one another on the terraces instead of singing together. The real wonder is that no one else seems to be seeing it. Of one thing you could be sure: my boys of old would have seen it all too clearly and whipped this evil up hill and down dale. Oh they would all have made a most devastating charge against these massing armies of evil. Of that you can be very sure.

Rowland first began his work in that church over the road until the church authorities threw him out because he insisted on preaching in 'unconsecrated' places. But the church remains both peaceful and prayerful, again reeking of floor polish and spruce with fresh flowers. There is a wire grille over the porch to prevent swallows nesting there but the door is usually unlocked and anyone can sit here listening to centuries of prayer and praise with just occasionally that great and inspiring voice breaking through it all.

'God pierces the very heart of the sinner and, inasmuch as sin has tainted his very marrow, in order to get at it he breaks his bones. Hence the Psalmist says: "Make me to hear joy and gladness, that the bones which thou has broken may re-joice."'

I can't say that Rowland ever gave me much trouble—unlike Howell Harris who, like Bishop Morgan, was almost always nothing but—except that he did suffer from frequent depressions later in his life, particularly when he believed that he had got preacher's block and took to his bed. Christian's Slough of Despond in Pilgrim's Progress was as nothing to Daniel's blues when he got going. These depressions used to tax all my ingenuity and I even found myself tickling his ribs or even slipping small drops of alcohol into his tea to brighten him up. This turned out to be slightly unwise since, before long, he became alarmingly addicted to tea, forever going on about its inspirational powers and insisting that he drank a gallon of it before going into the pulpit.

But even when in full flight, with his words cracking like lightning flashes over the heads of the congregation and with a gallon of my special tea sloshing about inside his belly, he still might dry up in the middle of a sentence, his eyes darting about in panic as his mind got blocked again. Then he would disappear from view, going down on his knees in the pulpit and praying that his flow might return. When this happened I might drop him a suggestion or two and, before long, he would be back on his feet like some great bird openly struggling with a huge, newly caught fish and holding it up for the delight of all.

His other odd fault was that he had a real faith in the ministry and prophecy of dreams which is almost as stupid as the absurd modern fashion of putting your trust in the predictions of some nutty astrologer. If he had a bad dream he was almost certain that it was going to come true in some awful way and he almost lost all power to act until he had gone to sleep again. I invariably managed to reverse the structure of the anxiety dream which had been troubling him in the first place. Reversing dreams may sound a complicated business but it is surprisingly easy. There again, I had better not give too many of my secrets away.

When this old, grey-haired Elijah finally died, at the age of 77, he said of his work: 'It is nothing.' He was buried near that chancel and had been a faithful warrior right to the end. I myself took his soul straight into the temple of God after he died and their hearts met in a most fantastic rapture of pleasure.

I suppose that it is somehow predictable that the Visitors' Book near the door of his church is full of lines invoking Rowland's spirit: 'May the Lord bless this land again as he did in the eighteenth century.' 'May God send us another Daniel Rowland.' A jet swooped low overhead and the sun slashed down through the stained glass. I heard again that powerful voice in the silence as those old hymns of praise drifted about in eddies. These were the sounds of the Great Awakening and many are asking if such sounds are going to echo through the land again.

The answer is that even I don't know because, unlike mad astrologers, angels cannot see into the future. But I will tell you this: revival only ever comes from prayer and the timing of any such revival is in the gift of God alone. Only He can order another devastating outbreak of the Holy Spirit. Only God can send another Elijah just as only He can decide when The Boss will return—as return he will since Biblical prophecy demands it.

Meanwhile my country of Wales and villages like Llangeitho are quiet just now. Dead lands are always quiet and so are whipped dogs. But so, too, is the eye of the storm.

It was again my trusty flame which cleared the way for me, taking me along roads with men working in holes, past electricity pylons and gangs of sparrows swooping through hedgerows and along the side of pebbled beaches until I came up onto the prow of a hill amidst drifting blue sea mists. The flame then began drawing the outlines of a small city with but two thousand inhabitants—the smallest city in Wales indeed— with long crouching terraces of brown stone houses along the main street. In one soft explosion of my gold rings I was down in the holy city of St David's.

There was a pilgrim cafe, now closed and being done up. A hand was stroking a cat sitting in a front window. An old lady in a blue coat and carrying a brown bag was struggling with her arthritis along the pavement. Flocks of crows scattered around the branches of one tree, making a fearful racket as they all swooped off to another. Here and there I picked up pockets of stewing tea. A few craft shops came next, followed by a fragrance centre and Digby's Brasserie. Outside the police station were posters offering rewards for information about a murder on the Pembrokeshire coastal path, a baby snatcher and a £50,000 armed robbery. A large stone cross stood in the square at the end of the road and, a few hundred yars further on again, was St David's Cathedral, deliberately built in a deep hollow so that it would not be visible to marauding pirates out at sea.

But even if I were blindfolded I would know where I was immediately since this city is special, holy, set apart. It is also unique in my life and career since it was on that headland over there that I first came here to Wales, born deep in a furious explosion of rainbows and almost dropped straight in the sea, way back in the fifth century. Hundreds, if not thousands, of rainbows were building up all the time along the coast at that time. Even the dimmest knew that something was up then. 'This land of Menevia is about to be given a new holy man,' the rainbows kept saying. 'So prepare yourself for another prophet—watch out for another human riddle hatched in the mind of God.'

All I can remember of that period was crashing through these coloured bars of flaming light. I wasn't even attempting to do anything: just being kicked through coloured vista after coloured vista until I found myself falling straight down into the sea. I panicked and tried to open my wings but to no avail since I didn't have sufficient height to get airborne, just wobbling one way and then another before coming down sideways with one hell of a crash and all but breaking one of my wings on that jagged cliff over there. Ah those were the days all right. Not one of us in the whole army had a clue what we were doing or how we were going to do it. I barely knew how to use a sword, let alone the flame, and even the very sound of my exploding rings made me jump.

I wasn't a volunteer for all this nonsense you'd better understand—although you've probably understood that already. I would have happily spent all my life messing about on Megiddo until The Boss came back but I was drafted without so much as a tiny query as to what I wanted to do. 'You're in the army now,' the suits said if ever I looked like making a complaint. 'And you'll do as you're told.'

Even so early this morning visitors were already making their way up and down the tomb-stoned slopes of the cathedral close. The cathedral is now receiving some half a million visitors each year and untold millions have already left their prayers here while, back in 1124, the Pope decreed that two pilgrimages to St David's was worth one to Rome. Many of them are taken around the city by Kathy Timmis who lives in nearby Goat Street. 'Interest in pilgrimage is mushrooming,' she says. 'I take them to other chapels here but it is the cathedral that they really want to see.'

Right next to the cathedral are the broken-jawed ruins of the Bishop's Palace, now the home of jackdaws whose staccato calls can be heard all along that wooded valley. Directly at the bottom of the close is the River Alun and The Penitents' Bridge which medieval pilgrims were expected to cross on their hands and knees. There is also the Sparling Bridge which was said to shriek whenever a corpse passed over it. I just don't know where all these dopey stories came from, if you are wondering.

Yet for myself I always look at the cathedral with a strange mixture of emotions since I spent oh so many bitter-sweet years watching it going up, falling down, being fought over and looted even by people who were there to look after it. Bishop Barlow once pinched all the lead off the roof in the sixteenth century to help provide dowries for his five illegitimate daughters. An earlier cathedral collapsed altogether after being built on nearby marshland and one gang of labourers was attacked by some pirates one day who just cut off all their noses. I was quite sorry about this when I found out about it since I understand that people are quite attached to their noses but I just can't be everywhere and again there were no S.O.S. calls on the prayer lines.

The Vikings almost completely erased it in the eleventh century when it was laid waste for seven years with even David's tomb covered with brambles. But it was the Normans who rebuilt it, making the spire short and squat so that it couldn't be seen from the sea. More than a little pettiness was invested in the cathedral too. There are now clock faces on only three sides of the tower since the people in the north of the city refused to contribute to the clock's cost.

But once inside the cathedral you can see how it has grown over the centuries out of a mish-mash of just about everything there has ever been in ecclesiastical architecture. There is the twelfth century screening, the fourteenth century choir screen, the sixteenth century ceiling and the twentieth century organ case. The oak ceiling, in particular, is one of the most perfect celebrations of the woodcarver's art while the stone columns of the nave splay outwards, giving a surprising effect of space and distance in such a small building. Golden splashes of light hung in distant purple darknesses. You can sometimes hear ancient voices too.

'The day is close at hand and I am glad to go the way of my fathers. Brothers and sisters, be cheerful and keep your faith and belief and do the little things that you have heard and seen through me.'

Yet it must be remembered that this is still a living church ministering to the needs of the community and an idle flick through the book asking for intercessions in prayer tells us much about the worries and needs of that community. They have asked for prayers for 'Daddy who does not believe in God'; prayers for Cambodia and Nelson Mandela; a truly Christian prayer 'for the man whose daughter died as a result of his cruelty' and a truly un-Christian request that a 'dear friend may open his wallet and bless me with his riches.'

Behind the main altar is a small chapel lit by mazy candlelight and holding an oak reliquary which contains the bones of St David himself. Ah my wonderful David; how I loved that man. I remember once thinking that if all Welsh men turned out like The Waterman, I'm going to be the shepherd of the greatest flock the world has ever known.

Anyway—as I was saying—it was just on the turn of the fifth century that I found myself half-concussed and spreadeagled on that cliff, worried that I had broken a wing with the other actually lying in the foaming sea. It was all so strange and this strangeness was heightened by a sky full of rainbows. But I slowly managed to get my act together, finding my wings and working out, by trial and error, how best to move around. All my movements come naturally to me now and I don't even think about them but there again I have had 1400 years of practice. But it wasn't always so and, in fact, on my first flight upwards with my wings I was all fingers and thumbs, even going backwards at one stage and crashing back into about the same spot that I had started from. It also took me ages before I learned that there were perfectly efficient and economical ways for an angel to fly without actually using his wings.

But I soon managed to get around and found that this headland was a starkly beautiful spot, powerful with the spirit of wild Wales. I had never seen waves rise and roar like that back home—you could watch the Dead Sea all the year around and barely see a ripple—and there was also a fascinating profusion of wild life wandering through those blackberry mounds. Even the hissing barnacles sang their own sad songs on the shoreline and there was no end of bird life overhead. Around early autumn one of the largest bird migrations in Europe all but blackened the sky. Finches travelled here from across the Bay along with thousands of chaffinches, nightingales, skylarks, blackbirds and redwings. In just one day I counted more than a million birds going past, some stopping for a rest but most going on to feed in the frog-choked marshes of Brazil or the sardine-thick seas of north Spain.

Yet as I began exploring my new territory of Wales I soon saw just what a mess it was and only wished that I could have migrated along with the birds, the only difference being that I wouldn't have come back and no messing about. The country was little more than an allotment in hell where every single inhabitant was being menaced by either war, plague or famine. Celtic chieftains were forever fighting and killing one another in the bloodiest and most meaningless of battles. Superstition and fear ruled every home and, such were the conditions, barely a third of all babies managed to survive and a fraction managed to grow to adulthood. Also pagan Druids with their 'sacred oaks' and fertility potions had control of the popular mind and, to make matters worse, tornadoes carrying plague germs were sweeping up and down the Welsh valleys.

I honestly just could not see what I could do in all this mess when, one day, I was just standing on the selfsame headland on which I had first fallen, doing nothing in particular and watching the continual and spectacular build-up of rainbows all along the coast when there was such a loud peal on the chimes that I all but lost my footing and fell straight into the sea. I had never heard a sound like it: so ravishing in its purity and so full with the promise of a coming glory. But, you must remember, I didn't even know what the chimes were supposed to mean then. They never explained anything at all to us in Megiddo before we got our marching orders; we were always left to work out everything for ourselves.

In the event I immediately followed the chimes to their source but five hundred yards away, coming to a small stone house where I stood in the corner, with one hand over my mouth and eyes welling with tears of wonder, as I watched a baby being born. I can't say that I have ever lost my sense of wonder at seeing anything at all being born but I knew that this moment was almost as special as that freezing night when The Boss was born in Bethlehem and standing here watching that baby inching out from between those heaving hips before unfolding into a bloodied, jellied flower and letting out a great scream I knew intuitively that my work had begun at last and that the dark reign of the Druids had ended.

The weather at the time also told me that God was near and watching everything closely. Forks of lightning were stammering silently on the horizon intermingled with huge shunts of noisy thunder. But a totally unreal light was shining down on this sweating woman and, despite the turbulence over the heaving seas outside, the atmosphere inside the house was as calm and sunny as a hot summer's afternoon.

It was in conversation with Victor and Macmac that we later finally put all the pieces of the jigsaw together. In response to the needs of the dreadful times God had decided to usher in a new Age of the Saints and each of the Celtic countries was going to get a new holy man who was both going to revive the one true faith and set up a brilliant counter-attack against all the forces of Druidical superstition and darkness.

(This idea of introducing a small group of men who would change and nourish a whole race over a long period is very much the way God works, by the way. Some of us angels have often gone in for the slam-bang approach—using our swords first and brains afterwards so to speak—but God's patience is as inexhaustible as His timing is always accurate. God does not believe in the concept of an overnight success; He always takes a long view on everything and, as He is not capable of physically destroying even His enemies, everything about His work and strategy is patient and long-term with a conclusion which almost no-one can foresee except Him.)

Our role in all this was to watch over this new group of men and it soon became clear, in more ways than one, that I was not to take my eyes off David for a single second. Nothing at all harmful was to befall him and, when he needed any wise counsel or instruction on anything, he was to get it. Absolutely no stupid pranks: just intensive care all the way. So watch your step or it'll be big trouble and possibly an 'interview' about your future as an angel with Michael himself.

At around this time Macmac also got Columba after following the chimes out to the isle of Iona just off Scotland and, later, he got Mungo who caused Macmac more than a few headaches with his habit of standing in an ice cold stream every day while saying his offices. You're going to lose him to pneumonia if you're not careful, I used to tell Macmac but got it all wrong again because—as I said before—Mungo died from the shock of sitting in a hot bath.

We Celtic angels were seeing a lot of one another at that time since the saints were great friends who often gathered down here in David's new monastery which was made up of circular huts and an oratory encircled by a high wall. I remember one day a whole gang of them walking along that coastal path—David, Columba, Mungo, Aidan and Patrick—all wearing their distinctive bracelets with their combs of bone in their long hair and grey habits swirling around their sandalled feet. They were all laughing and joking together with a gang of us angels fluttering along in the air behind them like the anxious chaperones of a Sicilian courting couple just prior to the wedding.

Not that any of them gave us a jot of trouble and, in all the many hours I spent with David, he gave me nothing but pleasure. As he grew up in these fields I might take the form of a dove and instruct him in the scriptures. I once even found a new spring for his monastery after the monks were complaining of a shortage of water during a summer drought. Or else I would hand him bunches of fresh flowers—daffodils were his favourite—but most of the time he was his own man growing up in his own way.

When he went abroad I went with him—we were allowed to roam through other countries more at that time as long as we didn't stay away from our patch for too long—and, when he returned, I also advised him on the running of his monastery here, first telling him how to set up the Opus Dei, a daily round of ordered worship. The monks ate herbs and, like David, drank only water. But it didn't seem to do them any harm and, in fact, it was David himself who insisted that no oxen were to be used in ploughing the fields since the monks could be their own oxen. There was one beefy character with brown eyes and a permanent smile, Steffan, who could take a plough and rip up a whole meadow in two hours flat and still barely break sweat.

Ah yes, my partnership with David really was made in heaven and he would always listen to me as we toured the country together founding new monastic settlements, healing the sick or fighting the current heresy of Pelagianism. The temper of the time was such that the people often wouldn't accept mere arguments, no matter how well they were constructed, so sometimes we had to achieve some sort of extravagant and theatrical effect too.

I guess the best example of the complete understanding we both had when we worked together came when David was forcibly denouncing Pelagianism one afternoon in Llanddewi Brefi and I caused a six feet mound to rise in the earth beneath his feet. We hadn't actually discussed this beforehand but, as soon as I saw that he was losing his audience, I thought I had better do something and, for no particular reason other than sheer theatrical effect, did that.

Then I turned into a dove and came fluttering down through the air to perch on his shoulder. That shut all those bored sceptics up in a flash I can tell you. There again I've always been a fan of good theatre, me. I've always felt the most miserable and unangelic jealousy that Sorroptus got Shakespeare.

But even when David was being quirky they were the most beautiful quirks. He was praying in his monastery one night when he heard a nightingale singing in a nearby tree. The bird's careless rapture so entranced and distracted him that he feared that he would never be able to pray properly again since half an ear would always be listening out for that nightingale's beautiful song. Accordingly he prayed that the nightingale would never again sing in his diocese and indeed one never did sing in the Pembrokeshire area from that day to this.

Yet I suppose the highlight of that whole early period was when I took three of those saints—David, Padarn and Teilo— back home to Jerusalem. It was one of those dream trips which kept getting better and better. At first they all had something of a language problem when they got there so I gave David the gift of tongues and he duly charmed everyone—even the uncharmable donkey men—as we travelled from Jerusalem out to Bethlehem then up to Nazareth and on to the Jordan and Galilee. We had no arrangements for food or water but at almost every stop people came out of their houses and gave all that was needed.

All the angels who weren't actually abroad on active service came down to see us in Megiddo and the Seraphim themselves laid on a terrific concert on the banks of the River Jordan. Even Michael himself put in a rare, if brief, appearance on our journey, doing his usual stunt of swooping down out of the sun with his enormous wings outstretched when we were all outside Jericho. We also even got an invite to the palace of the Patriarch of Jerusalem who duly made David an Archbishop and gave him a variety of gifts including a bell, a staff and a tunic woven of gold. Typically, David gave away his gold tunic saying that it just didn't suit him but you could see he was as pleased as Punch with his wooden staff which he took with him wherever he went. Well, what else would you expect from a dedicated follower of the son of a carpenter?

My brilliant Waterman finally died at the ripe old age of 147—which in itself must say something for a lifetime of herbs and water—and I just can't describe all the fuss when I took his soul up to heaven. Everyone who was anyone turned out for that—even all the cherubim with their great, glittering eyes and bodies of shiny wheels within wheels—and the music and festivities lasted for almost a week.

But, of course, we angels have always known and believed what many people—even Christians—usually find difficult to believe: that death is always a victory and triumph over life. The human body is merely a temporary husk and it is the personality of the soul that lives and works forever.

Certainly David's personality has continued to live and work on through Welsh history, even these many centuries after his death. He has given birth to numerous churches and all Welsh schoolkids get a daffodil on his birthday and it was a day off for them too, for many years. Yes, my great saint still lives and breathes in people's minds, says Nona Rees, a writer and

145

librarian who lives in Treasury Cottage in the cathedral close. 'By that I mean everyone here is still aware of David and what he stood for. He still embodies their approach to their own culture and feeling for Christianity. He is not a cypher but still someone who lives on in their psyche.'

So this day, late in the summer, I went back to that headland where I had first landed in Wales. The sea was still the same as were the big, bird-fluttered skies. On one side of me was St Non's chapel and, on the other, a retreat house run by the Passionist Fathers. There was also a small well, with a few fresh geraniums floating on the surface and some coins lying on its floor, marking the spot where David was born. The isles of Ramsey and Skomer lay out in the sea like ragged brown battleships waiting for orders to move in for an attack.

I wiped away a nostalgic tear after remembering my brilliant times with my Waterman and immersed myself in the well for a few minutes before wandering back up to the headland. A lovely warm breeze was drifting down through a swelling pink sunset but, try as I might that day, I couldn't see any rainbows building up along the coastline.

That last afternoon I spent at St David's was a bit of an odd one because I kept picking up the faintest of calls on the prayer lines but, whenever I was about to make a move in that direction, the lines went dead. These calls were almost impossible to describe except that I knew that some faithful soul was calling out for God's help. But, when they began again, they might well be coming from someone who wasn't quite human, I began thinking. They were almost like the troubled signals of a fellow angel but I just could not locate their source.

I drifted inland past the Preseli mountains hoping to pick up something but again apart from vague hisses of static, all the lines stayed dead and I finally set down in the arched ruins of an old monastery in Strata Florida in the Valley of Flowers. This was once a wonderfully industrious monastery with its own lead mine, fish farms and corn mills. In the early sixteenth century they even had their own public house in the monastery's precinct selling their own special beer which was so strong it painted Impressionist landscapes all along the length of the brain and was best drunk while already lying in bed.

I often came here to enjoy the monks' prayers but the aims of commerce and the ways of God are always inimical and it wasn't too many years before I was noticing a slow but steady process of corruption and a fine, prayerful culture becoming contaminate. The Abbot slapped two of his monks in irons for counterfeiting money down in the cellars but this was something of a smokescreen because I alone knew that the Abbott was in fact masterminding most of the clipping and coining himself. I just left the place to its own devices after all that started and it wasn't too long before the place ended up as rubble. Any monastery vitally depends on the good wishes of God but, when monks turn their back on God, He always gives them up.

There's barely any evidence of the old monastery now—except for a few ruined arches—but there is a more modern cemetery tacked onto the grounds which is in itself something of an oddity since, according to the tombstones, various London Welsh were brought back here from such places as Maida Vale or Putney. Also just near the yew in the middle of the cemetery is the 'grave of a leg' of Henry Hughes who lost it in a stagecoach accident and insisted that it had a proper burial. The remaining three quarters of him went pogoing off to America.

That yew also marks the burial place of another key figure in my report, one Dafydd ap Gwilym, a marvellous poet of the summertime who not only wrote with real feeling but with searing emotional power. George Borrow once actually kissed this yew but I just about managed to restrain myself because, as a Christian angel, I have always had the most ambiguous feelings towards Dafydd. While there is no denying the splendour of his verse, it has to be said that he was perpetually horny and not only are angels supposed to frown on all that business but they also, being the way are, can never quite understand it either.

For myself I have never understood why the eternal surge keeps surging, particularly given all the difficulties it always creates, but it clearly does, almost everywhere, without a break or time off for good behaviour and our Dafydd was the original salmon, prepared to defy any amount of gravity and scale the highest waterfalls in order to return to the spawning grounds of a young lady's arms. Many of his poems were based on the pursuit of the love tryst, even if these pursuits were usually unsuccessful and ended up in disastrous, if comic, failure. He just never let up for a second: one flash of a pretty face and he was after her, almost no matter what time of day or where he was. One poem was about him trying to crawl into bed with some wench in an inn but waking up everyone up in the process; another was about him fleeing the rage of his new sweetheart's jealous husband.

But what's the point of all this stouting around? That I've never been able to understand. A few minutes pleasure? Well I can understand that well enough but that brief bout of pleasure almost always leads to hours, days, weeks and even years of the purest pain and misery for almost everyone involved. Let it be firmly known that I am no prude but contemporary morality sensibly dictated that there should be no sex outside marriage simply because a carnal free-for-all in those pre-pill times would have resulted in hundreds, if not thousands, of illegitimate babies. Yet that was then and this is now. I'm not speaking for all angels but my postmodernist line on sex now is that it's all right with anyone you love as long as it's safe and there's no likelihood that anyone will get hurt.

But having entered that major caveat on Dafydd's work I would then have to say that old thunderthighs was also given the gift of bardic praise and is a central figure in that long and imperial line of praise poets going back to Taliesin and the court of Rheged. Occasionally I spent some time with Dafydd on his travels through Wales and it was one of my great pleasures to see the way the poetic emblems of his mind entered into a duet with a bird on a tree in a 'shroud of summer clover' and they would both serenade God with praise for the beauty of all His creation:

> Triumphant hours are the lark's
> who circles skywards from his home each day:
> world's early riser, with bubbling golden song,
> towards the firmament, guardian of April's gate.

Dafydd, like the Psalmists, saw God in all things; when he praised nature he praised Him who made it, although this was not Pantheism since, like all praise poets, he did see the creation and the Creator as separate.

> Music of a thrush, clearbright
> Loveable language of light,
> Heard I under a birchtree
> Yesterday, all grace and glee -
> Was ever so sweet a thing
> Fine-plaited as his whistling?

The poet—like the priest—always mediates the idea of God through his work. He praises the fine particularities of nature so that we might better understand and appreciate the glorious hands that fashioned them in the first place.

This praise tradition lives on today and, moving down through the Preseli hills in Pembrokeshire, I often pick up on the burly bearded figure of Bob Reeves striding over the ridges and exploring the savagely beautiful landscapes in which he lives and works. I am here with him now as he chooses and builds his words in which he will also convey the wondrous nature of The Kingdom. Here is a praise poet who has also become a remembrancer of the Pembrokeshire people; someone who draws on the past to replenish the present and mines his poetry out of the very earth of the living locality. He is not a formally religious poet but his work has muscle and fight with the deep feelings and wonder of God moving through every phrase and rhythm.

> Summer's sweet seduction.
> Bees drunk and giddy
> with excess, weave waterfalls
> of sunlight, slow and golden,
> heavy treasure of the hive.
> Larks hooked on soaring notes
> are reeled in by the sun.
> Lovers plead and promise.
> The Grass God dances on
> the hill, the world spins.
> Summer, such sweet seduction.

This damp, summer afternoon he was out in this land 'full of sea and light,' wandering directly above Fishguard which was slumbering around her curving harbour. Directly overhead buzzards were mewling like neglected puppies. Wild horses came wandering over to him, staring at him thoughtfully as if trying to work out if he was a threat before resuming their endless foraging. Nearby was a high mound of rocks standing on the bosom of the low body of the mountain. He was out here earlier this summer lying with his face to the sun when he saw a crow flying directly above him like a black cross. Way out over the water a storm was sweeping towards him, catching him in her hard, wet hands and flinging him about.

In a sense Bob has become a part of the land which he describes so well in his poetry. This relationship between a poet and the land has always been strange and complicated but, together with his wood carvings, such as the head of Brân from the Mabinogion and his current project—a huge head of The Boss carved out of the heart of an oak tree and so big it took six men to carry it into his work shed—he is using the land to create his art and, in this way, he is also entering into a covenant with God which is binding on both of them.

Out here, in the Preseli hills, 'between the kestrel and the mole' it is always a pleasure to see him wandering through the landscape which has sustained him for so long and so well. But there again I have always loved to be close to the mystical free-falls of a good poet's mind—and have often recollected those golden hours when I sat with Dylan Thomas in his little garden shed in Laugharne, my arms folded and leaning forward to listen carefully as he welded one word with another, shaking them about and pulling them apart until, after long laboured hours, they began fitting together into that which gives God His greatest thrill above all else—praise.

But today we are still basking in the glory of summer and, just thinking about it, Bob's mind was foaming beautifully with fine metaphors and similes. Ah now then, summer is getting your arm chilled to the elbow as you reach down for trout in cold mountain streams; summer is bruised grass and wild mint and definitely the smell of running water; summer is sleeping in the tall grass lulled by an insect choir singing hymns; summer is swifts weaving mazy patterns in the air and a green light under the tree but only before breakfast; summer is the hot, spicy smell of the earth and the elusive breath of gorse blossom. Ah yes, summer is larks and lavender and old men in even older sandals ...

Later he went over to Pentre Ifan, an ancient burial chamber of stones which are often dotted around these parts, all as mysterious and inherently improbable as the fare structure of British Rail. These stones even pre-date my arrival here and I've never been all that clear what they are supposed to be about but Bob likes to come here after dark to think about those strange, driven Beaker people who built chambers like these all those years ago. These stones are his Golgotha or place of the skulls. They tell him things about his past which he, in his turn through his work, tells the Pembrokeshire people.

151

I hear,
I hear them come,
I hear behind the wind
a thousand throats
scream sorrow
through a thousand
thousand years.

Bob was born in Neyland where his great grandfather sailed on the Irish steam packets. His mother was a daughter of a French fisherman who settled in Milford Haven and his Neyland childhood was special: 'Even now when the wind blows over the mud flats and shingle and weed, and the curlews and the oyster catchers make the air liquid and silken with their calls, I breathe deep and savour the salt and the sea and the childhood comes flooding back from a well deep within me ...' You see it's that deadly use of simple, musical language again and note the devastating use of that tiny word 'and'.

He crossed the river daily on the old 'paddle wheeled ferry steamers to school' and 'learned to swim from her shingle beaches, picked cockles and mussels and even, on a very low spring tide, oysters and queens, once I had been sworn to secrecy and shown where the bed lay.'

It is the sea which always draws him to her and, later that afternoon, I was with him down on the seashore in Pwll Deri where those great waves were still pounding the headland and three white seal pups were stretched out on the pebbles of one cove watched over by their mother. Way out in the Bay the bull's huge black eyes kept bobbing up out of the water and looking at her. Occasionally the bull swam in hoping for a bit of tickle and slap but the cow didn't want to know, lolling backwards and raising a flipper as if complaining of a headache. The bull then swam off again.

Bob loves the sea with its timeless roar and will sit for hours watching the seals going in and out. He will describe how seals sleep deep in the water, coming up vertically every five minutes or so to take a breath. Then there is the amazing quality of the light around here and the way salt carries on every wind. The suck and wash of the waves is another of his favourite phrases. 'This county is full of the sea. It seems the sea is always over the next hedge.'

That night he was down in his local pub, the Creselly Arms in Cresswell Quay; a very strange pub too, if only because they've got a side of bacon hanging off the rafter next to the dartboard where it is being smoked by many cigarettes. This economical method works quite well, it seems, and, while the regulars are having a pint, someone might start carving off a few rashers for a bacon butty.

But the undoubted star of the pub is Alice Davies, the former landlady, who still lives on the premises and is now the tender age of 105. She puts away three whiskies a night but is blind with her hands curled up with arthritis. Yet she is still as sharp as a tack and Bob likes to sit with her in the bedroom, beneath the congratulatory telegram from the Queen on her hundredth, and they talk about old Pembrokeshire when the Davies family sold coal in half hundred weight bags and people took them away on the handlebars of their bicycles.

She first met her husband Jim, she told Bob, more than a hundred years ago when she was four in the infants' school. She didn't marry him until she was 42 because she didn't want him interfering with her teaching. He came to see her at lunchtimes and was, quite frankly, a bit of a nuisance. What is more there was another suitor in the frame at the time: one Jack Jenkins. 'If I married Jack I was promised a fat pig and if I married Jim a new sewing machine,' she said with a bright chortle. 'In the end I went for the new sewing machine.'

Ah, great characters and a land of savage beauty: that's what Bob Reeves has to hand to use in his work. It might also explain why his work, in those wondrous, blue Preseli hills, is very fine indeed.

Later I stood alone on the seashore letting the cold waves wash around my feet. It was a full moon with wisps of black cloud being whipped through the moonlight by a brisk wind. An owl hooted and, from far away, there was the sound of singing in the pub. Just then a giant shadow seemed to be framing itself against the moon and I lowered my head a little in a cold spasm of fear thinking that a dark angel might be abroad in this lovely Pembrokeshire night.

This shadow seemed to be building into something the size of a mountain range, with its outline underscored by a thick pencil of moonlight, and my wings began fluttering uneasily in readiness for any trouble. I was holding up my flame ready to sketch in weapons of defence since there even seemed the possibility that Lucifer himself was materialising in that moon-soaked night. I've never actually seen him face to face but we've always been told to watch out for him and report his movements straight back to Megiddo. We are never quite sure what he is up to but what our intelligence does know for certain is that he is even now busy marshalling all his forces for the last great battle and that he is up to any stratagem or trick to separate people from their faith and destroy God.

But then the whole mountainous shape of that shadow changed yet again and I now saw the huge outline of a man wearing a long dark habit and holding a staff upright in his hand. The faces of others, unfamiliar but familiar, whirled around him in the moonlight like speeding planets around the sun. Now the hues of light were changing rapidly too and a glittering rainbow came gushing out of his left hand side joining his hip with the coloured surface of the sea.

Well, I knew who this was by now: this was my Waterman come with the others to be with me on my journey. I flung myself to my knees in the sea, overwhelmed to see my great man again but, no sooner had I looked up, than he had gone and taken his rainbow with him. Just those cold waves were washing around me and all that moved in the glowering moonlight was the hoot of the owl and the faint sound of singing still coming from that pub.

# Seventh Book

But it will again be emphasised in my final report that, while the work of Lucifer has advanced quite spectacularly in Wales—particularly in the mining valleys of the South—it is by no means complete. Even with all the major obstacles that have been strewn in my path like those two world wars, television and those execrable satellite and video industries—in all of which Lucifer's work has positively prospered—I have still managed to shepherd whole chunks of Wales successfully; one wide swathe of land in the west, in particular, leading from the market town of Carmarthen up to the shores of Cardigan Bay. The Baptist belt, they often call it: the main Bible heartland of Wales.

On a Sunday I might patrol this area on my flame, picking up on parts of chapel services or enjoying the odd prayers. On some days, if the weather is with me, I might be able to pick up on the prayers of five or six chapels at the same time and there are still certain preachers with whom I will sit in their pulpits if I think they might be in need of a spot of quiet encouragement or inspiration. And after the services you can still see lots of people standing around the chapels with their Bibles under their arms and chatting together about the sermon. The media always forgets about these sorts of people; the media is only ever interested in the spectacular and the noisy; the violent and the criminal. Yet parts of my territory are anything but and the people are still being fed by the Bible;

not as plentifully or in such large numbers as in the days of old, alas, but at least the food is still on offer to all who are hungry. Sunday also continues as the most precious day of the week in these parts. Family roots remain deep and ancestral voices are still listened to.

To get some measure of the kind of people they are in the Baptist belt there's probably no better place to go than the horse fair which takes place on the last Thursday of every month in Llanybydder. I'll always spend a few hours there if I'm in the area and often enjoy just being another flat-capped farmer, mixing with the others, as they scratch themselves, gossip or complain about lack of money.

From early morning the roads around the town are jammed with horse boxes as the whole world and his dog roll up for the day. Lemme see now ... over there are the boys from Nant Lwyd and just by here is David Griffiths who breaks in horses the Red Indian way. That man has just come back from Italy where he watched a thousand horses going to the slaughter and that man over there has silver hair and a beard so long and straggly it looks as if he is soon up for an audition for the part of John the Baptist.

Apart from the horse people there are also numerous farmers milling about, usually short of height and broad of beam, wearing their flat caps and carrying sticks. Many of the younger horse men sport ear-rings and huge sideboards in the gypsy style while a lot of the women have long blonde ringlets and seem to be asserting their independence—while also ruining their lungs—by chain-smoking cigarettes. You don't have to tell any of this lot what to look for in a horse either. They know that, first and foremost, a horse must have good feet and legs. Then they will look for a kind and generous eye since, just as in people, mean-eyed looks can often show a mean nature. They will also know how to work out a horse's age from his teeth and the colour inside a horse's mouth.

Around several hundred are gathering around the stables and auction rings this morning, patting the snorting horses and trying to figure out which of them are the best bargains. There are no flies on this lot and that's a fact. Horse people care as much about money as hill farmers. If you really want to know if one of them is dead, they say, put a silver coin in his hand and wait for a few minutes to see if his fingers close around it. If the fingers don't move he is truly dead. They also say that if you want to make copper wire you just drop a penny between two of them.

But, just being here and drinking tea with the farmers and tip-toeing around the smoking piles of dung or standing watching the stallions being paraded for stud in the street outside I couldn't help thinking again of my old favourite Christmas Evans. I kept seeing my one-eyed wonder of the pulpit leading his horse Lemon through the crowds, exchanging merry banter with the others or snorting derisively at the state of some of the horses they had brought here. He knew a thing or two about horses did Christmas.

For this is Christmas Evans-land and he was actually born in the nearby village of Tregroes; a small slumbering place tucked away in a fold in the hills near Llandysul. There is a plaque commemorating the centenary of Christmas's death on the school wall which now has 16 pupils but no longer any from the farms. The house where he was born on Christmas Day in 1766 no longer exists but an oak tree still marks the spot and I spent a long time leaning against the wall that day remembering that run on the chimes which first alerted me to his birth and the years of his youth when I was almost constantly busy on his behalf since I don't think that I've ever had to look after anyone who was quite so accident-prone.

It was a bit of luck that I was around at all but the first time he looked as if he was going to get into serious trouble was late one summer—around this time of year—when he was but eight years old. I just happened to be sitting on top of a hay barn watching the comings and goings in the farmyard when young Christmas climbed on the back of one of the big hunter horses. This hunter really did have mean eyes but, unlike other children, Christmas didn't know the meaning of fear—which accounted for most of his scrapes—and, next thing, he was trying to get this beast to ride out into the outlying field. But horses always know when they are being ridden by an uncertain pair of hands and the hunter duly turned around and raced back into the stable. Young Christmas would have got a face full of stable and almost certainly died had I not been there to whisk him off that horse and set him down safely on the ground.

I wasn't actually around when he next got into difficulties but picked up a frantic call on the prayer lines. He had been told to look after his uncle's cattle in Cwmtwyll but, as would be expected, began climbing the highest tree in the area when a branch broke beneath him and his head hit another branch. He managed to yell out the name of 'Christ' and I just got there to break his fall but he was still concussed and it was a few hours before I finally managed to get some passers-by to take him to a doctor.

I never had any direct evidence as such but it became increasingly clear that Splachnik might be at the bottom of all these 'accidents' and it wasn't long before I put an around-the-clock guard on young Christmas. Within a few months, he was standing on the edge of a swollen river one afternoon when the whole bank gave way and he found himself being sucked down into a whirlpool. I only just managed to catch his hand and haul him out, spluttering and crying but again grateful to some force beyond himself.

But we can usually anticipate trouble. I can often direct someone away from trouble like a falling slate or collapsing wall merely by turning them around or giving them a gentle push sideways. They never actually understand why they've changed direction for no apparent reason. In this way I saved Christmas from all kinds of difficulties before they actually befell him. But invisibility and discretion are always our watchwords. Only on very rare occasions have I allowed myself to be seen as I am. It doesn't do to go crashing around the place with fluttering wings and waving a big, glinting sword. That's not the way a proper angel should behave at all.

Yet, as it turned out, my many rescues were instrumental in Christmas's final decision to go into the ministry. All children live out their youth in a vague cloud of terror, hardly knowing what they are going to be doing tomorrow let alone next year but, every time I saved young Christmas, he developed a sort of religion of luck; he began believing that he was being safeguarded to live out some special destiny which in a sense, of course, he was. He did not forget those moments when my hand plucked him from certain death any more than Paul would have forgotten what God told him on the road to Damascus.

He went on to study under the pastorate of David Davies at Castell Hywel just up the road from Llandysul. Davies was a theologian and scholar who first translated Gray's elegy into Welsh and, in so doing, it is claimed, particularly by the Welsh, vastly improved it at the same time. Castell Hywel today is a pleasant holiday complex and the cries of children echo in the barns where Christmas read the Bible and first learned Latin by candlelight before setting off to begin his ministry in North Wales.

'We do have a ghost in the chimney here but we are not at all sure if it is the ghost of Christmas Evans,' Lisa Nunn tells visitors here. 'There was a heck of a lot of howling and moaning in that chimney but we haven't heard it for a long time now.'

After leaving Castell Hywel I began picking up that mysterious buzzing on the prayer lines again which had been bothering me from time to time over the past few weeks. There was something out there which was not quite human and in a lot of distress. But I just couldn't get a reading on it since, no matter which way I turned, it went away again and it sounded merely as if I was fiddling with the wavelengths on some old wireless, just the odd buzz which was then drowned by a lot of hissing or foreign shrieking or some weather forecast for the shipping. This was all very strange and I didn't know what to do about it, sometimes making moves in what I thought was the direction of the distressed force field only for it to disappear again.

But that didn't stop me quartering the country every few hours or so, moving over fields and past derelict buildings or even sweeping over whole towns but still finding nothing untoward. I kept this up non-stop for a night and a day, almost going over the area inch by inch but still picking up nothing until I resumed my journey again in the small coastal holiday town of New Quay.

It was a dull gunmetal dawn, with just the odd seagull wheeling overhead, when my flame set me down next to the lobster pots on the abandoned quay. The only sounds came from the sparrows foraging around the pots and the metal wires clanking against the masts of the moored yachts in the harbour. Already the fisherman Winston Evans, with his brawny sidekick Howard, was sailing their fishing boat, Catherine Arden, out into Cardigan Bay. On their first stop they pulled in the prawn pots, with all the prawns skittering furiously and sounding like heavy rain on a corrugated iron roof. The prawns were a translucent browny green with small black eyes and lots of whiskers waving around angrily at the effrontery of it all. Three black eels had also got into one pot as well as some butter fish and a few baby lobsters which were thrown back in to grow some more. Seagulls with beady yellow eyes, which missed nothing, kept flying around and around the boat.

New Quay itself is a series of scattered terraces curving around a headland. Over on one side is a small shellfish factory which looks like an old prisoner of war camp and on the other are the high white walls of the Black Lion pub. I am more than familiar with that pub since I spent a lot of time here watching over the safety of Dylan Thomas in World War II. He was trying to get out of the way of the war at the time, coming here with his family to live in that small asbestos and wood house, Majoda, just over the other side of the Bay on Llanina Point. I couldn't spend as much time with Dylan as I would have liked then—particularly when the Luftwaffe was busy bombing Cardiff and Swansea and I was doing what I could fielding those land mines—but I usually tried to be outside the Black Lion at stop tap to watch Dylan get back to Majoda since he had to go all along that high cliff-top and he was also almost always out of his brains on drink.

To be perfectly frank I don't know how I managed to keep him alive for as long as I did. He always drank too much and just didn't have the physique to take all that poison he kept throwing down his neck. It almost became a nightly routine for me to catch him along that footpath as he staggered home, then literally bend him double and pump his whole body up and down until I made him throw up almost every drop of alcohol he had put down inside him in the Black Lion's bar. I even, at one stage, made him throw up every time he took a single drink, hoping that that might discourage him from hitting the stuff with quite so much enthusiasm. But it never did. He just assumed that he was suffering from alcoholic gastritis which, like the weather, was always with him. It certainly never occured to him to actually stop drinking. As I said earlier there's not much we angels can ever do about alcoholism.

Then there was the added hazard of his violent fights with his wife Caitlin—particularly when they were both in their cups—and I was really worried that she was going to re-arrange the shape of his head with a hammer or something equally nasty so it came to pass that not only did I get him to throw up but then I had to give her belly a good pumping out too. Even so I had to hang around Majoda for an hour or so to wait for the worst of the alcohol to wear off. It wore off quicker with him, as it happened, because he, at least, always stuck to beer but when she hit the whisky there was just no stopping her.

And even after all that I nearly lost Dylan here one night to machine-gun fire, of all things. They'd been having some lively parties in Majoda and one local army man came back from the war in Crete and decided that his wife was getting up to no good in those parties. The army man duly went there one night and plugged Majoda full of holes, narrowly missing the poet and his family.

I wasn't within a hundred miles of the place at the time and the shooting was all but over by the time I got back there. The army man was clearly out of his mind—and drunk—and was taken away by the police. Dylan decided that he'd had enough of New Quay by then and left within a few days. The Thomas family duly returned to London and the unreliable custodianship of Sorroptus. 'You make sure to keep a special eye on him because he's important,' I kept telling Sorroptus. 'And remember: when in doubt pump his stomach out.'

But I must say that all my efforts on Dylan's behalf always seemed to be worth it. He wrote 'Fern Hill' here in New Quay and just the memory of those few days when those lovely syllables came bouncing out of his mind still makes me happier than a small baby. 'Fern Hill' doesn't actually mean anything at all but it is a celebration of youth and purity; it is a hymn of praise to God and his creation. Dylan himself said that he always wrote for the love of man and in praise of God; that's why they always insisted that I keep him alive for as long as possible. But his early death wasn't quite the disaster that it's often portrayed. His personality will live on, through his poetry, for all time; his work gave a modern re-definition to that old bardic art of praise.

This summer's day in New Quay turned out to be as splendid as anyone could possibly have hoped for with holidaymakers deckchaired together on the small beach, the sun glinting on the smooth sea and rows of guillemots standing guard on the ledges of the nearby cliffs.

Way out in the Bay Winston and Howard were pulling in their lobster pots, throwing a lot of the smaller lobsters—together with the numerous crabs—back into the drink and snapping rubber bands on the claws of the larger ones to stop them from getting into any damaging brawls with one another. You could see that the two fishermen were now working in a steady rhythm with the sea, winding up the pots, emptying them and re-baiting them before throwing them back in. It was a timeless scene of labour and movement which hadn't changed for generations.

By now the deck of the boat had come alive with all kinds of things creeping about. There was a giant whelk mooching about inside a bucket, an orange starfish hanging plaintively off the side of a lobster pot, a crab hiding in the corner unsure what to do next, any number of prawns lying on their backs with their little legs flailing about in the air and a huge eel trying to get the hell out of this mess, first sticking its head through a tiny hole in the gunnels and, finding that too small for its shoulders, finally twisting around the deck only to find a larger hole through which it squeezed and finally dropped back into the sea with a happy plop of release.

With not much luck with the lobsters Winston then let out his trawl net and, after an hour or so, hauled up a huge bundle of fish withallofthemjammedtogetherfarcloserthanthis. Hundreds of heads poked through the hissing holes, some having thrown up their guts in a huge lump of bloody jelly which dangled off their lips. Winston pulled the cod end clip and there was a slithering swoosh before the whole deck became awash with flapping brill, pilchard, skate, plaice and any number of dog-fish and dabs. Most of the dabs and dog-fish were thrown back in before the men began sorting and gutting the others.

The eyes and full lips of the skate opened wide with astonishment as the knife cut out their bellies and their red and purple intestines were thrown to the seagulls who fell on them in a squealing, squawking feeding frenzy. This was what the gulls had been waiting for all day. An even worse fate befell the dog-fish with their wise old eyes which had already seen much suffering and whose silver skin was already going alarmingly red as they twisted slowly this way and that in their death throes. They were picked up and roundly cracked on the head on the ship's rail. Then they had their fins sliced off and they were cut straight down the middle with their mouths opening into a huge silent scream as the knife reached the head. 'Oh blimey,' you could almost hear them shouting. 'Oh blimey why hadn't I gone down to the boozer with the boys or at least gone somewhere else when that damned net came around? Why hadn't I ... oooooooh ... Aaaaaaargh.' The death rattle of the dog-fish was then followed by the skin being ripped off their backs with the sound of a tearing calico sheet.

I never understand why people eat anything like fish myself—I mean to say fish have souls too—but nevertheless it was a beautiful evening with exuberant dolphins playing in water-splashed arcs around the boat and the sun now settling low over the headland, dotted with the odd drifts of yellow gorse. I was rising up to mingle with the sunset when it was my turn to be hooked—this time by a prayer trap on the other side of New Quay.

It was a moving scene because a mother and father were sitting on either side of a bed with their hands resting on a sleeping child who was blind. They weren't actually in the habit of prayer—I'd certainly never picked up anything on the prayer lines coming out of their small white bungalow—but they'd clearly decided to try it out anyway, both of them taking it in turns to pray for the healing of their child's blindness. I could tell that their prayer was faithful and believing too: angels always know about these things.

The bungalow itself had all the trappings of the middle class: clean and polished with the touch of a museum and furniture which was probably given to them when they were first married back in the early Eighties. The ubiquitous television sat in the corner of the living room but the motor of this family was overwhelmingly decent; not chapel-going themselves but having inherited the values of the chapel. In their prayer they were clearly trying to re-connect with the rather more stable world of their parents and grandparents.

The mother still looked quite beautiful—even if a little frayed around the edges—and, despite a receding hairline, he was still as handsome as he must have been when he was young. But there was a strong aura of hurt and disappointment about them since not only were they in pain over their child but in pain with themselves and one another. Their ten-year-old son had gone blind only a few years back and a multitude of tests and doctors hadn't found the answer to the problem. Now they had arrived at the final surgery of the last resort: they had opened their hearts to God in beseeching prayer and I had come here to do what I could.

Now I couldn't go around the place performing healing miracles like The Boss but there are certain things my complicated intelligence and gifts of understanding and tribal memory can accomplish. I can, as you know, fix broken hearts and sometimes revive a life if I catch the soul before it's gone. But there are more ways than one to cook a goose and, as I stood there listening to their prayer, it soon became clear to me why their child had gone blind. Children are wondrously sensitive instruments in ways that adults barely understand and it was apparent that this child had gone blind because there was something going on between his parents which he no longer wanted to see. In fact—although the parents did not even know it themselves yet—that child was on the verge of going deaf as well.

This 'something' between them was to do with an affair—although a 'fling' might be a better word for it—that the father had with another woman soon after they had got married. A lot of young men—particularly handsome young men—have difficulty settling down right after they've got married and many of them these days still dance off into the night trying to prove something or other. That's all this one did and for one night only but, unfortunately for him, he got caught out by some indiscreet gossip in the corner shop.

There was a possibility that they might get divorced over that but, as the wife was already pregnant, they decided to give it another go for the sake of the unborn child.

But here was the problem: even some ten years later she still hadn't forgiven him that fling. Her pride had been mortally

165

wounded and, while she had never openly admitted it because she hadn't quite seen or understood it herself, she had subsequently seized any and every opportunity to make his life a misery. She just could not forgive him and, after living in this poisoned atmosphere for so long, the child had finally responded to it by going blind. Now his wounded body was working on going deaf too. We angels know all about wounds; we know everything there is to know under heaven about human pain.

Forgive us our trespasses as we forgive those who trespass against us ... Forgiveness is at the heart of the Christian canon; it is almost as vital to the forgiver as the forgiven. Only in forgiveness can people ever experience the full majesty of God's mercy and I brushed my hand over that sleeping boy's cheek also praying that he would soon get well.

Well a situation like this might look a bit messy but it isn't really. I had ways of sorting out problems like this. When the father had finished his prayer I made the mother say: 'Martin, you know all that business with Maisy Bryant all those years ago? I want you to know now that I never once forgave you for all that. That resentment had hung in my heart all the years of our marriage and I've never been able to let go of it.'

He looked at her, rather shocked and even a little bewildered that she had seen fit to raise all that at this moment. She was a little bewildered too because she didn't quite know why she was saying all that at this moment either.

'I just feel,' she continued at my insistence, 'that I've put all that between us for all these years and I want it to stop. I want to tell you now—on the body of our son here—that I have forgiven you and I want you to put your hands on him and tell me that you have forgiven me.'

His face muscles were being pushed and pulled around by a mixture of shock and puzzlement. You could see that he was thinking that, even after ten years of marriage, he barely knew his wife at all. There are many men who don't know their wives even after thirty years of marriage, of course. 'Yes. I didn't realise ...'

'Please Martin. Please say that you'll forgive me for what I've done to you all through our marriage. There's something deep inside me that says I must try and remove this thing that has come between us ... please Martin ...'

Their trembling hands reached out to clasp one another's and then they both stood up and embraced, tenderly at first but then more passionately. I took this as my cue to leave since it looked likely that the sleeping child was going to have a new brother or sister in about nine months time. He wouldn't be cured of his blindness that day or even within a week but it was my guess that his eyesight would be fine within a month or so now that the blockage between his parents had been removed. It's all in a day's work of any hard-working angel really. Children blossom in love but, surrounded by bickering and resentments, they are the first to fall apart and die.

Stars studded the sky that night and I could see for miles as I returned down through the countryside from New Quay. It was a perfect night for flying although I sometimes liked to hold myself steady on the flame and enjoy the solitude of a lovely summer's night in which nothing moved except the long, silent slide of a shooting star travelling the length of the universe. Some say that shooting stars are angels going about their business but that's all nonsense. I guess that there's more rubbish written about us angels than almost anything else in the whole of creation.

But just then, down by the sleeping village of Llanpumsaint, I came across a sort of dimly-lit channel in the night sky which I can only describe as a complete oddity in the spiritual past and present of Wales. This luminous black hole, which stands directly above a couple of farmhouses and is smack in the middle of the Baptist belt, is often alive with, well ... er ... angels of foreign faiths I suppose you'd call them. Many is the time I've been travelling this way over the past twenty years and bumped into all kinds of fragrant and exotic spirits wandering in and out of those farmhouses.

They are all completely benign, mind you, and will often stop for a chat even if they speak in some of the strangest languages and, even with my gift of the tongues, I am totally non-plussed as to what they are going on about. One night I came across this huge spirit just sitting out there on that farmhouse with several heads and countless arms. He could see that I was a bit wary of him and explained, as casually as if he was giving me directions to the local bus stop, that he was some minor Hindu deity who was just passing through but had stopped off to enjoy the prayers.

But it's not just Hindu prayers that are said here since this is the Community of the Many Names of God: the multi-faith group of Skanda Vale who attempt to worship God from all kinds of directions and all kinds of ways which include Hindu prayers, Sanskrit verses, Buddhist chants and Christian hymns. What old Christmas Evans would have made of it all I shudder to think but I rather enjoy the work of this community myself and, like the other strange angels that call here from time to time, wish it every success. It's encouraging that my angelic counterparts also need to be sustained by prayer and that they too will always respond to faithful prayer in a positive and helpful way. There's much we have in common even if they do come in the oddest of shapes.

As it turned out there seemed to be a fair bit of angelic traffic moving up and down that channel that night with the odd flash of a long luminous body going down or some dark shadow with what looked like a dozen arms sliding up. When I got there, two Hindu devas were sitting on the farm-house roof. They were sharing a suspicious-looking cheroot and arguing quite fiercely but whatever the bone of contention they weren't going to let me chew on it and ignored me altogether as I settled down next to the chimney pot. I've never been too sure why they get out this way—they surely must have enough on their plate back in India or wherever—but it's always seemed a bit rude to ask and, anyway, there's clearly a lot more of them than there are of us. Perhaps they're sent out this way on some sort of Voluntary Service Overseas scheme: to broaden their outlook and all that.

I had already decided to spend a day hanging around here since, while it may seem inconvenient and even untidy for a Christian angel to be reporting on a multi-faith community in what is, after all, a Christian report then the work here at Skanda Vale cannot be ignored for a number of reasons. The main reason for their inclusion in my report must be that, while the Welsh chapels and churches are now floundering quite badly, this multi-faith community, with its reverence for all forms of life, keeps going from strength to strength. Here we learn just what can be accomplished with a bit of vision, a lot of prayer and abundant faith. The truly extraordinary feature of this community is that it works although there are probably some sceptics who would claim that a multi-faith community is one which is merely hedging all its bets.

But I suppose the success of Skanda Vale must also say something about the benefits of having a lot more angelic staff to shepherd it than almost any other group. One night during the Festival of Lord Ganesh there might have been a thousand people here with a good two dozen angels of various shapes and sizes up here on the roof all having a wail of a time.

But there is also a strong Christian element in the worship here. The eighteen or so full-time brothers have taken Franciscan vows of poverty, chastity and obedience and they have an exclusively Christian service every night. So I too have got to do my bit and, in some ways, it actually does fit in with the overall pattern of my work.

The two quarreling devas finally left without saying anything to me and it was still dark when the five o'clock service—or pooja, as they call it—the first of the day—began with the sound of bells and rhythmic chanting. The hollow wail of a conch signalled the end of some Buddhist chanting and the three dozen or so present moved on to a Sanskrit prayer. One of the brothers held up a flaming lantern made from purified ghee (clarified butter) which he kept moving around in circular motion in front of an effigy of Lord

169

Subramium. Around a hundred candles were guttering and flaming in the darkness as the group then moved on to The Lord's Prayer. Our Father which art in heaven ...

As the pooja ended and the darkness finally lifted on that fine morning you could begin to see the extent of the fields, woods and buildings that makes up Skanda Vale. On the left hand side of the entrance is a huge, tiered vegetable garden and, further along again, is a Port-a-Loo and a number of small, functional cabins for guests. Everyone is welcome but, if they stay, they must attend the five o'clock pooja and do at least four hours work here a day. In this way they weed out those who have come merely looking for a holiday. The sexes are not allowed to eat together and are told not to talk to one another either; in this way the brothers discourage the old malarkey which tended to rear its ugly head particularly back in the Seventies. First and last this is a working monastery of prayer, the brothers say.

There is a long climb up from the first farm-house along another alarmingly rutted track which takes you up to the next farm which, you soon see, is probably like no other farm in Britain. Llamas with their goofy smiles and propensity for spitting at the unwary come wandering across fields. In other paddocks are bulls, Shetland ponies and goats ripping up grass, brambles and just about anything else they can get near. There are the thin, sad calls of peacocks, the throaty warbling of many pigeons, geese which hiss at strangers menacingly and any number of dogs wandering about sniffing here or foraging for food there. All of them cry out occasionally and the whole farm sounds like some tropical jungle which, by some strange and mysterious accident, took a wrong turning in sunny Africa and ended up here in rainy Wales. A cat slides silently across the path followed by another and another.

The farm-house up here has a large whirling gold dome tacked on its end and, what is more, there is an elephant wandering around in the farmyard, busy sticking its trunk out towards any visitors by way of welcome. This elephant, Valli, a beast of considerable and long-lashed charm, also likes to show off to visitors by picking up the yard broom and using it to brush her large toe-nails. There probably isn't an elephant in the world more molly-coddled than Valli. Her keeper gives her a cup of hot tea—'No sugar because that's not good for elephants' along with the rest of the brothers at eleven o'clock in the morning. She is not allowed out of her warm shed in the rain—'Too much damp can give an elephant arthritis you know'—and her keeper understands the meaning of Valli's every squeak, rumble, trumpet and roar. 'You serve animals selflessly knowing that they can never thank you.'

The llamas were given to the temple by a local farmer on the verge of going broke; the many yapping dogs were picked up as strays around the towns; lots of the pigeons dropped in for five minutes and stayed, deciding that it was better life here than huffing and puffing in pigeon races around the country; some of the bulls were considered too dangerous or ill to keep on working farms and Valli was a gift from the government of Sri Lanka.

Here the veneration for all life is absolute. The gardener, Gwyn Williams, will take a torch out in the middle of the night in his vegetable patch to collect slugs in a bucket and put them on the other side of the stream because slugs can't then swim back to nibble his beloved cabbages. 'I also talk to the caterpillars and let them know that they're not wanted around here,' he says with a smile. 'It works too.'

Mice are trapped in humane jars but, when one of the brothers tried taking one of them to the other side of the stream, he not only discovered that the said mouse could swim better than Johnny Weismuller but he could run faster than Linford Christie because the mouse was back inside the farmhouse faster than the brother. The many cats would have kept the mice down but that's not allowed either so all the cats have been fitted with warning bells. Most of the cats here have a form of cat Aids and will be nursed here until they die.

Before lunch it is time for another of the five services of the day and, with the other visitors who turn up here almost constantly, there are now some forty gathered for the mid-day pooja in the lower temple. Here again the prayers are mingled in a lively, if bewildering, fashion as the flame is carried around the altar to bless the various sacred relics. The simple Sanskrit prayer says: 'From darkness take me to light, from truth to untruth, from death to immortality.' Towards the end of the service each worshipper symbolically washes his hair and face in the flame while also putting a dab of dust in the middle of his forehead, reminding him that it is to the dust that everyone returns.

So, in their roster of events for the year, there are all kinds of unlikely spiritual bedfellows from the Ganesh Festival with its breaking of coconuts, to Sister Topsy's birthday with a celebration by the river, the Subramanium Festival—with two weeks of poojas on the way God destroys evil in the world— and a celebration of Ascension Day, commemorating The Boss's assumption into heaven. Here you can learn about *dharma*, right living; *suprabatham*, the invocation to God at dawn; *prasadam*, food offered to the congregation and *wesak*, the celebration of Buddha's death.

This rather wonderful creation is the inspiration of one man— known to all as The Guru—who grew up in Sri Lanka, the son of a wealthy Buddhist father and a multi-faith mother who had a seven-sided temple built in her garden and would sit on a tiger skin and keep turning to look at the walls on which there were various relics of the different faiths. 'To meditate just shut your eyes and go,' she used to tell her son. 'Don't babble, just talk.'

He left Sri Lanka at the age of eighteen and called off in Berlin to listen to the Nuremberg trials and visit the Auschwitz death camp after the war. Then he came to London doing various jobs like working in Selfridges and sweeping up in the Sri Lankan High Commission before setting up a small multi-faith temple in his flat in Earls Court. Here he also did a lot of work among the growing drug addicts in the area. When they came to see him he would often be sitting on a chair with a huge dog on his lap whom he would talk to constantly. He always had lots of pets. 'All animals have God in them.'

Finally, after fifteen years in Earls Court, he found this farm here in West Wales—fortunately he always preferred the cold and the rain to the heat and sun—moving here in 1972 when he began building up The Temple of the Many Names of God into what it has now become. 'We must attack demon forces and establish spirituality,' he says. 'We are here to help people discover their own divinity. I never try to change anyone's faith. People come here to have their own faiths improved. They can take away as much—or as little—as they want.'

Visitors find The Guru a deeply likeable, chortling sort of man with sparkly black eyes and that strange blend of practical insights and mystical language that you often find in Indian wise men. They also find that he's got more charisma in his big toe than a train-load of politicians. He can absorb the contents of a book just by holding it in his hand, he says; he knows everything in the Bible but has never read it. He is very nearly blind but sees everything with his 'visionary eye'. Although he travels to Switzerland for one weekend each month to teach cookery he only eats a small piece of roti each morning and a spoon of rice each night relying on God to give him all the energy he needs.

One of the brothers fell off the top of a shed a few months back and smashed his pelvis. In fact The Guru told him off for his carelessness and pointed to the 'crying with pain' spot a week before it actually happened. 'He couldn't understand why I was getting so stroppy with him.'

The temple is now a registered charity which never solicits money from the people who stay with them but does accept donations. They have no income as such but also have very few overheads since they grow most of their own food, take water from a well, use no electricity and people have now given them enough sacks of rice to eat for at least ten years. All in all they need about £30,000 a year to keep going but could manage, if pushed, on £20,000. One substantial and surprise donation of

£40,000 enabled them to buy the other farm at the top of the hill.

Nevertheless they are now busy extending the range of their support for all life by starting to build a hospice for the terminally ill in one of their upper fields. Already they've raised £215,000 for this hospice—which will be the only one in Dyfed—and have already hired some nursing staff to provide a home visiting service. 'People would really prefer to die at home with their own things and pets,' says the Swami, Brother Justin. 'When people come here we want to give them a new lung to breathe. They may bring their problems here but they won't take them away again. No one preaches to anyone else and you just take away what you like. People come here to deepen their own faith.'

An orthodox Jewish couple likes to visit here and, perhaps predictably, a lot of Hindus come here and try to kiss The Guru's feet, much to his eternal embarrassment. 'I keep telling them to stop this feet-kissing business. I am walking around and finding all kinds of heads under my shoes.' One drunk rolled up here on Christmas Eve and slept on the floor until Boxing Day when he sobered up, was fed and duly went away again. Last year a man arrived here thinking it was a temple near Bangor, which is only about two hundred miles away, but he liked it here so much he stayed and, two weeks later, his brother came looking for him and stayed as well. Next thing the worried parents came looking for their runaway children and they stayed too—all celebrating Christmas together. Occasionally they are savaged by a cynical media on the basis of nothing at all but they live with it, wearily, as best they can.

By nine o'clock that night it was time for the Christian service in the lower temple. A woman brought a flute, a brother played a portable harmonium and another the finger cymbals. Hymns were sung with feeling followed by St Francis's prayer and a general chant to the glory of God. The service moved beautifully in the candlelight with strong echoes of many Christian services in other denominations. The brothers had simply picked the bits they liked from wherever.

Certainly I found the whole service a tremendous pleasure as I stretched out on that farm-house roof and when I feel any deep spiritual pleasure then so too does God.

The next morning was neither rainy nor sunny but a bit of both as I hung over a cliff next to the town of Tenby watching the sunshine trying, but failing, to break through the low, dark cloud as fat, white jelly-fish rose to the surface of the sea to feed. What, I have often wondered, is the point of jelly-fish? Who but God would have come up with the idea of a jelly-fish? They are almost entirely useless but, when you get close to them, you can see something both complicated and simple at the same time. Would The Guru insist that God was present in a jelly-fish? Yes, I suppose he would and I further suppose that he would be right too.

The sea itself was lumpy that morning and a small fishing boat, full of pilgrims, was bobbing over the waves in the direction of Caldey where I was planning to stop over next with the monks. But I was in no hurry and continued to dangle there, with my flame shunting gently, when a hanglider just came wafting through me. I do wish they wouldn't do that. Most things that fly make a lot of noise and give me time to get out of the way but these hangliders breeze straight through you without warning or so much as a by-your-leave. It's happened to me a few times now and, if they don't watch it, I'm going to turn into some giant bird of prey and see how they like getting swooshed about when they least expect it.

In fact I was half thinking of having a bit of fun at the expense of that hanglider when a call came through on the prayer lines. But this wasn't like any call that I could ever remember receiving. This was a huge blast for help which was so powerful and so redolent with urgency that it could only have come from a fellow angel. I knew then that this was who had been trying to get through to me for the past few weeks but this time the lines didn't go dead and I managed to get a reading on it straight away. The trouble was that it was taking me straight out to sea past Caldey Island and I always get a bit worried when I'm out at sea since the Bristol Channel isn't technically my territory. I mean to say no one has ever drawn up a map back in Megiddo detailing the exact extent of our territories inch by inch but I've always had an understanding with Sorroptus that all sea along here—outside the usual E.E.C. fishing limits so that islands like Caldey stay mine—is his.

But, judging by the powerful storms of anguish that were still blasting down the prayer lines, that might even be Sorroptus who had got into trouble. Come to think of it I hadn't actually clapped eyes on him since that punch-up with Klang and his popsie back in Presteigne.

The S.O.S. remained firm and strong as I continued feathering over the waves and saw Lundy Island—home of puffins and star of weather forecasts—heaving into sight. It looked like a granite fist thrusting straight up out of the sea except that its rocky crown was swathed in thick sea mists which were floating around and moving in all directions. But no sooner had I got to the shoreline than the S.O.S. call disappeared again leaving me to root around the island looking for whatever. The trouble was that I had never been out here before and the sea mists had enveloped everything to the extent that I had almost to go right up to them to see what was what. A tavern and a few houses drifted up out of the swirling mists. There was a farmyard and the arms of an aerogenerator revolving furiously and noisily. Some carrion crows sat on the roof of the farm-house, a few carp rose in a pond and a raven flew past upside down. That's as true as I'm here. I remember Sorroptus telling me about this bird out this way who flew upside down and there he was.

But, otherwise, nothing at all so I followed the main path all along the three-mile spine of the island to see what might turn up. Well there were lots of skylarks warbling in the warm, dripping air. Deer, horses and wild goats appeared out of the mists briefly only to disappear again and the eyes of watchful rabbits were everywhere. I also kept hearing the crashing of

176

waves on distant rocks as well as the throaty calls of lolling seals.

Well, there was clearly no future in any of this so I turned and turned again, deciding to hop it back to Caldey Island. But, just near the top of the island where the rocks tumbled down into the sea, a huge gap opened up in the mists and there I saw one of the most extraordinary sights of my long career. This gap in the mists was confusingly full of the most brilliant sunshine and, poking up from a hole in the rocks and about fifty yards up from the edge of the foaming sea, was a giant, flapping wing of an angel. This long luminous wing was speckled with blood and the rocks all around it were moving up and down as if warming up for some major earthquake.

What made it all far worse was that two dark angels were attacking this poor beleaguered angel, both of them swooping down out of the overhanging mists and striking at the bleeding wing so hard it rather looked as if they were trying to break it off which was probably what they were trying to do. One of the dark angels was Klang but I didn't recognise the other. Then it happened again; another blast calling for help on the prayer lines which was so close that it almost deafened me. A few more huge rocks fell away from around the struggling wing and Klang picked up one of them, flying up into the mist again before turning to dive-bomb the rock onto the ailing wing.

Rocks the size of small houses were crashing around in all directions with some tumbling down into the sea and others being dropped like bombs from above. At times it sounded as if the Greek gods were engaged in a furious and violent game of snooker. Muffled screams of the purest anger were coming from out of the ground as the trapped angel's wing shook away yet more rocks.

Well it was pointless just standing here—still less to try and follow any rules of engagement or turn into some fiery, frightening shape—so the flame sketched in my sword and I shook out my own mighty wings before flying up into the mists and then screaming down on top of these two thugs with

177

repeated explosions of my rings as my sword slashed through the air so fast its scream must have been heard a good two miles away.

It was just one of those days when you finally get lucky, I guess, because almost with my first stroke, I lopped off half of one of the wings of Klang's mate. He immediately lost control of his flight and went pirouetting down onto the rocks when he bounced around this way and that, spitting foul slime and the usual bad language. I can almost put up with the slime but it's the bad language that I always find difficult to take and, if he didn't watch his mouth, he was going to lose his other wing as well.

But first I had to deal with Klang and that wouldn't be quite so easy since I'd never known him to fall for a sucker punch like that. In the event I almost did get his nose with my first swipe but then the blade hit a rock with such force it jumped out of my hand, falling in a clanging shower of sparks down onto the rocks below. So it was wing to wing combat time again and I stuck him with a right and left before we both fell backwards on the shoreline wrestling with one another like a couple of drunken sailors on a wild night out after a year at sea. But this wasn't going to finish him off in any way. What I needed was my sword to chop off a limb or three and I looked around frantically but saw that it was lying on a rock at least a hundred yards away.

The next thing Klang resorted to his usual bits of dirt by head-butting me straight up into the air. He fair knocked all the breath out of me and I wasn't at all sure what was happening next what with all these sea mists as well. I was just lashing out blindly and not connecting too well either when I heard—through my concussion—the most ravising, if not welcome, words that I have heard for a long, long time. 'This is England,' a voice roared through the mists. 'And, as such, it is under the full protection of Sorroptus.'

Klang took one look around and shot off like a three-bob rocket, clearly deciding to make a bolt for it, but Sorroptus was on his tail in a flash and now it was all rather like a hundred thunderheads cannoning against one another as they both proceeded to knock the stuffing out of one another all along the length of the Bristol Channel. I suppose that I've seen those two fight hundreds of times over the centuries but I've never ceased to be amazed at the sheer size and fury of their brawls. They can go on for days and sweep the length of England as those huge wings lock in combat. Not that I could see too much of either of them that day because of all the mists.

For his part Sorroptus always reckoned that he had never known anything like the fight back in 1900 when I managed to see off Splachnik. That was one hell of a fight which sprawled all over Wales but I'll talk about that when I get there.

Meanwhile I went back down to the spot where the angel's wing had been poking up and began shoving away the various rocks piled up all around it. The other dark angel must have decided to swim for it because he was nowhere to be seen and, after moving another five or six boulders, I could actually touch the body of the angel who, as I suspected, had been chained up in his tomb which is about the only way you can ever immobilise any angel. There's a Biblical foundation to all this—and it's a very long story—but, while we can never be actually killed, we are always in deep trouble if anyone can manage to chain us up.

When I had made enough room to work in I broke one of the metal links with my flame and then another but it did take me a good two minutes to break the lot and finally enable him to emerge from his tomb. He wasn't best pleased either which wasn't what you might expect in the circumstances.

'Doesn't anyone anywhere listen out for any prayers of help anymore?' he asked, still spluttering and puffing with the indignity of it all. 'I might as well pray for help from a brick wall as pray for help from you lot.'

Ah yes, of course: it had to be didn't it? I had finally solved the mystery of the twenty-five-year disappearance of Victor.

179

# Eighth Book

Victor was in no fit state to fly anywhere after I pulled him out of that hole and, as he was adamant that he did not want to stay on Lundy for which he had developed an understandable loathing, I helped him back across the channel to Caldey island for some much-needed R. and R.

In fact I don't suppose there's a better place in Wales for a wounded angel to recuperate with those wondrous walks along the red sandstone cliffs; the black shiny heads of the kelp bobbing up and down in the waves and the cycles of prayers of the monks in the great monastery which sits in a dip between some wooded hills with its white chateau-like towers and red-tiled roof. Deep in a nearby woodland was a sparkly grotto built to the Virgin Mary and, further along the cliffs again, was a small solitary hermitage and a lighthouse. The distinctive flights of Manx shearwaters skimmed the waves and, down in the nearby coves, there were seals.

You could almost see Victor getting better in this earthly paradise and his damaged wing began healing up within hours of our getting there. The sun was also blazing down like a benediction and sometimes we lay together on a headland sunning ourselves or else we walked slowly along the cliff path around the island like a couple of old aged pensioners.

After Sorroptus had seen off Klang yet again he spent some time with us too and, if there wasn't a service with the monks to enjoy, we just sat together out in the fields yarning about this and that. We angels have never had enough fellowship together, in my view, particularly when out on active duty. Come to think of it I don't suppose we've met in any numbers more than three or four times—apart from back home in Megiddo—since we gathered for those little parties to chaperone those saints in St David's back in the fifth century. But fellowship is as important to the angel as it is to the normal human believer. We always need to nourish one another in fellowship; always need to build one another up with praise or warm words particularly if we've been going through a bad patch.

I must say that Sorroptus has always been a cheerful, up-beat sort of angel even if he does take a most questionable pleasure in fighting with dark angels. But Victor, perhaps again acquiring the characteristics of his fiery volatile flock, has always been rather temperamental—on top of the world a lot of the time but then crashing down into the dumps for almost no reason. You know how it is when the black dogs start yapping and you can't shake yourself out of a depression while talking a lot of packing it all in and retiring somewhere quiet and sunny.

Angels can't pack it all in and retire somewhere quiet and sunny, of course, any more than humans can decide that they don't feel like breathing anymore. But that was the continual drift of Victor's talk when I first got him to Caldey. 'I just can't take it anymore, Conker. There's no strength or fight left in me and I can't even face the thought of going back to Ireland let alone Belfast. I've been suffering something awful from migraine too. And amnesia has blocked out whole decades.'

But if you don't go back to Ireland they might give you somewhere worse,' I pointed out.

'Somewhere worse? What could be worse than Belfast?'

'Well there's always Beirut. They might well give you Beirut and there's hardly been an angel that's ever lasted for more than a week in Beirut. That place has always been a graveyard of the angels.'

'Take it from me Conker. Watch my lips. Beirut's a holiday camp compared to Belfast. If I was offered Beirut I'd leap at it with both wings.'

'Oh don't be so silly. You've had Ireland for exactly as long as I've had Wales. We've both put in centuries of work and all the signs are that The Boss is finally going to make a move. You wouldn't want to throw it all away just like that would you? Not now.'

'You just watch me. You just watch.'

But that was his mood in the early hours of our visit to Caldey since, the more we walked around the island, the more cheerful and positive he became. Sorroptus could always manage to get him to laugh too, particularly when he went on about all his flights with Klang and various other dark angels who were foolish enough to wander into England from time to time. Sorroptus chased one straight into Canterbury Cathedral earlier this summer, he told us, and, rather than risk a major fight in there, he had to spend ages trying to wheedle him out again before giving him a good bashing in the cathedral close. 'That's always the trouble with fighting dark angels these days. They know that, once they get inside a catherdral, they are more or less safe from my sword. I wouldn't even kill a baby dark angel inside a cathedral. It wouldn't be right and anyway just think what the Archbishop would say about all the mess.'

Late one afternoon the three of us were taking one of our constitutional hobbles around the island when I just happened to say that all the flowers mentioned in Shakespeare grew on Caldey and again that cheered up Victor no end since, as it turned out, he was a skilled and enthusiastic botanist. He showed us tree-mallow, vernal squill and sea-spleenwort and even discovered a primula which only grew in its true colour on the island. When it came to botany he was an absolute whizz, he said, even knowing that the gorse here was once fed to the cattle and used for heating the bread ovens. Now the monks use the gorse for making the perfume which they sell to the visitors.

I was most impressed and duly asked Victor: 'You wouldn't happen to know what jelly-fish are for would you?'

'Jelly-fish? I don't know anything about jelly-fish. What do you want to know about them for?'

'Oh I was just wondering what they were about that's all. What's the point of them?'

'There's something wrong with you Conker. I was always worried you had a few screws loose.'

It was only after Victor had been revived by several days of prayer and botany that he began to feel sufficiently strong to tell us what had happened back in Ireland and how he had ended up jammed down that hole in Lundy. And what a story it turned out to be.

Up until about twenty years ago he was doing the best he could in the beleaguered province of Ulster, he said, but everything took a decided turn for the worse after the British government began interning the IRA. Thereafter the international media came pouring into Belfast and, with everyone bandstanding for their benefit, he just didn't know where to turn. But that wasn't half the story.

Soon the city became engulfed in so much evil that barely anyone knew who was fighting with whom or why. People were getting shot routinely and the wrong people were always being blamed. Nothing was as it appeared and, what made it worse was that all the baddies were wearing suits and had degrees. Even the priests didn't know what was going on and, every time one opened his holy mouth, all you could be sure of was that he would somehow get in front of the television camera where he could be firmly relied on to grasp the wrong end of the stick.

In all the violence in the streets—which was being endlessly recycled and fortified by all arms of the media—faith was breaking down and there was barely any prayer back-up anywhere for Victor to work in. It was so bad that there were whole areas of Belfast that he could no longer patrol, still less protect. Even getting down a pavement became a nightmare unless he could find the shelter of a prayer. There were pockets of prayer but not enough to do any decent work in and it was getting so bad he was regularly spotting dark angels sitting on the terraces of the Falls and the Shankill. 'I just found I couldn't make sense of anything and spent hours walking around wringing my hands. There's almost nothing you can do in a household which is being irradiated by television violence almost every hour. Then the kids started bringing home those appalling videos. It was simply all too much for me. But this television service you know; it can take one murder and turn it into a dozen murders in no time flat.'

Both Sorroptus and I chirped with agreement at that one. In fact the iniquity of television was the one subject on which every angel agreed. Bimmimus had it right. When in doubt wreck the lot, he used to say.

Later still that afternoon Victor recalled that night when he was with St Patrick on the hill of Slane. I had noticed before that the tone of Victor's voice changed whenever he spoke of Patrick and he was clearly as fond of him as I was of David. Anyway Victor had been watching over Patrick as he stormed through Ireland, baptising thousands of converts, getting clapped in irons, laying curses on those who opposed him, turning poisoned cheeses into stones, blessing rivers and making them abundant with fish. But this night on the hill of Slane, Patrick entered into his final battle with all the wizards, soothsayers and witches who had gathered in the court of High King Laoghaire.

'It was a lovely dark evening with perhaps three stars glittering in the sky,' Victor told us. 'The custom of the time was that all lights in the land were to be extinguished until a flaming torch was carried from the king's hall. It was the way the people were supposed to show their homage to the corrupt old king. But it was Easter time and I stood with Patrick on that hill and he lit a Paschal flame, holding it up in the air and proclaiming the death and eternal resurrection of Jesus Christ. Then he lit a huge bonfire. It was this great act of defiance that announced that God's kingdom had finally been established in Ireland and was going to last for ever.'

But then Victor's voice began choking with a different kind of sadness as he told of how the kingdom had been visibly crumbling in Ireland. One night, he had been sitting minding his own business on one of the cranes of the Harland and Woolf shipyards when he spotted a squadron of some twenty dark angels flying across to West Belfast in the moonlight. He had never seen so many of them at one time and it came as a great surprise to him, particularly as he knew that we had once outnumbered them by about two to one. But then they started having babies, of course, so their numbers could be almost anything by now.

His shock at seeing the squadron was also considerably compounded by the fact that he had noticed that they had been flying in close formation around one of them who was exceptionally large. Victor went as close as he dared and found them all settled down for the night in a park at the top of the Falls in West Belfast. You could see the thickening tension in Victor as he described all that snorting breath and those slimy wings gathered around a large central figure who, Victor was reasonably certain, was Lucifer himself. Sorroptus and I stared hard at one another.

Well it all figured didn't it? Lucifer had to have his headquarters somewhere and where better than among the television aerials of violence-fouled West Belfast? Here he would be worshipped not just by his own but also be serenaded by the music of riot, arson and murder. Here his spirit really could run free in the children of disobedience and he could take particular satisfaction in watching the destruction of all faith and holiness. Here too he would have powerful allies: men in suits and with all the latest technology who would come to the people claiming that they were there to serve them. The more you thought about it the more perfect the place was for Lucy and all his cronies. I saw Victor's problem well enough and certainly hadn't a clue what I'd have done if the dark angels had decided to set up camp in the middle of Cardiff.

Victor added that he knew then that he had better get straight back to Megiddo and report to Michael. There had been plenty of precedents in history for sending in a battalion of angels to clean up an area, after all, but even if they didn't decide to do that, the fact that Lucy had possibly set up a new H.Q. in Belfast had to be reported back to base.

But now that he'd had plenty of time to think about it— more than twenty years of time as it turned out—Victor was reasonably sure that Lucy and the dark angels had allowed themselves to be seen by him in the Falls that night, knowing what he would do next since, the following day, Victor was flying home when he was bushwhacked by about six of them in the Bristol Channel near Lundy island.

He really didn't have much of a chance because four of them came down out of the overhanging cloud wielding chains and another two shot straight up out of the sea. Even so there had been one hell of a fight which was so protracted and violent that it actually caused a storm which, in turn, had messed up his calls for help on the prayer lines. At one stage he had two of them on each wing and they had obviously planned it well in advance since they all then chained him up and bundled him down into that hole in the rocks. I found myself wondering about Splachnik and if he had managed to escape from the chains I had wrapped around him.

It took over twenty years for Victor to dislodge some of the rocks piled on top of him but he couldn't shake loose the chains and, even then, his prayer lines still didn't work properly which accounted for all those mysterious buzzings that I had been picking up.

Oh it was one hell of a story all right but the only real question now was what was Victor going to do next. He was already feeling a lot better after his rest on Caldey and his first instincts were that he had better get back to Northern Ireland to check on what had developed in his absence before reporting back to Megiddo.

Needless to say Sorroptus immediately volunteered to ride shotgun, if Victor felt it would help, and you could see he was positively excited by the prospect of getting stuck into Lucy himself. 'No dark angel has ever managed to put a chain on me and that's a fact.'

Naturally I offered to join them too but, in the end, Victor said that, rather than risk anything happening to us, he would go back to Ireland alone to try and work things out for himself. 'If it's too bad we'll all have to go in mob-handed.'

'Well be sure to tell us where and when,' Sorroptus chimed in. There he was at it again: the only one keener than him on a spot of fisticuffs was old Macmac in Scotland.

Anyway the three of us then spent a whole day of prayer sitting in the rafters of the monastery and Victor took off first thing in the morning. Sorroptus said that he had some business up in Yorkshire and I resumed my journey and work on my report. Over the water in nearby Laugharne.

It's always been a place of sorrow and regret for me, this Laugharne by the sea; this town with but one main road and a ruined castle; this place where Dylan Thomas, my greatest praise poet lived towards the end of his life and was finally buried. I come here sometimes looking for his heartbeat and that's what I did on that warm grey summer's day, floating down through a pocket of honeysuckle and landing near a cemetery and on a field where a horse stood deep in a day dream next to a bandy-legged foal. In the far corner of the cemetery a man sat near a white tombstone, his shoulders slumped, weeping into a crumpled handkerchief.

A milkman was delivering his bottles along the main street and rooks flapped around the castle. A bus pulled up and a car drove away. I sat at the table in the window of Brown's Hotel listening out for my poet; just seeing him sitting there again, my dragon-tongued boyo with bulging eyes who, with a pint of beer in one hand and a Woodbine in the other, so briefly strutted around here under my care, either puking up over his shoes or spouting miraculous insights into death and all eternity. 'Light breaks where no sun shines.'

This town was his home; a 'pubbed and churched, shopped, gulled and estuaried one state of happiness' he called it where, more than forty years ago now, he sat in a small shed at the top of his garden and wrote much of his wonderful poetry. 'This place I love,' he said of this town with its castle, five pubs, a town hall, a Lord Mayor, a man who dressed up as a Wild West cowboy, a St Bernard (without brandy), a deaf-and-dumb ferryman, a visiting sea, a yellow Rolls-Royce—which was also a mobile fish and chip shop—and the herons whom, he claimed, he knew by their Christian names although there again, he could be a terrific liar.

Out on the estuary the river, swollen by some rain showers, was busy rebuilding and reshaping the sand and mud banks. Herons stood in pools and, out on the sands, oyster-catchers flew over the stooped bodies of the cockle-pickers. But Dylan really was the most complicated character who clearly still lives in the collective memory of the town under a variety of guises. 'Well, I'll tell you what,' said Stuart Lewis. 'What we classed him as was a layabout. Sat in Brown's Hotel all day he did. Never worked. Always seemed to look worse than he was. Always broke.' Three old-timers were sitting on a park bench and looking out at the sea. 'He was happy that boy. Never drunk, was he Fred? People were always saying bad things about him but the same people never met him. He was a tidy boy that one. Tidy.' In the pub a man lit a cigarette and then spent a full two minutes coughing his heart up. At the apex of each body-curling cough his tongue flickered out like an adder's. 'Dylan now,' he went on in between wheezes. 'That boy could drink. One night he was in here and passed clean out. Next thing he's up and asking how long he's been out and starts drinking again.'

Another wore a flat dirty cap with a torn raincoat and a huge set of ears. Verney was his name and he said he was 70 plus VAT. 'Oh Dylan, I remember him well. He came with all his stuff one day outside Brown's. I took it all on my horse and cart down to the Boat House and charged him three shillings and six pence. He paid me too. I liked him. He used to get drunk but so did we all.'

Laugharne has changed only in minor details since Dylan lived here and bought his chips nightly from the back of Arthur Jenkins's yellow Rolls-Royce. 'He loved his chips he did,' said Mr Jenkins, now a security officer in a local bank. 'Always there every night. A good bloke you know. A character. He would walk away from any fight and he always paid for his chips too.'

The yellow Rolls-Royce has long been sold. The cowboy has hung up his guns and the deaf-and-dumb ferryman is dead. The St Bernard has also long gone to the Great Kennel in the Sky, two of the pubs have closed but the herons are still in their pools and the sea is still visiting twice a day.

A few hundred yards along the cliff squats the famous Boat House—this 'sea-shaken house on the breakneck of rocks' which was 'high among the beaks and the palavers of the birds'—where Dylan sat in a garden shed, amid the sycamored trees and the multi-coloured Veronica and sailed passionately towards death praising God as he wrote in 'the singing light'.

His poetry had the condition of beautiful prayer and, in it, you could hear his heart singing out to other hearts. Those lines of his set up a communion in which all the things of God came swimming up. He wove his faith into the landscape; he understood the basic interconnectedness between all things. Poetry like his is as magical as it is unique. What he would do was take single words or ideas and let them germinate, either heroically or tragically, depending on what other words he decided to join them with. Some poets can write poems for a million years and never come up with a single memorable line. But every line Dylan wrote was memorable; he had a deep feeling for all words and no one ever managed to make such musical and attractive marriages between one word and another. His favourite line from the Bible was 'In the beginning was the word ...' Like the Psalmist he was always ready and willing to sing the Lord a brilliant new song.

Yet the real strength of his poetry was that he wrote it as a child and, in a sense, he remained a child all his life. He would suffer from the most childish fantasies about his womanising and prowess in bed but he was never any good at that. All he really wanted was a lot of mothering and was at his happiest when he was sitting in his bath, sucking boiled sweets or swigging on a bottle of pop, reading some trashy detective story while his wife washed his back. If he ever got cold when he was working in his shed he would call on his wife to bring him up a pile of pullovers. And she would have to put them on for him.

Today the Boat House is a sort of museum run by the Wales Tourist Board and, to be fair to the board, it looks exactly like a museum too: dull, colourless and desperately in need of a jazz band and one great wild party to liven it up. Upstairs there is a sort of art gallery and, in the main living room, there are horrible Habitat-style lights which would certainly have provoked derisive hoots of laughter in the poet.

Yet, just walking down below along the 'heron-priested and mussel-pooled' shore you can still find echoes of the incandescent images of his later work. There were tiny, white and dead crabs stranded in the grass. The very mud was hissing like threatening snakes and a light wind was making the sands whistle and dance. Shafts of sunlight caught in the wings of the oyster-catchers. Later still there was a sunset clotted with a few small black clouds and the aching calls of lonely cormorants.

Dylan said he came here one day, for the day, and never left. Got off the bus and forgot to get back on again. The insanity rate of the town was so high, he said, they had to lay on a special bus on visiting day at the local mental asylum. He had the usual Welsh penchant for exaggeration. But most all of the old crazies are now down in the cemetery along with Dylan while there are punks in the pubs, caravan parks, one-armed bandits and even a newly arrived transvestite who is causing much speculation amongst the boys in the bar.

'He should never have gone to London of course,' said the lady in the bar. Of course. I just could not keep an eye on him when he went to that city of the damned. Every good Welshman comes unstuck on Paddington station, particularly those as soft as Dylan who journeyed to the big city, broke and, in some vague way, hoping to live off women. Instead he was fouled up by parties, Bloomsbury and BBC producers— 'capital punishment' he called it. Everywhere he sold his work for a 'mouse's ransom' and scratched only breadcrumbs of happiness. Well that's alcoholism for you, I'm afraid. By the time he came to live here I realised that there was almost nothing more I could do for him and certainly gave up pumping out his stomach.

'But then again it was America that did for him wasn't it,' said Dai Rowlands. 'He was a beer man was Dylan. Just couldn't cope with all that American whisky.'

Ah yes, it was, it was. The beer was already killing him but it was the whisky that provided the final turn of the alcoholic screw. And so it came to pass that my little sentry on the edge finally fell over it and was brought down here to Laugharne— in a suit, dicky-bow and looking smarter than at any time in his life—stretched out in a box after drinking a few drinks too many in the fast lane in New York on November 9 1953. I shed a few tears at that funeral I don't mind admitting.

But he's still here. Listen now as night spreads over Laugharne and the last drunk has ricocheted off the last wall before falling in through his own front door. Listen carefully and you'll be able to hear the beat of my old praise poet's heart. It pounds down through those sleeping streets; it's there in those sacred front parlours; in the empty hoots of the watchful owl and that arthritic, polished pulpit in the brooding chapel. You can hear his heartbeat in that gurgling brook, the cats fighting in the dark and the girl with a face like a pretty parrot fish kept awake by her old man's snoring. It beats on in the locked and shuttered bar of the pub; in the chimes of all those grandfather clocks and on all those dusty Bibles on their desks permanently kept open at Revelation.

His burial place is marked by a simple white cross with paint flaking off it and some dead flowers. Nearby was a fresh mountain of flowers on newly-buried Trefor the Bus. Well at least our Rimbaud of Cwmdonkin Drive is now comfy. The wind rattled the leaves, making them burst into frequent rounds of applause. Across the lane, in a farmhouse, a light was still burning.

There's a secret place where I like to go and play when I am worried about anything; a huge stretch of sands some seven miles long and two miles wide, where huge winds come exploding in over the Burry estuary and I can roll around inside them, fighting against them and sailing with them, shifting one way and another as those winds go roaring on and on. The sands of Penclawdd they are called.

Before the sands themselves there's a corridor of marshland and gullies where packs of wild horses graze. The horses are always moving around on the marsh, black on green, and sometimes one makes a run for it and then they all make a run for it; about twenty of them leaping the gullies or struggling chest-deep through the sea pools. Just opposite, directly above the glittering, stirring line of the sea, is Llanelli.

Once out in those winds even I can feel fright and thrills as I let myself be bundled around in their rollercoaster currents. Yet sometimes I can find a still pocket between one and another and I will stabilise myself with my flame and enjoy the sight of all the gulls sitting around in silent conclave next to the shelter of a shingle bank or watch the horses run together or marvel at the way those winds have scoured the sands of everything except their form.

There's the wildest beauty out here for certain but great danger for people too. The cockle pickers who work the sands are always warning people about the tides since they can swoop in faster than walking pace. Even if you are a good runner you must know exactly which way to run since, if you get lost in the frequent sea mists, you can drown in that swirling tide—as many have.

Here and there are the ugly, rutted tracks churned up by the Land-Rovers of the new cocklers. The famous women cocklers of the sands of Penclawdd, with their trusty horses and carts, have long left the sands. They used these sands as the first form of Welsh social security after their husbands had been lost in mining accidents and, wrapped in their flannels and with their big bums sticking up in the air, they became a symbol of a terrible determination to survive. Now they have been replaced by men in Land-Rovers and the sands are no longer quite the same.

As I flew on down towards Llanrhidian there was a rumble of thunder and a stammering flash of silent lightning. I came down lower to the sands—even with all my flying skills this is no place to be out in a storm. But the thunder was not the overture to a storm; just the overture to yet more fantastic shunts of those great sorrowing winds.

Soon darkness would come and the rising flocks of the waders told of the turn of the tide. A late shaft of unexpected sunlight was picking up the wild horses on the marsh making them look fiery and almost Biblical. But at least—and as usual—I had completely forgotten whatever it was that I had been worrying about.

Further along up the estuary is the small town of Loughor which was once the fifth section in the Roman road called Via Julia. King Arthur and the princes of Glamorgan fought a lot of their bloody battles around this way but today, with its pubs, police station, castle and Welfare Hall the town is a slumbering place of the most marvellous ordinariness which the young leave for Swansea when they want any night-life.

But when the Welsh map of love is finally drawn up Loughor should be the new capital. Many still regard the place as the Welsh Bethlehem since it was here that the Holy Spirit made its last great and devastating move in Wales during the Revival of the winter of 1904. The Moriah Chapel—where all heaven broke out—still stands on the main road and outside is a memorial statue to Evan Roberts, the lightning conductor who stirred the nation's soul.

I want to spend some space recording this revival if only because it was the last time that I worked with any great and sustained energy in Wales doing what I do best. The revival also tells us much that is good and bad about Welsh spirituality since, while it sought to put God back on His throne in Wales, there was too much emotion at work and too heavy a burden was placed on one man. Put simply they just asked too much of him but, briefly, I did believe that Evan Roberts really was going to succeed and I did all I could to help.

Oddly enough his birth wasn't accompanied by any great run on the chimes and the first I picked up on him was when he was fifteen. I was passing by his house out on the marsh here and noticed the amazing and imaginative quality of his prayers. There was almost nothing like them at the time since he would first kneel for a good five minutes actively listening for the distant thunder of the hound of heaven. Then his mind would start constructing a Tent of Meeting around his house to protect his family, with his twelve brothers and sisters, from all the demons of evil. He was so good at prayer he also seemed to know when I was around, sometimes reaching out and trying to hold me in his hands. He was particularly anxious to use me to anoint his loved ones, particularly his brother Dan who was blind.

I kept an eye on him while he worked as a blacksmith and later in the nearby colliery but wasn't at all surprised when he decided to go to Bible College up in Newcastle Emlyn. I could soon see that he was special so I suppose my work with him started when I took him to see Seth Joshua at Blaenannerch one day. Seth was an itinerant preacher of the time with a tremendous talent for vivid oratory. He would talk of the valley of the avalanches with a huge precipice hanging over it. 'Walk slow and quiet brother lest the precipice fall. A curse, one swear word is enough to shake the mountain and grind you into powder. The ungodly are always walking in the valley of the avalanches.'

Evan sat down in the crowded chapel and Seth began tearing into those three Roman soldiers with their unmitigated insolence and blasphemous daring in the rough handling of the son of God. Just then I formed a golden halo over Seth's head and Evan sat bolt upright, feeling the old tribal passions boiling inside him as reality began dissembling. Then I made the air tremble with small flames and said to Evan: 'You too would be in this pit apart from God's grace.' People began moving towards the flames and Evan yelled out 'Let my people go. Oh please let my people go.'

'And I am telling you now,' Seth was then saying. 'I am telling you now that God has laid it on my heart that he is going to take a lad from the collieries—just as he took Elisha from the plough. He is going to take this lad from the mine and he is going to revive God's church.'

To revive God's church ... So the call had come at last and Evan stood up and shouted, 'So bend us now oh Lord. Bend us all now.' Barely had he shouted these words than he toppled forward suffering from a convulsion and Seth invited prayers for him. Within a few minutes Evan stood up wiping his mouth with a handkerchief.

And that's how the revival of 1904 began.

When he came back to Loughor Evan continued with a tremendous prayer life and he also discovered that he had been given the gift of healing since, just as Ananias had laid his hands on Saul, then too he laid his hands on his brother Dan and his sight was restored.

One Sunday early that autumn Evan announced in the main service of the Moriah that he wanted to conduct his own small service afterwards in Pigsah, the tiny mother chapel of the Moriah which was now only used for weekly Bible classes and Sunday School. Twelve young people—eight boys and four girls—went in there and sat on the long wooden benches with the yellow gaslights flickering on two of the walls.

'Anyone who wants to go home should go at once since I want all the doors locked,' Evan said. 'No one can enter or leave until the Holy Spirit has come amongst us.' He then paused but I was right by his side in case he faltered with any of his words, which he didn't. 'The Holy Spirit is the mind and strength and power of an active, holy God. The Holy Spirit brings you prophecies on the wind and tells us the deep things of God which are known to God alone. The Holy Spirit is a person in his own right, with his own purpose, who, said the prophets, would never leave you desolate. So I come to you. Yes, my children, I come and minister to you.' He clenched both his hands and raised them. 'So I want each of you to say "Oh Lord send the Holy Spirit now for Jesus Christ's sake."'

They were all made to repeat the line again and again until they could all hear a hurricane of their sins of old. 'Bend us in our sin, bend us in our shame. Bend us, you worthless servants. Break us all under the shadow of the cross that we may be born anew.'

At 4.35 a.m. the door of the Pigsah was unbolted and the first converts of the revival stumbled out, red-eyed and singing, into a grey dripping dawn.

The times were right for revival. There had just been a terrible train crash in Loughor in which fourteen had died and thirty five injured. The national rugby team had also lost heavily to England—in which I took a small part. Word went around quickly about this wonderful new preacher and, fanned by Press publicity, hundreds began coming to the nightly services which Evan began conducting in the Moriah. The services were lengthy go-as-you-please with Evan saying a few words, his singers breaking into a hymn and people standing up and confessing their sins. After the announcement of each new convert everyone waved their handkerchiefs and sang 'Diolch Iddo'—'Thanks to Him'—which became the great love song of the revival.

Today the Moriah is empty but well-preserved with a fine wooden ceiling and lots of polished wooden pews. A bunch of white chrysanthemums sits on the altar. They no longer have a regular minister and barely a dozen attend the services on

Sunday. But within days of Evan starting his new work you couldn't get in.

The miners also began services down the pits and the pit ponies, who normally moved only in response to swear words, were plainly bamboozled by all these new quiet gentle phrases. One miner used to take beer down below in his teapot but now he was going around saying that the Lord had converted him, his wife and his teapot. Absenteeism dropped as did crime. Even the rugby clubs—regular centres of violence particularly on the pitch—were disbanded.

Evan learned to speak with a relentless drive and, sitting up in the gallery of many a packed chapel, I was so proud of the way his words became the very motor of a service. 'God's promise is that where there is holy obedience which leads to purity of heart; where people bow their heads, broken-hearted in their sin and shame, to listen for the distant barks of the hound of heaven; when people do all this then so, too, will they be given a blazing vision of the truth of God and be guided through all the danger of their days by the radical power of the Holy Spirit.'

The stinging beauty of his words was such that he would make the congregation cower but then they might respond with a gusting hymn which would, in its turn, be taken up by the crowds outside. Evan would walk among them, kneel among them, sing with them then stride back to his pulpit where, with hands clasped together, he would lean forward over the people like the figurehead on the prow of a ship with his eyes closed and warm tears swarming down his cheeks.

Tribal passions powered these services for four hours or more. The services always had their own intelligence and always went in unforseen directions. Autobiographical confessions would be interrupted by a hymn. The announcement of another conversion would be followed by the mass waving of handkerchiefs.

'Sinners some day time will present you with a panoramic replica of all your sins. The mother who died of a broken heart years too soon. The father you drove out of your home. The girl you used and deceived. The poor man you stole from. The child in need you turned your back on. All these sins will be presented to you in full length and full height on the day you die, with your blood dripping like the drum of eternity on the endless torment of your damned soul.'

Broadoak colliery, next to the marsh, is now covered over by a small woodland but Evan's home, Island House, still overlooks the estuary with a burglar alarm and satellite dish on its walls. Nearby is the tiny chapel of Pigsah which Evan built himself; a fine, fit building with a lively congregation and Evan's own Bible, inscribed in his own hand, kept on the pulpit. But he would hardly recognise his home area now. Directly across the water are the steaming towers and pylons of light industry, including a condom factory which was recently closed and moved to Taiwan. There is also the Reverend James pub which, because of its unusual name, some people think is a chapel. They ring up the bar and ask what time are the services starting. One told the barmaid that he was about to commit suicide.

Together with his lady singers Evan moved out into the mining valleys of South Wales. Miners had always found theology entrancing and Evan believed that they would provide the bedrock of the revival. Soon the revivalists were moving from chapel to chapel in this poor, crowded world of the means test, zinc baths and damp marigolds.

'Of all the treasures that God gave us the soul is the greatest, more valuable even than all Solomon's treasures. A soul is not something to gamble with. You cannot redeem your soul after losing it. When you have lost your soul in the sea of sin then you too are lost for ever. Only with the passport of your soul will you one day rise again and be returned, in heaven, into the arms of those you once loved and lost. So who now will repent and save his soul?'

But for me the most memorable service came in Trecynon in the Aberdare Valley. Even now I can remember all the details of that tremendous service; the quickening of the blood, the mass testimony and the singing of 'Abide With Me'. The chapel was packed to the rafters as more and more announced their conversions and Evan finally stood to speak in the pulpit. He was a fine tall figure of a man with a pale face, hazel eyes and a large nose. He also had a strange way of waving his hand just under his chin.

'In the last days, we are told, certain things will happen. I read my Bible to mean that we are coming to the last days when the old will dream dreams and the young see visions. There will be bloodshed on the moon, a great darkness over the land and signs writ large on the sky. The moon ...'

It was just then that I had the fantastic feeling of the closeness and presence of God who was going to use me to tell Evan something. So I duly became the messenger and pinned a vision in the air directly above the heads of the congregation. I showed him a golden sea of light and made this sea of light move up and down like slowly swelling waves. Then a huge bank of shadow rose up out of this swelling sea of light and disappeared again. Next I drew a large black hand with my flame and passed it directly over Evan's eyes. He knew what this was all about all right: he caught it straight away.

'So he is coming then and will engulf all the world,' he shouted with the tongue of dragons. 'Lucifer and all his dark angels have finally escaped from their dungeon in hell and are even now preparing themselves for the last desperate rebellion against God. Beware, my people, arm yourselves with holiness, for this hurricane of evil will come and tear you apart in ways that you do not understand. This force will come as an organised intelligence scattering illusions at your feet. It will even be anxious to tell you that Satan does not exist. But he does, my people, and he is even now preparing to throw a cloak of the most violent perversion right over the face of the world.'

His voice then changed from dark warning to jubilant prophecy and he stood as erect as an oak. 'But this move to drive God from His throne will fail. This mighty struggle between God and Satan must fail in Satan's destruction. But it will only end when the powers of darkness seem to reign over the world. Only then—when we are weeping in our ruins and the very moon is ringed around with our misery and fear—will that bruised and torn Galilean rise again, arise again and deliver the world in the Second Coming. Yes, my people, that great day when the blessed will be separated from the damned and the dead be resurrected in joy. Repent and prepare for that hour when the Son of Man will come in all his glory. Are you ready if he comes tonight? Will you be ready if he walks in through that door this minute? Be ready my people. Be ready.'

Shouts mingled with praise. The congregation stood up declaring themselves ready again and again. But then, looking around that worshipping chapel, I remember seeing something most strange. I remember seeing a tall man walking into the top of the gallery dressed in a long grey habit. Another, wearing bishop's vestments, joined him as did another in a black gown and yet another with but one eye. Oh yes, now it was my turn to understand what this was all about. These were all Evan's spiritual forefathers, gathering to witness the birth of yet another mind possessor come with the thunder. Here were all the leaders I had shepherded over the centuries come to applaud another from that great praise dynasty. And we all just stood there basking in this new and beautiful breeze straight from Calvary.

The revival continued travelling through the valleys all that winter and Evan kept on patiently explaining a holy God's requirement that His people be holy too. He also arraigned sin, roused consciences and spoke of the coming apocalypse with power.

But, at its height, Evan became a tired and withdrawn man, going in for longer and longer silences in the pulpit and even beginning to believe that God had deserted him. He also started falling to the pulpit floor and letting out strange, agonised yells. It all got so bad that he was out walking on his own in the Garw Valley one day and I gave him a vision to cheer him up.

He was standing looking down at a cascading stream when I made it erupt into such a brilliant array of glittering light that he was forced to shield his eyes. I sang his favourite lines of scripture to him and made the spirits of the old saints rise up out of the hurrying water to warm him. He felt that his depression had been totally lifted and began jumping around in the stream like a salmon that had lost its sense of direction, flinging handfuls of water around in the air and praising God in a loud voice. 'God is great and I shall sing His praises forever,' he shouted. 'I will love the Lord my God until the day I die. Yes, until the day I die.'

He spoke well in the packed chapel of Pontycymmer that night with his short sentences cracking down on the heads of the congregation like whips. 'Though He may send thunder or locusts we will still love God. Though we may be thrown into thorn bushes or pierced with swords we will still love God. Though misery and darkness and the slime of Satan overtake us we will still love God. Even though we have lost our eyes and ears; even though every bone in our bodies be broken; even though blood pours from our every vein and we have fallen as low as it is possible to fall ... then we will still love God. Always love God, my people, and be certain that He adores every second of our loving praise. Know that the world is round and day follows night so that the sound of our prayer and praise will always be in His ears. The only command is to love Him and, through Him, each other.'

In Cwmavon the chapel was again jammed with people climbing in through the organ loft. 'The battle is fierce and we must take care of our bodies,' Evan shouted. A pane of glass was smashed. He commended this until, shortly, all the panes were shattered. Later he interrupted a hymn. 'No, no. God will not be mocked. There is a man here who will never be saved. He has disobeyed and it is too late, too late.'

He discovered a wonderful new singer in Annie Davies, a heart-stopping contralto, who held a big Bible to her chest and sang with head-shakings of grief. Evan's words duelled with her song to magical and devastating effect. The service in Treherbert just before that Christmas was one of the best. 'People say that the Revival will soon wear out. Let them. But remember that when a nation loses its vision of God then that nation will perish. When a nation perishes then so too will the people in it and violence will come to the streets and homes. This Revival will wake the very heart of our nation. It will shout our fear of God and love of Wales.'

Annie's voice began singing *Calon Lân* softly. Evan waited for her to finish the first verse and continued speaking with her voice fluting behind his words. 'Let it be known that, with the help of the Holy Spirit, we are going to restore this beloved land to its holy and sacred past. The music of the streets is going to be the music of prayer. The air of the land is going to be the air of love. Heaven makes no mistakes. The promises of the Bible will all be kept.'

That Christmas I tore around Wales like a mad thing, giving visions here and hanging necklaces of light there. Some of them were really extravagant too with pillars of fire over the Brecon Beacons; orange flames dancing in the night outside Pwllheli; red blobs revolving over the Cildwrn Chapel in Anglesey. I carried candles through the air to a chapel cleaner in Ynysybwl and spoke to miners down the pits.

Bookshops everywhere complained of a shortage of Bibles. Over half the pubs in Wales were tottering on the edge of bankruptcy. One Mountain Ash magistrate complained that there was now so little crime that there was nothing for him to do.

When Evan came to pray on his own in the Moriah chapel that Christmas I again rewarded him and his work with a beautiful but simple vision. I showed him a trembling hand just hanging in the air. A nail had been driven into the wrist with the blood seeping out of it, red and warm. The drops of blood fell downwards onto the pew in front of Evan making small soft splashes.

But when the revivalist party began moving around Wales again that spring Evan was soon back to his bad old ways, breaking down into sullen depressions and silences. There wasn't too much that I could do about them either. Such were his silences in the pulpit the Press began to dub him The Silent Evangelist. At some meetings he kept feeling oppressed by evil and, try as he might, he could not see any holiness or spirit of prayer in the crowds—just curiosity. His convulsions—brought on by an old pit accident—also came back with increasing regularity.

His real trouble was that he was too sensitive for this world and, hurt by the regular assaults on him in the Press, his shoulders became stooped, his hair greying around the edges and his once-sparkling eyes began to take on the full colour of stone. Here was a man sucked dry prematurely by the intense pressures of a revivalist's life and there was nothing at all that I could do.

After a seven-day silence in Neath he announced that it was all over and went to live in seclusion in Leicester. He died in Cardiff in 1955, where he had been living on charity, and a nation mourned.

Today he lies buried with his family in the graveyard at the rear of the Moriah Chapel. Sometimes I go to sit on his tomb where I remember the sights and sounds of that great winter of 1904. Here is a man who once opened the heart of a nation, it says on his memorial stone.

# Ninth Book

I can always tell when I'm approaching a major city because the air thickens both visibly and audibly with radio signals, telephone calls, television pictures and, of late, the direct and violence-packed beams of the distant satellites. On some days, depending on the weather and time, there's almost a traffic jam high in the air above a city and it's a bit like swimming through an electronic soup, particularly if I'm over the city the size of Swansea with her 172,566 souls, all scattered in their little terraces on the high amphitheatre slopes and the new buildings around the city centre.

It's not the prettiest of places either, flanked by half-built roads and forests of confusing road signs on one side and the industrially ravaged Swansea Valley on the other. Then there are all the buildings in the centre—mostly new and tributes to yuppy triumphalism—built after the city's heart was severely bombed during the war. But the sea is still the same, of course, still swamping the ragged curve of Swansea Bay twice a day, still nagging the city walls with her mumbling ozone words.

But today the crowds are out, with their little Union Jacks and best hats, because Princess Diana is visiting the city as part of one of her regular tours of Wales. For three days and a few hundred miles now much of the nation has been having nervous breakdowns on rainswept pavements as she swept by in her speedy Daimler. Choirs have serenaded her, harps have tinkled forth and grown men have cried. One man, with several rows of war medals, cried, pulled himself together and then burst out crying again.

And here she was with us now, blessing Swansea with her radiant beauty, either smiling wondrously at the cheering crowds or then looking around out of the sides of her eyes in the purest terror, as if a man in a peaked cap had just told her that they were about to turn off the palace's electricity for not paying the bill. Occasionally she might shift her body weight from one foot to another before cleaning one of her shoes on the back of her other leg. The elderly Welsh women, in particular, just love everything about her. She comes on as 'one of us' you see. If a pin was stuck in her she would indeed bleed. If she fell over she would indeed bruise. Ah yes. Everything was terribly wonderful as Princess Di went by in the Swansea drizzle what with all the children being kissed and babies poked and the Welsh, a radical race, re-lived the heady days of the Investiture of her husband as Prince of Wales.

The Princess's tour also underlined another strange feature about my patch; that it is, in fact, two patches. During the early stages of her tour in the northern rural areas the response was warm but fairly restrained. But, as soon as she got down to Swansea and the south, the traditional birthplace of socialism, everyone—but everyone—went bananas. Even when she spoke a bit of Welsh, sounding like a nice English girl speaking a bit of Welsh, they were collapsed with the honour of it all. 'Speaks like an angel she does. Just like an angel.'

Well I don't know about that. But there are, as it happens, a lot of Welsh in heaven. There is that joke, which perhaps I shouldn't tell, that, one day, St Peter himself got fed up with all the Welsh in heaven—forever orating windy sermons or singing melancholy hymns or composing tricky rhymes—that he ordered one of us angels to stand outside the heavenly gates and shout 'caws pobi: toasted cheese; caws pobi: toasted cheese.' The Welsh, with their mouths slavering, dashed out in one solid cavalry charge whereupon this angel slammed the gates shut and locked them all out. For a while St Peter found heaven quite an agreeable place again.

This is only a joke but it always makes me smile and no one knows better than me what a pain in the neck the Welsh can be particularly when they are down on their knees, in amongst the fag ends and chip papers of some damp pavement, in front of a member of the English monarchy—as they are now—giving her a variety of gifts which, so far this tour, have included a heifer, a ewe, several sticks of rock, a book of illuminated poems and a plastic coat hanger.

They also give her advice: 'Don't worry about the rain, girl. It's good for the complexion.' A few bounders did jeer her outside the Guildhall although she seemed to have a touching inability to tell the difference between those for her and those agin her. She greeted them all alike—with a bright smile and a sideways look of palatial fear.

After the Royal cavalcade had finally moved on, the city was still alive with shoppers and circling traffic looking for somewhere to park but, no matter on which corner I stand in this city, I always imagine that I've just spotted my favourite praise poet in the crowds. He always comes alive for me in these rowdy streets and takes on a real presence. Ah look, there he is now again striding through the new Quadrant shopping centre with his tousled hair and frog-like chin; that bulbuous nose driven out of shape by a mysterious accident; the Woodbine stuck to his bee-stung lips and the scarf twirled around and around his neck like a long-dead anaconda.

He threaded his way down through the shoppers to the Cross Keys pub where he stood at the bar staring around him at the drinkers sitting hunched over their pints, all trying to find shelter from the royal hoo-hah that had been going on all day outside. Pairs of old hands rested on the bar on either side of their pints. Just as in his old story 'Return Journey', Dylan took his own drink and sipped it before going over to one drinker after another asking if, perchance, anyone there remembered him.

Ah now then, one told him. You were a bit of a poet weren't you? Married an American girl and you were sexually prolific, as I remember. Most sexually prolific. I mean to say you're either in the Salvation Army or you're sexually prolific aren't you? Hah-hah.

Now they tell me—and it's only what I've been told—that you were a free-loader, another said to him. You know what I mean I expect. Short arms and deep pockets. A genius who liked his drop of pop but didn't like paying for it. That's the way it was with you wasn't it? There's a lot like you still around mind. You must have started a fashion.

Yet another wiped some beer off his mouth with his hand before letting out a loud belch. He thought for a bit and then took another sip of his beer.

I might as well tell you that I don't know much about poetry but I do know what I like. I can't say that I've ever read your stuff either but there again I don't suppose you've read any of mine have you? But there's none of us the same is there? None of us the same. And thank God for that, I say. Thank God for that.

Dylan listed a lot of old Swansea shops in his 'Return Journey'. There was Eddershaw Furnishers, Leslie's Stores, Tucker's Fish, Price's Fifty Shilling, Gregory Confectioners. But today, leaving the pub, he would find such as Oddbins, Our Price, Miss Selfridge and Roopa Jeans. He would also be bemused by the high-tech vision of the Leisure Centre, with its hydroslide and wave machine, together with the multi-million Maritime Quarter where his statue sits gloomily on a chair looking out into the rain.

But all this is nothing to do with my whirling imagination. The presence of my roaring boy on his runaway horse is almost everywhere you look. There is a Dylan Thomas Theatre, a Dylan's Bookstore, a statue to Captain Cat on the Marina and this statue of him on his chair. Dylan was always unfailingly rude about Swansea: 'this crawling, slummed, unplanned, jerry-villa'd town on the splendid-curving shore,' he described it and so the city has clearly taken revenge on him with this statue. One local artist says it makes him look like Harry Belafonte and another writer, Nigel Jenkins, swears it was modelled on Johnny Mathis. Others refer to it as The Portrait of the Artist as Someone Else. But, in fairness, the chair he's sitting on does look like a chair.

The Dylan Thomas Industry is the one industry which is booming in Wales during the current recession and his literary estate is on the verge of becoming one of the richest in the world based, as it happens, on one of the smallest bodies of work. There is now a Dylan Thomas Summer School in Aberystwyth in which the new captains of this industry lecture on everything from where he fought with his wife to which end of the pencil he used when he wrote his poems. A new recording of Under Milk Wood has been made by the London Taffia under the supervision of George Martin of Beatles' fame. Paul Ferris is working on a new biography of Caitlin. Under Milk Wood is today being performed in New York, Edinburgh and Hong Kong and, with every performance, another £30 goes into the coffers of the Thomas estate which is now earning some £120,000 a year with half going to Caitlin and the other to his children. Such earnings put him on a level with Sartre, Camus and T. S. Eliot.

They are also running special Dylan Thomas weekends out of Swansea's Holiday Inn, at £115 a head, in which they tour all the well-known Dylan Thomas haunts. Everywhere he fell over has become a hallowed spot; every pub he drank in a sacred shrine. Indeed only his grave in Laugharne, with its simple wooden cross, has been left untouched clearly because no one has yet figured out how to make money from putting a proper tombstone on it.

Ah yes—despite one of Dylan's best-known lines—death really does have a rich dominion. Death has indeed brought his family the bundles of money that so decisively escaped him all his life.

I walked up those Alpine slopes of the city—so steep it's a wonder everyone isn't disabled with advanced arthritis—to the Uplands area and Cwmdonkin Park which for Dylan, in his childhood, was 'a world within a world ... a park full of treasures and terrors'. It had begun spitting with rain and a teacher was screaming at a group of youngsters trying to teach them the wonders of hockey.

It was then I spotted him again: a be-scarfed figure hurrying down the curving path through the trees. He was always hurrying when he was young and it was only when he got older that he shuffled around the place with all the pace of a stunned slug. But in his youth in this park he was already looking at everything in a new way with new words. The children playing in the park were 'star-gestured' and as 'innocent as strawberries.' Then there was the sombre bell at closing time and the hunchback eating bread from a newspaper.

I spent a lot of time watching over him sailing his ship in the fountain basin. There was one old man here, in particular, who was forever bothering young boys so I always had to be on the alert when Dylan ever went anywhere near him. That old man used to faint a lot and everyone thought it was the drink. But it was just me up to my old angel tricks.

In fact I can still remember very clearly that huge and ravishing run on the chimes which told me that there had been another praise leak on October 27, 1914. I went straight to No 5 Cwmdonkin Drive—'a mortgaged villa in an upper-class professional row'—and watched my little genius being born in a bedroom with a hot water tank gurgling in the corner. There was no indication then of what he was going to become, of course. Truth to tell he screamed and dribbled so much there seemed no possibility at all that he was going to become a famous poet. A famous pithead rabble-rouser, more like, with lusty lungs like that.

But it didn't take me long to see the direction he was going and, most fortunately, the Christian influences on him as a child were strong. His family had produced active ministers who had run chapels in Swansea and he was made to go to Sunday School every week. He also liked to go and listen to the new would-be revivalists on Swansea Sands but they never produced another like Evan Roberts.

His father D.J. had no religious beliefs at all—he liked to stand at the window and shout at God if it was raining—but his mother put funny little prayers on bits of paper beneath the lino under the family bed. I was never sure why she hid them under the lino but that was the way it was in the Thomas household. They were all as daft as brushes and it was some wonder that Dylan wasn't dafter than he was.

But this Christian background rubbed off on Dylan in other ways too. He had no concept of property and never owned anything at all. Indeed it was a great pleasure watching this unusual child growing up in the city but I soon began noticing his growing and alarming addiction to alcohol. I made him more sick than at any time in his life after his first drink but that didn't help much; might even have made it worse as it happened because he had a positively Byronic attitude to suffering. 'Stay with me flagons because I am sick of love,' he would croon drunkenly.

Even by the time he was fifteen I had already begun pumping all that poison out of his belly on a regular basis. Already that early in his life I could see that he wasn't going to last long. He could go without it for days and even weeks but, as soon as he got alcohol into his bloodstream, he just could not stop. The very notion of just a couple of drinks was a joke with him; everytime he started it had to be an almost suicidal fall-down job. 'And for the next trick I'm going to destroy myself.'

Today students live in his old home at No 5 Cwmdonkin Drive and there are persistent rumours that the semi is going to be turned into a museum. The bedroom where he was born has posters like the Blues Brothers on the wall; papers are scattered everywhere and a pair of dumb-bells sit in the middle of the floor. A student, Jonathan Thompson, sleeps in this room and says that he has no time for poetry since he is far too busy studying business.

The hunchback and that dirty old man have also long left the park. Children don't sail boats in the fountain any longer but they do sniff glue in the shelter. The park keeper still rings his sombre bell at closing time.

Nearby is the Uplands Tavern which has changed considerably since Dylan first learned to drink here. There are one-armed bandits and quiz machines. The monotonous drone of disco thumps out of loudspeakers and drunken students are shouting at one another in The Dylan Thomas Snug Bar.

It was in that corner that Dylan learned to like 'the taste of the beer, its fine white lather, its brassed-bright depths, the sudden world through the wet-brown walls of glass, the tilted rush to the lips and the slow swallowing down to the lapping belly, the salt on the tongue, the foam at the corners.'

You can see, can't you, just by the way he describes the beer how much he was in love with it. He certainly never wrote about his Caitlin so glowingly. When he drank a pint of beer he was doing nothing less than making love to a beautiful woman. No—it was even better than that.

And it was there, amidst the disco thump and the shrieking students, that my delinquent praise poet came and sat with me again. He gave a deep Woodbine cough and raised his podgy fingers, with their chewn-off fingernails, in despair. His flies, as usual, were undone with urine splashes all down the front of his trousers.

Why, when he had been treated so badly all his life, had it all come to this, he wanted to know. Why hadn't it just been a little more comfortable? Did there really have to be so much pain when all he wanted to do was write a little poetry for the love of man and in praise of God? Where was the bloody sense in it?

I had a few answers, of course, but, in the circumstances, it seemed pointless to give them. Even after all this time my alcoholic bard had clearly not seen that the fault—if fault there was—resided in him. Only he was the architect of his own destruction. But he would never understand that simple insight so why upset him again?

I didn't know, I said when he looked up at me. I just didn't know.

You are probably by now trying to work out what I look like myself so I had better put the record straight before I go any further. I don't look like anything at all since I am pure spirit who is sometimes fire, sometimes wind, sometimes water and sometimes all three. I can—and often do—take on human form and will look like anything from a smelly hill farmer to the lead singer of Mott the Hoople. But mostly I am invisible spirit; one of the many atoms of the unseen who can feel pleasure and pain; who knows the meaning of jubilation and sorrow but who prefers above all else the sensation of happiness or joy. My errands of love or mercy are always performed for the glory of God. These are all difficult concepts I know.

So, as I move around the country, I can fly over the mountains and within the winds or even replenish my spirits by becoming water within water. Becoming water within water is another recreational pastime of mine—particularly on hot summer's afternoons—and that's how I enjoyed a few hours the following day: wallowing in the pools and waterfalls of the nearby Neath Valley.

It's a lot of fun bobbing around in the cold swirling pools of this valley river before sliding up the white curtains of the hissing waterfall. Directly under the waterfall is often the best place to be with the water smashing down on top of you and making the water all around steam as if boiling hot. All this raging water often catches the light and, holding hands, they do sparkling, fast waltzes together.

The Melin Cwrt waterfall near Resolven was looking dramatic that afternoon, driving through a gap on the top of a cliff edge and down some hundred feet of dark oblong rocks. This waterfall once powered a waterwheel used to produce pig iron for the nearby tinplate industry. You can still feel the energy that kept that wheel turning and I can frame myself in such a way that I too can go tumbling around and around like an old shirt inside a washing machine.

Further on up the valley, at Pont Melin-Fach, it can get even more exciting with waterfalls of every shape and hue almost every hundred yards or so. Rapids run into cascades and leap into cataracts before moving on into smaller waterfalls and then on into even greater ones. The further you go up the valley the wilder it becomes and I like to take my time as I move around and around each pool, enjoying the furious exuberance of it all.

Every waterfall has its own music, from the merry tinkling of the smaller waterfalls through to the louder chucklings of the larger ones, which seem to throw the very pebbles about, and then on to the thrilling bass thunder of the great waterfalls, full of determination and ancient defiance. But what is more beautiful than a frozen waterfall or one avalanching over a rock outcrop, aflame with the dying light of the evening sun? Who has ever failed to be moved watching the mighty drama of a salmon fighting again and again to overcome a high waterfall? Not even the steepest and most torrid cascades seem to deter them.

Sometimes, just for fun, I like to reprise the salmon jumps, as I did that afternoon, turning a bend in the river and coming face to face with a large waterfall. I inched towards the roaring curtain slowly in the driving water and what a huge curtain it was; a whole symphony of sound and movement playing every note furiously. Directly at the top of this waterfall the water slows and dawdles but no sooner is it on the edge than it flings itself in to the air as it pours down on to a boiling white grave in a screaming fury.

I launched myself out of this yelling grave like a rocket-propelled soul which can't get to heaven fast enough. But the water poured down on me hard and I allowed gravity to pull me back down again. Next thing I shot up head-first into the torrents again, twisting myself this way and that, letting out great Red Indian yells as I tried to scale the waterfall just with the momentum of my own leap and without using any flying tricks. It took me about five tries but I got there in the end and I lay there on the river bank with half of me still in the dawdling pool, resting from my exertions while also enjoying the unusual conjunction of the sounds of hissing and thunder coming up from the spray down below.

There are the deep and lovely things of God in every waterfall. Each sings a continual song of purity and renewal. They are constantly retelling the ancient myths of the hillsides as they roar out their magic spells. I love the spectacular Rheidol waterfall in Devil's Bridge and, of course, the high, foaming spread of Bishop William Morgan's in Llanrhaeadr-ym-Mochnant. But that one in the Neath Valley was all a hot and sweaty angel needed that afternoon and, as I looked about me at the profusion of birds and plants here, it also reminded me that water is always both the bringer and giver of all life.

Directly at the top of the Neath Valley we start to get our first sniff of the coal mines which have ripped the very bowels out of South Wales. We are not yet in the slag-sentinelled valleys of the Rhondda since there is still a rural feel to the landscape but there are pitheads and frozen landslips dotted around here amidst the winding terraces of the small towns. Already there is the tinge of something hard; something slightly dangerous begins hanging in the air.

But the humour here is cheerful for all that and the language vivacious. This is the world of The Rediffusion Man and The Man from the Pru. Welfare Halls echo to the sounds of the bingo caller and many of the chapels are just managing to hold on. Mean-eyed, scruffy sheep mooch around these parts looking for allotments to scavenge. I've actually seen some of them climbing on one another's backs to get into a patch of cabbages. It wouldn't surprise me in the slightest if I saw a sheep going down the road carrying a step ladder on his shoulder.

Max Boyce—Wales's leading entertainer and rugby theologian—lives in these sheep-haunted badlands in the small town of Glyn-neath at the top of the valley. You can easily pick out his house because it's the one with the most expensive car in the valley parked outside. Today it's a red Mercedes and the house is as near to the town's rugby pitch as it's possible to get without actually being on top of it. A sad, rackety spectator stand lies in the distance.

With his brilliant comic monologues about the world of Welsh rugby Boyce has managed that most difficult of all feats—particularly here in Wales—of being highly successful while still alive. He's had six gold records, a best-selling book *I Was There* and broke 17 box office records on a recent two-month tour. He's an immensely warm man, as sensitive as a canary in a coal mine, with round features, the largest smile in the business and pale blue eyes which can turn so sad he gives the immediate impression of being a little boy lost in Woolworth's. He also seems to have no cynicism. Everything is either 'great' or 'fabulous' or 'wonderful'. For his friends nothing is too much trouble.

The main body of his work is rugby-based while some of his fantasies are amongst the funniest ever penned. He tells of a secret factory for manufacturing outside halves and of all the fans at the match who 'all had doctors' papers ... but were in no pain ... we all had scarlet fever and caught it in the game.'

There was the fan in Ireland who fell into a barrel of Guinness and drowned. No, it wasn't a painful death. He got out three times for a pee. Also there was that coach that stopped 14 times between Neath and Cardiff on the day of a rugby international. Only one saw the match and that was on television in prison.

What he likes most about rugby is its sense of fellowship both on and off the field. 'Rugby fans are a gentle crowd. There's never any violence. We like winning, of course, but the important thing is that our visitors get a good welcome. If we lose I usually get better by Tuesday or Wednesday. It's watching all those recordings on the BBC I hate.'

Rugby, of course, is the unofficial religion in Wales and there is certainly the most jubilant sense of revival in the air on the days of the international matches in Cardiff when half the rugby loonies in the land turn up to the capital city decked out in red and white or disguised as giant leeks or daffodils. Phalanx after phalanx of jeering half-drunk fans will come pouring in from the railway and bus stations. The car parks will be full of men and women having largely liquid lunches out of their car boots and traffic wardens will be spraying tickets on to every sloppily-parked car like confetti. All this thronging movement will be heightened by out-of-tune buskers, evangelicals preaching the word of God off the top of milk crates and giant leeks hanging off lamp-posts shouting 'Oggey-oggey-oggey'.

The police are all on overtime on the day of the international, standing in silver-buttoned groups on corners protecting the statue of Nye Bevan in the shopping centre, watching out for drunken punch-ups in the pubs or the shop-lifting gangs who come to take advantage of the milling crowds and can clean out whole racks of suits from large department stores in the time it takes a detective to blink. By mid-day the city pubs are jam-packed with thirsty fans who always drink as if a drought is about to break out over the land. Virtually all the suites of the Marriott Hotel are taken over by groups entertaining their clients with lunch and a stand ticket to the match. It is almost impossible for real fans to get tickets these days since the ticket touts have moved into big business ... and throw in lunch.

But this doesn't stop the optimists ransacking the city for a spare ticket like demented bloodhounds. In his search for a ticket your Welshman is as heartless as a heroin dealer and as sharp as a second hand car salesman. He would exhume his grandmother if he thought a ticket had been buried with her. Max Boyce always reckons that Lord Nelson, atop his statue in Trafalgar Square, has got his hand inside his coat pocket because he's guarding his international ticket from pick pockets.

As kick-off time approaches these drunken, red-scarfed carpets all begin rolling towards the National Stadium leaving the city streets eerily quiet, punctuated only by the occasional roar or the sound of a distant massed choir.

The National Stadium is the shrine where my flock still worships with the fervour of old. Here the Allbright angels on the terraces will sing the great love hymns of William Williams of Pantycelyn. His most famous hymn 'Guide Me O Thou Great Jehovah' is a collective national plea for the bread of heaven of an incredible number of points, particularly in any game against England. And when ten thousand of us were massing around the slopes of Sinai as God gave Moses the ten commandments there had clearly been a huge mistake. Somehow Moses had been so full of fear at hearing God's words he had lost the eleventh commandment on his way back down. This was the tablet on which God had decreed that, in future, Wales will win all rugby internationals, especially the ones against England, by at least 80 points to three. You can give them three oh Lord.

As hymns duel with arias just before the kick-off you will be watching a passionate people preparing to engage in a passionate struggle which will recall some of the great services of the 1904 Revival. Burly hymns will burst out from beneath gusting roars. Flags will be waved in every part of the ground. Great spasms of emotion will go whirling around and around the stadium as the Welsh enter a deep and complicated tribal struggle which has always expressed their most beautiful ideals.

Rugby for the Welsh has become a genuine cultural artefact and standard-bearer of democracy. They built into the game notions of fellowship, song and the *werin*, the spirit of the common folk. Rugby became a life-enhancing force in every village and town when, both in defence and attack, they relived past battles against the auld enemy in their damp English castles.

Each season marks the start of the dark and difficult quest for the Holy Grail of the Triple Crown. Not for nothing has Wales won more internationals than any other country in the world. Wales is a small country and small countries need to be noticed. And look here now boys, we have got to stuff the English this coming season. But, if there is some terrible accident and the English stuff us the sheer melancholy of the occasion will give their song a finer rapture and surer edge. The fans will also finally engage in some real and fervent prayer for a change. This prayer—somewhere in the middle of the second half—will be a call that, in their darkest hour, God will watch over their place kicker and prevent too many embarrassing knock-ons. It will also be an utterly selfish plea that, at the very least, this impending disaster does not turn out to be quite so disastrous. I mean to say, oh Lord, I've got to face everyone in work on Monday morning.

But if the loss against England is indeed a disaster then just getting drunk is not nearly enough. It will mean the end of the world as we know it; it will mean that the sun will not come up in the morning ever again; it will mean the biggest wake since the death of St David. It will also mean that the referee was blinder and more prejudiced than usual or that the Welsh players were suffering from either travel sickness or food poisoning or bad beer or a fatal mixture of all three.

It will also mean that the Welsh can yet again call up their undoubted talent for myth and fantasy, pretending to a heroic grandeur when they are, in reality, being well and truly worked over.

My usual place during internationals is on top of the scoreboard from where I can enjoy the atmosphere as much as anyone. I know the singing is all for selfish motives and that the prayers are duff but the occasion is one of the most atmospheric in the Welsh calendar. Sorroptus comes down for the afternoon if we are playing England. We don't exactly wear scarves and swing rattles in the air but if, from time to time, you have ever picked unusually loud cheers or jeers, ironic or otherwise, coming from the direction of the top of the scoreboard, that'll be us in the angels' bob bank. Macmac comes if we're playing Scotland and Victor used to come here for any Irish matches before he got stuck down that hole in Lundy.

We get on quite well and there have never been any partisan punch-ups between us but I do have a weakness for teasing Sorroptus by asking him if he's getting fed up with all the splinters from handling the wooden spoon. Not that England have run away with the wooden spoon much lately since they have been getting worryingly good and the wooden spoon jokes have been on the Welsh.

But I don't think we'll ever have a team such as we had in the glorious Sixties and fabulous Seventies. Ah, how well I remember the first time I saw Barry John play. He was a one off that boy and I knew that we were going to prosper mightily with him at outside half.

It would be easy for us to interfere with the course of the match, of course. A rugby ball can bounce in almost any direction so we could always stick the elbow in here or there. But we don't. Yet, as these pages do amount to my true confessions, I had better admit that I did interfere with two rugby matches earlier this century and one of them was on orders from the suits up top.

I was told to make sure the Welsh didn't win their match against England in the 1904-5 season—at a time when Wales was beating England year in, year out—since, unknown to me, they had decided that not winning would thicken up the national sense of melancholy no end and prepare the country for Evan Roberts's revival. A dark hour always precedes every revival it seems; the darker the hour the greater the revival.

But then, by way of amends, I helped Wales notch up the only win against New Zealand's All Blacks the following year in what has been described as the 'greatest game of them all'. Teddy Morgan had scored a try for Wales but then, in the dying minutes of the game, the All Blacks were hitting back with everything they had and Bob Deans just managed to get the ball over the Welsh line to score. Fortunately Rhys Gabe was at hand to pull Deans and the ball back over the line. But the referee, John Dallas, wearing his street clothes and walking boots, didn't see this important pull back because, as he was struggling to get to the spot, I blocked his vision with a lingering sweep of my wing. All Dallas saw was a strange shadow and, in all the uncertainty, disallowed the try and ordered a scrum.

This 'try' has been a subject of heated debate, for close on a hundred years so at least I can now put the record straight. Deans scored, Gabe fouled him and I unsighted the referee. Hardly the right way for an angel to behave, I know, but the prayers to God to stop Deans were exceedingly strong and the country really did need a moral uplift at the time.

At the end of each international match everyone pours out of the ground and—win or lose—they then get drunk in the city pubs for which they have special passes or know the secret knocks on the windows. Here beer-sodden groups analyse tactics, review bungled passes or pick the team all over again. On international day everyone in Cardiff is an expert on rugby with more letters after his name than a chiropodist. That back now. He's got no vision. Can't seem to read the game at all. Max Boyce always has to go around in disguise after the game which, I suppose, is the price of fame. 'It's ridiculous I've got to hide away on international day but I get too much attention.'

Sorroptus and I also like to wander around the city after the match. Occasionally a pub door might fly open and there is the flash of a bouncer's tuxedo before a fan, full of hiccups and happiness, comes sailing out into the air only to land with a dull thump on the pavement. Other fans wander down into the dockland where—despite all the new developments—they can still drink themselves senseless in seedy pubs or clubs or else repose in the beefy, welcoming arms of one of the tarts who, despite more or less constant police harassment, still keep bobbing up on every corner like nettles after the rain.

This is a rugby international day ritual of long standing and, as far back as 1921, a World Health Report blamed an alarming increase of venereal disease in the Valleys on the fans going down into 'Tiger Bay' for their entertainment after internationals. The tarts were hauled in and given painful shots of bismuth with very long needles.

But late this international night the city centre now looks like the aftermath of the battle of the Somme. A few of the lads are struggling home through the litter and past the pavement pizzas of dried-up vomit. The statue of Nye Bevan has a red and white scarf tied around his neck and a traffic bollard on his pointing finger. The police are dragging another drunk into their van and, as they do so, they spot another likely customer urinating into a cash-point.

'But look here, ossifer, that's the way we always are on international day. I mean to say 'aven't you 'eard? This is our big day. But tell me one thing afore you fling me into that van. Tell me straight now. Who won?'

Summer has begun running out of puff by this time of the year with the nights drawing in and the rifle shots of the apples falling in the orchards where they are drilled hollow by slugs and wasps. It is the time of earwigs in the dahlias and bonfires in the gardens which burn with bright, fierce hearts. The tomato plants are withering on their bamboo supports in the greenhouses and daddy long legs gather to sun themselves in warm porchways. Today a brilliant sun was rising over the Bristol Channel making the passing clouds yellow-bellied as they passed overhead in twos and threes.

I had come drifting into the small town of Llantwit Major in the Vale of Glamorgan. There was a quiet and gorgeous mellowness in the streets with the leaves yellowing on the trees, a nip freshening the air and all the allotments amok with woodsmoke. Blackberries were thick and black, giving off that slight decadent aroma that comes from being baked to perfection in all those long hours of summer sunshine.

As I moved about in that glittering dawn most of the town was still asleep. Tiny snails with red and white shells were crossing the pavement and Johnny Jones's cockerel was greeting the day, but rather thinly, because the thing was now fourteen years of age and not what he was.

It's a most pleasant town is Llantwit Major with its shops, few pubs and, according to legend, its own witch, Mollen, who, balding and with but one tooth, roams the nights on a broom-stick on the look-out for any naughty boys.

As it happens I remember this place some fifteen centuries ago when it was just grass and woodland and St Illtyd arrived here to found the first university in the country. 'Now this Illtyd was the most learned of all Britons in his knowledge of the Scriptures, both the Old and New Testaments and in every branch of philosophy, poetry and rhetoric, grammar and arithmetic; and he was most wise and gifted with the power of foretelling future events.'

He also had the typical medieval saint's rapport with animals. Once, upset by the constant racket made by the crows, he gathered them together in his church and imposed a vow of silence on them. He also gave shelter to a stag fleeing from King Meridian and, thereafter, the stag stayed with him.

But his greatest glory was his university. Three thousand students were here, accommodated in seven halls. Eight hundred small cells were built on this spot, surrounded by the ditch and mound which comprised the sacred enclosure. They also built a tiny wooden church for prayer and meditation adapting the old regime of *laus perennis*—praise without end, which I had helped St David to introduce into his own monastery. The students were divided into twenty-four groups with each group responsible for one hour of worship and adoration, ensuring that my insomniac Father heard ceaseless praise all around the clock.

Education is important to the Christian ethic in a way it isn't to the Hindu or Buddhist. In education the Christian believes that the student can discipline his mind and creative imagination; he can come to terms with all his choices and choose sensibly; he can shape his imagination which will then take him out beyond the stars and enable him to become his own creator who will, in his turn, mirror the God who first created him. In fine education the Christian is finely released.

So the people who first came here to the university of the saints were, in a sense, the first to be released in an age of Druidical darkness. These were the first evangelicals called to do battle with the evil ignorance of an age. They were a mixture of poets, beggars and members of royalty. Three saints came here from Brittany—Samson of Dol, Gildas and Paul Aurelian—who, in turn, went back home to talk about the work of St Illtyd which is why his name is attached to so many Breton churches.

My Waterman also studied here as did St Patrick who was kidnapped here by a gang of Picts and taken off as a slave to Slemish. I would have intervened on Patrick's behalf but they ordered me not to bother. There was a lot of important work for Patrick to do in Ireland, it seemed, and anyway, by this time, Victor had been called up to look after him. Victor had even less of a clue of where Ireland was than I had of Wales. 'Island, what island? Hasn't the place even got a name?'

Today there's almost nothing left of Patrick's old university. It survived up until the Norman conquest but, apart from a few memorial stones and Celtic stone crosses, there are only a few mounds. But the church is spacious and lovely enough, set in a gully next to a stream with a neat cemetery dotted with palm trees.

There was a thick, low-lying mist when I was there and I was just sitting on the church's roof trying to re-create the old university in my mind's eye when I picked up some distant rumbles and shouts. At first I though it must be another of those jets since St Athan's RAF camp is nearby but those noises weren't at all mechanical and getting louder all the time. It would have helped if I could have seen something but the mist was now so thick I could barely see the palm trees in the cemetery below me let alone anything else.

The noises came closer and yet closer when, from right out of the mist, two pairs of interlocking wings went screaming past with all the burliness and authority of an express train at full speed. But it wasn't a coherent scream since, within it, were further sounds like wooden balls knocking over skittles in an alley. Whoosh, bang, whoosh, bang, bang, bang. I followed the noise at a discreet distance, careful not to get involved since, apart from the clear fact that it was one of us fighting a dark angel, I couldn't make out who either of them were.

Now the storm of sound was moving in the direction of Bridgend and, even though the mists were lifting slightly, barely all I could see were the thrashing tips of those wings revolving around and around one another. It wouldn't even have helped much if I had decided to get involved, particularly with my sword, since they were fighting at such close quarters and it was still so misty I could easily end up damaging the wrong side.

Whoosh, bang, whoosh, bang, bang, bang. The swirling dogfight began heading back towards the Bristol Channel with those fighting wings almost the length of small church spires. It was only when I began picking up the unmistakeable noises of wild tartan yells that I understood that this could be no other than Macmac. But what was he doing down here all the way from Scotland? And why was he scrapping on my patch?

But, much like Sorroptus, Macmac did so love scrapping with dark angels. It never crossed his mind to take out his sword and go for the quick finish. His idea of the most wonderful party was a twenty four hour fight with some luckless dark angel and here he was doing what he loved more than anything under heaven itself, rolling over the top of towns and farmyards, absolutely knocking the stuffing out of the opposition. Whoosh, bang, whoosh, bang.

Then the epicentre of the fight wheeled around again and they went crashing down the coastline until they passed over Barry Island with its holiday camp and funfair. Fortunately it was too damp and misty for many to be out on the sands even if a man out walking his dog did look up wondering what the hell was going on as his dog whimpered and cowered beneath his legs. But it wasn't so much the noise as the huge clumps of displaced air by those huge flapping wings that must have been the most bewildering. You don't expect to see small sandstorms on a beach on such a still, windless day but there they were billowing right up to the stone ramparts of the promenade. Seagulls rose up off the sands and flew away in alarm.

Somewhere down near Sully Island the dark angel clearly managed to shake off Macmac's assault and took off directly into the air in a long curving black flash. I came down slowly on to the island where I spotted Macmac sitting on a cliff edge, out of breath and grumbling to himself.

'Long time no see,' I said sitting down next to the tartan terror. 'What's going on then?'

'Oh, there you are. We've been looking all over for you. Where've you been?'

'I've been around. What's going on?'

'They've been shifting us around, that's what's going on. Lucy has been moving his troops and we've been told to wander around and find out what's what. I caught this one up near the Brecon Beacons and we've had one hell of a fight.'

'So I saw. But what's the matter with Scotland?'

'Nothing at all. They just told us to move around a bit. There's a build-up of those darkies going on and they think it might be in South Wales. But they don't know where and they're not sure.'

'Well I've not picked anything up,' I said feeling tense as I looked down at the brown waves breaking against the rocks. An old oil drum was bobbing up and down on the sea and, further along again, were two white polythene cartons. So it was clear, after all, that we were moving into the final days. We had always been promised that everything and everyone— particularly the opposition—would get lively in the final days. They had always told us that the build-up of evil would be terrific in the final days.

'They're around all right. They're around.'

'So what do you suppose I should do? I'm nearly through with my report.'

'Carry on man. Carry on. But they want to know immediately you spot any big build up of those darkies. Immediately do you hear? Are you coming up to Edinburgh for the rugby next year are you?'

'I might. Depends what happens down here.'

'Well, if I don't see you before, I'll see you then.'

# Tenth Book

The blue sky was clear of everything but hard sunshine and passing electronic signals as I banked up high in the air and just hung there, propped up by my flame, looking down at the three rivers—the Ely, the Rhymney and the Taff—all glittering with refracted sunshine as they rolled down through the main body of the city of Cardiff towards the Bristol Channel. As the three rivers threw off all this light they seemed to make the whole city float on a golden magic carpet. The city always looks at her best at this time of the year—with the seasons on the cusp—as she prepares herself for the rigours of autumn with her body still throbbing with the afterglow of summer.

From way up here everything was in splendid miniature and the large white buildings of the Edwardian civic centre looked like the white Legoland creation of some giant who would be returning at any second to move his toy cars and shoppers around the tiny, clean streets. There was also the improbable castle, the national stadium and all those outlying semi-detached suburbs where everyone had their 2 point 4 children and washed their cars on Sundays. The spiritual life of these suburbs is not exactly dead but nearly so. In the whole rather posh suburb of Rhiwbina I've only ever picked up the odd drifting smoke of a few lonely prayers and they were usually only for the success of some obscure Welsh book or other. There are a lot of poor writers in Rhiwbina.

Further out the three rivers were coming together in the city's dockland and rolling on into the Bristol Channel, creating huge rolling artefacts of pure light in the still sea and setting the ships and distant shoreline on a mesmerising bed of mazey, smoking silver. A one-legged seagull glided beneath me on motionless wings, shrieking loudly and neurotically the seagull news of the hour. There's nothing, anywhere, as batty as seagulls.

A brilliant last gasp of sunshine is usually part of summer's endgame at this time of year since, after weeks of drizzle, the schools' summer holiday is over and the children have to return to hot, airless classrooms with windows bright with the yellow glare of the sun. This is the time the luckless children look vacantly at Sir explaining the mysteries of maths as they daydream of being out in the streets robbing banks with guns, beating up their enemies. The playgrounds, during the morning and afternoon breaks, are alive with the leaps of hop scotch, whirling skipping ropes and the electronic buzzings of Game Boy.

This is also the time of conkers, those small shiny horse chestnuts that were named after me and, out in the many city parks, little boys and grown men with excited, barking dogs were busy throwing sticks up into the trees. Their rude sticks ripped into the branches and sometimes fell straight back to clout the throwers on the heads.

The recent rain showers had stirred the lakes and brooks in the parks too, making them sing, gurgle and flicker with iridescent tongues of light. On one willow bank in Roath Park two young lovers kissed and, out in the lake, fat carp rose to the surface to get more oxygen. A down and out, sitting alone on a park bench, with a flagon of cider parked safely behind his boots, muttered the truth of his lonely madness to himself.

All around the shopping centre there were lots of office girls in short skirts, shoppers with bulging bags and buskers setting alight corners with their golden showers of music. Today there was a wood-pipe mourning the loss of the mountains; a saxophone telling of smokey nights in dark jazz cellars and a hippy screeching Bob Dylan's 'Tambourine Man', probably for the millionth time, in a voice torn apart by a life of busking and special fags. Pigeons burbled noisily in the eaves of the market and clattering footsteps echoed down through the shopping arcades. New autumn styles were appearing in the shop windows while the house flies were slowing down in their thousands, braining themselves against windows and ending up dead on dusty sills with their little legs sticking up in the air.

Drifting down next to the Gothic spires of the castle I saw a salmon take a leap in the River Taff just in front of the weir in the castle grounds. Now here was a thing. This river has been dead for almost a century due to the coal silt from some eighty washeries up in the Rhondda valleys. The silt clogged up the fish gills and shut out the light. Then the plants and insects died. But now, with the demise of the coal pits, this river has become clear and clean again with a thick swarm of mullet coming up with the tides to feed in the centre of the city. The mullet moved through the dark, waving weeds when they were revealed in a sudden spotlight of shifting sunshine and people on the bridge were so happy to see them they nudged one another and pointed and wanted to wade out into the river and shake them by the hand. River wardens now watch over the fish closely since they face a new danger of poachers with plastic shopping bags.

A few Mallard ducks mooch around on these waters too and further upstream there's usually a watchful heron. Occasionally there is the blue flash of a hunting kingfisher and bobbing cormorants have returned to feed on sticklebacks. Even the odd otter has been re-colonising these once-foul city banks.

This same Indian summer was also sending its gaudy platoons of light scaling the large white buildings of the civic centre with its museum, city hall, law courts, university and Temple of Peace. Flower beds, as formal as drilling guardsmen, surrounded these sculptured Portland stone cliffs and, down next to the police station, a young lad smashed the windows of a parked BMW and made off with a black leather jacket.

Atop the city hall was a splendid stone dragon with talons outstretched and mouth forking fire. This building, perhaps the most triumphant expression of the former coal capital of the world, was built at a cost of two million pounds and many workmen's lives. As soon as it was built people came from all over the world to marvel at the English renaissance clock tower, its statuary of the veiled ladies of the four winds and the four golden dials of the clock itself. All five bells, made from the finest gun metal and tunes to give the hours and Westminster quarters, were dedicated to God.

But inside the city hall, on this Indian summer's day, the air was sepulchral cool, with shivering swords of sunshine slashing across the marble halls and stone staircases. Men in peaked caps hung around in corners watching out for whatever men in peaked caps watch out for. Over there was a bronze memorial to Captain Scott who sailed from Cardiff on the Terra Nova for his doomed expedition to the Antarctic.

Upstairs is another place I like to visit at night since there are a dozen or so statues in the Marble Hall called the Heroes of Wales. As you might expect St David is here with his hands outstretched as is Owain Glyndŵr, Dafydd ap Gwilym and my old *bete noir*, Bishop William Morgan. The likenesses aren't all that good—Bishop Morgan, in particular, was far more pugnacious and square-faced than he is portrayed here—but the spirit of these old Welsh warriors is undoubtedly there and sometimes I lie on the floor of the Marble Hall in the middle of the night and call out to them with my spirit.

This is no way for a rational angel to be carrying on, I know, but my mind and imagination can often conjure with the old dragon spirits with a few visual aids like this. I can even get the statues to move on their plinths and come alive with the spirit of Welsh Wales, reprising some great old sermon or indulging in a wild poetic flight. You should have heard them all on some nights. Dafydd ap Gwilym used to make a hell of a racket; I had clean forgotten quite what a boisterous Bohemian sort he was.

But I haven't tried that little spiritual conjuring trick with these statues for some twelve years now since it got out of hand one night and I had to put a stop to it. The suits always warned us about the dangers of trying any of those Ouija board tricks with anything at all and, for once, they were right. One night I brought their spirits spinning up from out of their prisons of white Serravera marble but, instead of behaving in the normal way, they all entered into some pre-arranged symphony of anguish. I'd never heard anything quite like it; a positive storm of grief and loss which, of course, was led by none other than Bishop William Morgan. The nation always dies in her heart at the end, he kept saying. When the nation's heart fails that's the end of her and her people. Even my Waterman was letting out the most terrible moans and I had never once heard him complain about anything at all. Not once. No nation in the world can keep going when her heart has failed.

They knew, of course; these old Welsh heroes understood all too well what's going wrong with this lost and wandering tribe of theirs.

But the architectural jewel in the city's crown is undoubtedly the great castle whose dull grey stones were now framed in this Indian summer splendour. Oh there's been strange goings on in this castle over the years but no one was ever quite so strange as the third Marquess of Bute who, thanks to coal, was once the richest man in the world. Together with the architect William Burges—and not a little help from opium—he created this fairyland castle with all its medievalism and expensive exoticisms. I can't say that I ever really had much to do with this strange man of ice and flame. He was religious but far too arrogant and rude for my taste. There was also one hell of a skeleton dancing around in his cupboard.

Now I suppose I had better be careful in blowing so many deep Welsh secrets but I think I'll open the door on this particular skeleton just slightly if only because it's fun. A lot of fun.

Basically what old Butey had done was take this mouldering Norman heap and, in 1865, turn Burges loose on it with an unlimited supply of money. What they would both do was meet up, smoke a quiet pipe of opium together and hatch the most extravagant designs by sketching them out on long rolls of paper. Burges's job was then to translate these opium visions into reality. He built towers where there were none. There was a Chaucer Room with designs inspired by Chaucer's books; a summer smoking room built in a zodiac clock tower; a lavish Arab Room with a ceiling covered with gold leaf and a huge library with books in every language except the one Butey hated above all other—Welsh. Fabulous designs and symbols of such as griffins were dotted on every wall and in every corner. Burges's trademark was a mouse and there were enough around here to start another plague.

The outside of the castle was smothered with vines to make wine and there was a real vine growing up out of the middle of the dinner table so that Madame could pick herself a fresh grape at the end of her meal. They even had the first central heating system in the land installed in the legs of the tables.

But, perhaps predictably, Butey, with his fine porcelain features and hollow cheekbones, was one of the unhappiest men alive. Some nights I dropped in on him and found him prowling the battlements and looking out over the city as he nursed his breaking heart. It was our old friend luurve again since this, the richest man in the world, had done nothing less than fall for one of the tarts down in the dockland. He visited her when he could but his wife—a cold and frightening woman who hated the Welsh as much as she hated this damp castle—kept him on tight lead. She did go to Deauville on her own for a spot of gambling and he really enjoyed himself with his tart down in Tiger Bay for two or three weeks. But all that came to an end when the harridan returned, usually having dropped enough money in the casinos to have kept a Welsh mining village in food for a year or two.

Then old Butey would be back on his battlements again, torn up with jealousy and pain particularly if he began thinking of any sailors who might be visiting his tart while he was stuck up here. Sometimes these pains were so severe he would squeal mutely up into the battlement night as if he had been gagged. Huge tears would also well up in his steely grey eyes which he would dab piteously with an antique silk handkerchief.

Now there have been occasions when I've been moved to fix a broken heart and, as I've indicated before, this has always been one of my specialities. But I could never do anything for daft old Butey. I never wanted to do anything for him come to that. In all justice he got exactly what he deserved since he never had the courage to break away from this million-pound Camelot with his frigid, tyrannical bitch queen and go to live with his heart's desire.

The trouble was that his heart's desire lived in one of the tackiest hovels in the docks and it was in such a state of dilapidation that even her bedroom had a big hole in the ceiling through which rain and sunshine poured in generous measures. She did once ask him for the money to fix the hole but he said that it would spoil the effect—whatever that was. You see what I mean? For all his money he was as mad as a hatter. Mills and Boon it wasn't, that was for sure.

But in the end he did what so many men, trapped in loveless marriages and wanting to be elsewhere, have done before him. He turned to drugs in a big way. There was one man, a retired Customs officer by the name of Pryce, whose sole job it was to keep a fresh and lively supply of opium coming into the castle. Pryce travelled the world looking for the best opium and it transpired that there was none better than could be bought in Burma. This Burmese opium was so good that Butey got high merely by looking at it and it wasn't too long before he was getting into it so regularly that he began looking like some forlorn wreck in a Shanghai opium den.

It had to be the strangest way for anyone to end up—let alone the richest man in the world. There would be his harridan of a wife, with her fancy jewels and ill-fitting wig, going down to the oratory to see if the master had finished his prayers and wanted his dinner. And there would be the master stretched out on the chapel floor, rosary in one hand and opium pipe in the other, stoned out of his skull and smack in the middle of some opium fantasy which almost always involved his dockland tart and their most romantic hole in the ceiling.

'Are you ready for something to eat, darling?' she asked him when he was in this condition one day.

'Not just now sweetness,' he replied after a lot of stoned mumbling and looking up at her with a wild, yellow look in his eyes. 'We're just waiting for the rain to come in through the ceiling.'

'The rain to come in through the ceiling?' she shrieked, getting all bilious in an instant. 'You've spent two million pounds on this awful castle and you still can't stop rain coming in through the ceiling. Let's go back to Scotland before I end up as mad as you.'

'After the rain has stopped, my sweetness. Let's just enjoy the rain.'

Anyway all that opium was too much for him and his addled brain in the end. He had wasted away so much he could have been carried away in a shoe box. When he did die, according to family custom, his body was buried in Scotland and his heart—what little there was left of it—was put in the family crypt in Jerusalem. More out of curiosity than anything I went to check out the family crypt one day and found that some Arab cigarette seller had set a stall in it.

There is a moral in all this but I can't quite work out what it is.


But today, just before noon, the splendid city pubs were beginning to fill up with the usual characters sitting in their usual corners. In the Old Arcade there was Nobby wearing a fine red dickey-bow and a party hat. You can always tell he's inside the bar because he always leaves a supermarket trolley, full of his possessions, outside. Then there might be Kung Fu Joe walking around and threatening to karate chop everyone in sight and you could always pick him out because he's usually got an arm or leg in plaster after being beaten up by someone who didn't see the funny side of his kung fu joke. Lots of former rugby internationals like Barry John hang around here in the bar also as does One O'Clock Bill who always starts an uproar at the stroke of one o'clock.

Outside, the street traders were flogging off whatever rubbish had fallen off the back of a passing ship and, just near the market, was the lovely St John's Church.

Cardiff has always been a well-churched and chapeled city and, over the years, I've had the pleasure of listening to such as Howell Harris, George Whitefield and John Wesley preaching here. Wesley, in particular, could give a wonderful sermon but, quite frankly, he was a bit too much of a prude for my taste. 'Yes, there can be dancing,' he said on one memorable occasion. 'But the men must dance with the men, the women with the women and it must be daylight and out of doors.'

Evan Roberts would never come to Cardiff, always complaining, with some justification, that the place was full of devils. They tried again and again to get him to speak here and again and again he agreed, only to drop out at the last minute claiming that the Holy Spirit had warned him off. The Holy Spirit had done no such thing of course: Evan was just a country boy who feared the big city.

I've always found it rather amazing to see the way the city has grown and developed with such commercial confidence since I remember it as a decidedly dim little place of dovecotes and scattered cottages with cows wandering down the unmade streets and fishermen in coracles working the river. There were two monasteries here: Grey Friars (Fransciscan) and Black Friars (Dominican) which, as far as I could work out, had abandoned the idea of prayer altogether. Everything revolved around the castle, of course, and I don't suppose I ever had so much as a spot of bother here from one century to the next.

There was one real headache in the middle of the sixteenth century in the shape of an appalling bishop who, despite the Reformation, could never quite decide if he was for or against

Rome. Bishop Kitchen was his name and he was nothing more than a gangster really, forever selling off Church assets to support all his whores and bastard children and ready to run before any stray ecclesiastical wind that suited him. He could even have been Lucy's first lieutenant of any note in Wales. Why they never allowed us to cook someone's goose by just letting them fall down several high flights of stairs I don't know. If I did mention anything like that they would say that's not the way we do things in God's army and I knew that I'd blown any chances of getting another stripe for another few hundred years.

Anyway, as if all that wasn't bad enough, Bishop Kitchen decided to set up his own little Inquisition, complete with a stretching rack that some dolt had brought back for him as a present from Spain. No sooner had he got this rack than he also found this poor fisherman Rawlins White, a devout Protestant and regular apple of any Lutheran eye. White was soon being stretched on this rack with the bishop calling on him to swear his allegiance to Rome.

White's prayers summoned me to his side immediately and I'd never heard such cries of pain. You could actually hear his bones splintering on that rack and I told him to tell the bishop anything he wanted to hear. White wasn't having any of that. He was one of those simple souls who believed what he believed and that was the end of it. In his boots I would have gone straight for some slippery pragmatism, but there you are.

This harrowing business went on for days and the bishop even got some thumbscrews from somewhere. I've never known anyone be tortured so much and I would have put an end to it in a second had Rawlins asked me, but he had his eyes firmly on martyrdom and there was nothing I could do about that. I did what I could to relieve his pain but he wasn't going to bend the knee to the Pope—no matter how many of his joints snapped—and quite soon the disappointed bishop could see that there was no point in pursuing the matter any further.

Rawlins White got burned at the stake for heresy in the end—right on that spot where that street trader is busy selling towels near St John's Church. Even when he was almost a cinder he was still refusing to acknowledge the authority of the Pope but, in one of life's sick ironies, it was only a few months before that gargoyle bishop decided that he wasn't going to be obedient to Rome after all and went back to Canterbury. There were the strangest people running around Wales in the middle of the sixteenth century, I can tell you, and they were all running around inside the church.

But, needless to say, Rawlins White had one of the most astonishing welcomes ever in heaven. Anyone burned at the stake for his faith was guaranteed a good reception in heaven, no matter what side he was on, but so many cherubim and seraphim turned out for Rawlins that it quite took my breath away. Even Michael put in an appearance for that arrival and nodded at me before I took the fisherman in to see God. There's not many times I've ever seen Michael throughout my career and that was about the only time that he had ever acknowledged my existence.

But for every great success there's always a great failure isn't there? Certainly one of the biggest mistakes of my career— apart from getting posted to Wales in the first place—was made in connection with Cardiff and its Llandaff Cathedral. I still run the events of that dreadful night through my mind again and again, wondering how it all could have been so different. I've never really been able to work out if it was my fault, as they subsequently decided when they put me on a fizzer, but almost every second of that dreadful night is still vivid in my mind.

Llandaff cathedral was an old favourite of mine and was first founded by St Teilo as a small church way back in the time of St David. Teilo had been much inspired by our trip together to Jerusalem and, no sooner had he got back to West Wales than he told David that he had work in South Wales. This small church at Llandaff was his first building.

It finally fell into ruin but the invading Normans rebuilt it as a symbol of psychological domination and Urban, the first Norman bishop, arranged for the bones of St Dyfrig to be brought down here from the island of Bardsey thus making him the first Bishop of Llandaff and providing the shrine with some authentic relics to attract pilgrim money. To be perfectly honest I don't know whose bones they did bring to Llandaff but they certainly weren't Dyfrig's. Not that it mattered much. All those shrines in those days were nothing if not symbolic. Between all of them they had enough bits of the true cross for Noah to build himself a new ark and, if I told you where some of those 'holy' bones had really come from and whose bones they actually were, you just wouldn't believe me. The best that could be said of some of those 'holy' bones was that they would have made a good glue.

But St Dyfrig, let's remember, was a big name at that time who enjoyed star status in medieval legend since he had also been the Archbishop of Caerleon who had crowned King Arthur. He was the 'Dubic, the high saint, chief of the church in Britain' in Tennyson's 'Coming of Arthur'. His chapel still stands on the left of the cathedral's altar, an enchanting spot of old shadows and stained glass.

But even after the Normans sorted the building out it had endless problems over the years, being torn apart by storms and earthquakes and once used as a beer house for Cromwell's troops. The chapter library books were burned and the font became a pig trough. In 1656 troops shot at some parishioners taking communion in the Lady Chapel and, in 1703, a storm brought the tower tumbling down through the roof. The nave walls collapsed too and, soon, ivy was growing over the sad rubble prompting one to describe it as 'this poor, desolate church of Llandaff'.

It was restored yet again in the eighteenth century and then got into trouble once more during the Second World War.

As I have mentioned before that war was a most frustrating time for us angels since they told us to stay out of it. Now it's not for us to question their orders so that's more or less what

238

we did. Not that we exactly went to sleep, of course. We were still obliged to listen out for—and respond to—prayer; still expected to shepherd the faithful in trouble and still supposed to act as agents for God's goodness and love wherever and whenever we could as long as we didn't interfere with the war. Yet they did give us one direct order—watch out for any cathedrals on your patch.

Sorroptus watched over St Paul's in London for almost the whole duration of the war; in fact that's about all he did watch over since, come D-day, St Paul's was virtually the only building left standing in London after all those destructive nights of the Blitz. He either hung directly over it during the air raids with his great wings outstretched or else he actually caught those land mines on their little green parachutes and moved them over a bit to drop into the Thames or somewhere else out of harm's way. I must admit that the work called for marvellous and sustained patience—with not a little skill—and Sorroptus was duly decorated for all his efforts on behalf of the Cathedral Guard when the war was over.

Yours truly, on the other hand, got busted for his efforts on behalf of the Cathedral Guard. There are various ways of looking at the whole business but I suppose I have to admit that, when all's said and done, I cocked it up.

There were really three cathedrals that I had to worry about in Wales—St David's, St Asaph's and Llandaff. But there was almost no threat to St David's or St Asaph's during the war—apart from the remote possibility of the Luftwaffe losing their way to Liverpool and dropping off most of their load before coming home—so I concentrated most of my Cathedral guard duties on Llandaff here.

Yet before I explain what happened I had better say now that I did misjudge the difficulties of moving around the city skies at a time of war. All those barrage balloons didn't help, of course, and neither did all that pounding ack-ack which kept giving me a headache. But my main difficulty came from the rapidly changing light—or, to be more precise, the lack of it.

Flight for me is not as easy as it might sound—even with my flame and exploding rings. In fact all my flying apparatus is finely tuned to the light and so it follows that, if there are rapid changes of light or complete darkness, then so too adjustments have to be made in my flying apparatus which are often dispositional but not always so. Sometimes I do have to think quite hard about flying adjustments. It's not like driving a car.

So, during the war, I was actually having to think a lot because there was always a black-out at night and I never had so much as a candle flame or bicycle lamp to work with. Every move had to be thought about and the point about thought is that it slows you down. Thought can also affect your spatial ability and awareness.

But then, when you're moving around at night in a war, everything can change with a flaming incendiary or the sudden appearance of whirling searchlights trying to pick up passing planes. We're only talking nano-seconds here but even a nano-second is extremely important to an angel's efficiency as will soon become clear.

Anyway we come to the night of January 2, 1941, which was clear and star-studded and, in many ways, good for flying around in. The air raid sirens began blaring over the city roof-tops and I rose up over them, stretching my wings out wide and limbering up for a busy night.

I suppose I had better also clarify a small matter at this point. They did tell me to watch out for the cathedrals and I'm sorry—I am very sorry indeed—but there was no way I was going to hover over that cathedral while the rest of the city was getting bombed to bits. I've never understood how Sorroptus could do it but it just wasn't in my nature to sit back and watch my capital burned to toast particularly when the Germans began sending down their land mines on parachutes and I found that I could clear away whole bundles of them from different parts of the city without too much difficulty.

This was my flock after all even if I always took particular care to keep the cathedral within my sight.

At around six o'clock a shower of incendiaries came down on Queen Street and Tudor Road and I darted around doing what I could even if my flight was very jerky and uncertain as I got to grips with all these high walls of fiery light. Then the searchlights came on and I was easily able to pick up most of the drifting land mines on their parachutes. I shoved them that way and this but couldn't pick them all up because I also had to keep my eyes on that cathedral spire.

Then another wave of Luftwaffe bombers moved across the sky and I don't suppose that I have ever been busier throughout my career, flashing across the houses and pushing the bombs out into the parks or guiding them down into rivers, even leaving a few dangling up a tree while also trying to keep a weather eye on the buildings in the civic centre. But even so I had to miss out on quite a few and they went on to kill a total of 156 that night with 427 injured. There would have been a lot more deaths if I hadn't been skidding around frantically that night and that's a fact.

As the death toll rose then so did my panic and, spotting three land-mines drifting down towards the suburb of Fairwater, I dashed straight for them, catching two of them by the parachutes and taking them out to the river Ely when I turned to face yet another incendiary ball of flame.

It was a nano-second—and maybe two—but, as soon as I had made my flying adjustments and got through the flame, I saw that they had hit the cathedral on the south wall. I hadn't even spotted the mines coming down and it was just sheer ill luck that the incendiary had gone off at precisely that second. Sheer ill luck.

What was left of the cathedral was a hell of a mess and I hovered over it bleakly, feeling the fall-out of the explosion still in the air and watching the masonry still tumbling this way and that, as I wondered what kind of deep trouble I had got in now. Some angels had got Beirut for far less than this.

But, as it turned out, my punishment was far more subtle and far-reaching than even I had thought possible. I lost my only stripe and they confined me to barracks in Megiddo over the next Christmas period. But then, rather more omniously, they also told me that my real punishment would come when Llandaff cathedral was rebuilt.

I didn't know what they were talking about at the time but it soon became clear when they re-built it on its present spot in a deep hollow surrounded by the graveyard. Around the outside wall they restored the small carvings of sovereigns' heads beginning with Richard III and going right on to Elizabeth II. It is said that, when the walls are full, there will be no more kings and queens of England. Medieval and nineteenth century features were also carefully restored but then came the rub. They decided to break with the past and, where the medieval builder had once put his rood-screen between nave and sanctuary, they stuck up this enormous parabolic arch of reinforced concrete. As if that wasn't bad enough they then pinned on this arch a huge unpolished aluminium sculpture of The Boss, otherwise known as Sir Jacob Epstein's Majestas.

And it's there now—as it will be forever and ever—a permanent reminder of my inability to take orders and stand guard on a cathedral when I'm told. The Shame of Conker, they should call that sculpture, something I'll always have to live with. Ah, if only people of Wales knew the whole story. If only they knew the half of it ...

This Indian summer's day was beginning to break up over the city but, even so, it was still surprisingly warm as I stood under the railway bridge at the north end of Bute Street. Girls on high heels went clattering down the pavement and every now and then a train rumbled overhead. The smell of brewing beer hung in the leaden air and the occasional ship's hooter echoed over the rooftops.

Of all the strange areas in my strange patch I was now on the edge of the strangest of them all. Tiger Bay, the popular

Press once dubbed it; a bopping Hell's Acre, full of clamour and surprises, with so many competing faiths and sheer contradictions that it often baffled even my intelligence. I still like to take a regular swing down through the Bay but I'm never sure what I'm going to find or who I'm going to meet. I've bumped ito the strangest of angels down here: caterwauling divas and rip-roaring characters like nothing you've ever seen in the pages of the Bible.

But, on the other hand, I've also come across whole pockets of unexpected tenderness in this unique, multi-racial community. I've enjoyed services with the Sikhs and the Moslems. I've attended the Vespers of Love with the Greeks and kneeled with chanting Buddhists. Oh they've always had the lot down here and I've enjoyed them all. Angels never lay claim to exclusive authority over forms of worship and have no truck with religious rivalry of any sort. We understand that God's people can deal with religious truth in any way they apprehend it. A few faiths—no names, no pack drill—have gone up the pole to be sure but never too much so. Even in the most eccentric of faiths you will always find the fingerprints of the one true God if you look hard enough. The real differences are almost always in the trimmings.

I suppose that almost the first thing you would have to say about the Bay is that it has a marked physical isolation form the rest of the city. Just standing near this bridge at the top of Bute Street you could see that it was fenced in by a railway line on one side, the River Taff on the other and the Pier Head and the Bristol Channel down the bottom. Even the iron stolidity of this bridge seemed to underscore the Bay's sense of isolation and, in a sense, this bridge has always been a sort of Welsh Checkpoint Charlie.

I've known this area right from its tumultuous beginnings. Every nook and cranny has been familiar to me and I've seen things so foul down here that I would never put them in any report. But, just walking down from the bridge and into the Bay itself, even I can find it difficult to remember the old order of things since the demolition ball has wiped out whole communities and streets. All around weeds are flourishing in rubbled wastelands and the old terraces have been replaced by the sheds of light industry.

Irish Town—gone. The old Salvation Army hostel—gone. The Charleston Club—gone. The Cairo Cafe—gone. The Adelphi pub—gone. All of it ... gone, gone, gone.

Most of the houses are new with many disfigured by those foul satellite dishes each as distinctive as the mark of Cain. There's also those wretched video shops which still get me gagging and feeling faint if I'm not careful. Right over there are the twin towers of Loudon Square flats—built in the Sixties—and now abandoned by everyone except students, the unemployed and the similarly desperate.

But even without its old suit the body is much the same. There's still a thriving community here in which three generations of some fifty nationalities have come together to fight and love one another. Ah yes, there's never been anywhere quite like the Bay and that's a fact.

I remember the time before the turn of the century when the docks were full of windjammers and dozens of paddle steamers came pounding in and out of the Pier Head. Bute Street in particular was always amok with tradesmen and sailors, musicians and prostitutes, all going about their business to the sound of rattling trams. The Quebec pub just by here had some wonderful barrelhouse jazz and it was in there that I first formed my love for jazz. The smells of chop suey drifted out of the Chinese block and there would be a couple of fat prostitutes joking with some yobs from Swansea as gossiping women and washing hung out of the windows and snot-nosed kids teased sailors long gone mad outside the Mosque ... It's all still here ... somewhere ...

Directly past the new Salvation Army hostel is the long low scar which was once the Glamorganshire Ship Canal. Barrel-chested, sweating horses used to pull barges piled high with iron and coal along this canal. The first on the right is Greek Church Street which still has its impressive Greek Orthodox

244

Church, just about all that's left of a flourishing Greek community. I often like to sit in on the services here, particularly the beautifully-named Vespers of Love at Easter. I can't say that I ever understood what was going on but, there again, who ever understood what was going on in a Greek service? The minister, Father Anastias Salaptos, still lives here with his family.

'The Greeks first established a community in Cardiff in 1873,' he will tell you. 'This church was built in 1906 and, with a Greek ship coming in every day, the whole community established itself around it. But by 1960 the work stopped and so did the ships; now we get one ship a month. My people here have moved out into all parts of South Wales.'

Every colour and nationality pitched up in Bute Street with barely a shilling in their pockets and a gambler's hope in their hearts. In No 157 Bute Street, according to Kelly's Directory, there was Michael Eraklis, hairdresser; no 159—Miss N. Lavinski, seaman's outfitter; 106—Louis Fenech, cafe; 163—M. Kleanthous, boot and shoe repairer; 164—Cuban Cafe; 166—Seng Lee's laundry; 169 and 179—the Loudoun Hotel; 171—Rainbow Cafe; 172—Mediterranean Cafe; 173—Jack's Cafe; 174—Coronation Cafe.

They came running here from a world in turmoil. They were escaping from war, from tyrannies, from troubles with nagging wives and men in bowler hats. They poured in from boats and trains. Betty Hassan's father was a Somali who went through the First World War. Later he was in the navy and met her mother.

'Tiger Bay was a beautiful area to life in and there was no racial discrimination of any kind,' she remembered. 'There were Germans, Greeks, Jews, Norwegians and Dutch. You name it and they were here. The people were peaceful and you felt safe. Nobody ever bothered you. There are still a lot of Somali people here and the situation out there is very bad with the war going on. The president is no more than a Papa Doc and the people have to become free from that regime. There's also a lot of forgotten children in that forgotten war. They have no toys or clothes or anywhere to sleep. They are living rough and running between the war zones. I want to set up a children's village; something which will be theirs, not just the bush or a begging bowl.'

Ah the expression of concerned love has always been the sweetest music to my heart. There have been many grave and beautiful people in the Bay who have performed the gravest and most beautiful acts. Right here was the Rainbow Club where Shirley Bassey had her first singing date. The club for all the children of the Bay was founded by Margaret Capener who saw a rainbow forming over the city one day. She thought of the last line of D. H. Lawrence's The Rainbow and how it had come to represent a living, multi-coloured truth. 'There can be a rainbow,' she said.

But perhaps the real love story of the Bay, which tells everything about the great spirit of racial hope that the area came to represent, is told by Mrs Olive Salaman, a Welsh girl from the Valleys.

'I lived in the Rhymney Valley. There was no work about and I got a job in the Cardiff Royal Infirmary for one pound a month. I didn't go out for two months but one day went to the pictures in town and took a wrong turning when I came out. I ended up down in Bute Street and asked this man the way. This was Ali Salaman, the first coloured man that I had ever met. We married when I was 16 years and three weeks old. We had twelve children who are all married now with their own children. Only one of my children married a Moslem. The rest married every race going.

'I never knew a great deal about religion but came to love the Moslem faith. Ali was a good living man, a very religious man. He had three big warehouses in Bute Street and converted one into a Mosque. One Christmas Day these filthy tramps turned up wanting dinner. He told me to give it to them. "But Ali," I protested, "these men are filthy." But this Moslem insisted that was what Christmas was all about— giving to people like that.

'When he died everyone was there from the highest to the lowest. From the Cairo Cafe to the Empire Pool the police lined the streets and saluted his coffin. So who couldn't be a good Moslem married to a man like that? I was most fortunate in loving a man like him.'

The dark had settled her skirts over the dockland by this time with the orange sodium street lights neutralising every living colour all around them. Television sets flickered in the living rooms and, down on the corner near Custom House, the brilliant flare of a struck match highlighted a tart's face in a shop doorway as she lit a cigarette.

The Bay is not the same though; it's just not the same. Just roaming the darkness around Loudoun Square I could feel that there was something deeply and profoundly wrong and, down one dark alleyway next to the community centre, I spotted some scuffling shadows. They weren't the shadows of people either and, with my flame spurting softly, I prepared to draw my sword as I entered the alleyway, seeing nothing but hearing an amplified burst of wings coming from somewhere distant. I came out into Bute Park, doing one of my smoke 'n' mirrors movements as I crossed the grass over to the wall on the other side, appearing and re-appearing but still not picking anything up. The playground was empty with some litter and orange peel scattered near the swings. An old woman carrying an apidistra plant came walking out of the darkness. This was no place to be on her own but she seemed unconcerned so I tailed her until she got home safely just in case.

I crossed back over Bute Street, taking a quick look along the railway track and over at the dockland cranes. But I still couldn't find anything. I didn't like it at all; the whole area seemed to be lying under a long and growing shadow but I couldn't make out what it was. It was almost as if I could actually see the love draining out of this community like blood pouring out of a wound in someone's side—or hands—or feet.

But the law of love hasn't always ruled down here—far from it. A few hundred yards back up Bute Street used to be No 250—once a lodging house for West Indian seamen which later became the Charleston Club. No 250 Bute Street was also the scene of Britain's first race riot.

It was a hot Wednesday night on June 11, 1919. The First World War had ended and unemployment was high in Wales. In what became a time-honoured tradition, the Press was putting the blame on the twelve hundred black seamen who had settled in the Bay.

A gang of whites jumped a group of blacks in the city centre. Bystanders joined in. A shot rang out and a soldier was wounded. The blacks ran for the safety of the Bay and were chased by a gang of Army lads. Shots were fired by the bridge and running fights started all over the area. Three blacks ran into 250 Bute Street chased by some 20 whites who dragged them out and beat them up. Hysterical crowds roamed all over the Bay that night and a gun battle started. The police later confiscated a revolver, a razor, a pile of bludgeons and a length of brass wire with a plate on each end. Twelve men were charged. Fifteen were injured including a policeman. One man died.

The next day the local newspapers called for all blacks to be returned to America and the West Indies. A councillor also complained that they were actually being allowed out of the dockland and into respectable areas of the city.

These riots were just a small hiccup, of course, particularly if you compare them to later, more savage, riots in the Eighties in Brixton and Toxteth. But I remember thinking then—or at least feeling then—that I was actually watching the first dragon's teeth of violence being sewn on my very own patch. These riots were surely going to be a pointer to the future and those dark angels were almost certainly at work in there somewhere. But who really knows where a dark angel works? The evil within which dark angels work has always deceived almost everyone. Even I am never quite sure what they're up to or how they operate.

Having said that I've never actually caught a dark angel down here in the Bay but I am getting more and more uneasy that they are around all right. Those scuffling shadows could easily have been a couple of dark angels and futhermore I'm sure they're in all those flickering televisions; they're there in those satellite dishes and, somehow, they are deeply embedded in that long and growing shadow that I've been complaining about.

But come on now, Conker boy, shake it off. Let's press on and this report will be over sooner than you think.

Burt Bray, a staunch member of the Loudoun Square Methodist Church, has lived in the Bay for almost sixty years. He can recall other troubles here when he was a boy. 'I remember that there was some other trouble around 1924. They were employing cheap labour with the coloured seamen and getting rid of the whites. Policemen were stopping you going into the docks but it only lasted a week or so. I remember troops being billeted in some meat warehouses in Tresilian Terrace in case the situation broke down but it never did. I have always loved living in this area. I was superintendent of the Sunday School in Loudoun Square and used to run the Boys' Brigade. I met a man the other day who lives out in Llanrumney. He said he still remembered the songs I taught him in Sunday School. So we must have dropped the seed somewhere. My wife and I think that we were fortunate to have lived here. We wouldn't have wanted to have lived anywhere else.'

So we're getting the picture of the Bay as a giant bowl of minestrone which had everything thrown into it. The Italians brought ice cream and arias. The Chinese brought in laundry and chop suey. The Greeks had their kebabs and bouzoukis. The West Indians their mangoes and calypso.

But what art form is more eclectic and drawn from so many different cultures than the sound of my beloved jazz? Jazz was the burly sound of the Depression: a mixture of instruments and styles which came to speak so vividly of the variety of man. Virtually every pub down here thumped to its sound and it still lives on, particularly in funerals when old jazzers will be honoured with a band following the coffin playing that heartbreak of all heartbreaks: 'The Old Rugged Cross'.

If jazz is from anywhere at all, of course, it's from the West Indies. The West Indians have always loved its exuberance and shuffling rhythms. Some two thousand have come to live here, mostly from Jamaican backgrounds. As well as their own musical traditions they brought with them exciting forms of worship. Carleton Thomas is the minister of the Pentecostal Church in Angelina Street.

'A lot of the early elders of the church here found that they were not welcome. I don't know why. In the Caribbean the churches are alive but, when they got here, they couldn't find their kind of fellowship. They had to start their own prayer and Bible meetings. We are a Pentecostal group and preach the full Bible. It's a live Church led by the Holy Spirit. We believe in tongues, healing, deliverance from different problems. How we worship is an expression of what's inside. The idea is to care for the total person, the total man.'

Across the road from the Pentecostal Church is the Alice Street Mosque and it has to be said that the Moslems have had more than their fair share of troubles over the years. There was the time the local kids kept pinching their shoes and throwing them over the rooftops while they were at prayer. In the Fifties there was a huge row after they began slaughtering their sheep in the street since it was upsetting the children, some locals complained, not to mention the sheep. There was also another terrific row when the cemetery people could not—or would not—dig their graves facing Mecca.

They even got into bit row amongst themselves which got so bad over the years that the Moslem community split into two. This row was complicated and tied up with Middle Eastern politics although it officially began when one group claimed that the old Peel Steet Mosque did not face Mecca. They imported one of the biggest set of compasses in the world to resolve that dispute but they never did.

The Moslems in this Mosque gather here every day for zawya; chanting, prayer and the settling of disputes. The Imam sits in the corner intoning prayers from the Koran—Seven times a day do I praise your righteous judgements —and incense hangs above the thick carpets as the others stretch and submit themselves to the Inscrutable and Autocratic Majesty of Allah. One member faces Mecca and stands upright, the palms of his hands raised to the level of his ears. God is greater than all else. Arms lower and the right hand is placed over the left arm. Glory and praise to thee O God. Blessed is thy name and exalted is thy majesty. Body bends forward and hands are placed on knees. Glory to my Lord, the exalted. He kneels upright, lips muttering, eyes closed. Two flies are rising up and down the window above lots of other dead flies, sometimes buzzing fiercely before turning one another over and over. Quietly does it, the Moslems are praying ...

Sheikh Said Hassan is the Imam here who will tell visitors: 'I've been in Wales since 1941 but was born in South Shields in the Thirties. The Moslem community was not very well organised there and we worshipped in a converted pub. My father went away to sea during the last war and he lost his life so a religious leader from Cardiff took me there to learn the faith. My mother had been born in Wales and was a Christian who converted to Islam. Eventually I settled in Cardiff so I'm a bit of everything really—part Yemeni, part Welsh and part English.'

Yes, they all talk a lot about the old days down in the Bay. In fact, I've often observed that, the stickier the present becomes, the more they talk about the old days. The young—especially the Rastafarians—are taking up increasingly alienated stances which is bringing them into conflict with the law. It is no longer much fun representing the long arm of the law down here but it was not always so.

Sometimes I've come across an old Moslem angel when I've been down here and he also likes to talk about the old days. He's not too active any more and I've never been sure if he was ever issued with so much as a sword but I've occasionally bumped into him on the corner of Alice Street where he might be puffing on a cheroot as he talked about this and that.

'The main problem now is that the community has become ossified and there is little ambition or leadership,' he once said in the strangest of Cardiff accents. 'The old radicals are mute and the young are merely angry with their ideas becoming progressively more criminalised by a corrupt media. There is very little hope for them now and, where there is little hope, there is also a breeding ground for violence.'

He's just waiting around now, he will tell anyone who passes. But he never exactly spells out what it is that he is waiting for.

But, disappointingly, he wasn't on his usual spot that night since I would have loved to have discussed that ominous shadow that I had been feeling everywhere. He would have almost certainly known what I was talking about since the same angel had been around far longer than me. There was talk that he had even known Mohammed. But it was only talk.

By now the streets were dark and their silence was broken only by the odd ship's hooter. A man came out of the darkness and hurried across Bute Street when he disappeared again somewhere near the new Glamorgan County Hall. They are well into a new multi-million pound development on the site of the old docks, hoping to turn it into a new Venice. Some hope.

I was drifting down towards Mountstuart Square, the old commercial heart of the docks, when there was that strange sound again ... there was that scuffling business ... there was that scuff ... there was that ... Parts of my consciousness began flickering with light and dark shadows like an old movie that had come to the end of its reel. Reality began breaking down and I was going hot and cold and couldn't even seem to get the right words ... there was that scuffling ...

I turned and turned again, vainly trying to shake out my wings so that I could just fly somewhere safe and put myself together again. Next I tried my flame but nothing worked and I didn't seem to be able to move anywhere. All that happened was that I was finding myself encircled in an ever tightening darkness.

But then these dark circles fell away and, to my absolute horror, a woman's naked body rolled down in front of me in a brilliant pool of light. I turned my head away but forced myself to look at her again. There were cuts all over her; no, not cuts, stab wounds ... lots of stab wounds. I recoiled backwards unable to take any more of this deepening nightmare. Nothing like this had ever happened to me before and I didn't know what to do about it. Everything went dark again but then I seemed to be released and all was back to normal. But, come to think of it, there was something that could affect me like this ... but no. Steady on now Conker. Don't even think about it. A police car went past me with the smooth, escalating whine of changing gears.

Down here, I recalled with some effort, was George Street where the Spanish had once gathered. They called this place Little Madrid and the air was always full of the sounds of flamenco and laughing children particularly on fiesta days. But the demolition ball and English marriages soon put an end to this community.

And here was the massive Stock Exchange of Mountstuart Square; a kingdom now ruled by emptiness and weeds and a far cry from the days when gas lights sputtered in every corner and up to five hundred shipowners, jobbers and brokers worked the huge ornate wooden floor in the coal book which made the city what it became.

I moved on down towards the waterfront when it happened to me again: something falling on me and imprisoning me in circles of darkness. There were flashes of that stabbed body again and a slipstream of familiar laughter passed over my head. Ah, so it was becoming a little clearer. This time I managed to break out of the dark rings with one quick explosion of my gold rings. My fluttering wings were also at the ready as the flame drew my sword.

At my feet the tide was coming in and the whole basin was getting full to brimming in the moonlight. The wind was humming in the telephone wires overhead and the moored boats were rising up on the encroaching water. A newspaper moved past me slowly, going up on one side before falling over on the other like a slow-motion acrobat.

Just then my blood ran cold when I spotted them sitting out on the wooden mooring towers all along the side of the dock: six or seven dark angels just snoozing there, the most I have ever seen in one spot. This Himalayan range of evil was spread right along the several hundred yards of lapping water, all of them motionless except for the odd fluttering of their wings. The moonlight caught in the patches of slime underneath their roosts. What were they doing here? I swung my sword back and for in the air wondering what my chances were of getting them all—the one after the other—while they were asleep.

But then a large shadow swooped across the face of the moon and I knew that my chance of getting even two or three of them were remote since that was a dark angel flying around on sentry duty. They would never dream of leaving so many open to sudden attack, and if I moved on one, the sentry would certainly shout a warning and they would all be on me in a flash. The only sensible course of action seemed to be to make a strategic withdrawal and warn the others.

I had the feeling that these dark angels were all going to get their comeuppance soon but, in the meantime, I'm almost ashamed to say that, with a soft explosion of my gold rings, I slunk away like a thief in the night.

# Eleventh Book

Autumn had finally begun her great golden romp over the land and a market had been set up in the grounds of Chepstow race-course. I've always loved markets. Their exuberance, vitality and colour have barely changed over the centuries. Close your eyes and you could be in any tented market of the Middle Ages.

Crowds milled past stalls selling magnetic window cleaners, iron kitchenware, silver balloons, dance and party frocks, children's books and badges, cannabis-flowered T-shirts and women's nighties. Such markets are also a good guide to all the drek of the modern world from naughty underwear to cheap horror videos; from Coca Cola towels to jeans with Teenage Mutant Turtles stamped on them; from sweets of every description to clothes which will fall apart at the first wash. You will also notice how those skilful Indian entrepreneurs have completely taken over the leather and rag trades, laughing a lot in their stall but with their big, black eyes missing nothing. There is a lot of theft in modern markets but even Fagin's little apprentices would have been hard pushed to pinch anything from beneath those black eyes.

This stuff ain't been stolen, it just ain't been paid for. There were leather jackets, fur coats and trendy track suit bottoms. Today we ain't selling them, we're giving them away. Bodies pushed forward in anticipation of a 'never-to-be-repeated, once in a lifetime' bargain. A wailing child was given a good smack.

Don't unwrap these before you get home will you? Why not? Because they're rubbish that's why not.

The town of Chepstow itself is built on the steepest slope rising out of the River Wye. It's an even bigger jumble than the market with shops thrown in with old buildings and gabled houses stretching around a leisure centre. A beleaguered stone Roman gate still stands in the middle of the main road after being bumped and chipped by almost a century of traffic. The Silurians built the earthworks of this town, the Romans fortified it, the Saxons traded in it and the Normans built its castle. Now it looks as if it's falling apart from old age and traffic stress but somehow managing to hang onto a few precious bits of dignity and self-respect.

In Hawker's Street there was an ancient inn 'The Five Alls.' The name derived from the five portraits on the sign: the king—'I govern all'; the parson—'I pray for all'; the lawyer—'I plead for all;' the soldier—'I fight for all' and the devil—'I take all.'

Yes Lucifer certainly does and, as I set off towards Tintern, I began worrying again about all those dark angels I had spotted on the waterfront in the Bay. I had become so worried about them I didn't know what to do and had not even reported their presence back to H.Q. let alone communicated it to the other angels as I should have. But it was clear that the dark angels weren't just going to run away and that they were building up in such numbers for some reason. But what reason? And why here? Why me?

The other item which kept replaying itself in my mind was that slipstream of familiar laughter. Now I'd had some time to think about it I was becoming more and more convinced that my old enemy Splachnik had in fact escaped from his confinement in that lake as I had guessed earlier this year. He was out all right. Well we'd got Victor out of that hole in Lundy and so, it made sense that they'd get Splachnik out too. No one knew the territory better than him after all; he knew everything about Wales that any alien invader would need.

And Klang would be bound to be in the middle of it all somewhere, too.

The encircling darkness and that image of the murdered woman began making some sense. We angels have always specialised in visions of love and beauty but the dark angel has always dealt in hatred and murder. Now, by the look of it, they had found a way of laying their favourite imagery of death on me. *On me!* Endless fear is also a key item on the dark angel agenda. Their first move has always been to try and get someone worried out of their mind and then, if they can introduce an element of panic and anger, so much the better. Fearful irrationality has always been the name of their game. So keep a cool head now Conker boy.

So I consciously tried to bathe my mind in beauty as I wandered along that road to Tintern. I decided—as St Paul once advised—to fasten my attention onto whatsoever was pure; whatsoever was lovely; whatsoever men were of good report and, quite soon, I could actually feel myself getting better. I could feel my nagging fears and worries begin to drift away and my mind was actually healing which is, of course, one of the reasons why we should read the Bible regularly.

Two hot air balloons were floating peacefully over the Wye Valley with the rich yeasty smell of autumn wafting out of the woods. But the falling leaves were the real glory of the day, drifting past me in ones, twos and great rattling storms. They went tumbling over the roads and scratching the surfaces like the faint rasp of fingernails on blackboards. Many danced sudden demented jigs in the draughts of passing cars. Then another breeze broke loose yet another gold crackling shower.

The woods themselves were rioting splashes of browns and reds. A magpie foraged in the branches and faraway was the aggrieved clinking of a blackbird. Autumnal woods have always had a wonderfully invigorating effect on my spirits and there have been times when I've stood in them and let out great whoops of laughter as I've flung the dead leaves up into the air. If you ever spot a laughing fountain of brown leaves in the middle of a shaft of sunshine in an otherwise dark wood that'll be me enjoying the autumn.

I came near to Tintern, every now and then catching a glimpse of the River Wye curling along the valley floor. But then, all at once, my spirit was transported back through time since there, squatting in a clearing, were the ruins of Tintern Abbey, guarded by the river and framed in a huge orb of autumn sunshine. The ruin was almost disdainful in the knowledge of its complete beauty, merely sitting there, serene in the mellow certainly that often comes with the very old. Certainly you felt the power of its charm immediately; you understood the magnetic pull on painters and poets to those 'bare ruin'd choirs where late the sweet birds sang.'

The abbey was roofless with rows of gaping glassless windows. The huge seven-light window on the west wall, stood erect against the clear sky like a huge pair of closed pincers. It was just near here that Wordsworth had composed his lines on Tintern Abbey. Turner came here in 1790 to paint an ivy-clad ruin lying in glorious shafts of light. By 1800 it was busy tourist attraction, surrounded by beggars and bringing boatloads of visitors along the river from Chepstow, all escorted by innkeepers from Ross and Monmouth 'so that the ear was not painted by he coarseness of language so frequently heard from the navigators of public rivers.'

But I can still picture it when it was a working abbey echoing with prayer and Gregorian chant. Even as I approached it I saw again those golden days when the bells summoned the tonsured monks to prayer. Those monks worked hard all around the clock, copying manuscripts, teaching the novices, sleeping in that large dormitory over there, eating in the dining hall, which was along here, and caring for the sick who, alone, were allowed to eat meat.

Their prayers were still moving through the air as I stood in front of those windows which had long lost their stained glass but now contained something larger and lovelier in those ravishing views of river and wood. Sunshine smashed down on those broken pillars, fallen bosses and promises of eternal praise. Prayers were being chanted again at Lauds as I went along the side of the nave where there were bird droppings and tiny fluffy pancakes of white matted feathers.

This abbey owed its beginnings to a murder after one Walter de Clare slew his wife, Eva, in Chepstow Castle. Her ghost kept coming back to torment him so, on the advice of a priest, Walter became a pilgrim crusader. But he was still racked with guilt on his return and he poured all his money into building this abbey, inviting the Cistercian monks to join him for the first service in 1131. Later the building was expanded by the fifth Earl of Norfolk, Roger Bigod, who employed the finest craftsmen to create this exquisite poem in stone.

The Cistercians worked the abbey for close on four hundred years and I spent many happy hours here particularly during The Great Night Silences which began with Compline or evening prayer. Bells rang here right through the night as I remember: small bells which struck off the hours; larger bells to mark off the beginning and end of prayers and even larger bells which all but shook the walls down at midnight.

I liked to lie on the roof listening to all those bells or the sounds of the winds moaning down the valley and my favourite moments came at Matins at 2a.m. followed by Lauds until 3.30 a.m. and then Prime sung at 5 a.m. It would still be dark as the monks came over for the services with their warm breath pluming against the cold air. They would also don their hoods which was meant to re-inforce their isolation from the world and their oneness with God.

No sooner had they all taken their places in the choir stalls than all the candles were put out except one and I always found it both relentlessly beautiful and moving as they chanted the psalms and sang the hymns while their black cowled shapes kept revolving around and around that one guttering candle. Gregorian chants mingled with readings from the Scripture as these men came together to give God the worship that He so loves to receive. In an age of growing darkness the monks of Tintern were keeping alive the flame of faith.

But they lost their faith in the end. They turned their back on God and, when they did that, God gave them up. Alien ideas began infiltrating this place of prayer and the men drifted away in pursuit of filthy wealth and foul lust. They were even bringing in local girls for their own pleasures and, as wc know, the mind of the flesh is always death. There was no possibility that I could interfere and all I could do was watch mournfully as the place fell apart at the seams.

Barely a handful of monks was left by the time Dissolution came and the abbey was handed over to Henry VIII. The abbot was given a small pension and told to be off on his donkey. The lead was stripped off the roof. The huge stones were used for nearby buildings and such valuables as remained were given to The Treasury.

But it was no bad thing at the time. The wealth from the monasteries secured the monarchy in a dangerously unstable period and the whole body of the church had anyway become helplessly diseased and corrupt. It wasn't just the monks of Tintern who had gone bad; almost all of them had gone down the pan.

Today the public can hire a Walkman cassette player at the ticket office at Tintern which will propel them through the medieval heart of the abbey by guiding them around the ruins with the sounds, music and prayers of old. This Walkman takes people to every corner of this great place which took 32 years to build and was once the richest monastery in Wales.

But there's not much to see and the imagination has to do most of the work. The only tomb left lies under the north arch: Hic: Iacet; Nicholas: Landaverists—Here lies Nicholas of Llandaff. Certainly the Walkman gives no real idea of the prayerful majesty that was once Tintern. But there again it's almost impossible to give any real idea of the real majesty of faith once it's gone. Real faith has to be seen and felt to be believed.

But all is not lost. Lots of birds have made their home in this ruin: mostly drop-out racing pigeons fed up with tearing around the country in stupid races and preferring instead the quiet amiability of retirement here. So there is that.

Brilliant autumnal sunshine continued to light every tree and the leaves fell this way and that as I continued my journey by drifting down with the leaves at the beginning of Llanthony Valley just north of Abergavenny. Smoking chimney pots poked up out of the roofs of the woods and a woman was sweeping up leaves in her garden, making one small pile before carrying on to make another. One yellowing leaf had caught on the edge of a glittering cobweb where it kept twirling around and around helplessly like a man on the gallows.

Those falling leaves were everywhere. They fell on to the road and fields and all along the River Honddu, causing endless problems for the trout farm right here at the start of the valley. The river actually fed all those boiling fish ponds but brought so many dead leaves with it that the manager Andrew Osbaldston had to get up three times a night to unblock the pumping machinery. Leaves don't just fall for a week or two, he reminds visitors. They began falling some three weeks ago and continue until Christmas when he will get his next good night's sleep.

Some trees were already bare of their leaves but others had still held on to almost all theirs. They were every shade of yellow and brown, catching the sunshine and turning it into an autumnal sparkle. That day the leaves of a poplar were falling as furiously as the sparks of a Roman candle, drifting down on to the river, some riding the surface like speedy yellow coracles but others sinking down into the clear water where they bowled over and over the pebbles.

It was just then, watching those underwater leaves, that I, in my turn, first became aware that I was being watched from the woodland on the other side of the river. I could see that he wasn't too keen on showing himself, just bending slightly to get a better look at me through the gathered tree branches. Then he did one of my old smoke 'n' mirrors tricks of disappearing into thin air but I knew that he was still out in those woods even if I wasn't sure if I should go over to him.

Nevertheless I had felt an amazing surge of excitement. His sheer size had given him away, of course, since I knew immediately that my watcher was no other than St David. This valley had been one of his old stamping grounds and he'd had a hermitage here. He also drank water from that river and this was the place where he first ate all those foul leeks which the Welsh became so fond of they made their national emblem. I'd always preferred the daffodil myself but no one asked me.

But it was possible, of course, that this reappearance of St David had only been a trick of the light. He might have merely been an intensification of my feelings; someone whom I desperately wanted to see walking the Welsh earth again. The land had never been so full of hope as it had been when he was around you see. But today it has probably never been so full of fear and despair.

Certainly the interplay of darkness and light has always been a major feature of this valley which is so deep that the sun always arrives late and leaves early. Even this early in the afternoon the one side was almost as dark as night while the sun thwacked against the other side, throwing a huge halo of golden light around Cwmyoy Church.

This church is one of the strangest and wonkiest in the whole of Wales. It was built on a landslip which is clearly still slipping, so everything is out of joint and people almost feel quite drunk as they make their way unsteadily up to the crooked altar. They have even buttressed one end of it to keep it stable but there was clearly no buttressing on the cemetery gravestones which all look as if they've just been knocked around by a hurricane.

I explored the cemetery a little, enjoying the fantastic battles of the plants which you always find in such places. There's cow parsley battling with the nettles, dandelions staving off the ivy, ferns in hand-to-hand combat with the cowslip, brambles fighting with the laurel. Nettles always grow well in cemeteries since they thrive on the sulphates of human bones.

But then I saw that some bulky figure stooping down to look at me again. He was about a hundred yards away and this time I shrank back into the cold cemetery shadows, still uncertain what to do since that certainly was David and he would have come over if that's what he'd wanted to do. There was now an added problem since it was also clear that he had some company—one Bishop William Morgan, unless I was very much mistaken, and Ann Griffiths. There might have been two or three others in the background too; a veritable gang all keeping an eye on me. But why? I couldn't make any sense out of it and decided that it would be best to ignore them at least until their intentions became clear.

I moved slowly back down to the main road and thought that I could still see a few trailing me from the cover of the woodland. They were running as fast as they could but David wasn't among them. Come to think of it, David was always too graceful to run anywhere which, in no small measure, accounted for his amazing age. Keep mentally active and physically indolent: that's the secret of longevity. Athletes always wear their bodies out years too soon.

But, once back on the main road, the sounds of running feet had gone and everything was as peaceful as it had always been.

Only about 120 people actually live in this valley which is some ten miles long. At this time of the year, with the summer and her tourists behind them, they will be beginning to act more like a community with choirs, whist drives and pantomimes in the Memorial Hall. Farmers will also have been out on The Gathering; rounding up all the stray animals at the end of the season.

A few have also been feeling low lately and I've picked up some pleasing prayers for an improvement in their health. Barbara Smith of Bethos has just had a hip replacement and Stan Walker has been off work for some time with problems with his neck. The farmer, Bruce Davies, has also been laid up on his sofa, to his intense frustration, with a pulled leg muscle. They had one of the wettest summers ever this year and they couldn't get up all the potatoes so he's got to get them all in soon or they'll go rotten. Actually, to be perfectly honest, he now wished that he'd become a trout farmer. 'You should see the money they make. We don't make anything like that out of potatoes.'

Further up the road a magpie was hopping around on sheep's backs in a meadow trying to find something interesting to eat in their fleeces. Sometimes the bird got tossed off but he didn't seem to take any offence, merely hopping on to the next sheep and now trying to find something interesting in the corner of one of the sheep's mouths.

I passed over a stone bridge when I glanced down a slope and found myself looking at an old and well-loved face with but one eye. But it wasn't so much the one eye as the whole fierce look which I recognised immediately; that look of tender ferocity which was uniquely Christmas Evans's. I took one step towards him and then another but the face disappeared.

Yet I wasn't as scared of these strange goings on as I might have been in some other part of the country. This was, after all, the holy Llanthony Valley where it was unlikely that evil or dark angels had made any headway or set up any sort of base. I would have been absolutely astonished to have spotted a dark angel flying over this sacred and haunting landscape where the old tribal elders were clearly still living and breathing.

Little, of course, could be more haunting than the ruins of Llanthony Priory now looming over me with its broken ruins and surrounded by green and gold mountains. Horses grazed in nearby meadows and from somewhere in the distance was the furious barking of a dog. They built this priory in the twelfth century and I liked to come here too, enjoying the work and services of the monks. But they went the way of Tintern in the end. There was just something poisonous in the air and silly chroniclers put it about that 'Christ and his angels slept.'

This simply wasn't true at all: people don't seem to understand that if someone wants to do something there is almost nothing at all we can do about it. If they choose the way of sin we're absolutely helpless. We're not the agents of a dictator any more than the dark angels are the agents of a God of love and freedom.

After Dissolution the priory was sold to a servant for £160 and an eighteenth-century owner turned the south tower into a shooting box. Later the poet Walter Landor owned the priory but he couldn't get on with his neighbours and left in high dudgeon. 'I hate and detest the very feature of the country,' he moaned. 'I can never be happy here, or comfortable, or at peace.'

Now the priory must be a unique holy ruin since it contains a small hotel and a pub wherein it is possible to get very drunk very quickly.

Darkness fell, claiming both sides of the valley and, as I stood in the middle of the ruin, I watched the headlamps of the passing cars lighting up the high arches of the ruin, making them shiver and dance before letting them disappear into the darkness again. Little boys with Dracula masks and wearing capes looked around corners, for this was Hallowe'en night.

Just then I felt David's hand clamped on my shoulder. I didn't turn around but could feel him there well enough; knew that it was him all right; sensed great and unbearable anguish moving through him like iced acid. Oh yes, I knew my Waterman well enough to know what he was feeling without having to ask. The burden of his anguish was right up there in the cold night air, heavy and eloquent enough without me having to look around. I simply bowed my head and let a tear fall for him.

The road through the valley, with no street lights and more holes than an old string vest, pre-dated even the Priory ruin. Two cars hoping to go in opposite directions immediately amounted to a traffic jam, not much helped by the ducks and quail that seemed to go wandering unconcernedly everywhere.

In Capel-y-Ffin Church there was an inscription on a tombstone which has always brought a great joy to my heart: 'Noah Watkins, aged 8, died in 1738. This child said that he would not take a hundred pounds in money for breaking the Sabbath but keep it holy.'

Right here is another important landmark in the spiritual history of Wales—the new Llanthony Abbey, built in Victorian times by Father Ignatius Lyne who wanted to introduce monasticism into the Anglican Church. The monastery began going up in 1870 and I remember taking a quiet interest as the main church was built and the trees and shrubs planted. Like Christmas Evans before him Father Ignatius raised all the necessary money from preaching tours. They also kept cows here, harvested their own hay and grew their own flowers and vegetables.

Father Ignatius loved this valley with a rare, if somewhat overwrought, passion: 'How glad everything is looking Now the noisy Honddu shines like silver in the sun and joins its music to the sheep's bleat, the oxen's low, the birds' song, the bees' hum, the breeze's breath. All nature seems triumphant in its wild glad freedom here, and oh the wild flowers simply resplendent in the gay garments of glory . . . How majestically the cloud-shades were floating upon the mountains; how calmly the moonlight lay in the valleys; like tricklings of quicksilver the streamlets glistened on the rocky beds. Like a rush of molten silver seemed the Honddu in moonglow; solemn were the dark shades of the Abbey buildings cast broad and long on the Abbot's meadow, the ineffable beauty of the mountains brooding over all.'

But he spoke quite well and was such a saintly person with a high forehead, soft brown eyes and hands with long fingers which seemed made for prayer. I loved to hear him give a sermon with his quiet voice, full of suppressed laughter, which, on occasion, turned to absolute fire if he got worked up about something.

But the real problem with starting a monastery—as he soon found out—was finding the right monks and he had far more

266

failure than successes in that department. He once admitted that out of fifty postulants he could only hope to get three good monks and, as he was so often away on preaching tours, it wasn't long before this monastery also began going the way of all flesh. At the end of the day there was just no prayer in it. If Ignatius was away I could have sat on that roof from now until Christmas and not picked up so much as a line.

Another of the visitors here, who always gave me the greatest of pleasure, was the clergyman and diarist, Francis Kilvert. Oh how I loved everything about that man, particularly his clear, crisp writing style full of lovely images and vivid detail. His pen worked the broadest canvas from crowd scenes to sharp insights into people's personalities; from stunning invocations of landscape to faces so pretty you wanted to kiss them. There is no better guide to the life and times of Victorian Wales than the diaries he kept in his vicarage in nearby Clyro.

There were moments when I would play with the workings of Kilvert's imagination when he was walking the countryside around here, sometimes enabling him to see nature in a new and revelatory way. He never actually knew it was me, of course, but I was once highly amused when he wrote 'an angel satyr walks these hills'.

He wasn't slightly prudish—which is often the great sin of a clergyman—and we both enjoyed and celebrated human beauty—particularly in young women and girls. Modern commentators have often tried to make something nasty and even sinister out of his so-called 'erotic sensibility' but that's just the way of the fallen modern world; the way in which these commentators have become obsessed with sexual inconstancy and perversion in all its forms; the way they seem desperate to throw a dark cloak of scandal over everyone and everything.

Certainly Kilvert didn't have much sympathy with monasticism even though, oddly enough, he got on quite well with Father Ignatius. They used to spend a lot of time laughing and teasing one another. Kilvert found Father Ignatius's trusting innocence in everyone particularly naive and indeed it was this innocence which enabled the corrupt monks to cheat him right, left and centre.

They buried Father Ignatius beneath a cross of stones in the monastery here and it was on his grave on this gorgeous autumnal day that I stood watching a tremendous red and yellow sunset exploding up out of the Black Mountains. Clouds the size and shape of ruined castles clotted the dying embers of the sun and bats came fluttering out over tinkling watercress streams.

I thought of St David and Christmas Evans, wondering if they would come and visit me again. I was sure I could feel the presence of Bishop Morgan and Ann Griffiths too but they may just have been shadows flickering in that Llanthony sunset. But then, yes, that was Dylan Thomas and Evan Roberts moving out of their caves of praise and walking towards me. Francis Kilvert came to stand at my side and I was picking up the magnificent voice of Daniel Rowland, all of them, fiends for love, come to fight against the evil tide and gathering here in the beats of my frightened, breaking heart.

How long now oh Lord? How long before Christ and all his angels make their final and devastating move to reclaim the earth?

And as I gathered the spirits of all my old praise warriors to me and as I felt them coming to re-arm me I also felt that something was struggling to break out from the very ground beneath me. Even the stones of the cross were cracking together as if some huge bird was struggling, but failing, to rise up out of the earth and fly. I looked about me frowning and wondering what was going on now. It was getting that you had to have nerves of steel to be an angel these days. In this fraught, post-modern age you were just not sure what was going to happen next.

Then, with some more sharp cracks and soft rumbles, the spirit of Father Ignatius began rising up from beneath his stone cross. It was little more than a tight, dark shadow but it was him all right. Something caught in the back of my throat, which might have begun in terror but then ended in delight, and I shook out my wings rising up with Father Ignatius's spirit and taking hold of it.

We held one another tightly and then, on slowly flapping wings, we both headed up towards Gospel Pass and straight into the brilliant eye of that resurrection sunset.

Big skies and wind-ravaged moors. Litter scattered around a sign warning dire penalties for the dropping of litter. A down-pouring of waterfalls and a booted procession of oilskins. Limestone gorges and the charging of soldiers.

There's not a lot about the Brecon Beacons that makes much sense. You climb up its highest peak at Pen Y Fan and you might as well be standing in the bob bank at a rugby match. You are feeding off the silence and a platoon of some twenty Paras go running right through you.

Gurgling lollipop-cold streams and a tickle of trout. A munching of sheep and a ruin of Iron Age hillforts. Mountain ponies standing motionless in the shelter of a hollow. A muttering gathering of Beaker ghosts and a monolithic assembly of old, tired stones. Remember that ancient Welsh law carries the death penalty for anyone disturbing these stones.

I was strolling higher and higher up Pen y Fan now gazing out at the 500 square miles of the Brecon Beacons National Park. These mountains have a much quieter charm than the more rugged splendour of the mountains of the north. Indeed, from up here, they looked like a series of hump-backed whales diving back into mist-shrouded seas before being frozen by the hand of God for all time.

There used to be a couple of thousand mountain ponies grazing around the Beacons but, over the past five years or so, they have dropped to fewer than a hundred. Their welfare is looked after by the wondrously bewhiskered RSPCA inspector, George Mossop, who is always whizzing around the Beacons in his little white van. The word soon goes out on the tom-

toms that Mossop is on the mountains, he will tell you, and almost immediately every animal in sight starts to get better fed.

But these are dangerous weeks for the mountain ponies since the roads are being gritted in readiness for the onset of winter and the ponies go looking for the salt which gathers around the cats' eyes on the roads. That's when accidents happen and, when car hits pony, there's not much left of either of them. If there's one thing George hates it's having to shoot a pony and put it out of its misery.

A rumble of distant thunder and a few spots of rain. It rains a lot out here which is why there's eighteen supply reservoirs sitting out there like overblown puddles. In fact it even rains up here when there's not a cloud in the sky. Snow streaked the grass over there, the first of the year. Way back in 1724 Daniel Defoe said that the Beacons were 'horrid and frightful, even worse than the mountains abroad.'

The oilskins thinned out and the sun burst through the rain shower. A good moment for prayer I was thinking when a huge gang of Paras come pouring over a ridge, heading straight down towards me as if re-enacting one of their better moments in the Zulu Wars. They were carrying full packs and rifles. Their shaven heads resembled sides of bacon and there was a murderous look in their eyes as they charged straight through me. The strong will live and the weak will die, they like to say in the Parachute Regiment so they were out here doing Basic Wales—making 17-miles runs over mountains, mountains and yet more mountains.

I came out onto the summit of Carn Du which, at 2,863 ft., is one of the highest spots on South Wales. Right at the very top there was lots of churned-up black mud as if a circus had just left town. About a dozen youngsters were digging drains for the National Trust with a huge cold wind blowing straight up their backsides.

But I've always felt cold up here too since this was the scene of the greatest and most miserable tragedy that I've ever been involved in. It still makes me quite sick to think of it all and I can barely relate the story's basic facts without that old terrible sorrow—and not a little anger—flooding back.

It was August 4, 1900, when a Maerdy miner decided to take his five-year-old boy, Tommy Jones, to visit his grandparents on a Brecon farm. At about six in the afternoon they set off for the farmhouse only to be met by young Willie John, Tommy's cousin. The two children ran off towards the farmhouse to warn of the visit but, about half-way there, Tommy got scared of the dark and, crying, ran back to find his father. He was never seen alive again.

The father and grandfather began the search almost immediately as did the soldiers in the nearby camp. By the next morning almost everyone in the locality had joined in the search and I was alerted by a sudden, huge burst of activity on the prayer lines. We were still in faithful times at the turn of the century and, if I were to try and describe that particular burst of prayer, I would have to say it was like being a mile or so from a football ground after the home side had scored an important goal. Indeed as the days went by this roar of prayer kept getting louder and yet louder so I had no choice but to respond with everything I had. As the police, farmers and soldiers went through the Beacons almost inch by inch I was there too, zipping past them and pouring through ferns and searching the gulleys. It looked as if he had fallen off one of the footbridges over one of the streams and I even became water and went into the water but still couldn't find any trace of little Tommy.

It was clearly important that someone found him—or his body—since all sorts of scandalous rumours were flying about and the finger of suspicion was being pointed repeatedly and wrongly at the gypsies whose camps were being searched again and again. This is an old Welsh tactic: when in doubt blame a foreigner.

But the blunt fact of the matter was that none of us could pick up so much as a sniff of the boy. I couldn't understand it at all since I searched the area carefully but little Tommy might as well have stepped on some visiting spaceship. His father had been out in the Beacons for several weeks but, even when he was sent home to Maerdy, he couldn't sleep or relax and was soon back out here scouring the mountains again. I was as miserable as him and, in the end, all I could do was trail around by his side, providing whatever comfort I could— which wasn't much.

Sometimes the red-eyed father just lay down on the mountain and wept into the earth. Then I would spread myself over him, trying to warm him with a little hope in a hopeless situation.

But the the strangest thing happened. A Mrs Hamer dreamed of the spot where Tommy would be found and indeed it turned out to be along that ridge further down from where those youngsters were now digging drains for the National Trust and directly above the lake of Llyn Cwm-Llwch. Mrs Hamer took a group straight to the spot where they found the remains of Tommy's body. He had died through exhaustion and exposure, the inquest found.

Yet what I couldn't work out was why we hadn't discovered his body days earlier: the father and I must have passed that spot a few dozen times on our aimless wanderings. Maybe we hadn't looked properly since this was a very high point for a small boy to have reached, even in the panic-stricken dark. He had climbed 1,300 ft. and had walked at least two miles from the spot where he had gone missing.

The real question though was why hadn't I found him? I mean to say human beings—particularly upset human beings —are fallible but I was supposed to be an angel who knew a thing or two about searches and such-like. There was no excuse at all for my failure.

The next day, still baffled by my apparent incompetence, I went back to the spot where they had found the body and examined the ground minutely. The first thing I noticed was a slight brown circle around the actual spot in the moss and heather. Then my sense of smell picked up the unmistakeable whiff of acid slime. That was the slime of a dark angel that was. Instinctively I took two sharp steps backwards and all became clear.

A dark angel had found little Tommy before anyone else and had covered over his body so that it couldn't be found. Dark angels have their own chameleon ways of doing things and you would actually have to step on one to know he was there. This one had probably lain over Tommy right through the three weeks of the search until he had been disturbed by the revelatory flash of that woman's dream. But by then it had been too late.

Now there was only one dark angel who would have done anything quite as dreadful as this and, with pure murder in my heart, I immediately set out to find him.

It was clear that Splachnik wasn't going to hang around after doing something like that but, even so, I didn't think it would take me as long as it finally did to catch up with him. I scoured all his known Welsh haunts like the screaming furies, going back to them again and again at different times of the day but not picking up so much as a trace of his horrible laughter. I even ransacked parts of the English border and Klang must have tipped him off because I couldn't locate him anywhere there either.

But that's always been the way of real evil hasn't it? It comes and goes, particularly when you least expect it. And then, when it's right under your nose, it's more often than not disguised as something else. The one feature of evil that's always puzzled me is the way that it often gets men of intelligence and influence to serve its purposes. Evil can even take in the very elect of God.

After about a month of sweeping the country I finally gave up my search for Splachnik, concluding that he must have gone away to start trouble in some other part of the world which would have, at the very least, meant a lot less work for me for a bit. But then, later that same year, it was a brilliant autumnal day and I was cruising down past the edges of the Radnor Forest when I spotted Splachnik just sitting in a tree, talking to himself and staring into space. Had the leaves not been falling I would probably have missed him altogether. But there he was—as large as life and twice as nasty.

He spotted me almost as soon as I spotted him and was off in a flash, scurrying deep into the heart of the forest with me on his tail in a furious explosion of rings. Twice I grabbed him and twice he slipped out of my grasp as he desperately tried to shake out his wings to get airborne. The trouble was that he was constantly hampered by the surrounding trees which weren't helping my cause much either since I then tried to cut him with my sword but ended up felling a whole pine. Splachnik had also resorted to his old trick of throwing off his terrible, corrosive slime but I was determined to cook his goose this time and didn't let that bother me.

An old man was walking along a forest path at the time and I shall always remember the look on his face as his jaw fell open and knees began knocking as he looked up as this huge noise of two brawling angels went cartwheeling past him.

I caught Splachnik by the throat next but again he managed to wriggle out of my grip and, stumbling into a clearing, found that he had enough room to take off. He could fly too, that one—not like some of them—but he had barely gone a mile or two before I was on him again and we went fluttering and crashing across the length of two counties, locked in ferocious combat. No one could see us, of course, but the damage to trees and buildings was immense including one church spire in Llanbister which was knocked out of true.

After about half an hour of this Splachnik was weakening badly and I had cornered him against the cliff of an old slate quarry where, taking my time to catch my breath, I was just standing in front of him with my sword drawn and poised. He knew—as well as I knew—that I couldn't actually kill him but I could cause him and his wings untold damage with my sword which might take him years to recover.

He was just looking at me with his hissing yellow eyes. His small red mouth was also wheezing for breath and then I spotted a long rusty chain lying next to the rail track. I looked at the chain and then at him and it was as if he had read my thoughts since he took off at about a hundred miles an hour except that I jumped straight into his path and, as he hesitated looking for another way, I sliced off one of his wings with my sword. Now he didn't seem to know what to do and within a few seconds I was whirling that quarry chain around and around him until I had tied him up into a neat metal bundle.

'Time for a long, long rest boyo,' I told him, picking him up and flying his struggling body back to the Beacons where I took him back to the scene of his crime before taking him down to the bottom of Llyn Cwm-Llwch where, just for good measure, I piled several large boulders on top of him. 'Now pick your way out of that lot.'

And today I had come back here, standing next to the obelisk which they had put up in memory of little Tommy and looking down at the small lake in which I had buried his murderer. Small flashes of sunshine broke through the clouds and glazed the surface of the lake making it look as if it was on fire. In places the sunshine seemed so strong it almost made the water look as if it was boiling.

Well there was only one way to find out if he was there or not and so I went straight down into the lake to have a look around. A few fish dashed away from me and within a few seconds I discovered that the boulders had been moved and those chains of his had been broken. The dark angel had indeed escaped. Splachnik had risen.

It was a much chastened and thoughtful angel who continued on his journey through Wales. So where was Splachnik now? Had he got anything to do with all those dark angels building up in the Bay? What exactly was he doing? You could bet your very life that he was up to no good somewhere.

My anxieties weren't helped by the weather either. Winter foreclosed on the land within days of the end of autumn, turning everything to a rotten mush as it sheeted with freezing rain almost every hour. The sound of rain was almost everywhere: it poured off roofs and into water butts; it washed across roads and down drains; it dripped off the bare branches of trees and on to the ragged brown tongues of bracken. Nothing escaped its wet and relentless clamp.

And as I stared about me, across rainy fields and into dripping woods, there was only one shape I was looking for: the slightly stooped slimy shape of Splachnik talking to himself or dreaming of yet more evil plots.

But there was still my report to finish, of course, and so I had to practically drive myself on through the constant rain showers, this time to the old farmhouse of Pantycelyn which I finally located sitting on its own way out in the middle of nowhere.

This one was the home of one of my most famous hymn writers William Williams and I could see him again now, at his desk in the window with a quill in his hand and gazing out at the wandering chickens and a yapping dog in the farmyard. Some 6,000 visitors came here last year, on his bicentenary. David Lloyd George has signed the visitors' book in the farmhouse as has Lord Tonypandy. Not that there is much that belonged to the great man left to see except his 250-year-old grandfather clock, which grandma still winds every night before she goes to bed, and his china teapot which is kept polished and burnished in the display cabinet. But his old bed is still out in the shed and there is a portrait of him in the living room with a somewhat hippy hairstyle and looking quite cock-eyed.

He sat at that window for much of the day and almost all of the night because he had problems with his bladder, if you really want to know, and could never remember the last time he'd had a decent night's sleep. This bladder trouble ensured a prodigious amount of work which included more than 90 books and hundreds of those wonderful love hymns.

But Pantycelyn here never really became a shrine like Llangeitho, perhaps because Williams, apart from his bladder, was quite normal unlike the tempestuous Daniel Rowland. Nevertheless his hymns shaped the very emotions of the Welsh who still glory in their power. Williams's choral poetry became the very blood of the tribe and he was thought by some to be the first poet of European modernism. He celebrated creation and the order of the material world. His hymns were aware of time and the infinity of the universe. He was always thinking of the hills where the Psalmist lifted his eyes: 'I see the black cloud is now being turned to flight and the wind from the north by small degrees begins to turn.'

His was the poetry of the common man and he also churned out an almost endless stream of books in an attempt to make 'Godliness attractive'. His Life and Death of Theomemphus followed a soul through the Methodist Revival. Here was another man at a time of violent social change essaying the true nature of revival and rebirth; here was another who, with Rowland and Howell Harris, entered into a brilliant triumvirate and put together a social order which was to last two hundred years. Ah, how I loved all these men; they were one-offs without whom I would have done very little except wring my hands helplessly. It is one of God's mysteries that IIe can only effectively work through man; in a sense His work is but a constant search for the right personalities who will, in their turn, push forward the boundaries of the kingdom.

As it happened I converted William Williams myself with one of those simple heart warmings that was so much in vogue with us angels at the time. Warm them up and imbue them with a sense of melancholy and wonder is about the long and short of it. They don't know if they're coming or going and simply submit to the complex and wonderful mystery of things. Simple but effective that one. I also did that with Howell Harris and, after I'd explained how it was done, Sorroptus worked much the same trick on John Wesley.

But when Williams did get moving he tore through Wales in a punishing ministry lasting 43 years and covering more than 150,000 miles on horseback. And all this, remember, at a time when the roads were barely roads at all, littered with rocks and plagued by footpads. It took ten days to travel from North Wales to London by stagecoach.

Williams was a man of peculiar tenderness with a highly charged preaching style who could make people weep with his words and stirring imagery, particularly when he got onto the gory details of the Crucifixion which even made me wince no matter how many times I heard them. I remember him one year, when he was preaching on the resurrection of the dead from a window in a Merthyr chapel, holding a huge crowd out in the cemetery so well that, when he reached the climax of his sermon, everyone moved sharply in terror lest the ground opened up and the dead rose there and then.

His life and work, according to T. Gwynne Jones, a poet, had 'subdued chaos, conquered sin and ascended to Heaven. He has done more. He has overcome self and wretchedness, has known what it is to long with a consuming passion for the clean white flame of absolute invariable goodness and purity; he has realised the utter abandonment of himself to one whole saviour.'

The present fifth generation of the Williams family here in Pantycelyn is not particularly musical however. Cecil sings a bit and the eldest daughter plays the organ. But they do still maintain a strong link with the local chapel.

But moving back across the sodden countryside, I came to the former home of Howell Harris, almost the only remaining key figure in my spiritual history who has not yet been covered in my report. Men like Harris have been done a grave disservice by the leaden pens of many historians since he was a wonderfully vivid and turbulent personality, much given to new and crackpot ideas, whose sheer ebullience and inflexible courage I found so irresistible I converted him with another heart warming in Talgarth churchyard.

Thereafter he travelled thousands of miles on horseback, speaking to hostile mobs and getting himself arrested, stoned, beaten and thrown out of town but still coming back to haunt them like a bad hiccup, railing against all the 'ale-house people, the fiddlers or the harpers' or else preaching the wild word of God. Those were stormy times for all unlicensed preachers, who were forever being threatened with public prosecution and even pursued by the police. I tried to watch over them as best I could but it was very difficult and one of his pals was actually killed while preaching in Hay-on-Wye.

Harris, Williams and Rowland nourished the Welsh as no three men had ever done but Harris split with Rowland on doctrine and came back here to his 'castellated monastery' at Trefecca with a gilded angel on the roof where he set up a 120-strong community of ideal friends sharing all their possessions—a precursor of Robert Owen's Co-Operative Movement—with their own chapel, library and dovecote. They all rose at four in the morning and went to bed at 10 at night, working all day with no recreation and breaks only for meals, Bible study and prayer. A constant hive of industry, they also did spinning, weaving and bookbinding.

It was his sheer bloody-minded drive that helped to wear him away in the end and, at the comparatively young age of 59, I took him across the Jordan. Some 20,000 turned up to his funeral and three clergymen tried to read the service at his graveside but kept breaking down. This was a real man, a terrific fighter, another one-off. Needless to say the welcome in heaven was terrific.

Later Trefecca became a college for training Methodist ministers but today this 'castellated monastery' is a conference centre in which many of the ideals of Howell Harris's community live on. Able to accommodate around a hundred residents they have various courses here for such diverse groups as the intercessors, Quakers, youth workers, the retired, fans of ancient music and those in need of HIV counselling.

There is also a small museum with such artefacts as Harris's travelling pulpit, his sword and guns from his period in the Army in the Seven Years' War, his prayer bells, candle snuffers and an 'electrifying machine' which looks a bit like an old-fashioned record player and, it was thought or rather hoped, could cure up to 45 ailments from baldness to deafness and bruises. 'The old ethos is still here,' said the new warden,

Gwilym Ceiriog Evans. 'People can still come here to share their beliefs and social concerns just as they did in the days of Howell Harris.'

Hovering outside Trefecca that night, where they've still got that 'gilded angel blowing the trump of doom' on the rooftops, I picked up a most unusual burst of sounds on the prayer lines. It was so unusual—so grief-stricken somehow—I turned and turned again, even shaking out my wings in preparation for I knew not what. With two huge thrusts downwards I rose some twenty feet up into the air and just hung there. Several more thrusts took me ever more higher and I rode the night breezes as I took another reading on that great and heartbreaking sound.

Its source wasn't too far away either and I was there almost immediately, on top of an old chapel just north of the village of Glasbury, high up on a lonely hill and looking down on the curling River Wye. This building was another key icon in our chapel culture: Maesyronen, one of the oldest chapels in Wales, built in 1696 and where the old religious dissenters once came to worship in secret. It was certainly one of the most beautiful too with stone-flagged floors, mullioned windows, an old pew table, three box pews, a pulpit and lots of memorial tablets around the walls.

The lamps inside the chapel had been lit and crowds of dark shadows were moving around in the orange glow. There was another terrible burst of prayer which shook me rigid. I could barely move any closer to the window. The thrust of the prayer was a call on God to be their rock; it was a plea that He shepherd the people safely through the gathering storm. It might even have been the prayer of an army preparing for one last battle.

I suppose what struck me most was the real and fervent quality of the prayer; these people knew what they were doing. They were almost professional. And then at the end of the group prayer for help I picked up the rich sound of a voice that I knew so well.

'It is finished. The powers of darkness heard the acclamations of the universe and hurried away from the scene with a death-like feebleness. He triumphed over them openly. The graves of the old burial-ground have been thrown open, and gales of fire have been blown over the valley of dry bones, and an exceeding great army has been sealed to our God as among the king in Zion, for so the Bond was paid and the eternal redemption secured.'

Even as Christmas Evans had finished his lovely and powerful old sermon I came down next to the wall and pressed my nose up against the window. A man with a long thick beard was now mounting the pulpit and preparing to read from the Bible and, unless I was very much mistaken, that was Bishop Morgan setting out all the pewter vessels on the old oak table in readiness for communion. Voices cried in the winds outside and I could feel my heart racing and bleeding, just racing and bleeding. Reality was breaking down and old Conker was finding it difficult to carry on. Oh I'd had enough of all this . . . enough . . .

I knew who they were; these were all the tribal elders who had been haunting and bothering me all year. These were my old praise warriors to whom I had once ministered and who had all now escaped from heaven to take a final communion together. But why?

Could it be that the word had got out about all the dark angels gathering over Wales and they had been told to carry me along with their prayers as I prepared for the final show-down? Could it be that their spirits were being released in readiness for another great and devastating outbreak of the Holy Spirit? Who knows? I didn't and certainly no one was going to bother to explain anything to me now. The Megiddo suits had never once explained anything to me and they certainly weren't going to start now.

I recognised the distinctive bulk of Saint David and the tall impressive figure of Evan Roberts. Iolo Morgannwg was there too as was Ann Griffiths and Daniel Rowland. But there were other lesser-known ones there like Seth Joshua and, unless I was very much mistaken, that young girl directly beneath the pulpit was Mary Jones who had once made that epic journey over Cadair Idris to see Thomas Charles.

Ah yes, of course, that bearded figure about to start reading from the Bible must be Francis Kilvert. Bishop Morgan began pouring the wine into the communion cup as Kilvert read from Peter.

'But the days of the Lord will come like a thief, and then the heavens will pass away with a loud noise and the elements will be dissolved with fire, and the earth and the works that are on it will be burned up. Since all these things are thus to be dissolved, what sort of persons ought you to be in lives of holiness and godliness, waiting for and hastening the coming of the day of God, because of which the heavens will be kindled and dissolved and the elements will melt with fire. But according to his promise we wait for new heavens and a new earth in which righteousness dwells.'

There was little I could do except be with their spirits so I entered their prayer too that the stage might finally be set for the foot of the Boss to come down through the clouds of heaven. I didn't know when it would happen but I did know that, right on the second the foot did appear, all the angels working and patrolling the world would hear a ravishing peal on the chimes such as they had never heard before.

But how long now oh Lord? Just how long?

# Twelfth Book

It's a most strange place this Pontypridd, this Istanbul of the Valleys; a begrimed casbah built in the middle of a traffic jam, where lots of spivs flog off rubbish cheap in its lively market and those from the Valleys meet those from the south for a sort of eisteddfod of trade, low-level crime and traffic fumes.

Even ghosting along the curving terraces, on those Alpine hills scattered around the River Taff, I am never too sure what the place is about. It was once a home of prayer and the Temperance Movement but that's all long since passed away. Now I am more likely to pick up a prayer from someone who wants twenty three points on his pools coupon or a full house at bingo or that the club committee won't ban him for too long for fighting in the lounge. Evan Roberts once spoke in some of these chapels but now most of them have fallen into dereliction or are used as carpet warehouses. Otherwise the 33,500 inhabitants have the use of 63 bus shelters, 13 allotments and five public urinals.

But there's no one anywhere in Wales who is quite so funny and exuberant as these people from Ponty. You get to laugh a lot in Ponty unless you are playing against the rugby team which is famous for its brutality. On these noisy corners language has been given a whole new wash and brush-up. Making love is described as 'having a bit of a rub'. A man might be so boring he'd put a 'glass eye to sleep'. When a man was dying his 'tools were on the bar'. A Ponty definition of good fun is for a few men to grab a newly married man, hold him down on the bar floor and give him a good love bite to take home and explain away to his wife. One man, who was knocking a huge hole in the front of his house to make way for a picture window was asked if he'd lost his key. Stand at the end of one of the terraces and shout 'Yes' and you can be sure a dozen heads will come out of the doorways and shout back 'No'.

Ponty has characters on every corner who understand everything about life. Pubs like The Globe are the liveliest and The Grogg Shop, with its eccentric owner John Hughes and his caricatured clay models of famous names is arguably one of the most interesting anywhere. The House speciality is little clay sheep with THANK GOD I'M WELSH or BAN MINT SAUCE written on their sides.

But there is a dark side to Pontypridd too and perhaps there is nowhere with so little history but such a shady past. One Billy Mannings held up a bank with a water pistol and made off with a sack of money. In another epic moment in the annals of Ponty crime, two masked men burst into a post office brandishing toy guns at the counter clerk. While one was demanding the money the other was down on his knees picking up the birthday cards that he'd just knocked over. 'This is not a stick-up,' the chief gunman shouted rolling around his eyes in exasperation. 'This is what I call a cock-up.'

If we are talking about characters, however, I would have to say straight off that the strangest and most wonderful character that Ponty ever produced was Dr William Price who wandered these streets in the nineteenth century with his long white hair and beard flowing down all around him like some Old Testament prophet who had just missed the last bus to the Promised Land.

Now I always had a soft spot for nutty old Dr Price and, in fact, protected him more than once when a mob was threatening to tear him apart limb from limb. He had the kind of personality that upset people usually because he made them realise how dull and colourless most of them really were. A hippy long before the days of Bob Dylan and LSD everyone got out of the way when Dr Price came striding down the pavement in his green trousers, white tunic, crimson waistcoat and fox fur hat with the legs of the poor beast dangling down over his forehead.

You might have thought that he would have fitted in well with my gang but his ideas were far too eccentric to be of any use to a conventional, hard-working Christian angel like me. He always said that he was an atheist and there wasn't so much as a ripple on the chimes when he was born but I kept an eye on him anyway since he was, as they say in Ponty, a real character. But then, to my mounting horror, he got into all that Druidical stuff, going up to the stones on the common just above Pontypridd, where he worshipped the sun, practised fertility rites and all those other holes-in-the-head.

But, if that's the way they want to carry on, I can't interfere and can only hope that they manage to get sensible one day. Not that William Price ever got remotely sensible: he just kept getting madder and madder.

I found him on that corner near the bridge once preaching free love to a crowd which, as you can probably imagine, didn't go down at all well with the chapel elders. He also busily condemned the institution of marriage and had a string of mistresses even if he did marry his young housekeeper at the age of 81 after she threatened to leave him. Something of a pioneer health fanatic he was a vegetarian who loathed smoking and was so fastidiously clean he never wore socks and would scrub all his coins before putting them into his pockets.

But the balloon went up over his life when he publicly burned the body of his five-month-old son, Iesu Grist, in a barrel of oil. A policeman kicked over the funeral pyre and Price was locked up. At the inquest Price was allowed to take his son's body away providing he buried it properly. On his way home Price stopped to feed his cow and was busy chopping up swedes when a curious crowd which had followed him decided, in the way that crowds do, that he was chopping up his son. That's when I stepped in.

They were throwing stones and clods at him and I had to field the more accurate shots, even, at one stage, sucking the oxygen out of the air around one farmer who looked as if he was about to do something very nasty to Price with his pitchfork. I practically carried Price to the Bear Inn when another crowd attacked his home and I again had to protect his wife from all the missiles. But then she produced a gun from somewhere and clearly demonstrated that she was more than capable of protecting herself without any help from me.

Price was later sent for trial on charges of attempting to burn the body of his child instead of burying it. He loved this period since his chief hobby was litigation and, in the event, was found not guilty. Thus began the practice of cremation in this country and Price's very last words before he died at the age of 86 with a glass of champagne in his hand, was a fervent plea that they wouldn't stick his body in a hole in the ground.

Instead he had a theatrical cremation in Llantrisant and some 10,000 bought tickets to see it. His influence on his home town, to this day, is so durable that 1,500 now elect for cremation in Ponty each year as opposed to the 200-odd who have asked to be stuck in a hole in the ground. If you're at all curious on what attitude I take to it all it makes no difference to me. The body is merely a husk which is on loan on a temporary basis, as far as I'm concerned, and, after death, it doesn't matter a fig to me what happens to it. I only ever deal with the glorious soul after death which is quite different and distinct from the tawdry matter of the body.

Ponty has had great moments, however. The Welsh National Anthem was written here in 1856 by Evan James and his son. I was present at the time even if, as I have already explained, neither of them—not even me—could have even guessed what that strong melody would have gone on to become.

But the town has always been notable for music, producing some particularly fine singers. Stuart Burrows and the late Sir

Geraint Evans came from here. And that wall over there finally fell over after it was propped up for so many years by the pop singer Tom Jones when he was unemployed.

Everyone still likes to burst into song in Ponty—especially when they've got a few pints inside them—and on market day you might see whole groups of traders serenading one another as they attempt to sell a variety of rubbish to the amused customers. Sometimes I've sat on top of the faggots and peas stall, enjoying the myriad smells and picking up the most intriguing bits of conversation. 'Do you know that Edith Evans has never been the same since she had her bust bronzed,' was one of my favourites. Or there was: 'Whose coat is that jacket?'

The rain had got the River Taff to burst her banks again on the day I was there but the townsfolk had lost none of their humour as a foul brown tide washed through their living rooms. They were still busy cracking jokes about how they were going to get Noah to build them a new ark or wondering aloud if they could get a lifeboat to come and pick them up and take them to the pub for a pint.


I ghosted on up through the Valleys, taking readings on the high volcanic walls and twisting this way and that with the gentlest explosion of rings, floating past the pigeon cotes and over the winding terraces, the ruined Miners' Welfare Halls and the hissing fish and chip shops, occasionally stopping to linger awhile on the top of a crowded bus shelter or sit on the wheel of the winding machinery of some abandoned pit working.

I do not spend much time in this part of the world through choice. These were once brilliant, vibrant communities, built around the mines, convinced of the new political creed of socialism and living in the fear and shadow of the Lord. I can remember times when I would travel the length of Wales just to attend a meeting in one of those Welfare Halls, enjoying the political rhetoric and naked displays of a caring social conscience. There was a passion in those meetings which could melt Arctic ice flows and some of those early political orators were as good as any to be found in the chapel pulpits.

These imaginative, insecure people took education as seriously as their work down those dark and dangerous mines. Every Welfare Hall had its own miners' library with some of the biggest and most comprehensive collections of socialist literature. Their reading rooms in the Welfare Halls were sacred places where you would not so much as dare to whistle or talk. These communities were also the homes of the Penny Readings and the meetings of The Hearts of Oak. Here a clever body of men struggled against the hated coal barons and, in the process, gave birth to ideas that both changed the world and forged the early character of the valleys.

Small villages like Maerdy in the Rhondda Fach valley produced fiery, articulate leaders such as Noah Ablett and Arthur Horner. They became such an influence that the village became known as Little Moscow. There were competitions for boxers to go to the Soviet Union; 'Lenin weeks' in the coalfield; funeral wreaths in the shape of a hammer and sickle and a communist football team. A reporter from the South Wales Daily News wrote of 'lawless Maerdy' and 'the red reign of terror', describing how strangers were called 'spies' and how children wore red sashes at funerals.

But the real character of such villages was not forged so much by the politician as the pulpit. Maerdy alone had eleven chapels including Calvinistic Methodists, Congregationalists, Strict Baptists and Wesleyans. The chapels provided the organising loci for all such villages and are the key to the understanding of the Valleys. It was the nonconformist ideas of those chapel preachers which, in turn, formed the very seed bed of socialism. Some early chapel theoreticians argued that Karl Marx had worked on the same loom as Isaiah; that, in the love of God and brotherhood of man, both the preacher and the politician were talking about the same thing.

Yet there's little but melancholy and loss in these Valleys these days and I find that I can't settle down almost anywhere around here for more than an hour. Instead I tend to drift around in any moving patch of sunshine, passing over the terraces and the stern black geometery of the abandoned pitheads. I roll along in these drifting shunts of sunshine, cartwheeling down the valley walls only occasionally stopping to listen to a prayer except that there aren't too many of them to be heard around here any longer.

On some days you can actually watch rain clouds building up over the heads of the valleys and they will then come marching down the high slopes, sheeting rain over the wandering sheep and piles of pit props alike. But then sunshine will burst through the massing rainclouds, making wisps of steam drift up from the tops of the pigeon cotes and allotment sheds. Sometimes this sunshine can be so ferocious it creates the illusion that the whole village has been set on fire. Even the coal tips look new, with the brown bracken shivering beneath a gloss of gold and, on such bright moments, the housewives peg out their washing, bringing the back gardens alive with the sound of their booming sheets.

But then it will rain again and, just being there, I'll feel like crying along with the rain. It is impossible to describe the sense of desolation and sadness that always overcomes me as I ghost over these terraces, noting the burglar alarm boxes and the nests of satellite dishes dotted just beneath the eaves; seeing the way that bolts and chainlocks festoon the front doors. Even the main doors of those once-holy Welfare Halls are now often made of cast iron after repeated break-ins and the one-armed bandits just inside their front doors are routinely padlocked inside a cage so that you may not rob what robs you.

Lawlessness now reigns in these valleys. The shadows of the dark angels fall over every home and, while some of the old still fight something of a rearguard action, most have now given up and lie like whipped dogs in front of their televisions while so many of the young are busy tearing the place apart. These have become sick communities. Many understand what's happening to them but do nothing about it. They just check their burglar alarms and locks before switching on their televisions or slipping a video into the VCR hoping that everything will work out all right. In time all these nasty things will, quite simply, disappear.

They have often told us back in Megiddo that there are no such things as no-go areas on an angel's patch. We have always been told to put our personal feelings aside and undertake regular patrols everywhere. But it's terribly hard for me here and I have to admit that I have never patrolled these Valleys intensively. In fact, to be honest, I haven't been around here for a few years now, possibly afraid of what I'd find. I feel that, in a sense, I've failed at everything here in the Valleys. There is almost nothing that amounts to anything successful here that I could point at and claim was down to me. I would make it my only no-go area in Wales, if I could, but I can't.

A dry cold Saturday night when I next made a patrol there with a grapefruit moon pinned to the sky above the terraces and the twanging sounds of a rock 'n' roll band tuning up behind the curtains of the stage of the Welfare Hall. I like clean fast rock 'n' roll but, if this is the band I heard when I was here last—and it rather sounds like it—it's all crash, bang and wallop on three chords.

The tables in front of the stage were filling up and small queues of people were forming to buy tickets just near the gents lavatory since every social event in the Valleys—no matter how large or small—must be preceeded by a few hands of bingo. A hand of bingo is now the modern form of saying grace.

Outside, all along the main street of the mining village, the pale glow of many televisions was flickering in the lace curtains of every living room. This distinctive flicker has always reminded me, in a curious way, of the flicker of death. At the moment of death I have often spotted a flicker like that; ghostly, evanescent, final . . .

The orange light of the sodium street lamps shone down on the parked cars, neutralising all their colours and making them seem the same. Some starlings were squabbling together in the eaves of the Welfare Hall and the silence of the streets was finally broken by the amplified voice of the bingo caller reading out the all-important numbers from his glass box of bouncing table tennis balls.

A police car accelerated smoothly down the main road and skinheads gathered around a Space Invaders game in the fish and chip shop alternately jabbing at buttons with fingers tattooed with SCUM or HATE or else kicking the machine itself with their Doc Marten boots and making its very insides rattle. The bingo numbers came drifting out into the night and hung in the very air as dolefully as someone reading out the list of the Jewish dead outside Treblinka.

It is on nights like this that I often find myself thinking of the sheer fun and joy that I had watching over Dylan Thomas while he was working on Under Milk Wood. Everything about that play was funny and joyful, written with a lot of affection and even love. Those marvellous characters would pop up from everywhere in Dylan's wonderful imagination and many was the time when he would take his cigarette out of his mouth and look around with his bulbous eyes as he wondered where all that faint giggling might be coming from.

Well Dylan wouldn't have much to be funny or joyful about here. All the love has seeped out of these streets. Around the back of the general stores there was a lot of soft cussing as two youths were trying to jemmy open the back door which was covered with so many chains and bolts that they were even now talking of going down to the garage to steal some 'oxy' equipment to burn their way in.

In the bar of the one pub a few old-timers were kicking their heels and talking, as they do incessantly, of the way it was and the way it has become. 'Duw, all our family went down the hole and what with strikes and stoppages we all grew up in real poverty,' said Wynn Thomas. 'But all we used to do was go out and kick a football around. We never thought of thieving anything—not like the young of today. And not only did none of us ever commit anything like rape, we didn't even know what it was.'

Further along the road another two youths were busy stripping lead off a chapel roof and, on a patch of waste ground around the back of the Welfare Hall, with the sounds of the bingo caller exploding against the walls, some six other youngsters were taking it in turns to inhale on a bag of glue. None of their eyes could focus on anything at all and it would have been impossible for any of them to have managed to stand up on his own two feet. One of them did indeed try to stand up to dance around the waste ground when the rock 'n' roll began playing inside but, giggling insanely, he missed his footing on a few empty cider bottles and soon fell over again, bashing the side of his head against a rock.

Outside the chip shop the skinheads began kicking a tin can up the pavement until the can got lost inside a pile of rubbish and, disconsolately and with much swearing, they all wandered back together to stand in the light of the chip shop again. Their clothes were of torn denim and they had shaven heads with rings in their ears. Chains of safety pins dangled around their shoulders. A warning shout came out of the darkness and they all began running together up the pavement but saw nothing. They stood together peering out into the moonlight before running back to their spot outside the chip shop where they stuffed their hands down into their pockets and stared down into the gutter a bit more.

As the rock 'n' roll band continued with its extremely rough and ready set I knew that I had to leave this place. I just couldn't bear watching these people, who had once been so great, dying like this in a long hard season of crime, boredom and despair. These valleys were now nothing more than those old valleys of bones first foreseen by the prophets and there was no evidence or sign of any resurrection anywhere. Just like Joshua you could scan the horizon for a long time waiting for rain clouds in this valley of death.

Many blame poverty and unemployment for this appalling state of affairs but, while a factor, they are certainly not the main reasons. These Valleys have long known everything about poverty and unemployment but crime has only firmly settled here in the past twenty years—about the same period as television.

Here families were once so poor and undernourished at the turn of the century that, of every eight children born, only four survived. Inadequate medical care meant that many, many women died in childbirth. The boys had little hope of a decent education and the girls none at all. In every family at least one daughter remained unmarried to care for the parents in their old age and self-induced and dangerous abortions were frequent. Whole families were stricken by rickets and tuberculosis. In Merthyr in the 1926 strike, unemployment rose to 82 per cent but still every front door was left open and only a tiny handful of the hard men ever did battle with the police.

Those old mining villages knew everything there was to know about hard work. Some still remember the days when the hooter would sound after a fatal accident and the whole pit stopped working to march back to the village with the body. Many was the time when even I had to avert my gaze as those cleats of all those hobnailed boots cracked against the cobbles as the men marched back through the town and the widow was presented with what was left of her dead husband in a sack.

There are still miners in the Welfare Hall who talk of rats swarming around the ponies' stables underground and the taste of black pats in their sandwiches; of zinc baths hanging off nails in damp marigold gardens and having money stopped for candles, oil for the lamps and chalk for marking the drams. Tell them a story about hardship and they always know a worse one. They know horrifying stories of boils the size of rugby balls and lying on their sides to hew coal in six inches of water. They remember shaking Robin's starch on the baby's bottom because there was no talcum power and using baked bean tins for sand buckets on the miners' annual outing to Barry Island. They have seen the men of their families dying by inches, their lungs choked with dust.

Many of the older ones also understood the secret language of the pit props: of how their creaking would tell that there was water around; how hard the rock was coming down or whether to make a quick run for it. Oh aye, life was always hard and dangerous down the hole.

But still there was no significant crime.

No, no. These people of the Valleys are dying because they have turned their back on God and all His holy laws. They no longer understand a holy God's requirement that His people be holy too. And when any people ever do that then God always gives them up. He leaves them to wallow in evil and lawlessness until they cry out in prayer for Him to take control of their lives.

Oh here I go again, railing against the sins of my flock when I probably should have done more about it all myself. Maybe Bimmimus was right after all; maybe I should simply have gone around and fixed every television in every valley and then we would have had a far different picture wouldn't we?

But the real trouble with getting myself locked into all this angry argument on a Saturday night in a mining village in South Wales is that I then know that it is time to leave and that I should perhaps get over to Caldey Island for some rest and recreation with the monks before carrying on to finally finish my report.

The real trouble is that I've spent too many hours weeping over the Valleys; I've never really been able to accept that such a great people have taken such a tragic wrong-turning.

So I was ghosting around those forlorn terraces again, not absolutely certain what I was going to do next when, just near the fish and chip shop, that strange feeling I last had down in Cardiff docks returned. Again it was as if someone was busily fitting dark clamps on to my consciousness and my thought patterns began stuttering and stumbling. Almost as if sensing a great and immediate danger I could feel my wings fluttering on my back, trying but failing to open as my flame began trying to sketch in my sword which again never seemed to quite work, flashing upwards but then disappearing into a small shower of sputtering sparks.

Just then a naked man and woman rolled down in front of me and, to my mounting horror, she began chopping at his face and chest with an ice pick. I couldn't seem to tear my eyes away as she kept stabbing him again and again. It wasn't even possible for me to move properly and again there was that faint slipstream of familiar laughter hanging in the air overhead as I lifted my sword to defend myself only to find that it quite simply just wasn't there in my hand.

The naked couple disappeared when I took one hesitant step forward and then another. Those dark rings were still being clamped on my mind—one being taken off and a few more being put on—when there was another explosion of bright, brittle light and a man was hitting a woman around brutally, striking her hard and often and, even though I tried to interfere, I couldn't seem to grab hold of his arm, just couldn't seem to be able to protect her; just didn't seem able to do anything at all really.

I had to escape from all this; just had to get the hell out of here but, even with repeated explosions of my rings, I couldn't get any height. Now it was as if someone—something?—was hanging a huge stone around my neck since I was feeling heavier and heavier as a car came spinning through the air towards me being pursued by another car with a man leaning out of the driving window blazing away with a chattering machine gun. The illusion of that spinning car was so realistic that even I jumped out of the way as it went sailing past my head and down past the chip shop.

Oh this was all getting too much for me and, with yet more explosions on my rings, I struggled to get my wings open, straining this way and that like a huge, wild beast as my wings hit against the walls of the terraces next to me and the telephone wires above. No one would have seen much but there was certainly a fearful racket as a few faces appeared in the lace curtains and even the gang of skinheads left their spot outside the chip shop to come and investigate the noise for themselves. But they couldn't make it out at all, staring at the spot where I was fighting to get airborne with crashing wings and muffled explosions before looking at one another with a baffled curiosity.

By now I was making more noise than forty angels and even knocking a few slates off a roof until, yes, I did finally manage to free myself of my invisible anchors and began climbing up the back of the sky, feeling those dark clamps falling away from my consciousness as I looked around and below me at the disappearing outlines of the village with just the orange necklaces of the street lights winding this way and that along the thin valley roads.

My ears picked up a strange plunking sound and I held myself steady—a motionless Spitfire in the moonlight—since, for one terrified moment, I thought something else was going to happen to me until I realised that it was only the sound of that rock 'n' roll band in the Welfare Hall storming to the end of their predictably rough set.

I swear to you this job is not fit for man nor beast. No one has ever had to put up with what I put up with and there's not even a token pay packet waiting for me at the end of the week. With three huge downwards thrusts on my wings I powered up into the rock 'n' roll night, intent on getting away somewhere—anywhere—until I had calmed down.

As it turned out I didn't get all that far after all since I had lost a lot of my strength from using my wings to fight against those invisible weights so I ended up spending the night sitting on top of the derelict Thomas and Evans pop factory tower just over the valley in Porth.

And it was there that I began seeing exactly what it was that had been attacking me since, in a sense, it was also what had been so busily and devastatingly attacking the rest of the Valleys. For what had been coming after me, I was deducing, was a series of evil images which had all, in their different ways, been coming after my battered flock too. These were the very same images of crime and violence which had so completely destroyed the old chapel culture of the Valleys. And not only was this violent and criminal imagery breeding violent minds it was also breeding criminality and vandalism on a scale both unknown and unprecedented in the history of the world.

Bits of the jigsaw were finally moving into place as I looked out over this tiny township of Porth with the twisting river on the one side and the railway line on the other. I managed to sweep up a drunk off that line by that junction a few years back. Two or three seconds later and he would have been a goner. Pigeons sat around unconcernedly on the stained brickwork next to me.

There was a mind and philosophy at work here which was steadily growing more identifiable and discernible and, sitting up there with the pigeons, I began seeing all too clearly exactly what that mind was all about. I'd had sniffs of it often enough in the past, of course, but now it was all busily sketching itself across the wide Valley sky.

This mind was one which tirelessly lionised the individual and was obsessed by crime and sexual inconstancy. This mind declared that conventional morality was redundant and ran in constant pursuit of the perverted, the morbid, the cruel and the violent. Some called this philosophy Romantic but, whatever it was called, it well described the thought processes of the mind of the modern media which was busily attacking a fallen world.

Where once this mind was difficult to find it was now impossible to avoid. The films of Sylvester Stallone and Arnold Schwarzenegger were powerful celebrations of the violent individual. Tabloid newspapers in particular were obsessed with sexual inconstancy and you can find the redundancy of conventional morality and obsession with crime in most Hollywood films in general and the Mafia films of Martin Scorsese and Francis Ford Coppola in particular. The year's most popular video, Basic Instinct, was an extended celebration of violent perversion. The fingerprints of Rambo were all over the Hungerford massacre and the influence of Scorsese's *Taxi Driver* was everywhere in the attempted assassination of President Ronald Reagan.

Modern news gathering was also nothing if it was not in constant pursuit of the violent. Foreign news is little more than a search for war. Wherever there is violence anywhere in the world there is usually a television camera or six whirling around it. So there it was stretching across all those Valley lives, busy generating ideas and imagery which was having destructive consequences for everyone.

But now, not content with laying waste the world, this mind was beginning to attack angels like me. *Angels like me!* It was now stepping up the sheer scale of its attack and doubtless targeting all God's angels. That's how powerful this mind had become and there was now barely any shelter for anyone. Even all the angels were soon going to be on the run from this evil, and who was going to save the world then?

All I did know, beyond all shadow of doubt, was that all the dark angels were but the agents of this mind; that they were all out there busy extending its influence even if it seemed to be managing quite well on its own. How long now oh Lord? Just how long before this great tide of evil can be firmly and finally repulsed by the transcendental of the Second Coming?

The drought goes on without any sign of an end. The bones pile up on the valley walls. Thoughts of a worried angel sitting on an old brick stack in the middle of a long, dry season.

Now that the old giants of the pulpit have disappeared only good writers with trenchant pens have any possibility of digging these dead people out of their premature graves. Only good writers with that old unflinching courage and spiritual insight which were once such powerful forces in the pulpit here can attack this mind by constantly re-defining the condition; changing the way we think with new ideas; holding up that troubling and damning mirror.

But where would they be? There are plenty of humorists in these Valleys who can wrap up any and every problem in a joke and even a few good folk singers who can tell us something about the times. But where are those deadly writers who can tell the bitter truth since, unlike the mealy-mouthed and publicity-mad politicians, they are not looking for votes?

There is, as it happens, one young writer in the Valleys whom I've been keeping an eye on. In fact I've been keeping an eye on him for a long, long time since there was a lively peal on the chimes when he was born and I once brought him back to life with one of my little angel tricks after he had all but drowned in a river when he was a kid. He writes with a thrilling passion and energy and not only does he seem to have spotted the real beast running amok in the Valleys but he's gone after it with a gun.

Ed Thomas is his name and I caught up with his new play, The House of America, in a theatre in Cardiff recently which overwhelmed me with its power and truth. The play is set in the Valleys near a drift mine and we meet a family which has lost its identity and very soul. This family, we soon discover, is so completely in the grip of American fantasy it is literally rotting away. The husband is thought to have run away to America and the children all want to go there to be with him. They read only Jack Kerouac and listen to American music. All their dreams end in New Orleans.

The mother likes to watch The Godfather on video; she loves the very crackle on the television screen late at night, calling it Mr Snow, her only friend. Her favourite singer is Frank Sinatra.

The play, punctuated by bursts of white televisual light, telling its own story of a drift towards death, finally moves into incest and murder which, in this context, is entirely appropriate. The family is not, of course, a real Valley family but a metaphor for what's going on in the Valleys. A people who no longer know who they are will surely die like this, the playwright is saying. A people who turn their backs on their roots and get taken over by another decadent culture will surely end like this.

Ah, how I've always loved the truth-teller for all this is exactly the truth of what's going in the Valleys isn't it? There are now regular and horrifying attacks on old people with some being murdered and one even scalped. Gangs are attacking one another with shotguns and baseball bats. Simply nothing is too hot or heavy as this evil mind busily colonises these ancient hills of coal.

And what is the nature of this evil? Well, as Ed Thomas suggests, it's largely—but not exclusively—this destructive Hollywood fantasy which is being spun everywhere by the mind of which I have been speaking. It's the Romantic creations of Rambo and Hannibal Lecter; it's the glorification of crime in Goodfellas and the hymning of the lawless joy-rider in Terminator; it's the promotion of violent rape in Basic Instinct and the relentless vandalism and violence in Lethal Weapon. It's the Romantic mind of Hollywood that's pulling these Valley townships apart and writers like Ed Thomas have spotted it.

Ed Thomas, who is still a tender 31, has already experienced the mindless wrath of those who still seem to believe that everything in the Valley gardens is lovely. About twenty walked out when he staged his House of America in Ystradgynlais and a further five cancelled their orders for meat from Ed's father, a butcher in Cwmgiedd in the Swansea Valley. Even his own mother was worried about what she had given birth to but then came to understand the truth of his work.

'I don't know who I am,' Ed will say to anyone who asks. 'We Welsh have become almost invisible; we have no modern mythology so we absorb American culture. Others have a foothold in the world but we have no icons of our own; we don't even have the beginning of them unless you count Tom Jones. But I've tried to reclaim my own Welshness; it's there for anyone to demand.'

That lovely spirit of my old praise warriors still flickers on, you see; it often takes on different forms but it's out there, ready to scorch the land again. But how many more need to be burgled and murdered, I wonder, before even the stupid come to understand that the land is being Americanised by a corrupt media? How many gang fights with baseball bats does it take? How many rapes need to take place before it is understood that

300

youngsters are doing this because they are constantly watching films about it? Those kids are getting those videos and watching them again and again—no matter what their age.

Only the steadfast few left in the chapels probably now understand that the only reasonable option that seems to be left for these Valleys, so rotten and devastated by sin, is that God scorches every wall clean with huge balls of purifying fire.

And so, still sitting on that stack of bricks in Porth that morning, I can't say that I was shocked or even particularly surprised when I spotted at least a dozen dark angels flapping slowly, black and blue, across the clear winter skies.

Pointless to attack so many, of course, even if I had the inclination which I hadn't. They were flying in the direction of the Penrhys housing estate which was as likely a place for them to gather as anywhere, I suppose. If I told you what happened on that estate you wouldn't believe me but you've only got to look at the broken windows, the vandalised bus shelters and the double-locked garages to get the picture. This is a neighbourhood watch area. Beware of the dog. I had long suspected that dark angels might well be hanging out somewhere like that.

But, before I get completely distracted by the not unexpected show of the opposition, there is, come to think of it, another perfect metaphor at hand for this, the death of the Valleys.

Let me take you back to the day when the Valleys broke their heart and I very nearly broke mine. There was nothing at all I could do to mend this particular heartbreak since it engulfed everyone—whether they lived here or not.

I was in Cardiff at the time, sitting on the top of the City Hall, when I picked up a strange and plaintive burst of anguish on the prayer lines. It was almost like nothing I had ever heard before—a great chorus of pain—so I went immediately to investigate it and found the air amok with young souls.

A huge tip, I saw, had burst its sides with an inner explosion of water, sending thousands of tons of black slurry down on to a small school in Aberfan. Already men were gathering to dig out the buried school—already using the standard mining technique of digging for a minute or so then all stopping to listen for any sounds from the survivors.

But I didn't have the time to stop to listen out for anything since many of those young souls were still flapping about in the air, waiting there for me to harvest them. I have never worked so hard and fast, swooping them up in bundles and taking them straight across the Jordan. They were all clearly ready for me when I got to the gates of heaven too, taking them in as fast I could go before I went back for the others. All children are accepted in heaven; they are always blameless and without any sin of any kind.

It wasn't even a job for which I could use my wings, which would have been too cumbersome, so I kept flashing back and forth with my exploding rings, picking up another bundle of them which came up later than the rest. They were alright as soon as I got to them; still stunned and worrying about their parents but I have ways of calming them down, telling them that everything is going to be fine and that they would all be back in the arms of their families and loved ones soon. There are no coal tips in heaven.

I have never known what's on God's mind when such disasters happen; never understood why He allows them but it's not for us to try any independent thinking or ask any awkward questions. We have anyway all learned often enough in the past that there is a reason for everything which all becomes clear sooner, if not later.

I harvested more than a hundred souls on the bleak and bitter morning in the Valleys, only stopping work when I knew that everyone had been accounted for. It was then time for a rest and I sat on what was left of the tip looking down at heartbreak such as I had never known.

The miners were still digging around the engulfed school as more and more ambulances and emergency services arrived to help the beleaguered village. Blankets were held up as they dug out yet another broken child's body and, when a blackboard was moved, a teacher was found holding two children in his arms. The pain and shock were unbelievable and I cried along with everyone else; we share in grief too and later I went along the terraces, listening to prayers or trying to sing a song of healing love to the hearts which had become understandably bitter with my Master.

Later that day darkness fell and sodium lamps were put up over the school as the digging continued. That foul slurry was the hardest ever to dig; a smelly black glue which was being chained away in buckets by hand. Crowds of weeping parents gathered outside the Bethania Chapel waiting to identify the bodies of their children who had been laid out on the pews. Oh my people

Even today I still cannot go back to Aberfan without the memory of that grim morning coming back in every detail.

But the point, surely, is that the Valleys have again been engulfed in a black tide, no less destructive and no less murderous for not being able to be seen. You can see and smell a tip. You can count the lost lives and even measure the loss. But who can count the lost lives and measure the loss in every home when they are being run almost every hour of the day by a relentless black tide of violence, crime and perversion?

The children are again being drowned and destroyed in this new tide of black slurry and even the few teachers who are still fighting it, who are picking up a few children in their arms behind a blackboard, are also being engulfed too. Young arsonists have been repeatedly burning these Valley schools and if a school, with all its accumulated values, is destroyed by fire or a renegade tip, then the effect is still much the same.

So the old bitter lessons are not being learned and my flock is continuing to die in a mass grave with thousands of satellite dishes and television aerials as tombstones. This once-great tribe now knows more about the life and works of Rambo than Karl Marx; they have given away their libraries and barely know the difference between communism, fascism and rheumatism.

But I had to make that savage journey to Penrhys, of course. I had to make that one final pilgrimage before my report was complete. It's strange how this my final—and greatest— obstacle had come at the end but there was no avoiding it or putting it off. If all those dark angels had made camp there amidst the poor and unemployed I had to know about it. We all had to know about it and I had to do something about it.

Yet, somehow, I couldn't just burst into the estate, forlornly wandering those desolate valleys for a day or two, trying to arm myself for the coming battle with prayer and holiness. Sometimes I practised drawing my sword on some lonely allotment or valley slope with the sheep foraging all around me as my sword flashed in the air, cutting through it with swishing swipes so loud that even the sheep stopped their munching to look up, wondering what was going on.

If the dark angels were in there I would have to fight them and it would be the bloodiest of encounters. I would probably metamorphise into a fiery red dragon for the battle too; a lot of fiery snorting would give me a definite edge since evil, lacking any real and definite conviction, is always essentially cowardly at heart. It is just possible that I could frighten the wits out of them and that alone would give me a decisive advantage in any fight.

I also discovered a little trick which was strangely replenishing and that was to visit a lot of those abandoned valley chapels and merely stand in the ruined pulpits, enjoying the voices and hymns of old, feeling again the flame and flood of famous revivals. These are imaginative leaps but I can do them easily when I concentrate really hard. I can go back there and hear the hymns surging up into the rafters; hear those startling voices cracking down on the rows of empty and dusty pews.

'It is finished. The powers of darkness heard the acclamations of the universe and hurried away from the scene in death-like feebleness. He triumphed over them openly. The graves of the old burial-ground have been thrown open, and gales of life have been blown over the valley of bones, and an exceeding great army has already been sealed to our God as among the living of Zion, for so the Bond was paid and the eternal redemption secured.'

In Cwmavon the chapel was packed again with people. The heat and excitement was as intense as it was unbearable and a voice shouted from the gallery: 'Someone has decided.' The sounds of Diolch Iddo echoed up into the Valley night and there was another tumultuous waving of handkerchiefs. 'Another has yielded.'

'There is to be no singing. It has become too terrible to sing. There are two brothers here who are not at peace with one another. The two of you must stand up and declare your love for one another.'

> Guide me oh thou Great Jehovah,
> Pilgrim through a barren land:
> I am mean but Thou are mighty,
> Hold me with Thy powerful hand.
> Strong Deliverer.
> Be Thou still my strength and shield.

'Don't say hush to anyone. A drunken man has come to this meeting and been sobered up by the Holy Spirit. He must not be interrupted.'

Then, In Abercynon, another great and well-loved voice came rasping up out of the mildewed darkness: 'In the regions of ice and snow immense pieces are gradually loosened by the rays of the sun. A huge precipice hangs over at this moment. Thunder is unnecessary—the cornet of an old beggar is enough, or the bleating of the sheep in the distance and then the terrible avalanche. The ungodly walks through the ravine of avalanches. God's threats hang overhead. Walk slowly and quietly, brother, lest the precipice fall. A curse, one swear word is enough to shake the mountain. Watch, be careful. "On whomsoever it will fall it will grind into powder." Turn the stone into a foundation. The stone will be on thee or under thee for ever. Under thee as a foundation, on thee as eternal destruction.'

And so it came to pass that night that I was finally ready to climb the great mountain, first watching the sun go down over those valley volcano homes before taking to the slopes where already I was beginning to pick up the fluttering sounds of alien wings. The dying sun was still giving a lingering kiss to the tops of the distant hills of coal as I advanced slowly, my purple flame sputtering and hissing, ready to draw my sword at an instant.

Soon the tops of the Penrhys houses hove into view and everything that I steeled myself to find there was there in the dimming, silvery sunset; a squealing of hissing, tinny voices with the occasional boom of dark wings overhead. But, on turning the bend in the hill, it was all far worse than I had expected because there were dozens and dozens of them, sitting up there on those beleaguered rooftops with huge patches of slime glittering hard in the dying light.

Three of them came flying down the valley, banking up high before crashing down together and actually knocking a few others off. A fierce fight followed with the displaced ones trying to get back on to their roost, their noises sounding like a strange combination of fierce shrieks and manic laughter. Another larger one came gliding overhead and, although the growing darkness made it difficult to be positive, I was pretty sure that was my old adversary Splachnik.

In any battle Splachnik was going to be the first to get it in the neck; that was a racing certainty.

I thought of my old preachers in their pulpits of fire. Again I heard those old hymns when, all at once, there was a huge and brilliant flash of white light into which gangs with snooker cues and baseball bats began running towards me. Oh no. They were at it again and I could feel my very blood running cold and my very soul getting heavier and heavier as I drew my sword ready to fight darkness with light. There was a lot of hooting and a screaming woman ran across my path being chased by a man who was stabbing her repeatedly. Now there were dark sounds and shuffling movements behind me too so I turned again with my sword at the ready wondering where the attack was going to come from next.

Then, that brilliant flash of light disappeared as quickly as it had come and I found myself standing next to a vandalised bus shelter. Directly above me five dark angels were circling around in the silver skies like vultures looking down at carrion. Everywhere I was picking up the smell of burning sulphur and scorched grass. A crowd of youths were standing outside the pub swigging on flagons of cider. Well, Conker boy, you are going to be mincemeat soon enough but you are going to go down fighting. No point cowering behind this bus shelter: get out there and hit them with everything you've got.

Just then the shuffling shadows behind me seemed to be coming alive. So what was going on here? One shadow was drifting across the road towards me and another was wafting up behind. I raised my sword but lowered it again in pure hopelessness. You cannot fight shadows. Even I cannot fight shadows. But then these shadows began taking on a human form. I gave a soft shout of thanks since I immediately saw that one of the faces had but one eye. Then there was another wearing a bishop's mitre and I nodded at him, telling him that I was glad he was here. Another appeared and it was Daniel Rowland. I understood then that this was nothing less than all my old praise warriors coming to help me in the hour of my most desperate need.

Anne Griffiths materialised out of the drifting darkness and I recognised the peculiar gait of Evan Roberts too. Howell Harris emerged looking distinctly combative and even Dylan Thomas was there shyly sucking on a cigarette and clearly uncertain how he had found himself in such strange company. Then William Williams turned up and Thomas Charles. I greeted each and every one of them with a warm and holy kiss.

But there was still only a silence between us—what was there to say?—when the darkness parted again and a jaunty figure came striding down the hill, looking splendid in a white tunic and a fox fur hat. 'Ah, it's Davey Crockett,' said Howell Harris. 'Come to fight the Injuns.'

So there we all were on this strange and tense Penrhys night; all the old praise warriors of Wales come together to do battle with the forces of evil which had colonised this great and blessed land.

But then, as Christmas Evans led the prayers, I could feel myself growing in power and strength. The very night seemed to be fluttering with centuries of prayer and hymns as many of the dark angels, sensing that there was trouble afoot, took off from their rooftops roosts and wheeled around overhead, calling to one another in panic-stricken shrieks.

Born up on the magic carpet of my people's prayers I had gained ascendancy again and, as I finally led my group up the final few hundred yards into that fallen estate, I could feel every part of me changing and replicating with explosion after explosion of my gold rings. I had never seen my flame quite so large and fierce either, hissing like the furnaces of a steel works with a huge purple heart. My sword just seemed to be getting bigger and bigger too when the very night darkened as Splachnik came dive-bombing down on our prayer party, screaming and spitting like a crazed banshee.

This attack was the biggest mistake of his long and evil career since such a huge burst of prayer came up from behind me that his flight path was all but stopped and he just seemed to hover there, neither going forwards or backwards, with slime dripping hard off his all but motionless wings. I then struck directly at his chest with my huge sword and not so much sliced him in half as made him actually burst like a bomb with the sky full of his dying screams, blood and falling black feathers.

So the first and most decisive strike had been delivered and, with all my rings continuing to explode, I rose up over this valley night watching all those other dark angels rising up ever higher, presumably to get out of the way of my avenging sword. Now I was going to attack each and every one of them, one after the other. There was no need to change into a dragon now; everything I needed I had. With the prayers of my people behind me I was unbeatable by anyone and anything.

Down below me the streets of the estate were empty and quiet with all those black feathers falling everywhere. The youths outside the pub were silent and looking up at the sky. A dog was running around barking at the strange feathers as they drifted down around him and the television aerials and satellite dishes. Directly opposite them, on another corner, my praise warriors were still carrying me aloft with their prayers; still arming me with their powerful passion and pride.

'To redeem men,' Christmas Evans's voice was saying. 'I will be incarnate in the Son of God. I will be the Lamb slain in the life of this graveyard world.'

But, even then, I could see that the army of dark angels had recovered from their initial shock and were gathering together to attack me. But, if they were frightened before, they became even more frightened when I addressed them with a voice that was as loud as the night was quiet.

My words went booming and ricocheting down every bend in the Valleys, travelling through the old mineworkings and along the roofs of the terraces and the Welfare Halls. These words told everyone with eyes to see and ears to listen that battle was about to be fully and finally joined. These words were also full with the promise that all life would soon return to these Valleys of lawlessness and death and that, soon, a foot would be set down among them which would be accompanied by such a great peal on the chimes that they would be heard in every corner of their graveyard world.

'This is Wales,' I shouted with repeated and extravagant flashes of my great sword. 'This is Wales,' I shouted again with such a fury that it broke up that massing attack by the dark angels almost before it had begun.

'This is Wales and, as such, it is under the full and continuing protection of I, Conker . . .'